John V. Gunnison

The Ninth Wave

HOUGHTON MIFFLIN
LITERARY FELLOWSHIP AWARDS

To E. P. O'Donnell for *Green Margins*
To Jenny Ballou for *Spanish Prelude*
To Robert Penn Warren for *Night Rider*
To Clelie Benton Huggins for *Point Noir*
To Dorothy Baker for *Young Man with a Horn*
To David Cornel DeJong for *Old Haven*
To Maurine Whipple for *The Giant Joshua*
To Mary King O'Donnell for *Quincie Bolliver*
To Helen Todd for *A Man Named Grant*
To A. Fleming MacLeish for *Cone of Silence*
To Donald MacRae for *Dwight Craig*
To Joseph Wechsberg for *Looking for a Bluebird*
To Ann Petry for *The Street*
To Beatrice Griffith for *American Me*
To Elizabeth Bishop for *North & South*
To Helen Mears for *Mirror for Americans, Japan*
To Arthur Mizener for *The Far Side of Paradise:* A Biography of
F. Scott Fitzgerald
To Anthony West for *The Vintage*
To Fred Ross for *Jackson Mahaffey*
To Rebecca C. Patterson for *The Riddle of Emily Dickinson*
To Madison A. Cooper, Jr., for *Sironia, Texas*
To Charles Bracelen Flood for *Love Is a Bridge*
To Siegel Fleisher for *The Lion and the Honeycomb*
To Harold Livingston for *The Coasts of the Earth*
To Milton Lott for *The Last Hunt*
To Edward Hoagland for *Cat Man*
To Eugene Burdick for *The Ninth Wave*

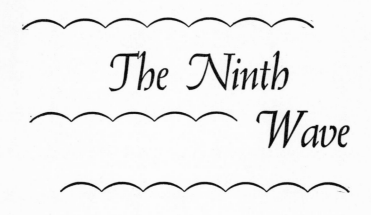

The Ninth Wave

BY EUGENE BURDICK

HOUGHTON MIFFLIN COMPANY · BOSTON
The Riverside Press · Cambridge
1956

For *Carol*
and *Marie*

"Those who have only empty space above them are almost inevitably lost in it, if no force restrains them."

EMILE DURKHEIM, *Suicide*

CONTENTS

CONTENTS

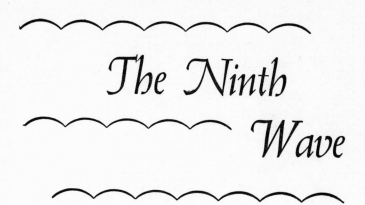

The Ninth Wave

CHAPTER 1

The Ninth Ninth Wave

A Buick drove up behind the circle of Model-A's that were parked at the top of the cliff. One or two of the cars had neat chrome-plated engines, powerful squat carburetors, wire wheels and twin exhausts. The others were dilapidated and broken down. All of them, however, had braces on the tops where the long surfboards were slung.

Mike opened the door of the Buick and at once passed from the smell of the woman, the odor of perfume and deodorant, into the hot odorless sunlight. He turned and looked at Miss Bell through the open window.

"I'll see you again, Mike . . . very soon," she said expectantly, half whispering.

"If I can get away," Mike said, hedging. "Busy this week. I have to . . ."

"If you have time for surfing you have time to see me," Miss Bell said sweetly, but there was the corroded edge of a whine in her voice. Mike smiled at the way the flesh around her mouth worked in tiny flat jerks. "Please now, Mike."

"O.K. I'll try. I've got some work in chemistry to catch up. Maybe by Friday."

They talked for a few more minutes. Mike could feel the sun starting to open pores on his back, through the thin cotton of his T-shirt . . . the tight blue jeans over his legs turned warm. He was bored, but it was pleasant to talk to her. Some angle of the car caught the sun and reflected chrome brilliance in his eyes so that all he could see of Miss Bell was a black faraway figure. She receded and as her figure grew more doll-like and remote it took on a reprimanding, hostile look. Mike squinted his eyes to keep the blue refracted light from the Pacific from blinding him entirely.

Her voice took on its piping schoolteacher's authority. "You just must be more considerate of me, Mike. You must."

"Why?" he asked idly. "Why, Miss Bell?"

At once the remote doll-like figure collapsed into a posture of apprehension. Miss Bell's voice lost its crisp quality and quavered.

"Well, don't you care, Mike? Doesn't it mean anything to you?"

It is so easy, he thought, so easy to make her drop that cool note of authority in her voice. He reached out and touched her shoulder and at once she leapt back into proper proportion, was neat and full-sized in her flowered silk dress.

"Sure I care," Mike said. "I'll call you later in the week."

"For sure?" she asked.

"For sure," he replied.

He turned away from the car and started toward the edge of the cliff. He heard the Buick start and then turn slowly. Mike smiled out at the blue Pacific, noticed a tanker, hull-down and far at sea, smoke from her stack smearing the blue-white sky.

When he got to the path that led down the cliff he stood for a moment while his eyes cleared of the glare. At the bottom of the cliff there were two umbrellas, shabby and stringy. Anonymous legs stuck out of them. A few surfboards were scattered around. The sand was white and washed looking, picking up all the sun in the cove.

I know, Mike said to himself, that you look clean from here, but when I get down there you will be jumping with sandfleas, a regular layer of them, just off the sand . . . hopping, jumping, screwing around. Jumping into the air and rubbing their legs. But I like it. Sandfleas don't bite, they just tickle.

As he started down the narrow curving path he could see that most of the boys were far out in the cove. Very far out, as if they were waiting for the occasional big hump. Their boards rose and fell, they sat with their feet up, some of them wearing straw hats to shield their faces from the sun . . . tiny, lazy, Mexican-looking figures.

One of the boys was eating from a paper bag and Mike was sure that it was Hank Moore. It was just like Hank to take his lunch out on the board. That was what was confusing about Hank, Mike thought. He was like an old lady before he got in the water. Cleaning off his board, testing the water with his toe, edging slowly into the water and not diving sharply in like the rest of the boys. Hank would go out slowly on his board, not yelling like the other surfers, but picking his way out cautiously, watching the waves, protecting the brown paper bag which held his lunch. But once he had eaten his lunch out of the brown bag, wadded it up and thrown it out on the water, Hank changed. He sat stubbornly, endlessly waiting for the ninth ninth wave. Some of the other boys would get excited, mistake a big hump for the ninth ninth, but never Hank. He always knew when it would come; he never took a smaller wave; he always waited for the big one. They all believed that every ninth wave was bigger than the preceding eight, and every subsequent ninth wave was bigger than the one before it, until the biggest wave of all was the ninth ninth.

Mike wasn't sure if the system was accurate, but he did know that there was always one wave a day that was bigger than the rest. The other waves might be big and sometimes they were really huge and you might get excited and think that one of them was the ninth ninth. But not Hank. He always knew when to wait. He always got the biggest wave of the day.

Some days he would sit quietly, glancing over his shoulder at the humps, watching them come working up out of the ocean, not moving for three hours. Then finally, he would turn around, start to paddle, and it would be the biggest wave of the day. If he picked his board up and got out of the water that was a signal there would be no other big ones that day. Hank read the weather reports in the papers because a storm far out at sea would often mean big waves and every day, winter or summer, that a storm was reported Hank was down at the cove, looking out to sea, waiting.

As Mike came down the steep cliff he watched to see how the waves were shaping up. The coast was flat and even except for this cove which had been carved by waves into a huge U-shaped indentation. The swells rose quietly and smoothly from the flat ocean, beginning at the very edge of the horizon. In even lines each wave moved toward the shore, increasing in speed as it approached shallow water and beginning to steepen. Then as the waves reached a certain point of shoal water they turned a concave face toward the beach, reached higher and higher and began to feather with foam at the top. Along the rest of the coast they pressed powerfully against the rocks and sand without breaking, but as they came into the cove the feathering tips broke forward and the entire wave crashed over and rolled like a long, noisy, incredibly powerful cylinder toward the shore.

Mike could see that the waves were big, but no one was taking them. They were waiting for a ninth wave. When it came, swelling up big and green, sucking up all of the water in front of it, slanting sharply into the sky, the lines of surfers kicked their boards around, lay on their stomachs and began to paddle slowly, looking back over their shoulders. Only one person did not move in the line and that was Hank Moore. Monkeylike he reached down a hand, touched the water and moved his board away from the nearest person. Then he looked out toward the sea. Mike began to trot down the path, suddenly anxious to be in the water.

When the wave reached the line of surfers several of them backed water, afraid to try it. Several more skewed their boards sideways when the wave began to feather and prepared to smash forward. In the end only two or three boys actually rode the wave through its crash and only one of them was able to control his board and finally get to his feet.

As Mike rounded a boulder his view of the cove was cut off. When the ocean came in sight again Mike was much lower, walking steadily downward into the hot reflected sun, the densing odor of seaweed and iodine, the sudden streaked smell of long-burned charcoal. This descent into the odor, the heat, the smell of sand, was as pleasant as the first second when he dove into the water. He walked slowly, controlling his urge to get quickly to the beach. He felt the muscles of his legs strain with the slight effort of holding back as he descended.

When he got to the sand he took his shoes off, slid his blue jeans off and stood up with only his swimming shorts on. He walked toward the nearest umbrella.

"Hi, Mary Jane," he called to one of the girls.

The girl rolled over, shaded her eyes against the glare. Here at the bottom of the cove, cut off from the wind and picking up all the dull reflection from the sand and water, it was hot with a dead pleasant heat that pulsed rhythmically as the waves shifted the air and made it heave and swell. Mary Jane's nose had sweat on it and the edge of her bathing suit was rimmed with moisture. She stared for a moment, expectant, a smile on her lips but unable to see him. Mike stood still and waited. He knew what she was seeing. When you lifted your head suddenly and looked into this dull, glaring sun people looked like black solid shadows, faceless, formless, only the edges of their bodies glowing with an astral brightness.

Then Mary Jane recognized Mike.

"Hello, Mike," she said. The other two girls under the umbrella looked up, their faces surprised; suddenly unfocused and confused. They did not smile and the smile faded from Mary Jane's face. Their faces were bruised somehow with a hard memory; a curiosity that changed to irritation.

"Where have you been, Mike?" Mary Jane said. "Waves have been good all day. Some really big ones. Tommie said they were eighteen feet high . . . base to feather."

"I've been riding around," Mike said. He squatted down on his heels. The sandfleas started at once, a blanket of tumbling, falling, jumping, writhing black dots; falling to the sand and then springing wildly back upward. He felt a light, delicate itch start over his feet, reach up to his ankles.

"Riding?" Mary Jane asked. "Riding all morning?"

Now the bruised, disinterested look was gone from their faces and was replaced with curiosity. Their eyes were wide with interest, although their lips were drawn thin with some sort of disapproval. Mary Jane's lips drew back and showed moist teeth and pink soft flesh in the corners of her mouth.

"Yep, just riding," he said. "Out toward Long Beach, past the docks, then over here. Nothing but riding."

Oh, he thought, you'd like to ask, wouldn't you? You'd just like to screw up your courage to say "Who with?"

He squatted there in the sun, feeling like a roadblock in the easy flow of their serenity, sensing the curiosity well out across the sand like a physical substance. Squatted there, his knees drawn under his body, all his muscles taut, his arms dangling, he felt powerful and poised. He closed his eyes and for a few moments he dozed. When he opened his eyes the girls were pure black figures. Gradually they swam into perspective.

The girls were tense with elaborate disinterest. Mary Jane yawned, then opened her mouth as if to speak, but stopped. Mike smiled at them and quite suddenly their faces looked outraged.

"I think I'll try some waves. Can I borrow somebody's board?" Mike said.

"Board?" Mary Jane asked, her voice round with surprise. "Sure, of course, see Bill Flatter over there. He just came out."

The quick first impression of antagonism had vanished from all the girls' faces; they were tense now with curiosity. As Mike stood up the girls twitched with irritation. Mary Jane scratched at her ankles, her eyes following Mike.

"Bill, can I borrow your board?" Mike asked a long, very tanned boy.

"Sure, Mike," the boy said waving his hand, his black eyes searching Mike's face once and then falling away. "Remember, she's heavy in the tail so ride her a few inches more forward than you'd do normally."

"O.K. Thanks," Mike said.

He picked up a long narrow board, natural mahogany-colored on the body of it and trimmed with blue at the edges. His fingers unconsciously ran over the wood, measuring the smoothness, judging the quality of the board. He swung the fifty pounds of it over his head and walked toward the water. It's a good one, he thought. That Bill Flatter makes a good board, heavy in the tail or not heavy in the tail.

When he got to the water Mike stopped and stood on a rock where the water was only a few inches deep. Usually he would wait until a wave deepened the water and then with a sweep he would throw the board on the shallow water and swing himself aboard and with one movement be heading out to sea with only the tips of his toes wet. But today he waited a moment and then put the board on the dry sand.

He walked to the water up to his knees, waited for a wave and with a clean strong dive dove over it and into the water. He let his body glide, held himself straight and stiff. Then he stood up and made a curious unpremeditated gesture: he wrung his hands over his head and then threw them down to his side and at the same time looked up at the people on the beach. They were all watching him.

Mike felt a surge of surprise. The gesture was so strange. He was not sure why he had done it. It seemed vaguely propitiatory like the sign he imagined a priest would make over an animal sacrifice, or the motion that a magician makes after a trick, the jerking wave of hands as if to cleanse them; to take a curse off.

Mike looked away from the people under the umbrellas. As he walked to the board the sandfleas jumped on his legs and stuck to the moisture. He waded into the water again to drown them. Then he lay flat on the board and headed for deep water.

It took him ten minutes to work out through the waves. The waves were big and as the lines of broken surf approached he dug his hands powerfully into the water and then came up on his knees so that his weight went toward the rear of the board and shot its nose up over the foam. When the nose was over the foam the body of the wave would hit the board and smash it forward with a whipping action.

There is a point in the surf where the waves have just broken and the tons of green and white water are falling almost straight down. One must cross this point between waves or the surfboard will be thrown backward or turned over. Mike waited cautiously until there was a lull, then shot forward over the shattered hulk of one wave and slid up the side of another wave before it broke. Then he was in the clear water beyond the surf line.

There were almost a dozen boys waiting on their boards. Some of them were lying flat on their backs, others were sitting with their feet dangling in the water. Mike saw that half of the boys were from Manual Arts High and the rest he did not know. He saw Hank Moore and paddled over to him.

"Hey Hank," Mike called. "How're they humping? Been waiting long for one?"

Hank Moore swung around. He was a short, stocky, freckled-faced boy. Although his hair was blond and his eyes light blue he had a perfect Semitic face. Hank looked coolly at Mike. He's bright, Mike thought. He's got intelligence.

"They're good," Hank said. "Long wait between big ones, but when they come they're really huge. Must be some sort of funny storm out at sea. Never saw such big ones mixed up with such little ones. About every other third ninth is big and then every ninth ninth is a big baby. Pretty soon there'll be a really big one."

Mike splashed his hands gently into the water and his board skimmed over the surface, jarred against the end of Hank's board and the two boards were held together by the slight pressure. Hank was sitting neatly in the middle of his board, his knees pulled up under his chin. The top of his board was covered with intricate lines where the salt water had dried on it. Hank never dove off his board or played around in the water. For him the water was only a means of getting out to the waves and he disliked swimming. Hank was talking to a boy Mike had never met.

"Where've you been, boy?" Hank asked, looking at Mike. "You've missed some good ones. Farting away the day in L.A. when you could have been down here."

Mike grinned back.

"No. I've been for a drive. Just riding around Long Beach, Pedro, Wilmington . . . just got here now. Nice day for riding."

"Riding in a Buick, I'll bet. A blue Buick." Hank said and his voice ended in the slightest burr of a snarl, so faint that only someone who knew him well would know that he was angry. "Riding in a Buick."

"Yep, in a blue Buick. And stopping and eating four hamburgers, and two Mile-Hi cones and shooting a rifle twenty-five shots at a gallery. Doing that and riding in a Buick that'll do fifty-two miles an hour in second." Mike stopped and looked coldly at Hank for a moment. "Your ass, Moore. Right up your ass."

Deliberately Hank reached out a hand, stuck it in the water and moved his board away from Mike's. He did it as a rebuke.

Mike felt a sense of excitement; an excitement that was really a spasm of triumph. Even old Hank, he thought, even old Hank is that way. He pushed his board forward so that it touched Hank's board again and smiled at Hank.

"Look, Hank, grow up," he said. The strange boy stared in bewilderment. "You're seventeen years old. Grow up. She knows what she's doing. Don't worry about her. Just worry about yourself."

"You son of a bitch," Hank said.

Mike watched Hank's strange Semitic face, with the sharp flat planes and the odd blond, twisted hair and the light blue eyes. Hank was angry, but Mike knew that he was also confused.

But Mike was not confused. Not me, he said to himself, not me anymore. Carefully, picking the words, he phrased the meaning to himself. He was excited.

You, Hank and all of you, you think that some day you're going to stop worrying. You think that you'll get older and just by getting older some day that god damn worry and uncertainty in your guts is going to stop. You think that you're going to come in out of the worry and the fret and the doubts, like stepping out of the sun into the shade. All that has to pass is time. You think you don't have to do anything; that it will just happen. Well, it won't. Absolutely, positively, without fail, it will never happen. You'll always be the same, you'll always be miserable . . . right at the core, you'll be miserable. And you'll spend most of your time trying to escape that fact. That simple little fact.

Intuitively, on some obscure level, Mike knew he had discovered something valuable. He knew he had a tiny fragment of insight that at once made orderly and understandable a lot of things that had been chaotic. Also, and this with a kind of disappointment, he knew that he could use his special knowledge. Also he knew he would add to it. He would find other things.

Sitting on the gently heaving board, watching Hank's face, Mike spoke a law to himself: Everyone is scared.

Mike sat and stared at Hank for a moment.

"What's he so tough about?" the strange boy asked Hank.

"He's not tough," Hank replied. "He's just a cocky bastard. Not tough though."

"Well, what's he so cocky about?" the strange boy asked. He looked sideways at Mike and Mike grinned at him.

Hank lifted his head from his knees and turned toward Mike. "He screws the English teacher. That's why he's so cocky." Hank said it coldly.

"Big hump, really big hump," someone shouted.

"Big hump, big hump," everyone in the line said, taking it up like a chant. The boys who were dozing came awake and began to kick their boards around so they faced the shore. Everyone began to chatter with excitement. The strange boy was talking to Hank, but looking at Mike. Mike swung his board around and then looked over his shoulder. He could see at once that it was huge. It seemed to take something away from the two waves in front of it so that they were small and shrunken and behind them the big one humped up, already so high that it was losing the blue color of the ocean and taking on a green thinness as the sun came through it.

He looked quickly at Hank. Hank stared for a moment at the wave. He pulled his shorts up tight. He looked over at Mike and for a moment, just the slightest fraction of a second, something dark flitted across Hank's eyes and then was gone.

It's the big one for the day, Mike said to himself. And Hank is scared of it. Like he's scared of all the big ones.

Watching it, Mike felt the usual slow chill of fear. At some point the big waves were always like that, so awesome that he felt as if he would like to dig his hands in the water, shoot the board out into the safe water beyond the surf line. And then there would be the grind of satisfaction, as he made himself stay there and move his hands to put himself in the proper position to catch the wave.

Most of the skill in surfboarding depends on catching the wave at precisely the point where it has reached its highest peak, is be-

ginning to feather at the top, and is ready to let all the tons of green
water it has held in a curious rhythmic control for so many miles
crash downward. A second too early and there is nothing for the
board to ride. A second too late and the board is submerged in a
lather of foam. Some people are never able to catch this knack, this
ability to sense the precise moment when the wave will crack and
let its water spill.

The wave moved from the middle distance with a rush; drew itself
from a hump into a towering cliff of water and now, like strange
plants frozen in old green ice, Mike could see pieces of kelp in the
water, every thread of their filigreed detail caught for a moment in
the sunlit water. The water was soundless at this point, but Mike
felt a pressure rise in his ears and head as the wave gathered itself.

Mike felt the water fall from beneath him as the huge wave rose.
He looked over his shoulder and saw its green, soft and ominous bulk
take shape above him. The wave was pure and undiluted; not a trace
of foam in it. He gave a couple of strokes with his arms and the
board began to move ahead. He looked sideways and saw the scared
white faces of the other boys. Most of them were backing with their
hands, making sure that they did not catch the wave. Hank, however,
was crouched on his knees on his board. With his hands he was
crumpling up the brown bag which had held his lunch while he
looked over his shoulder at the wave. His face was rapt with attention and something more; a sort of tough angry belligerence. Hank
threw the paper bag away without looking at it and then took two
strokes in the water with his hands.

Mike felt his board lift and savagely he cut the water with his
hands. Midway in the fourth stroke he sensed that he had it; felt
the body of the wave grip his board and he began to move forward.
He looked sideways and saw that only he and Hank were still riding.

For a few seconds the wave rushed silently forward. Then a thin
vein of foam gathered at the top of the wave and formed a lip which
bent slowly forward. The speed of the wave increased. This was the
critical second when the surfboard would not only be moving forward
at great speed, but would also drop down the face of the wave as it
crashed over.

Mike glanced sideways and looked at Hank. Then suddenly Mike
stood up on his board, still looking at Hank as he did it. This was
not the time to stand up, for usually one stood up after the wave had
broken and the board had smoothed out. Mike had never stood up

at this point, and he was not sure he could keep his feet in the next few seconds. Hank looked at him without blinking and stood up also.

For a moment they stood calmly as the wave moved forward. The only noise in the vast moving green world was the hissing of the boards over the water. Then from deep in the wave came a sound like rocks rolling together and with a curious lunge it broke. A great green tunnel of roaring water was formed in front of the wave, foam gathered as high as Mike's waist and the board almost dropped away from under his feet. With a slight liquid shock the board landed on solid water and although Mike's feet slipped for a moment he remained steady. He looked sideways and saw that Hank also had survived the crash of the wave.

Mike's board chittered with speed, slapped a thousand blows against the water. They were rushing toward the blue water of the cove and the noise was enormous.

That's right, Mike howled to himself. I screw the English teacher. Just what all the rest of them would like to do. But I'm the only one that does it and I'm wiser than the rest of you because of it.

The surfboard shook with speed, the water hissed and roared, foam tossed up over his shoulders. Words rushed through his mind, piled incoherently on one another, forming impressions and all this mixed somehow with the taste of salt on his lips and the noise in his ears.

You all think you'll get better as you grow older, but I know you won't. Because I know Miss Bell who is twenty-eight, which is very old, and I know that she lies naked in a bed and cries when she calls me in. I know that right in the center she is rotten with fear and because of this I know that we will always be that way. That it won't change when you get to a certain age, but it will always be the same.

The wave was dying now and in a few seconds the board came to a halt in a few inches of water. Mike stepped off and looked over at Hank. He felt suddenly depressed, sorry that he had this piece of knowledge that none of the rest of them had. And he was sorry because he knew he would use it. It was as if he already knew how unfair was his advantage.

"That was pretty chicken, Mike, standing up before the wave broke," Hank said. "Trying to delight the girls, eh? You did it because you're chicken, that's why."

"Sure, Hank, that's why. I'm chicken," Mike said, but he laughed and Hank looked up quickly, his face confused. "You just go on believing that."

Mike picked up his board and laid it on the sand and in the hot sun the wood began to steam and the salt traced out a pattern on the board.

"Hank, can I ride home with you?" Mike said. "Don't have a car today."

"Sure. I'm going right away. Hurry up."

CHAPTER 2

Make Birds Touch Wings

THE WESTERN MOTEL was built halfway between Long Beach and Los Angeles. At first it was in the open country and its occupants were riggers from the oil fields and an occasional tourist. It was a poor place in which to put a motel and it should have failed, but history caught up with the Western Motel and made it a success. The tall, spidery oil derricks marched closer to it every year. Then in 1922 the land speculation started, in some way became a bubble and around the Western Motel there was a vast pattern of brightly colored tents with men in derby hats giving away sandwiches, cold pop, taffy candy and one free lot if you bought another for $500. A sign saying "Los Angeles — Population 1,500,000 by 1940!!!" was placed along the highway in front of the Western Motel. The Western Motel prospered and the owner, a Texan, responded by building an elaborate façade around the original kernel of each unit of the motel. One was converted into a nipa hut, another an igloo, another a tiny colonial house, another a replica of Monticello. And through the years the Western Motel continued to prosper.

Inside the Monticello unit of the Western Motel Mike was lying on the bed. On the wall was a mirror and he could see himself when he turned his head. He was entirely naked and in his mouth he had a cigar. His hands were behind his head and occasionally he would blow a cloud of thick white smoke to the ceiling. It was hot and he could feel drops of sweat trickle through the hair on his chest. He had strong, powerful legs and big hands. His face was regular, but not handsome because his jaw was too large and his nose too broad. He had short brown hair. Mike winked at himself in the mirror.

"Mike, don't lie on the bed naked," Miss Bell said from the bathroom door. She was wearing a loose silk wrapper. "And you shouldn't smoke cigars. You're too young."

"I like cigars," Mike said, without taking the cigar from his mouth. "If I'm old enough to do this," and his hand circled and took in the room and Miss Bell, "I'm old enough to smoke."

Miss Bell flushed and she walked over and sat on the edge of the bed. Without her glasses on, her eyes looked soft and unfocused. She had an attractive face, although her figure was starting to soften. Her breasts were still large and firm, but her hips bulged the kimono slightly. Her fingers were fattening and a ring almost disappeared on her left hand.

She eats too much, Mike thought. He remembered the countless hamburgers and Mile-Hi cones and malted milks they had eaten together. She always ate with a breathless laugh, repeating that she shouldn't, but always ordering a hamburger or an extra little paper bag of french-fried potatoes.

"What are you going to do in the fall?" Miss Bell asked. "Have you made up your mind?"

"No."

"Why don't you go to college, Mike? You're a good student."

"But why go to college? What good will it do me?"

"It will broaden your horizons, it will . . ." She saw the look on his face, faltered a moment and went on. "It will help you to get a good job when you get out of college."

"Did it broaden your horizons?" Mike asked. "Your dad went to college. Did it broaden his horizons? He still got cleaned out on that Belgian hare proposition."

"I never should have told you about the Belgian hare business," Miss Bell said. "That doesn't mean a thing. Today you can't get a decent job unless you have a college education."

She had told Mike about the Belgian hares several weeks before. During the late 1920's all of Southern California had been swept by an excitement over Belgian hares and newspapers carried advertisements of prize bucks and does. It was alleged that the skins of the hares would sell for fabulous sums and thousands of the hares were bred all over the state. Brochures were circulated which stated that the pelts would be made into exquisite fur coats and much was made of the fine sheen and long hair of the hares. Miss Bell's father had resisted for months, but finally a man he knew made $2500 with the hares and Mr. Bell purchased a matched buck and doe for $1750. They were beautiful creatures, with huge soft eyes and moist noses and he carefully nourished them in his bedroom. But a month later the excitement died, the brochures disappeared, there were a few stories in the papers and Mr. Bell sold the hares to a poultry store for seventy-five cents.

"I can get a good job without going to college," Mike said.

"Doing what?" Miss Bell said.

"In the studios, they pay big money there," he said tentatively. "Or working out at the aircraft factories."

"Oh, Mike, that isn't big money, those aren't big jobs," Miss Bell said. "Those are the little jobs. Law, medicine, business executives; those are the big jobs. You can't get one of those jobs without going to college."

"You can make money without going to college," Mike said. "I know that." He puffed on the cigar, felt a drop of brown bitter juice gather in the corner of his mouth, but let it stay there. "You can make money lots of other ways without having a college degree. Did Henry Ford go to college? Or Jim Farley? Or Charles Lindbergh?"

"There are exceptions, Mike," Miss Bell said. "I admit that. But they're flukes. Most of the big jobs go today to men who have a college training. Certainly most of the famous men in the United States have gone to college. I can prove that."

"How?" Mike said. He took the cigar out of his mouth and looked over at her.

She put on her glasses. Her eyes came sharply into focus; her face looked thinner. She walked over to the bureau and opened the little night case she had brought to the Western Motel. She took out a thick book.

"Now don't be angry, Mike," she said. "I brought this from the school library just in case you raised the question. You never take what I say. This is a copy of *Who's Who*. It's a list of all the famous people in the United States. Just name me one person, any person and if he's famous he'll be in this book." She paused and added with triumph, "And you'll see that most of them have gone to college."

"What if he isn't in the book?" Mike asked. "How do I know they've got all the really famous people in there?"

He bent forward, took the cigar out of his mouth. The little trickles of sweat ran down his chest, gathered around his waist, ran down between his legs.

"If they're famous they have to be in this book," Miss Bell said and laughed. "That is the definition of being famous . . . being in this book. If you aren't in the book you aren't famous."

"Yeah, says who?" he said, but his voice faltered. He stared at the book in her hand.

"It's just so, Mike." Miss Bell said and now she was speaking in the voice with which she talked in the classroom: even, confident, assured. "This is the book where they gather the names of famous men. They are experts at it."

"O.K., O.K.," Mike said. He took the cigar out of his mouth, threw it toward the wastebasket in the corner. It fell in neatly and in a moment a tendril of blue smoke came straight up out of the wastebasket. Mike leaned back on the pillow and closed his eyes. "O.K. What does it say about John Cromwell?"

He could hear her flick through the pages, run them through her smooth expert fingers with a hissing noise. Her fingernail scratched down a page. She came over and sat on the edge of the bed.

"Here it is, John Cromwell," she said. "Read it."

She laid the book on his chest. He opened his eyes and picked it up. Her finger was under a name. He read slowly.

CROMWELL, *John W., lawyer, b. San Francisco, 1895. Stanford University, Stanford Law School. m. Susan Donner; s. John Jr.; Timothy; d. Maria; Assemblyman, 1928–32 Sixth District; Congressman 1932–35, Ninth District; Phi Beta Kappa, Sigma Kappa Alpha, Beta Sigma Chi, Bohemian Club, Pacific Union Club. Articles various law journals. "Torts and the Common Law," "Hobbes and Natural Law." 2323 Hyde St., San Francisco.*

"See?" Miss Bell said. "He went to college. Stanford."

"Yeah," Mike said slowly. He ran his eye down the page, read other brief biographies.

"Why did you pick him?" Miss Bell asked.

"I heard him talk once in Exposition Park," Mike said. "God, could he talk. He was talking to a Mexican picnic. They were celebrating a revolution or something. Or the anniversary of a revolution. Something like that."

"What did he talk about?"

"I don't remember. It doesn't matter. Something about the glorious revolution." Mike slowly sat up in the bed. "But Jesus he had 'em. Really had 'em in his hand. I was standing in the crowd and they said he was the son of a real old rich California family. He looked crummy. His suit all covered with cigar ashes and he scratched all the time. It made them laugh. I even laughed. He was comical. He just stared out at the crowd and let them laugh. But when he talked. By God, they stopped laughing quick enough."

"Don't say 'God' so often, Mike," Miss Bell whispered. "It's just a habit. Doesn't sound nice."

"When he started to talk he was like a preacher," Mike went on. "Just like a preacher, except that he made you feel bad. As if you'd done something wrong. God, half those Mexicans were crying by the time he finished. I never forgot him."

"Well, name anyone else, Mike, just anyone at all that is famous in his field. He'll be in this book and nine times out of ten he will have gone to college. You just can't get into an important job if you don't have a college degree. Name another person."

"O.K., O.K.," Mike said. "That's enough. I'll go to college. I don't know how or on what, but I'll go."

"You will?" she said uncertainly.

She licked her lips and took off her glasses. Suddenly she looked disappointed, the sort of dull surprise of a person who pushes against a door he thought was locked and finds that it is open.

"Where will you go?" she asked. "Stanford, U.S.C., California?"

"Stanford," he said although he had never thought about it until a moment ago.

"That's out of town. I'll miss you. You'll be gone for a long time."

"Sure. I'll take Hank and go to Stanford."

"Hank Moore?" she said. "I thought he didn't like you. You're always arguing. I don't think he likes you."

"Doesn't like me?" Mike said. He leaned up on his elbow and stared at her. Then he laughed. "O.K., maybe he doesn't like me. But he'll go with me. We get along all right. Even if we're not best friends we got . . . we got respect for one another." Then, because his last words made him suddenly shy, his face went hard. "Don't worry about Hank. He'll go with me."

Her eyes misted as she looked at him.

"I'll miss you," she said. "You were my best student. I guess you're

the best student Manual Arts High has had for a long time. Everybody
says so."

"Sure, everybody says so," Mike said ironically. "What do they
know?"

I ought to be good at Manual, he thought, there aren't many good
ones there. That huge sprawling school was designed for the production of mechanics, printers, welders, typesetters, linotype operators,
bookbinders, molders and auto repairmen. The same families that
insisted that their sons take a training course for a trade also insisted
that the school offer a college preparatory course. So there were
always a few tiny classes which studied Greek, Latin, English composition, modern languages and the other college preparatory courses.
Among this little group Mike was the undisputed leader.

"Those lunkheads. What would they know?" he went on. "The
competition isn't very tough at Manual," he said.

"Will your folks be able to help you at Stanford?" Miss Bell asked.

"Are you kidding?" Mike laughed. "They don't have a penny. I've
had to earn all my clothes money and spending money since I entered
high school. You know that."

"Look, Mike, I'll help," Miss Bell said. "I've still got some money
left from what Father left when he . . . died." Her father had committed suicide the day after he sold the two Belgian hares to the
poultry shop. "I'd be glad to do it."

Mike watched her soft, nearsighted eyes search for his face, her
lips twitching as she tried to read his expression. He smiled at her
and her eyes widened and his smile was echoed in her face. No,
Miss Bell, not this, he thought. For months I've taken hamburgers,
malted milks, gabardine slacks, small change for rubbers, movie tickets,
your car and books from you. But this is different.

"No, I'll do it alone," Mike said.

"Don't be silly," Miss Bell said. Her voice was a little desperate.
"I'll make it as a loan."

"It's not my conscience," Mike said. "I just don't want help from
anyone."

He sensed that this was the first loop in a snare. It came across
the air of the hot room, rested about him with a thin delicacy that
he knew could become a tough web of obligation as it was joined by
dozens of other loops of the snare. Her smooth plump face worked
as she tried to read the expression on his face; her lips smiled tentatively, then collapsed.

"Please, Mike, I'd like to help," she said.

Mike sat up, reached over to the table for a White Owl. He slid the cigar out of its cellophane wrapper, put the band around his little finger and lit the cigar. He opened one side of his mouth, let a thick white curl of smoke float up past his eyes. Miss Bell's eyes squinted as she tried to see through the smoke.

For a moment he thought of asking her to come to Stanford; to teach up there. He could have the Buick, the hamburgers, the free food. And she would always be waiting, her lips ready to tremble, her hand ready to guide him to her body. Always ready. And then, for no reason that he knew, almost by instinct, he rejected it all; became protective.

"No. I don't want your help or anyone's help," he said sharply. "First I'd take the money and then I'd take the Buick and pretty soon you'd want to move up to Stanford to be close to your investment and protect it. I don't want to be anyone's investment."

Miss Bell felt the loop of the snare draw tight and snap. Her face grew hard, her eyes narrowed to hard black points, she sat up as if she were in front of her class.

"God damn you, Mike," she said. "You owe me something. You can't talk to me like that. Sitting there naked and talking like that; it's just not right. Pull something over yourself," she finished with a shrill voice.

"I don't owe you a god damn thing, Miss Bell," Mike said. "Not a god damn thing."

Mike reached forward and pulled her gown down over her shoulders so that it fell down her arms and she was naked to the waist. She raised her arms once to cover her round full breasts and then, the hard look fading from her face, stared at Mike and in confusion at her breasts. She took her glasses off. She let her arms fall.

"You don't even care," she whispered. "I've almost ruined myself over you and you don't care. If they ever hear about this at school I may lose my job and still you don't care. Not the least bit."

"They know about it," Mike said. "But they won't fire you. They won't even mention it. They'll try to cover it up, ignore that it ever happened. You don't have to worry."

Miss Bell seemed numb with despair or boredom or shock. She stared down at her breasts.

He caressed her absently, for he was thinking of the family. He was thinking what they would say about his going to college. Es-

pecially what his father would say . . . his father who had only three
moods, none of which Mike had understood.

In the first mood his father locked his legs around the polished
wood of the cello and his stubby fingers suddenly became light on
the bow. As the rich fat music flowed through the house his eyes
became soft and remote and seemed not to see the dirty wood stove,
the half-empty milk bottles on the sink, the grease-soaked papers
containing chunks of food, the leanness of his children. Almost in-
variably it was Bach that he played, over and over, working with a
ceaseless patience at revising the suites for the violin and cello. Occasionally he would stop, bend forward and with a tiny sharp knife
scrape a note off the page and with a beautiful round hand draw
in another.

Always he would practice in the kitchen and then everyone must
leave the room. Sometimes he would begin to practice late in the
afternoon and continue until it was eight or nine and the four children and his wife sat on the back porch waiting for the notes to
stop so they could eat supper.

He had taken pupils, but none of them lasted long. The operator
of the ice plant down the street sent his daughter and Mike's father
had given her three lessons. She had grasped the bow in her fat
fingers and sawed resolutely at the strings, her frightened eyes following Mike's father rather than the music.

"Do you have no ear for the music? Are you not aware that you
are breaking the notes?" his father would shout at the girl. "This
is not chopping chips from a log, this is making music from a bow
and gut strings. Try again, but for Christ's sake go easily."

The girl's eyes would grow larger and her knuckles glowed red
as she tightened her grasp on the bow and her knees locked tighter
around the cello. During the third lesson he had grabbed the bow
from her hands and began to talk to her in a low intense voice.

"It is like two birds, my child. The bow is a bird and the cello
is a bird. Bring them together softly, make the wings barely touch.
Do it gently and the birds will make music for you. Forget the
muscles of your arms and legs. Close your eyes and do it softly."

The girl closed her eyes tightly and brought the bow down on
the tight gut. The notes croaked leaden and broken from the polished
brown wood of the cello. Her eyes popped open and she looked frantically up at her teacher. He leaned over and taking the bow and
cello from her turned away.

"Go tell your father you cannot play the cello. Tell him you have no ear for music, your fingers are stiff and clumsy and you have an empty head and he has scared you too much at home," he said without looking at the girl.

When the girl left he flexed his fingers for several minutes and then bending over the cello played for six hours while his family stood on the back porch listening to the rich fat music that flowed underneath and through the door.

In his second mood Mike's father was apoplectic and red-faced over the table, pounding savagely with his fist as he told of the iniquities of the capitalists and the cunning evil atrocities of the monopolies. As the dishes chattered on the table he thundered the sins of America's wealthy few. Each of the laws to protect property seemed to be a goad in his flesh. In this mood the children who could crept quietly from the room, but those under his eye sat silently with their shoulders hunched over, their eyes big in their heads and nodding dumbly like a claque of infants. His father would stand in front of the tiny row of children flourishing a newspaper, waving the crinkled paper in his hand.

"Look, here it says that income taxes are to be reduced. See, here it says it. Read," and he would shove the paper under the eyes of the children who looked with glazed, frightened faces at the maze of type. "The income taxes for the rich are to be reduced and all the time people starve in the streets. The filthy sniveling bastards, the vultures. Every ounce of fat on their bodies is a pound of flesh from our bodies."

His voice raged and was heavy with a vitriolic hate. The little claque nodded pointlessly and his voice went higher and more bitter. Occasionally his wife would interrupt.

"Not in front of the children, John," her flat voice said. "They're too young, they don't understand."

"No. Not in front of the children," he roared. "They don't understand hunger or cold? They don't know what it is to belch cold potato soup for thirty days in a row? Do you think they can't see their toes sticking from their shoes?"

"But they don't understand," her flat voice went on. "It's too much for children to know." She would bend her head over into her hands and begin to sob, a sound as flat and dull as her voice. Even now Mike could not remember his mother, she was a gray formless shadow, her personality so thinly drawn beside the titanic rages and great hates of her husband that she almost vanished.

"They can't learn too young. When children are undernourished in their mother's womb they know these things by intuition," the father said, but now his voice was lower and his face was suddenly tired. "They know these things as intuitively as I know my music." He turned and looked at the children and their heads bobbed knowingly at him and then bent back down to inspect their knobby knees, afraid to look at his face. He wadded the paper in his hands, dropped it to the floor and as he walked toward the door he became smaller, more crushed, seemingly almost to shrink in size as he walked. The sudden deflation of pressure, the crumbling of their father would bring tears to the children's eyes and they would sit in the little row, their shoulders shaking delicately, making flat small sounds to match their mother.

In the third mood, the best one, Mike's father was tender and kind. He would take a child on each knee and gently talk to them of a world where there was no law and every man was every other man's brother. He talked softly of Kropotkin, a Russian nobleman, kind and generous and loving every man in the world. He talked of St. Simon and of Eugene Debs, whose picture was cut from a newspaper and was growing yellow and dried out over the kitchen sink. He told them of Joe Hill and the Wobblies who went out against the guns and bayonets of a superior enemy bceause they wanted to see justice done to all people. To the children it was a lovely fairy story where huge men with beards and strong knotted muscles were infinitely kind to women and children. The children smiled at one another and boldly squeezed their father's arm and ran their fingers over the curly black hair on the back of his hands. He rocked back and forth and when he had finished his fairy tales he would begin to hum a strange exciting song to which they added their piping small voices . . . "Arise ye prisoners of starvation, arise ye workers of the world . . ."

When the four children played by themselves they fought to play Joe Hill. The winner would be chased by the other three who were "Salt Lake City Special Deputies," and Joe Hill would dodge around the house throwing imaginary balls of wet phosphorus into wheat fields, binding bundles of dynamite to railroad car wheels, throwing kerosene on cribs of corn. Finally the deputies would capture Joe Hill and would stand him against the house with a bandage over his eyes. As they crouched down with their sticks leveled to fire, Joe Hill would strip the bandage from his eyes and look straight at them. Then they would make popping noises with their tongues and Joe Hill would buckle against the side of the house and finally slide in a crumpled

heap to the ground. Then they would start the game over and someone else would be Joe Hill.

Mike thought of a Christmas many years before. They had never
had presents or a Christmas tree, for Father had stated that they
were symbols of a corrupted ideal. Even when Father had a good
job at the studios or the Hollywood Bowl or in a string quartet they
did not have presents, but spent Christmas Day behind the curtains
of the home watching the other children in the neighborhood run
their cheap, painted bicycles and toys up and down the sidewalk.
This Christmas mother had promised them a Christmas tree and presents and the children had carefully not mentioned this to their father.

It was late Christmas Eve when Mike had been awakened by a
sound like tiny crashing cymbals from the living room. He had
walked quietly to the door and opened it the slightest crack to see
into the room. The first thing he saw was a small Christmas tree
upside down in the far corner of the room and around it in perfect
little splashes of blue, red and green glass were the shattered Christmas
tree ornaments. They lay beautiful and sparkling on the floor, each
one smashed into a circle of fragments. The glass head of a reindeer
was the only intact piece in the wreckage. Mike's father was standing
in the middle of the room, his hand still in the air after throwing
the Christmas tree against the wall. He was smiling, a thin, gray
smile that had nothing of humor in it, but much of pleasure and self-
righteousness.

His mother was standing crouched over in front of the tree facing
the center of the room where his father stood. Her lips were drawn
tight and thin so that her teeth showed. She was talking in a low
fierce voice, just opening her teeth enough to let the words out. All
Mike could remember of her face was the lips and chin and the
white teeth.

"God damn you, John Freesmith. If I had the strength I'd claw your
eyes out," she whispered at him. "You've beat them down so often
with your crazy talk of injustice and your beautiful bloody revolution
that's going to make all men brothers they don't know where or what
to stand on. You're making them confused, almost crazy. You just
keep cutting the ground out from underneath them."

A fleck of spittle ran down her chin and with an incredibly sharp
motion she jerked her hand across her lips and went on talking.

"I don't care about the food and this house, but you have to leave
them something to live on. When they're older let them become

anarchists or revolutionaries and begin to hate, but now those ideas are just dry bones that mean nothing to them. Oh, for the sake of Jesus Christ, let them have something."

Mike's father stood startled in the middle of the room, his eyes bulging slightly as he listened. Occasionally he looked at the shattered Christmas tree in the corner and flexed his fingers with that quick expert way he had. Finally he began to talk. He talked of the brotherhood of man again and how Christmas had corrupted the ideal, but Mike could tell he was uncertain. He hesitated over the words and tried to rephrase the arguments in a new and more persuasive way.

Mike's mother stood listening to the words flow from his mouth and finally she gave a shudder and turning toward the broken tree buried her face in her hands. Then the old flat dull cry began to tear out between her hands and as soon as both Mike and his father heard it they both knew she had surrendered. Suddenly his father's words became confident again and began to flow faster and after Mike had closed the door and crawled in bed he could hear the confident monotone drone on through the dreary Christmas night . . .

Miss Bell was quivering. Her neck was pink and on her cheek Mike could see a round bright spot. He put a hand over her breast and squeezed. She shuddered and a tiny, sharp yelp of pleasure came unexpectedly out of her mouth. She turned and stretched out beside him on the bed and put her arms around him.

"You won't forget me," she whispered harshly, "I won't let you. I just won't let you. Ever, ever, ever . . ." Her fingers dug into his back.

Mike laughed, his hands full of her flesh, automatically caressing. He laughed for he had already forgotten her, quite literally for a moment he could not remember her name and he had no memory of her face or body or actions. She was already forgotten and he was thinking of other things.

CHAPTER 3

Across the Grapevine

HIGHWAY 99 between Los Angeles and Bakersfield cuts directly across the Tehachapi Mountains in a twisting narrow road which was known as the Ridge Route. At the bottom of almost every elevation there was the huge burned-out hulk of a truck which wore out its brake-shoes on the descent and had to crash off the road. On the Bakersfield side of the Ridge Route, beyond the Grapevine, is a smooth long strip of asphalt which drops gently toward Bakersfield for twenty miles without a turn in the road. Here is where the great semi-trailers are in the most danger, for the slope is so gradual that unless the driver drops down into a lower gear every few miles he is soon going so fast that his brakes are crisped black at the first touch and the truck runs away. On the long slope the runaway trucks reach eighty or ninety or even one hundred miles an hour before the driver will run the truck off the road. The straight rows of eucalyptus trees that line the road are scarred and battered by the accidents and occasionally an entire tree will be destroyed or stunted.

In the summer the wrecks are marked by enormous clots of alfalfa that look as if they had been exploded over the landscape. In the spring the wrecks will scatter carrots down the road and occasionally an egg truck will crash and gobbets of egg yolk are splattered over the fields, the roadside cafés, the black asphalt and passing cars. When one of the milk trucks crashes there is a sudden eruption of milk running down the side of the road and then, with incredible speed, the flies arrive in great dense clouds.

Hank Moore and Mike came down the Grapevine in Hank's
Model-A on their way to Stanford. Hank kept his long thin fingers
on the gearshift and when it wobbled too much he double-clutched
and slid it into second gear. Then the Ford would tremble, the rear
wheels would shriek against the asphalt and the car would slow down
to forty-five miles an hour.

"How much money have you got, Hank," Mike asked.

"About five hundred bucks," Hank said.

Mike whistled.

"Where did you get that?" he asked.

"I had it. Had it around for a long time."

"I'm damned. Old Hankus with all that money and no one knew it.
You're a funny one. Live by yourself in a boardinghouse, don't have a
family, only work a little bit and you've got five hundred bucks. I
work every Saturday and all summer and all I've got is two hundred
bucks. And fifty of that my mother gave me. I don't know where she
got it. Come on, Hank. Where did you get that money?"

Hank looked over at Mike and grinned.

"Maybe I'll tell you later. But I didn't steal it. It's mine. I earned
it."

"How long will my two hundred bucks last at Stanford?"

"Not very long. Tuition is $115, room and board at Encina is $120
a quarter. Books will cost a little. You haven't got enough to last
even a quarter."

"I'll make it do. I've got ways. I understand you can sign a note for
the tuition and pay it off when you graduate. So I'll have enough for
the first quarter."

The eucalyptus trees whirred by, big shreds of bark hanging from
their boles, putting a pungent oil smell out into the air. They passed
a truck going very slowly and as they went by they saw huge round
bottles labeled ACID nestled in excelsior on the bed of the truck.

"Look, Mike. I don't want a lot of talk and crap about money when
we get up there," Hank said and his voice was sharp. "I'm going to
have enough other things to worry about. We'll pool our money and
I'll let you know when we start to run out. When that happens we'll
talk about money. Not before. O.K.?"

"That wouldn't be fair. You're the guy with most . . ." Mike started
to say.

"Don't give me that crap, I said," Hank cut in. "Just say yes or no.
If I put in more money than you I'll get a good return on it. One way
or another."

"What do you mean by that?" Mike asked.

"For one thing I'm depending on you to pull me through some of the courses. The ones in English and history and that sort of thing. I don't do very well in those." Hank hesitated and then went on. "I didn't tell you, but I'm going to take a pre-med course. There will be lots of chemistry and biology and that sort of thing. I want to concentrate on those. You pull me through the other courses and we'll forget about the money. Just say yes or no."

"Yes."

From behind them they heard the shrill, peculiarly heavy whine of truck tires going too fast. Hank looked in the rear-view mirror and pulled far over to the right. The truck flashed by them; too fast to see anything except a white blob of a face, a long stack of red bricks and the blur of wheels. As it passed they heard a harsh long-continued grind, the raw smash of metal against metal, and then a snap as the transmission refused to slip into a lower gear.

"He must be doing eighty," Hank said quietly.

"His brakes were gone," Mike said. "You could smell them as he went by."

The truck quickly grew smaller, seemed to fade away. The red bricks shimmered for a moment and then the truck disappeared around a slower-moving truck. Faintly, but still with the savage tear of metal gnashing, they heard the truck try to go into gear. Each time it snapped out. Then even the sound was gone.

"Mike, what do they do when you get to Stanford?" Hank asked. "I mean do they have someone to meet you, to show you around?"

Mike looked over, startled.

"Hankus, no one is going to say hello, goodbye, or yes, no, kiss my ass," Mike said. "They'll take your money, stamp your cards and that will be it. What did you expect?"

"I didn't know what to expect. That's why I asked. O.K. Now I know."

"You know, but it doesn't make you feel very good," Mike said. He put his hands behind his head and leaned back in the seat. "Well, it makes me feel good. I don't want anyone to shake my hand and show me around and then feel that he has done me a favor. I want to arrive and look around and know that every person I look at doesn't give the slightest damn about me. No obligations, no debts. Then you can do what you want."

"What do you want to do?" Hank asked quietly.

"I'm not sure. But when I decide I want to be able to do it. I want to be able to look at every person and figure they are enemies and then decide what I want to do. I don't want to be tied up with some of them." Mike hesitated, reached for adequate words. "It sounds a little crazy, Hank. I know. But I've got a theory."

"What's your theory?"

"I don't have it all worked out yet. Just part of it. But I'll work out the rest of it. But right now I know I don't want to feel obligated. I don't want a lot of this phony friendship crap. Later when I know more I'll tell you the whole theory."

Hank looked over at Mike. Mike was looking straight ahead and he had an odd half-smile; the lips drawn back as if to smile, no real humor on his face. Really, Hank thought, it's like the beginning of a snarl, but when Mike does it, it looks attractive. He knew that Mike would never tell him the rest of the theory.

Ten miles later they passed the semi with the bricks. When it hit a tree at the side of the road the bricks had kept moving and sliced off the top of the cab. There was an ambulance there and someone was picking wet fragments off the stacks of bricks. A bored cop was motioning cars past. A man and woman had stopped their car and were quickly loading some of the loose bricks into the back seat. A cop ran toward them and waved them away. Hank drove quickly past and a few miles later he took the turnoff for Coalinga and Blackwell's Corners.

They drove for a half hour past old oil well derricks. The derricks were oil soaked and great clots of dust stuck to them. Beneath most of the derricks was a neat shiny engine which drove a pumping arm slowly up and down. The various pumps were connected by a pattern of pipes which led to large shiny tanks. There were no men in the oil fields for these were old wells and needed little care. They slowed down for Taft and then shot down the road toward Coalinga.

"Hank, where did you come from before you came to L.A.?" Mike asked.

Hank looked at Mike and saw that he was smiling, but he saw it was a different smile now.

"North Dakota."

"Really? I thought you were from New York or Chicago."

"That's because I'm Jewish. Everybody in California thinks that Jews come from Brooklyn or Chicago."

"Was your name Hank Moore in North Dakota?" Mike asked. "That isn't a very Jewish name."

"It isn't Jewish at all. My name has always been Hank Moore though. I had a father who thought if you called things by different names you might eventually change them."

"And he wanted to change things?"

"Sure. He wanted to stop being a Jew and be something else. I couldn't blame the poor bastard. When he was a kid his father took him out on the road to sell hardware, cheap jewelry, perfume, everything. Dad was no good at it and somehow he got into the hotel business and drifted from town to town. Finally he wound up owning a railroad hotel in this town in North Dakota. Ever seen a railroad hotel? Well, this one was a beauty . . ."

It had twenty-eight rooms and was just fifty feet from the railroad tracks and a set of switching spurs. It was a square ugly old building that had been painted once, but now had only a few shreds of paint up around the eaves and in spots where the sun never hit. In the winter the wind came solid and cold off the prairie and the half-inch boards of the hotel seemed barely able to keep it out, really to only break the flat blast of it. In the summer it absorbed all the heat in the sky; filled itself with moist-packed hotness during the day and held it tightly throughout the night. When trains went by the hotel chattered, light bulbs flickered and water spilled out of glasses that were too full. There were no fans in the hotel and each six rooms shared a toilet and bath. The washbowls had deep yellow scars in them where dripping water had built up a slow growing stain.

Occasionally a commercial man would come there by mistake, but he would never stay longer than one night.

Hank's father sat behind the desk in the lobby. A naked electric bulb shone down on his balding head and threw his watering eyes into the shadow. He had long sloping shoulders and big muscles, but his body had the wrinkled baggy look of an athlete who has suddenly stopped exercising. His skin drooped off his arms in sheets and was dry and scaly. The skin on his face was a collection of sags and folds that pressed down on one another. He never spoke to anyone. Occasionally he would reach an arm out and stop a brakeman or engineer who hadn't paid for a few weeks and hold his palm up. The men would laugh and give him whatever change they had and he would enter the sum in a large notebook which he kept in a childish scrawling hand.

Once a month his father caught a ride in a caboose to Bismarck, and was back in two days. After each trip he would take a slip of

white paper carefully from his pocket and drive it on the nail of a
spindle that he kept in the back of the unlocked safe. Hank had
looked once at the pieces of paper. The old ones on the bottom were
browned with age, while the ones on the top were crisper and newer
looking. At the top of each slip of paper was the letterhead, "Dr. J. J.
Locke. Specialist in Men's Diseases. All Consultation Private, No
Painful Operations Necessary." And then the line, "Laboratory Report."
Under this would be a line in handwriting. "Wassermann test, plus."
Occasionally the slips of paper would bear a prescription for pills
and his father would take the pills for a few days and then forget
them. A drawer under his desk was full of little blue boxes which
had forgotten pills in them.

Hank could not remember his mother. She had disappeared somewhere long ago.

Hank had worked in the hotel when he was a boy. He had peeled
potatoes in the kitchen, pounded the thick red strips of tough meat
with flour, opened cans of pale string beans and helped serve the
food in thick porcelain bowls. He had cut hundreds of pies into dry
crusty triangles, each with a lip of thin sugary goo on its edges and
served them to the men in the dining room. Sometimes when they
could not get a chambermaid he made the beds and swept the corridors. The floors were old soft wood and they smelled of Lysol. The
bedrooms smelled of tobacco and coal and dried grease. He liked
working in the kitchen best because he could talk to the endless
stream of Chinese cooks that worked there. They came in, silent,
yellow and smooth skinned, cooked for several months and then moved
on. One had been a college boy from Columbia on his way back to
China. He had talked patiently to Hank about Confucianism, explain-
ing over and over in his singsong voice that it all hinged on the
love and respect for one's parents. Hank had laughed at him and
finally the cook had left one night after slapping Hank with the flat
edge of a knife.

When Hank was eight he had asked his father about going to
school. His father had turned his heavy, shiny head down from the
height of the stool and looked over the counter at Hank. He had
scratched his head and a few white scales fell from his fingernails.
Finally he had turned his hands up in a noncommittal gesture and
shrugged his shoulders. So Hank had forgotten about school until he
was thirteen.

When he was not working in the hotel Hank hung around various buildings and offices in the town. The best place was the rear of the taxicab office where the tobacco-stained politics of the town were decided. In front of the taxi office there was a neon light that blinked steadily, day and night, summer and winter, "Taxi. Five ride for the price of one." In the rear of the office there were a half dozen chairs with smooth leather cushions on them. The chairs were occupied by three scrawny-necked merchants, who were brothers, and the fat-jowled chief of police. The chief was related to one of the merchants. In the '28 campaign they had put a picture of Al Smith underneath the spittoon and all you could see was the fringe of Al's head. Across the white part of the sign someone printed "A Dirty Cat-licker." The spit splashed brown stains over the picture and by election time it had vanished beneath a hardened scum of old tobacco-specked saliva. When the election was over Hank had removed the poster and looked at the circle that had lain under the spittoon. There was a bright circle of a man's face with a bright politician's smile on it and the then hardened brown juice, framing it all. He cut it out with a razor and took it back to the hotel.

In the taxi office they had a file case full of little half-pint bottles of corn whisky and when an election got close, which was seldom, they would send the three taxicab drivers out into town. The drivers would scour the town, making their tiny bribes with the bottles. They would sweep the pool hall, the hotel, the several Negro families along side the railroad track, the farm boys in town for election, the whores, everyone before them into the polls. They would come just before the polls closed, a waving, yelling froth of men and women. They would flow into the polls and vote. The drivers would herd them in gently, joking with them and making sure that they knew where to put the X. No one ever cheated when they got behind the black curtain; none of them got that drunk, not on a half pint of whisky.

The town regularly spent $43,500 a year and the three turkey-necked merchants and the chief controlled every cent of it. They noted it down on the back of envelopes and shifted the figures around and laughed a good deal. Once they gave the chief $1200 to go to an F.B.I. course in Washington, but he had a few drinks on the train and went to New York and stayed in a big hotel with a famous movie actress for a week. "Forty dollars for black lace panties and eighty-five for good bonded bourbon," he had told the merchants when he returned and they had filled the back of the office with laughter. He never did tell anyone the actress's name.

Hank learned about business and high finance from a Jewish tailor. His name was Cohen and he had a little shop on the main street. He had lost his wife and four children in a pogrom in Poland. The mob had closed in dense and black on the ghetto, moving down the streets with a soft tinkling of broken glass and a great roaring sound. Cohen had hurried his family ahead of him as long as he could and then the youngest boy had said he had a stitch in his side and wanted to stop. In a second of panic Cohen had left his wife and four children huddled together against a wall as he ran ahead to search for a hiding place. He heard the strange lowing, eager sound of the mob and then as he ran back toward his family he saw the mob reach them. There was a nameless, odd, sharp snapping noise as the mob absorbed his family and he knew instinctively that they were all dead. He ran toward the mob, a thin scarecrow of a man, hoping to be killed, to be kicked to death, to suffer for a few seconds and then be gone with his family. He muttered curses through his stringy beard as he ran shouting in a high messianic voice for revenge and threw his skinny arms wildly in the air.

The mob hesitated as they saw him. The low ominous howl diminished and they stared at him with bewilderment. By the time he reached them they were no longer a mob, only stolid businessmen, housewives, laborers, electricians, fishmongers. He threw himself on these individuals, hoping to be picked up and beaten and killed. But they pushed him away, the bright excitement fading from their eyes and replaced by a look of boredom. The crowd split up, began to walk away and there was no way that he could arouse them. He was never able to find the bodies of his family, for as if the mob had been a huge animal they had been absorbed, digested, and vanished away.

Since the pogrom Cohen had always felt threatened by crowds. When his tailor shop had three or four customers simultaneously his eyes began to bulge slightly and he breathed quickly. Hank was in his shop one day when the Rotary Club came out of the hotel after their luncheon, their feet scraping on the pavement, their voices laughing, the sound of a crowd of people in motion. Cohen's head snapped up, his needle gleamed in the air, he seemed to stop breathing for a long second. Hank listened with the Jew's ears and a shiver of fear ran down his back as the businessmen laughed, shuffled their feet, lifted their voices in raucous jokes.

"It's the Rotary Club," Hank said, leaning toward Cohen. "They've just finished their Tuesday lunch."

"Ya, ya, of course," Cohen breathed, "only the Rotary Club." His lips curved into a smile although his eyes were brilliant with fear. He did not relax until the last sound had left the street.

Hank was in Cohen's shop on a Fourth of July. Across town a band was playing, firecrackers popped and a parade was beginning. The sounds drifted lazily through the hot summer air, people put chairs on their lawns to watch the parade pass, the pulse of the town was slow. Cohen sat with the cloth close to his face, stitching rapidly and talking into the cloth.

The parade rounded a corner far away and suddenly, by some odd refraction of sound, in the tailor shop Hank and Cohen could hear the shuffling of the parade, slow, steady, cadenced. The music stopped for a moment and down the hot dead air of the town, caught between the unpainted buildings, came the sound of marching feet. The sound of feet was not obscured by the music, but was a raw, solid sound with a vitality of its own. Cohen looked over the piece of cloth, his eyes glittered with terror. He put the cloth down and stood up.

"I'm going for a walk," he said and started for the rear door.

"I'll go with you," Hank said, but the tailor did not even hear him. He walked quickly, staring straight ahead. He stumbled once over a sleeping dog and swung his head vaguely toward it when it barked in pain. Hank walked beside him. They were at the edge of town and still the sound of the parade had not diminished, but seemed to throb and swell as if the parade were growing in size. At some point Hank stopped thinking of it as a parade and thought of it as a mob also.

They both walked faster and faster and when they got to the edge of town they cut across a field of rye. They were almost running as they crossed it and when he looked back Hank could see the erratic, zigzag path they had left, as if two small and insane animals had passed through. They splashed through a small creek and were oblivious of the mud that caked on their shoes. At some point the sound of the parade died away and they began to walk at a normal pace. Late that night they re-entered the town and Hank went quietly to the railroad hotel.

Ever since that night Hank had known that he was a Jew. The crazy, stumbling flight through the town and across the fields was a kind of ritual; an initiation; the assumption of a burden; a primitive act of faith. Hank was thirteen years old at the time.

Hank learned about love and the family from the girls at the hotel. Some of them were plain dumpy girls who worked in restaurants or in stores and others were simply whores, who wore flashy clothes very tight across the hips. And the professionals wore furs that Hank could not forget. They were skimpy fox pelts with the heads still attached. The jaws were strengthened by a spring and each of the mouths bit into the tail of another and they went over a woman's shoulder in an endless circle of biting foxes. Even before he knew what the girls did in the upstairs rooms of the hotel Hank hated them for the furs with the little glass eyes, tiny varnished claws and red biting mouths.

The girls drifted into the hotel around nightfall. Some of them went steady with one man; others simply sat in the lobby and waited for an invitation.

Because of the thinness of the walls, the open doors and the loud voices, what went on in the rooms between men and women could not be avoided. The sounds of it echoed in the corridors and the men talked about it in the dining room so that to Hank it was like the Lysol smell of the floors or the loose scabs of ancient paint on the outside of the hotel. It was part of the hotel; part of its dark smelly substance.

When he was eleven Hank had seen Old Kelly, the oldest engineer on the line, beat up one of the girls. She had run out into the hall and Old Kelly had caught her at the foot of the stairs. They had stood there, both of them naked, Old Kelly hitting her the way men hit one another, straight solid blows on the lumpy body of the woman. It made a sound like someone kneading bread; not a slapping sound, but a dull, soggy, damaging sound. The woman had scratched out at Old Kelly, but finally had fallen forward into his arms, so that he could no longer hit her. Hank had watched them make their stumbling broken way back to the room.

Once two of the girls, a little older than the rest, had stopped him in the lobby. They were both very drunk and ready to cry. One had patted him on the head and said, "A little boy I might have had." Hank had knocked her hand away and backed off, angry. The two girls had cried, looking hopelessly at one another and at Hank. Big tears soaked their way through the powder and rouge and dropped pinkly and aimlessly from their chins. Their grief had been so great that they had staggered out into the night, without waiting for their railroaders to arrive.

By the time he was thirteen Hank was too big and gawky to sit in the corners. They ran him out of the taxicab office and the pool hall and Cohen asked him one day why he didn't get a job. The girls in the hotel began to get angry with him for looking at them. Hank decided to go to school.

Hank enrolled in the local high school. He was the best student they had ever had. He finished the first two years of work in a single year. But at the start of his senior year he discovered mathematics and poker and quit school.

As soon as he learned mathematics in school he began to calculate the odds in the poker game that went on day after day down at the hotel. He took a statistics textbook from the library and with the deck of cards out in front of him he figured various combinations. He memorized columns and columns of figures and odds and chances until gradually he forgot the columns and knew by merely looking at a hand how it could be improved, how it compared with other hands and how a kicker would help it. Then he went down to the lobby where the men played poker and watched them. He moved from one man to another, watching their hands, checking their chances with his statistics. He noticed how some men place a chip over an ace when it comes to them down; that few men look again at their down card in stud if it is a face card; that most men swallow when they make a good draw; that the time to win in a poker game is late in the evenings when players are anxious to win back losings. The statistics he had learned rapidly, but the way men play took longer. At the end of a year he thought he knew enough to play.

One night he asked the men if he could play and they laughed and let him in. He bought five dollars worth of chips, a little stack of white and red, that when held between his fingers ran only up to his second knuckle. He lost rapidly until he had only three white chips and one red chip left in his fingers. Then he got over the confusion caused by the smoke over the table, the eyes, the rapid flicking of the cards and he started to win. He played cautiously, like a very stingy old man, and by midnight he had won six dollars. He was sixteen years old.

After that he played three nights a week. He carefully calculated his winnings from each man so that he never won enough from any one to anger him. His winnings were steady and constant, never varying more than fifty cents from the sum he predicted for the night. In a few months he had five hundred dollars in a cigar box in his room. The cigar box bulged with old tattered one-dollar bills, slick new fives, an occasional ten and a pile of silver coins.

One day he heard a fireman state that the landlord's son was too

good at poker not to be a cheater. Several of the other men nodded
agreement. That night he got into the game on the first hand.

Carefully and very slowly he began to boost the bets. He made
all of the men commit themselves equally and by midnight a few of
them were beginning to sweat and the smoke around the shaded light
was thick and yellow. By three o'clock the pots were averaging over
fifty dollars each. The eyes around the table had turned red and the
floor was littered with sandwich crusts and empty whisky bottles.
Hank had won four hundred dollars by then. He went relentlessly
after the rest and by dawn he had all the money on the board and a
note from one of the railroaders that he owed Hank $66. Finally he
played them for their change, for the nickels and dimes in their
pockets. He played one engineer for his Waltham and stuck it in
his pocket when he won. Some of the losers began to complain, but
Hank ignored them and went on playing. Toward the end he made
such large bets that even men with good hands could not afford to
back up their cards.

When he had all of the visible money on the table he said he was
going to the toilet and left the room. He went to his room, packed
a wicker suitcase full of clothes and climbed out a window. He
walked to the railroad yard and swung up into an empty boxcar. The
next day he was in Bismarck . . .

"Why did you come to Manual Arts High after all that?" Mike
asked when Hank was finished. "You could be a professional gambler."

"Too boring," Hank said. "Gambling is the hardest way in the
world to earn a living. Show me a gambler and I'll show you either
a man bored stiff or a knucklehead . . . or both."

"Do you ever hear from your father?"

"No. Not a word."

"Why don't you write him? I heard Jews were supposed to be
great family people . . . always taking care of one another and watching
out for other members of the family."

"Sure, Mike. You hear a lot of things that aren't so," Hank said
and grinned. "That's one of them. I'll tell you some more later."

A mile ahead of them a Portuguese sheepherder was trying to
move a thousand sheep across the road. Like a formless tide the sheep
ebbed onto the highway and then stood there motionless as the sheep
dogs circled and barked. Hank slowed the car and came to a stop a
few feet from the closest sheep.

"Well, I'll be damned," Mike said. "That guy probably had all week to get those sheep across the road and he has to pick the time when we are passing. What's wrong with that crazy guy?" He glared out at the sheepherder, his face working with anger. Suddenly he turned to Hank and his face wore the wolfish raw grin that Hank hated. "It's like everything else, Hank. You have to get out and fight for what's yours. I'll get us through this god damn herd of sheep. Just follow close."

"Get back in the car, Mike," Hank yelled. "It will only take a few minutes for them to cross the road."

Mike grinned back over his shoulder. He walked toward the sheep and began kicking them. The sheep squealed in surprise, pushed sideways and away from the car. Mike walked steadily forward, kicking, pushing, cursing. The Portuguese sheepherder swore and shouted, the dogs barked and ran in frantic circles. Slowly the Model-A with Mike leading the way pushed through the dusty panicked herd of sheep. Finally they were through the sheep and the road was open.

Mike got back into the car. His face was streaked with sweat and dust.

"That's the way to handle 'em, Hank," Mike said breathlessly. "Men, women, sheep, horses and dogs all need to be pushed a little."

"And even if you're not in a hurry you have to get out and kick them?" Hank asked. "Just to be kicking?"

"That's right, even if you're not in a hurry," Mike said. He looked slyly sideways at Hank. "But, of course, I'm in a hurry."

"I know, I know," Hank said.

The car sped down the road and began the long climb into the brown soft hills of the Coast Range.

CHAPTER 4

The Experiment

MIKE GOT a job as a guinea pig the second month he was at Stanford. On the bulletin board on the English Corner there was a sign that stated that subjects for an important psychological experiment were wanted. The pay was fifty cents an hour. The sign directed applicants to see Miss Bird in the Psychology Department.

Mike saw Miss Bird and was hired. She told him where to report for the experiment and the next afternoon he climbed to the top floor of the Psychology Building. He walked down a long corridor lined with rat cages. He could see hundreds of pink eyes glittering in the semi-darkness and a wave of sound preceded him. It was the scurrying of thousands of horny feet. The smell of the rats was thick and hot; like rotted cereal. In one cage there were six rats with neat scars down their skulls. Something had been cut out of their brains for they stayed frozen in one position, unable to move, although their eyes glittered wildly when Mike put his face close to their cage. One rat had been placed with its forepaws tucked under its chin and it squatted on its hind legs. Once it shivered as it tried to move and its eyes rolled, but it remained motionless . . . only its hair rippled.

Mike turned away and walked down to the room where the experiment was being conducted. Two people were in the room and they were both wearing long white coats. One was a middle-aged woman, the other was a young man with protruding eyes.

"Are you Mr. Freesmith?" the man asked. "I'm Dr. Sutliff. This is Dr. Urich."

Mike shook hands with both of them.

"Could you for the next week every afternoon be available?" Dr. Urich said. She had a foreign accent and spoke very slowly. "Two hours every afternoon?"

"Sure," Mike said.

They led him over to a large table at the end of the room. On the table was a large black box with a naked electric light bulb protruding from the top. There were two windows in the front of the box, one covered with a red card, the other with a blue card. In the center of the machine was a small funnel. Mike sat down at the chair in front of the apparatus.

"The object of the experiment is to see how many times you can cause the light to go on," Dr. Urich said in a slow precise voice. Mike sensed that this was a special voice, developed just for giving instructions to subjects. "The light can be illuminated by pressing one or the other of the two cards. Every five seconds a machine within the box automatically changes the cards, giving you cards of different colors. It also changes the window, which will close the circuit and cause the light to go on. So every five seconds you will have a fresh choice. Each time you illuminate the light a penny will drop out of the funnel. You may keep all the pennies you earn. If they do not equal fifty cents an hour we will make up the difference. Do you have any questions?"

"No."

"You may begin."

Mike pressed the red card in the left-hand window. The light did not go on. The machine whirred, two new cards, orange and yellow, dropped down into the windows. Mike pressed the yellow card. The light did not go on. The mechanism whirred again and the cards were changed.

Mike hesitated. Something was wrong. He pressed the right-hand card again. A penny dropped down the funnel, rolled slowly on the table and slowly spun to the surface between his hands. Mike looked down at the penny. The mechanism whirred. He pressed the right-hand card which was black. Again a penny came down the funnel and the light briefly glowed on top of the box.

Forget the cards, he told himself. They're not important. What is important is the mechanism. Forget the cards.

Then, quite intuitively, he was playing the two people in white coats. They must have set the mechanism to work in a certain pattern. The thing to do was to find the pattern. Hell with the cards, Mike thought. Play the people.

Mike pressed the right-hand window two more times and the light did not glow. Then three times it did glow and the pennies rolled down the funnel. Then three times he failed.

That's it, he thought. The pattern is once right, once left; then twice right and twice left, then three times right and three times left and so on.

He pressed the right-hand window four times running and each time he won a penny. Then he switched to the left-hand window and pressed it four times and each time a penny rolled on the table. Then the right-hand window five times. Then the left-hand window five times. The pennies jingled on the table, grew in a heap between his hands. Once a penny rolled out on the floor, but Mike did not notice it. Also he did not notice the color of the cards and he did not look up to see if the light went on. He only watched the funnel to see the little jump that the pennies made when they were ejected onto the slippery metal slide.

He pressed the right-hand window six times, but the fifth and sixth time the penny did not drop down. Mike hesitated. Something had changed. He switched to the left-hand window. It paid twice and then twice it did not. The mechanism had switched to four times on each side. Instantly Mike had it. The mechanism was set to alternate from side to side until it reached five times on each side and then it went down again; four, three, two, one. When it reached one he guessed that it would start up again.

Mike played that pattern and he was correct. Each time the penny jumped onto the funnel, slid down onto the table and rolled to a halt between his fingers. Mike chuckled and played the pattern and each time he pressed the windows he felt he was defeating the two people standing behind him.

For twenty minutes he played without an error. Dr. Urich spoke to Dr. Sutliff. Mike did not listen, but he could tell they were arguing. The stack of pennies grew in front of Mike. The light glowed regularly on top of the black box. Dr. Urich's voice grew slightly shrill.

Dr. Sutliff coughed. He had moved directly behind Mike. Mike looked over his shoulder.

"That will be enough for today, Mr. Freesmith," Dr. Sutliff said.

"I thought you wanted me for two hours," Mike said.

"For our purposes that will be enough today. Tomorrow we will want you again. The apparatus will be the same, but the circumstances will be different."

Mike pushed back his chair and started to stuff the pennies in his pocket. Once he looked up and Dr. Urich was watching him closely, antagonism in her eyes. She smiled over the antagonism. The pennies filled one pocket and half of another. Mike walked lopsided out of the room.

When he was outside the door he paused. He looked at the rats with the thin red wounds in their heads. Through the thin plywood wall he heard Dr. Urich talk.

"He does not play the colors at all," she said. Her voice was full of complaint. "It was exactly as if the colors he did not notice."

"He figured out the pattern we set in the mechanism," Dr. Sutliff said.

"But he is the only one. All else choose by the colors. This will the figures badly skew. How do we explain?"

"We'll alter the mechanism tomorrow and then see how he does," Dr. Sutliff said.

"Why would he not do as the others?" Dr. Urich said. "It was plain that he should choose by colors."

"It's a stress situation. The pennies are positive motivation to take the pattern rather than respond by colors. It's just funny that he is the only one that concentrated on the pattern."

Mike put his finger through the wire of the cage and pushed gently against the rat standing on its hind legs. The rat's eyes bulged, its fur bent away from his finger, but the rat's body moved like putty. Mike pushed it to one side and the rat stayed in that position, bent at an impossible angle, its tiny claws tucked under its chin. Mike turned and hurried off down the corridor.

The next day when Mike reported for the experiment there were two more subjects in the room. One was a girl named Connie Burton and the other was a boy named Bill Evans. The girl was attractive and she was wearing a cashmere sweater and Mike guessed she was doing the experiment for some other reason than money. The boy was skinny and very embarrassed.

Dr. Urich gave the instructions again.

"Each of you has operated this apparatus before. Today the mechanism has been altered so that a new pattern is operating. You will decide among yourselves which window you will choose on each try. You may choose the window on whatever basis you wish. But you must all agree on the decision. If you are not agreed you can make no choice. None of you may press the window until the other two have agreed to your choice. You will share the pennies that you earn. Please make your discussion audible for what you say will be recorded on a wire recorder."

A paper in her hand rustled, she coughed and the room was quiet. Bill Evans looked at her with agony.

"Do we start now?" Mike asked.

"You may start now," Dr. Urich said. She walked to the back of the room and joined Dr. Sutliff.

The three students looked down at the windows. There was a pink card in the left window and a blue card in the right window.

"Let's start with the pink card," Connie said.

"Why?" Mike asked.

"Well, we have to start somewhere. Also I noticed when I did the test alone that pastel-colored cards turned on the light more often than darker colors."

"What about you?" Mike asked Bill.

"I don't remember," Bill said. "I just picked the color I liked each time. It's supposed to be a test in color perception so I tried to wipe my mind clean and pick the color I liked best between the two cards."

"Who said it was supposed to be a test in color perception?" Mike said.

"Nobody." Connie said. "But you can see that it is. That's why the cards change. What else could be the point of having the cards change?"

Mike looked slowly from the boy to the girl.

"Look, isn't the point to illuminate the light, to make the pennies come down the slide?" he asked.

"Sure, but we ought to do it the way they want us to do it," Bill said. "They're trying to learn something about colors and we ought to decide on the basis of the colors we like or something like that."

He looked over his shoulder. Dr. Sutliff and Dr. Urich were in a shadow and he could not see their faces.

"He's right," Connie said. "We ought to do what they want. We really should co-operate. It's an important experiment."

"The important thing is to illuminate the light as often as you can," Mike said. "That's all they've told us. Let's do that. O.K., you can disregard the cards then. They're not important. What is important is the mechanism inside the box. Every time it changes it makes one or the other window the right choice."

"What about the cards?" Bill asked.

"Forget the damned cards," Mike said. "Use your head. Someone had to fix the mechanism, put a pattern into it. If you discover that pattern you can make the light go on every time and you'll get a penny every time. Right?"

He could see that it had never occurred to either of them before. The girl saw it first and she started to smile, but almost at once she looked over her shoulder at the rear of the room.

"What if there isn't any pattern in the mechanism?" she said. "What if it's just a random choice?"

"That's probably what they think it is," Mike said. "But making things random is hard. Whoever set the mechanism probably did it a certain way just out of laziness. Or because he thought we would concentrate on the colors of the cards. Do you agree that if there is a pattern in the mechanism and we can find it out that is the quickest way to earn the pennies?"

Faintly, like the sound of a machine heard through a thick wall, Dr. Urich was talking urgently to Dr. Sutliff.

"Well, logically I think you're right," Connie said. "But I don't think that's what they want us to do. The cards are there for a reason."

"Who cares what they want us to do?" Mike asked. "Let's do the best thing. We could have pressed the window twenty times by now. We're just wasting time. Look, I'll start to press the windows and find out the pattern of the machine. If I don't find it in a few minutes we'll try another method."

He leaned forward.

"Remember, Mr. Freesmith," Dr. Urich's voice said softly, "every one of the subjects must agree to letting you proceed."

Mike looked first at Connie and then at Bill.

"How about it?" Mike said. "Are we just going to sit here or are we going to do something? They don't care what we do. They said we can do anything we want." Bill was sweating in the dull yellow light. "Anything is better than nothing. Is it all right for me to go ahead? Do you agree?"

Bill glanced once more over his shoulder and then his face dissolved in confusion. He nodded agreement at Mike. Mike turned to Connie. She nodded.

Mike began to push the left-hand door. He pushed it twenty times

in a row. It only paid off six times, but at the end of that time he
had found the pattern. He pulled his chair closer and began to play
his system. Once he had to alter it when a slight change was made in
the pattern.

Behind him he could hear Dr. Urich arguing with Dr. Sutliff.

Mike pushed one window after another and every time a penny
rolled down the slide. The heap of pennies grew between his hands.
At the end of twenty minutes he pushed the heap of pennies aside
and Connie and Bill began to stack them. He did not take time to
explain the pattern which he was playing to them. They became
bored and once he heard Connie yawn. Bill stood rigidly beside him,
stiffly stacking pennies into little piles of ten.

At the end of the hour the table was almost covered with the little
piles of pennies. Dr. Urich and Dr. Sutliff came up from the back
of the room and thanked them. Dr. Sutliff put his open notebook
down on the table.

"Thank you very much for your co-operation," Dr. Sutliff said. "It
was very good of you to give us your time. I think you will discover
that you have earned a good deal more than fifty cents for your
hour's work." He smiled thinly. "Your co-operation was very helpful."

Dr. Urich was standing to one side. She looked steadily at Mike
and her face was strained with anger. When Mike caught her eye
she flushed and looked down at her hands.

"Will you want us tomorrow?" Mike said.

"No. Not tomorrow," Dr. Urich cut in. "Not ever again, I think.
We must revise the experiment on the basis of today's results."

Mike edged over to the table and he glanced down at Dr. Sutliff's
notebook. On the top of the page was the title of the experiment:
"Color Apperception: The Latent Tendency to Overselect Dark Colors."
There was a notation of the scores that Connie and Bill had made on
previous attempts. Connie had guessed right forty-two per cent of
the time. Bill had guessed right thirty-eight per cent of the time.
Mike glanced down the page to a section of notes written in ink and
bearing the date of that day. He read it quickly:

*The three subjects did not make the selection on the basis of
color preference, but seemed to make what might be called a
political selection. Subject 34 dominated the group and insisted
that the choices be made on a basis other than the color of the
cards. For this reason today's results are being discarded as being
atypical and aberrant. Subject 34 will not be used again in the
experiments.*

Mike turned away. The pennies had been divided and each of them received 205 pennies. Mike took his, put them in his pocket. He grinned at Dr. Urich and walked out of the door. In the corridor he stopped for a moment to look at the catatonic rats. The rat with its paws under its chin was still slanted sideways. Mike gently bent the rat forward until it was on all fours. Then he pushed it over to the water spout at the end of the cage. The rat's tongue shot out, licked at the water and Mike left after it had consumed a half dozen drops.

Mike was almost at the foot of the stairs before Bill Evans caught up with him. Bill was breathing hard, but his face was bright with excitement.

"I wanted to thank you," he said hurriedly, not looking at Mike's face. "I hate both of them; Dr. Urich and Dr. Sutliff. I hate them and that damned test. It made me nervous. I've been doing it for weeks. I always get about the same number of pennies. Never over fifty an hour. They always acted so damned superior. I'm glad we did it the way you wanted. Did you see how mad Dr. Urich was? Serves her right. I'm glad. Really glad."

He jingled the pennies in his pocket and smiled quickly at Mike and then looked away.

"Anyway thanks," Bill said. "I'm glad we did it. I got so I was hating the two of them. I feel better now."

He turned quickly and trotted away. Mike never saw him again at Stanford.

Mike walked slowly across the Quad. Something is wrong with the two professors, he thought. There was something important they were missing. They were testing for something little, something screwy, unimportant. And something big was involved.

He turned the experiment over in his mind, tried to find the correct words. They slipped away from him, remained just at the edge of his mind. He walked by the chapel, past the clumps of palm trees and around the tall thin hulk of the Hoover Library.

Then it came to him. He stopped. A girl drove by on a bicycle and he was only aware of the spinning wheels, the clank of the chain, the flash of her plaid skirt.

The important part of the afternoon's experiment was this, Mike thought, and the words went like a written sentence across his mind: one person can make a decision faster than a group.

That's it, he thought. That's Freesmith's First Principle of Human Behavior: One person can make a decision faster than a group. That's exactly, perfectly, precisely, absolutely it.

He walked on toward Encina Hall. He was almost there when he thought of Bill Evans and another principle crossed his mind. Freesmith's Second Principle of Human Behavior: The weak person wants to be delivered from the superior person.

Delivered to what? he asked, as if the principle had been stated by another person.

It doesn't matter, he said. Deliverance is enough.

CHAPTER 5

Close to Your Vest

THE FIRST QUARTER Hank did not go to three of his classes. He stayed in his room and read anatomy, physiology and biology. Two nights before an examination he would read over Mike's notes on the course. Then Mike would ask him questions on the course. The night before examinations they did not sleep at all. They went over the notes endlessly.

In the morning they would leave Encina and walk out for breakfast. Dawn turned the hills across the Bay a soft suede texture. The big sandstone buildings around the Quad had a queer ugly unity and often there was the salt smell of fog in the air. They walked through the lonely world like men about to make a conquest. Their eyes glittered from too much coffee and too little sleep. When, finally, they picked up their bluebooks and sat down to answer the questions it seemed incredibly easy and simple.

At the end of the first quarter they received their grades. Mike put the cards on the table in their room and studied them.

"Not good enough, Hank," he said. "My grades are good enough to get a scholarship next year. I've got three A's and and one B. You've got two A's and two B's. You'll have to do a little better. Right now you're on the borderline."

"I'm happy," Hank said. He was reading his Gray's and had it open to a diagram of the delicate, intertwined, complex muscles of the ankle. "I'll get three A's next quarter and I'll be qualified for a scholarship. Don't worry about me."

"The old cigar box is getting low," Mike said. He walked to his bureau drawer and took out a battered White Owl box. He opened it and took out a stack of wrinkled bills and poured a mound of coins onto the table. He counted it rapidly. "Two hundred and sixty-seven bucks left. That's all." He scooped the money back into the box and threw the box in the drawer.

"We can get through the winter quarter, but we'll be broke by spring quarter," Mike said. "It's the incidentals that run up. Laundry, haircuts, books."

Hank looked up from his book.

"I eat too much," Hank said apologetically. He kept his finger on a plate in the book. It was squarely over the long thick purple sweep of the aorta through a skeletonized neck and down into a yellow muscle-streaked chest. "I'll cut down."

"You can't cut down," Mike said. "You're hungry so you've got to eat. You don't get any fatter so it must be going into energy or some damned thing. But you can't eat less."

Hank was vaguely ashamed of his appetite. He would eat the huge starchy meals they served in Commons, take seconds, and then two hours later he would feel a sharp pain in his stomach and in a moment he was ravenous. A Hershey bar, a huge handful of peanuts, a few apples, almost anything, would blot out the appetite and in a moment he had forgotten it completely, could work absorbedly until the next attack of hunger. But if he did not have the food at once he became dizzy, his attention dissolved and he felt a sharp anxiety. Sometimes he even woke up at night and staggered around the room, half asleep, looking for a candy bar or a bag of peanuts or anything. If there was nothing in the room he would put on his clothes and half sick with embarrassment and anger would walk down to the all-night restaurant and eat a mass of fried potatoes and toast and then walk back to the campus.

Hank worried because the enormous amount of food never made him any fatter. His face was thin, his ribs stuck out. He longed for a layer of fat over his bones.

"I know, I know," Hank said. "But maybe I could cut down on the food between meals."

"You can't," Mike said flatly. "We've just got to get more money."

Hank's face went hard and tough and defensive.

"Look, Mike, I told you no crap about money. We made an agreement."

"But we need money for the next quarter."

"You said we had two hundred and sixty-seven bucks."

"It'll be gone next quarter when we pay tuition. What about the spring quarter?"

"We'll worry about it when the money's gone," Hank said.

His bleached thin features relaxed. He murmured a word softly, looking down at the book. "Aorta, aorta, aorta," said with the bemused repetition by which a child chants a word into meaninglessness or twists it into a special emphasis.

"Hank, why don't you get into the poker game Hollis has in his room every night?" Mike said. "If you can play like you said you can you'd win plenty."

Hank turned the page, read a few words and then looked up at Mike. Mike knew he had not heard him. He was repeating another word, worrying it to death.

"Poker, Hank," Mike said. "Get in the poker game in Hollis' room. A lot of those eastern prep school boys play there. They've got money. They play for big stakes."

"Phagocyte, phagocyte, phagocyte," Hank murmured. Then he heard what Mike was saying. His odd blue eyes snapped open, he swung his feet to the ground. "No. Don't mention it again. I hate poker. No more crap about money. Understand? And especially not about poker money."

Mike left the room and walked down to Hollis' room. Hollis had money. Everyone in Encina knew it. Hollis never mentioned it, but they could tell. They could tell from the framed photograph on his wall which showed him with his arm around the shroud of a very large yawl and wearing shabby sneakers. They could tell also from the blazer he wore which had an intricate little device over the heart and a Latin motto stitched in white. They knew also from the thick white envelopes on his desk which contained invitations to debuts in San Francisco and Boston and New York. It wasn't until years later that Mike knew that the soiled white buckskin shoes and the slip-over Brooks Brothers shirts and the use of the phrase "Nanny used to say . . ." were also signs. Mike thought that Nanny was a nickname for his grandmother.

Hollis looked up when Mike came in the door. He had a thin, very tan face. He seldom smiled.

"Hello, Freesmith," Hollis said. "No openings, but there might be later. Make yourself at home." Hollis looked at the six men sitting around the table and his voice became harsh. "Osborne, you can take your shirt off if you want, but you can't stay in this room if you do."

Osborne, a big muscular boy from Ohio, stopped with one hand still in a shirt sleeve.

"Hell, Hollis, it's hot in here," Osborne said. "All this smoke and stuff."

"No one sits around in my room in an undershirt or naked to the waist," Hollis said. "Take your shirt off if you want, but get out if you do. Go ahead, Holloway, deal the cards."

The cards spatted on the table. Osborne hesitated, his face anguished. Hollis looked at the first card. Osborne slowly put his arm back into the sleeve. He left his shirttail out as if to defy Hollis, but Hollis did not even notice.

"How much are the chips worth?" Mike asked.

Hollis looked up from the table and found Mike's face in the dim light ringing the table. He smiled.

"Not much," Hollis said. "White chips are a half dollar, red chips a dollar and blue chips two dollars. Of course we could always sweeten it up a bit if anyone wanted to. But we just try to keep it friendly."

The other boys at the table smiled, but they did not look up from their cards. Mike guessed that they found it expensive to play. Most of the pots wound up with around fifty or sixty dollars on the table. No money changed hands, for Hollis acted as bank and merely made a notation on a slip of paper when players bought chips. At the end of the night he calculated what everyone had won and lost.

Hollis won the hand and while the cards were being shuffled he looked up at Mike again.

"I understand that you Los Angeles people do things in a big way though," he said. "You probably wouldn't want to play for little old stakes like these."

The men around the table laughed. Some of them pushed back from the table, gave Hollis soft encouragement.

Mike smiled at Hollis, but he had made a decision. He waited until the laughter died away.

"Those stakes are rich enough for my blood," Mike said. "But I'm not the poker player in our room anyway. I'll tell you, though, you won't get Hank to play for those stakes."

"A pity," Hollis said. "All these run-down Easterners could stand a transfusion of real red Southern California blood."

He did not look up from his cards. Mike knew he did not want to go on with it. Mike slipped it in softly.

"Not Hank," Mike said. "He won't play for chicken-shit stakes like this. That Hank is a real poker player. He plays poker for really big money."

Hollis looked up from his cards. The other boys; stopped talking. The dealer paused with a one-eyed jack about to drop from his fingers. Mike went on reflectively.

"No, these stakes wouldn't interest Hank. Not him."

"I think we could make it interesting for Mr. Moore," Hollis said. "Why don't you just step down the hall and invite him to play? He can . . ."

"He won't," Mike said. "Not for stakes like these. He's heard of these stakes. I don't think he'll play with you."

"Tell him he can name the stakes," Hollis cut in sharply. "Whatever he wants."

"No, no," Mike said as if Hollis were being very dense. "You don't understand. Once you play for really big stakes kid stuff like this is out. You're bored. I wouldn't want to ask him."

Mike walked to the door and opened it. As he closed it behind him he had a diminishing, angular, smoke-obscured view of the room . . . the overflowing ash trays, the blank faces of the boys, the white shirt fronts, the hands holding the fans of cards. Then he heard a collective exhalation of breath and Hollis said, "I'll be damned." Then the door closed.

Hollis stuck his head in their room the next night.

"Moore, would you like to play some poker tonight?" he asked. "Nice bunch tonight. They can probably play for any stakes you want."

Hank looked up, startled.

"No. I don't want to play poker," he said.

When Hollis had left Hank turned to Mike.

"Who was that?" he asked.

"Hollis. He is the guy I told you about. He has a poker game every night in his room."

Hank had already lost interest and was turning over the pages of Gray's.

The next day at lunch in Encina Commons, Osborne and Hollis sat at the same table with Mike and Hank. There were eight men at each table. The food was brought in big white porcelain bowls and each man helped himself.

Hank ate quickly, neatly and fiercely. He seldom talked at the table and he seldom listened to what was said. He was on his second helping of creamed chicken over biscuits before he knew something was wrong.

He noticed everyone except Osborne and Hollis was silent. Hank looked at the boy across from him and at once the boy glanced away. Hank turned and looked down the table at Hollis.

"It's simple, Osborne," Hollis was saying. "I'll repeat it. Only a crude anti-Semite would believe that the Jews have all the money because they are greedy. The fact is that the Jews have all the money because they never take a chance on losing it. They just hold on. If you hold on long enough to all the little bits you can collect pretty soon you've got a big wad. It's just that simple. The Jews just freeze the money when they get ahold of it."

Hank felt his fork break through the crisp crust of a biscuit. Without looking down he scooped the food into his mouth. He looked at Hollis' tweed coat, the striped tie and the coarse, expensive-looking Oxford cloth shirt. A pinpoint of hunger started up somewhere in Hank's stomach. He reached out and quickly spooned more chicken onto his plate.

"Go on, Hollis," Hank said. "Tell us more."

"That's all there is to it, Moore," Hollis said. "You heard it. It was plain enough."

Hank nodded. His mouth was full and a bit of biscuit hung from his chin. He added some lima beans to his plate, spread buttter on a biscuit. His teeth bit into the lima beans; reduced the soft pulpy substance to liquid and felt it go down his throat. He felt a necessity to cram more food down his throat.

He looked at the red embarrassed faces of the other people around the table and the hunger grew until he knew that he could never ease it. He took two more gigantic bites of biscuit, scooped up some chicken on his last biscuit and pushed it into his mouth. He chewed slowly. When his mouth was empty he looked down the table at Hollis.

"Hollis, I know you're trying to be tough," Hank said gently. "But you don't understand. I don't care one way or another about being a Jew. I just don't react to it. I'm a Jew, but I'm not a patriotic Jew. But I don't like you. Not because of what you said about the Jews. Just because you're a pretty crude guy. I guess you were trying to be tough so that you could shame me into playing poker with you. O.K., I'll give you your choice. I'll play poker with you or I'll take you out behind Encina and pound the shit out of you. Which will it be?"

Hank turned back to the table and began to eat the bread pudding dessert. Hollis' face turned a slow red that gleamed through the tan.

He looked at Osborne, but there was no help there. Everyone at the table sensed how neatly Hank had trapped him. If he picked the poker it looked as if he were afraid to fight Hank. If he picked the fight Hank wouldn't have to play poker and the whole conversation between Osborne and Hollis was a silly stunt.

"I'll do both of them," Hollis blurted out. "I'm not afraid of you, Moore."

Hank looked up and laughed.

"One or the other," he said. "I haven't got time for both of them."

Hollis looked around the table once more.

"We'll play poker tonight," he said slowly.

Mike counted all the money in the cigar box. It came to two hundred and fifty-two dollars. Hank reached across the table and picked it up. Mike put the coins back in the box and closed the drawer. A thin tinkle of pennies and nickels echoed in the room. Hank smiled.

"Let's go," Hank said.

They walked out of their room, down the corridor, and into Hollis' room.

There were six of them waiting around the table. They were all eastern boys. Three of them were wearing seersucker suits and all of them wore ties. They looked up curiously at Hank, smiled at his sweat shirt and blue jeans. Hollis did not introduce Mike or Hank to the men at the table.

"We pay up at the end of the evening," Hollis said crisply. "By check or cash. It doesn't matter."

Hank slumped into the empty chair. His long white fingers hung on the edge of the table. Mike stood behind him and for the first time he was aware that in the dim light around the edge of the room there was a ring of freshmen. They were pressed against the wall, sat on the two beds, crouched on the dresser. They sat quietly, but their eyes gleamed in the reflected light. Mike could not recognize any of them; all he could see was the pairs of eyes and the occasional shift of hands as someone lit a cigarette.

"What stakes do you want to play, Moore?" Hollis asked.

"Are there any house rules?" Hank asked.

"Do you want some?" Hollis asked.

"Yes," Hank said quietly. His face was back out of the light, only his long limp fingers showed. "Dealer's choice, but games limited to five- and seven-card stud and five-card draw. No jokers. No wild cards. No misdeals . . . every card is played even if it is misdealt. Three bumps. Declare a time limit at ten o'clock with the big loser setting the time."

Mike heard the men around the room take a collective breath. Hollis looked slowly around the table.

"That seems all right," he said. "What kind of stakes do you want?"

"Anything you say."

"How would one dollar for whites, three for reds and five for blues be?" Hollis asked.

Hank did not say anything. The white fingers reached for a cigarette, struck a match and suddenly Hank's face was illuminated by the small light from the match. He blew out the match and threw it in an ashtray.

"Well, how about two dollars, five and ten?" Hollis asked. "That all right?" His voice was a little tense.

"Anything you say," Hank replied.

"That's it then." Hollis said. "How much do you want to start, Moore?"

"Five hundred dollars," Hank said.

The eastern boys stirred in their chairs. Hollis hesitated and then counted out five hundred dollars in chips. He stacked up thirty-five blue chips, twenty reds and fifty whites and pushed them over to Hank. Hank did not touch them; he just let them rest between his hands.

Hollis counted out five hundred dollars in chips for the rest of the players without asking them what they wanted.

You better be good, Mike thought. You've got twice in chips what you've got in cash. You better be good.

"We won't cut," Hollis said. "You can deal first, Moore."

He broke open a deck of Bicycle cards and threw them over to Hank. Hank peeled off the two jokers and dropped them on the floor. Hank shuffled the cards slowly. He did not do it skillfully. He held the two halves of the deck together and riffled them and then pushed them awkwardly together. Mike felt a slight pang of doubt.

"Five-card stud," Hank said. "Everyone ante two bucks."

Hank pushed two white chips out onto the table. His fingers tightened, he held the deck flat above the table and the cards started to fall. He dealt three down cards and stopped with his hands in front of Hollis, a card held in his fingers.

"Go ahead, deal," Hollis said.

"You haven't anted," Hank said.

Hollis looked down. There were seven white chips on the table. Hollis flushed and pushed a white chip onto the table. Hank dropped him a down card and went on with the deal.

When everyone had their second card Hank put the cards down and looked at his hole card. He raised the tip of the card so that Mike could see it. Hank had a king down and a queen up.

A man with an ace showing bet a red chip. Four of the players went along. Hank folded. Osborne won the hand with two jacks.

The next dealer played five-card draw. Hank drew four low spades and the ace of hearts. He discarded the ace and drew a jack of diamonds. On the first bet after the draw he folded.

Hank lost also on the next two hands which were five-card stud. Then Hollis was dealer.

Mike watched Hollis shuffle. He did it expertly with a gamblers riffle; the cards hissing through the air and then a long stream of them falling quietly into his hand.

"It's draw," Hollis said.

He dealt the cards rapidly. Hank had a pair of treys and an ace of spades and two other low cards. Hank held the treys and went along with the opening bet of five dollars. He drew three face cards and did not improve his hand. However, when the betting started he raised the first ten-dollar bet by fifteen dollars.

Easy, boy, Mike thought. Only four hands and you've already lost about a hundred dollars. Two treys are not much in this game.

Hollis raised Hank twenty dollars and two other boys went along. Hank raised twenty dollars and everyone folded except Hank and Hollis. There was almost two hundred and fifty dollars in the pot.

Hollis won with a straight. He raked in the chips and his tanned face was creased with a smile.

Mike bent over and whispered in Hank's ear, "Take it easy, Hank. They don't bluff very easy. You're down a hundred bucks already."

Hank did not move his hands from the table, but he turned his head and looked up at Mike. He answered in a normal voice that everyone in the room could hear.

"You've got it wrong, Mike," he said. "I have to find out who is willing to buy a pot and who is going to really win one. Now I know."

The players looked up angrily, tried to find Hank's face in the gloom. They looked at his hands and one of the players swore.

"We don't need any kibitzers, Freesmith," Hollis said. "Let Moore play his own cards. After all, he's the big gambler from L.A., isn't he?"

The ring of men sitting in the gloom back of the table laughed. The players looked up and grinned.

"Up yours, Hollis," Mike said.

"Don't be vulgar," Hollis said. "Just let the big-time gambler play his own cards."

Mike looked down at the back of Hank's head, then down the dark reach of his arms where the light suddenly caught the elbows and hands in intense white detail. Hank had not moved during the conversation.

By ten o'clock Hank had lost three hundred and forty dollars and had won only one small pot. The other players had relaxed and between deals they began to tell short stories about summer vacations and rumours about the fraternities. At exactly ten o'clock Hollis held out his hand.

"It's ten, Moore, and you are the big loser," he said. "How much longer do you want to play?"

"Twelve," Hank said. "I'd like to knock off for ten minutes right now and have a cup of coffee."

As they walked down to the coffee shop in the cellar of Encina Mike talked earnestly to Hank.

"Look, Hank, you're in over your head," Mike said. "Play close to your vest and if you get back even just ride along. Remember we don't have enough money right now to pay off what you've lost."

"Don't worry, Mike," Hank said. "The big winner in a poker game is the man who wins in the last hour. All you need is a couple of big pots."

"Sure, but you haven't even won one big pot yet," Mike said.

"That isn't important. You have to spend a little time finding out how the rest of the people play. That costs a little money, but it's worth it in the long run."

"Have you found out anything?" Mike asked. "Hell no."

"I have," Hank said. "For example, the three boys in the seersucker suits are cheating. When one of them has a good hand he signals to the other two . . . pulls his ear, yawns, scratches his armpit, stuff like that. Then the other two keep raising the bets to build up the pot. It's the only simple way to cheat in poker there is. It gives you just the slight mathematical edge that you need."

"Well, for Christ's sake let's call them on it," Mike said. "Let's sock one of the bastards and call the game off."

"Don't get excited, Mike. Now I know when one of them has a good hand. I'm better off than they are."

Mike started to talk again, but they walked into the coffee shop and the other players were there. Mike and Hank sat in a booth by themselves and drank their coffee and then walked back up to Hollis' room.

The first game was five-card stud. Hank got a king down and then his first up card was a king. Hollis had an ace up. The rest of the up cards were low. Hollis bent forward to look at the other cards and his face came down into the light. He tugged at his ear lobe.

Mike looked at Hollis carefully. Hollis was now wearing one of the seersucker coats. Mike realized that he must have changed with one of the other boys during the coffee break. Slowly it washed over Mike that the seersucker coats were part of the plan; they were a sort of signal. The three players in the seersucker coats supported one another in the betting, but all of them must be in on it. Mike had a quick, grinding impulse to reach across the table and slap Hollis in the face and tell him that he knew they were all cheating.

Hollis checked. The next player in a seersucker coat bet ten dollars. Someone else raised that five dollars. Hank went along.

Mike wanted to bend down and tell Hank what was happening, to warn him that they were sandbagging the betting, but he was sure that he could not control his voice. He gripped the back of Hank's chair.

Use your eyes, Hank, he thought. Don't you see that Hollis has aces back to back. He just gave the signal.

On the next card Hank drew another king. No one else improved their hand. Again Hollis checked and one of the other players bet ten dollars. Someone else raised. Hank went along. So did everyone else.

On the fourth card no one visibly improved his hand. Hank bet twenty-five dollars on his two kings showing. Hollis raised twenty dollars. Four of the players folded.

Mike rapidly counted the chips. There was almost five hundred dollars in the pot. When the last cards were dealt Hank had not improved his hand and, apparently, no one else had. Mike's stomach was knotted hard.

"It's up to you, Moore," Hollis said. "You've got the two kings showing."

"Thirty dollars," Hank said.

"Raise you thirty," Hollis said.

"Thirty more," Hank said. "If it doesn't drive you out."

Hollis saw Hank's raise, but the other player folded. Mike realized that Hank had Hollis beaten; that there was no possible way that

Hollis could win. Mike looked down and saw that Hank's hands were still on the table, the way they had been all evening.

"What do you mean, drive me out?" Hollis said. Slowly his face puckered with cunning. "You don't think you're bluffing me, Moore? You're trying to buy it, aren't you? Just like you said I was earlier."

Hank did not reply.

"Well, I'll tell you, Moore. Just for this one hand and just to show you that we know how to give a big L.A. gambler some fun I'll raise you one hundred dollars and give you the right to bump if you want."

Hollis leaned forward, suddenly triumphant. His face came into the light, lean and tanned, and he grinned at Hank. His smile faded as Hank counted out ten blue chips. Then Hank counted out another ten blue chips and threw them on the table.

"I raise you a hundred dollars, Hollis," Hank said.

Hollis put in ten more blue chips. The pot was almost a thousand dollars now. The room was very quiet. Down the hall a door slammed, bare feet sounded on the corridor floor; disembodied, wet, lonely. A shower hissed somewhere.

"Show your cards, Moore," Hollis said.

Hank was opening a fresh pack of cigarettes. He went on with it. He neatly tore the cellophane back, ripped the paper and pulled out a cigarette. He lit the cigarette. Then he reached down and turned over his hole card.

The three kings burned on the table.

Hollis whimpered.

The rest was easy. Hollis bet frantically, desperate to win back the money he had lost. He no longer looked for signals or gave them. He snatched up his cards, glanced at them and if they were bad his face collapsed. He bet too heavily, too soon, when they were good. The other players played aimlessly, staring at Hollis and not knowing quite what to do.

Hank only went along with three hands in the last hour of play. But he won all of them and they were the three biggest pots.

Hank won eleven hundred dollars that night. Hollis wrote him a check, his hand trembling as he wrote. The whole room held its breath as Hank took the check, turned and left the room without saying a word to anyone.

When Hank and Mike were in their room Hank handed the check to Mike.

"Put it in the kitty," he said.

He walked over and picked up his physiology book. He put his feet on the desk and opened the book. Before he started to read he looked up.

"Mike, I know you rigged that game with Hollis," he said. "Don't do it again. I won't play next time. I don't like Hollis, but I won't play him again. Him or anyone."

"You're right. I rigged it. Maybe I'll do it again if I think I can get away with it," Mike said. "You scared the hell out of me for a few hours, but it was worth it."

"Don't do it again."

"Don't try and scare me," Mike said. "You didn't have to play if you didn't want to. You won't have to play the next time. Don't try to load your problems off on me. I rigged it but it was a pretty damned obvious job of rigging and it didn't fool you a bit. You played because you wanted to."

Hank looked steadily at Mike for a moment. Then he grinned.

"That's why I like you, Mike," he said. "You are so lacking in morals yourself that you can always spot immorality in someone else. You're right. I didn't have to play. It's just that I couldn't resist playing Hollis. But I won't play next time. Even if you rig it very smoothly."

Mike knew that Hank meant it. At once Mike gave up any thought of ever trying it.

"O.K. How about calling a cab and riding down to Paly and spending a few bucks on some ham and eggs," Mike said.

They went to the all-night diner and each had four eggs, ham, pancakes, hashed-brown potatoes and toast. Hank ate a second order and then they walked slowly back to the campus.

Mike remembered the poker game long after the money was spent. He remembered it because Hollis tried to become friendly with Hank. He invited Hank to go East with him for the Christmas holidays. Hank refused. Hollis sent Hank a set of cuff links and six shirts with French cuffs for Christmas. Hank hocked them for ten dollars. When Hollis' family came to Stanford in the spring he proudly introduced them to Hank and for two days Hank rode around the Peninsula in a rented Cadillac showing the family the sights. Hollis tried to get Hank pledged to his own fraternity and was outraged when he discovered that they did not pledge Jews and Hank would not join anyway.

Finally Hank got bored with it and told Hollis to stop coming around. Hank said it in front of Mike and Hollis was embarrassed. Hollis smiled wistfully at Hank and then he turned and with his confident, easygoing walk he left the room.

Mike took a piece of paper off his desk and slowly wrote a single sentence on it: "Freesmith's Unnumbered Principle: People appear to love the man who humbles them." He looked at it for a moment and then shoved it into the desk drawer; along with the other abandoned pieces of paper that contained similar sentences.

CHAPTER 6

Hot Bread and Butter

*I*N THEIR junior year Mike and Hank rented a small cottage behind a professor's house on the campus. The cottage was isolated from the professor's house by a thick hedge, a lemon tree and two apricot trees. The cottage was very cheap. It rented for sixteen dollars a month.

In their sophomore year they had both gotten scholarships which paid for tuition. They still had to pay for books, the rent on the cottage, laundry and, finally, food. The food was the worst. By their junior year they had spent almost all of the poker winnings on food. And most of the food had been eaten by Hank.

Hank became hungrier all the time. Even when he had eggs, bacon, fried potatoes and toast for breakfast he was hungry by the middle of the morning and had to eat three or four doughnuts and a few cups of coffee. It was the same in the middle of the afternoon. He would stand by the counter in the soda fountain and rapidly eat three large ice cream cones; his teeth crunching the soft shell of the cone, not tasting the ice cream, but forcing it down his throat as fast as he could. Vanilla, strawberry, chocolate, coffee, rocky-road; he ate all of them with equal eagerness. He was unaware that he hunched his shoulders when he ate, bent slightly forward, as if protecting the food he was eating or sheltering it from the view of others. All he knew that when he had eaten he could go back to his books and study again.

But it was the nights that were difficult. They would be reading in the cottage and around midnight Hank would look up from his books.

In front of him was the evidence of the night's work; pencil drawings of intricate ganglia, cross sections of muscle tissues, the beautiful and exotic shapes of bacteria. He wanted to go on with the reading, but he could not. Somewhere, at the very outer edge of his consciousness, the thin taut membrane of his attention had been slit. It was tiny and faraway, he could almost ignore it, but that was impossible. Hunger came gushing in on him. His mouth started to water, his stomach turned tight with hunger, his intestines growled. He looked back at the book and the words were dim and blurred. His fingertips trembled slightly and he knew he could not read until he had eaten.

He stood up and spoke in a voice that was falsely casual.

"I'm going over to the Cellar for a bite," he said. "Want to come along?"

Mike would shake his head and Hank walked over to the bureau and took two dollars out of the cigar box. Forty-five minutes later he would return and slip into the room. He picked up his book. For a moment he was aware of the hard round knob of his belly pushing against his belt, a strange distension that would vanish in an hour and leave him skinnier than before. Almost with disgust he thought of the hamburgers, malted milk and pie that he had eaten. Then he would be lost in the book again and would not think of anything until three in the morning when he stood up, stripped off his clothes and fell naked into bed. In the morning he would step out of the bed, brush his teeth and with the sweet minty flavor of the toothpaste still in his mouth he would be ravenous. He would trot down the street to the Cellar.

Hank tried everything to cut down his appetite. Once, for a three-week period, he took little cellulose reducing pills, followed by three glasses of water. The pills expanded into a huge mass in his stomach, his belly bulged out round and turgid. But the hunger was still there, cutting through the soft watery mass of cellulose. He had to eat, forcing the food into an already full stomach and he felt distended, unnatural. Another time he tried eating fruit and nuts because someone told him that these would reduce his appetite. He ate peaches, oranges, apples, bananas, grapefruit and pears. He ate them until the juice dripped off his chin and he broke out in a rash. But they did not reduce his appetite.

In the end he gave up and attempted to keep a stock of food in the cottage. It did not matter what the food was, just so there was plenty of it. He ate soya-bean cereal with buttermilk, yogurt and cheese. The cottage was littered with the moist paper cartons in which delicatessens sell their yellowish potato salad, milk bottles, soda-cracker crumbs, the skin of salamis, crusts, apple cores and banana peels.

Even so there were nights when there was no food in the cottage, for Hank did not think of food when he was close to a grocery store. He discovered slowly all of the restaurants in the town that were open all night. His favorite was a Chinese restaurant that served a huge bowl of fried rice and shreds of pork for fifty cents. When this was closed he ate at a drugstore which featured a hot roast beef sandwich which floated in a circle of solid, glycerinlike gravy and was flanked by two round balls of mashed potatoes.

"We have to do something about our food costs," Mike said at the beginning of their junior year. "If we can cut down on what we are spending there we can get by the rest of this year and our senior year on what is left of the poker money."

"What about hashing?" Hank asked. "Lots of guys have hashing jobs. Just wait on table and you get your lunch and dinner."

"But what about the rest of the time? What do we eat then?" Mike asked.

Hank squirmed in the chair. He looked down at his fingers. They were dirty. His stomach convulsed, saliva gathered in the back of his mouth and poured around his teeth. He was hungry. Like an animal, he thought. Like a slobbering, damned animal.

"I said no crap about money, Mike," Hank said. "For Christ's sake we've still got money in the cigar box, haven't we?"

"Sure. About three hundred bucks," Mike said.

"Well, let's worry when that's gone."

Hank looked back at his book, picked up his pencil.

"No. We'll worry about it now," Mike said. "If we wait until next year it'll be too late."

"I'm not going to worry about it," Hank said. He refused to look up from his book.

"I'll worry about it," Mike said. "I just want to make sure you'll go along with whatever arrangements I make."

"O.K., O.K. I'll go along," Hank said. He started to copy the complicated, beautifully involved bones of the knee onto a fresh page. "With anything. Stop talking about it."

Mike got Hank a job in a bakery. It was a perfect job. Hank only had to work from eight at night until midnight. When he came to the bakery everyone else had left. Hank's job was to operate the bread-wrapping machine. The cooling loaves were neatly stacked in a huge rotating rack and Hank had only to load the machine with wax paper and press the button. The loaves came pouring out the side of the machine, each of them neatly wrapped. Every fifteen minutes a bell rang and the machine needed more wax paper. The rest of the time Hank could read. It was perfect.

When Hank came to work the first thing he did each night was to take a loaf of hot bread and cut it in half. Then he went to the refrigerator and took out a cube of butter. He put the cube of butter between the halves of hot bread. The butter melted into a warm, yellow pool. When he bit into the bread he could smell the warm yeasty odor and the butter ran between his fingers. He usually ate two loaves of bread and butter during his four-hour shift. When he left at midnight he carefully selected a big sack of coffee cakes, doughnuts, rye bread, cookies and cupcakes. During the day he ate out of the bag, washing the food down with a few quarts of milk. He never became tired of the bakery goods. During the time he was working at the bakery he actually saved money.

Mike had intended to get a job hashing, but something happened. Mike got into a controversy with Julius Mardikan, an Armenian graduate student from Fresno. Mardikan was the section leader for one of the sections of a large upper-division history course. Mardikan was short, fat, very bright-eyed and a promising Ph.D. candidate. He received two hundred dollars a quarter for teaching the section and he was happy.

Hank and Mike were both in Mardikan's section and for the first month they listened placidly to his lectures. In the second month Mardikan began to lecture on Luther.

"Before Luther the medieval society was unified and solid," Mardikan said. "Although people were born into a rigid society they knew exactly where they fitted into the society and they were happy. Everyone had a sense of security, of belonging. Everyone accepted the status quo."

Mike sat up in his chair and put his hand in the air. For a few moments Mardikan did not see it for he was talking with absorption, almost love, of his favorite period in history. Finally he saw Mike's hand.

"Yes, Mr. Freesmith?" he said.

"Do you mean that in the medieval society there was no discontent and no unrest?" Mike said.

"Scholarly work indicates that there was very little unrest and discontent during that period. Certainly it was a much calmer and more satisfied period than the present."

"Scholarly work on what?" Mike asked. "How do the scholars know this? What do they look at?"

"Religious documents, psalm books, monastery records, records left by merchants. That sort of thing."

Mardikan spoke more slowly and cautiously, careful of a trap, his bright eyes narrowing with concentration.

"What would a psalm book or a merchant's record tell you about the way people actually felt? Couldn't they actually be miserable and unhappy even if the merchant's records showed a profit?" Mike asked.

The class laughed. The smile vanished from Mardikan's face. His teeth separated and showed his tongue. He licked his lips and looking away from Mike spoke very slowly.

"The work of Max Weber for one and Tawney for another would seem to indicate very precisely that the medieval man was a very secure and intact sort of person," Mardikan said.

This was not altogether true, but Mardikan did not know that. Later he came to know it well. Mike wrote "Weber" and "Tawney" in his notebook and then looked up.

"I don't believe they were right," Mike said. "People were always pretty much the way they are now. Probably always will be."

"And how are they now, Mr. Freesmith?" Mardikan asked.

He was surer now. He felt that he had control again.

"People are . . ." Mike hesitated. Then he went on. "People are scared. I don't know if that means they're insecure. I just know they're scared. And I think they always have been."

The class murmured its disapproval. Mardikan smiled.

"I'm sure Mr. Freesmith that the scholarly community would be grateful for your profound views on this matter," he said.

The class laughed. Mike smiled. The discussion went on to another subject.

That afternoon Mike bought Tawney's *Religion and the Rise of Capitalism.* He checked out three of Weber's books from the library. The next morning when the section met Mike put his hand up before a word had been spoken.

"Mr. Mardikan, do you know what *jacquerie* is?" Mike asked.

Mardikan hesitated. The smile froze on his face and then was fractured by his nervous tongue.

"In a general sense," Mardikan said. "Yes. I know very generally."

"*Jacquerie* is agrarian or peasant revolution," Mike said. "During the medieval period there were over two hundred examples of *jacquerie* in Europe. Peasants revolting and killing their lords, burning up the manor houses, raping the women, taking possession of the land. Does that sound like a secure and happy society to you?"

The class stared at Mike. Mardikan pressed against the blackboard. With his fingers he turned a piece of chalk and it became soggy in his hand.

"A few cases of peasant revolt do not mean that the total society was demoralized, Mr. Freesmith," Mardikan said.

"Of course not," Mike said. "But do you know that there were also countless cases where the people stormed the monasteries and burned them down and threw the monks out into the snow? What about that? And did you know that almost every feudal estate had a police force? That most of the gallant knights spent their time either fighting the serfs or plotting against their boss?" Mike lifted a heavy red book and turned it slowly over in his hands. "It's all right here in this book. People then were just like people now."

"I don't think, Mr. Freesmith, that a few scattered pieces of evidence are enough to overthrow the well-considered views of the best historical scholars," Mardikan said.

He was sweating though and when the class was over and he stepped away from the blackboard he left a round black shiny circle of sweat and his tweed jacket was covered with chalky reversed words which he had soaked off of the blackboard.

From the start it was a losing battle for Mardikan. Mike began to read everything. He read anthropology, sociology, psychology, mathematics, philosophy, ethics, history and logic. He stole books from the library, bought used books in Palo Alto, borrowed books and bought still more books. Some books he glanced at, threw under his bed and never opened again. Some books he read twice. A few books he read over and over, marking the pages, scribbling in the margins. Mike's eyes became red from reading and he was quite unaware of it. The cottage began to overflow with books. They spilled off the tables, squashed the salami skins into the rug; they slid under the bed and gathered dust; they were stacked under the washbasin and were covered with water stains.

"I thought you were going to get a job hashing," Hank said in the middle of the year.

"Sure, I was, but I don't have time now," Mike said. "I've got too much to read. No time to work."

"Why do you want to prove that Mardikan was wrong about medieval society?" Hank asked. "You keep after him like it was a battle."

"Battle?" Mike looked up with surprise. "You're crazy. I don't give a damn about Mardikan. Also I don't care about the medieval society argument any more. I'm reading other things."

"What other things?"

"Lots of things. History, sociology, just about everything. I just realized this year that there was something in books except fiction. I never thought before that the people who wrote all those books believed them; that they studied history or people or situations and then tried to write about them in books. I thought they invented it all out of their heads."

"Is it pretty good stuff?" Hank asked cautiously.

Mike looked up and thought for a moment. He shook his head.

"Most of it is crap. Real crap. Every once in a while one of them puts down something honestly. It sounds hard and real. Then he takes a look at it, realizes how grim it sounds and rushes to cover it over with a bunch of crazy interpretations and explanations. Some of them never say anything real. They just write. Like I said, most of it is crap."

As they talked Hank realized that Mike really did not see that he was engaged in a battle with Mardikan. Actually he was hardly aware that Mardikan existed. The Armenian was just someone on whom he could try his ideas and reading. But everyone else saw it as a battle. Students from other sections began to drop into Mardikan's section and sometimes the room was overcrowded. Also graduate students started to come to the section meetings.

The section became fabled around the campus. The pattern of the section became set. Every day Mardikan walked in, leaned against the blackboard and looked around the room. Mike's hand went up in the air. Mardikan called on him and the struggle commenced. Mike brought old and obscure books to class; he quoted from notes; he referred to little-known periodicals; he challenged the authority of great and well-known historians and discovered almost anonymous sociologists and supported their interpretations. The class was confused, but they were delighted. At the end of every hour Mardikan came away from the board with a slight moist sound and left the glistening mark of his nervousness on the hard black material.

Mardikan capitulated in the middle of the third quarter. They were discussing anarchism and Mardikan was defending the viewpoint expounded in the textbook which had been issued to the class.

"The textbook is wrong when it states that anarchists are optimistic about human nature," Mike said. "The anarchists are as pessimistic about human nature as Spencer or Malthus or Adam Smith. They . . ."

"That is not the generally accepted view," Mardikan said. He was tensed against the blackboard, his hands held rigidly in front of his waist, the fingers spread defensively. He fought against Mike's words, the way a small overtrained terrier will fight against a tough mongrel. "Generally there is a view . . ."

"A general view that is held by people who have not read the anarchists," Mike said. The class took a sudden breath. Mike picked up a small bound copy of a newspaper. "Right here it says something that is right on the nose."

"What are you quoting from?" Mardikan asked.

"The newspaper put out by the Society of Egoists," Mike said.

"All right, Mr. Freesmith. There is no need to read from it," Mardikan said. He began to gather up the papers on the table in front of him. "That is all for today."

He walked out the door, his shoulders slumped forward. He stumbled on the door jamb, recovered and disappeared into the corridor. The class got up silently and left.

Mardikan went to the chairman of the Department of History and asked to talk with him.

"It's no use, sir," he said. "I can't keep up with Freesmith. I have orals to study for, my wife is pregnant, I take time out for meals, I read the daily newspapers. Freesmith doesn't do any of those things. He just reads and he understands what he reads. Oh, I'm not sure he understands what he reads, but he can use what he reads; he knows how to manipulate it. I can't keep up with him. I want to drop out for a year and then I'll pick up my studies again."

The chairman looked at Mardikan's fingers, at his tired face, at the dull eyes and he told Mardikan that he thought the year's leave of absence was a good idea.

In the summer vacation between their junior and senior years they went to Santa Barbara and worked. They hoed beans, picked lemons, curried polo ponies in Montecito, cleaned fish at a fish-canning factory and were bar boys at a big hotel during Fiesta. They wound up the summer with eighty dollars in cash, a half case of bonded whisky they had stolen from the hotel, two cashmere sweaters they found in the lockerroom at the polo grounds, a pair of hand-tooled shoes that an Englishman had placed outside his hotel door not knowing that they would fit Mike, and a case of canned tuna which was a gift from the owner of the fish-canning factory.

When they got back to the cottage at Stanford Mike looked at it as if he were seeing it for the first time. He looked at the heaps of dusty books, the bits of food on the floor. He noticed a stream of ants flowing in and out of an old box of crackers, each ant waving a tiny shred of cracker above its head. He noticed that the clothes hanging from hooks needed cleaning and he wondered how long they had been that way.

Mike got the cigar box out and counted the money. There was less than a hundred dollars.

"O.K.," Mike said, almost as if he were talking to himself.

"O.K. what?" Hank asked.

"O.K., I'm going to go to law school," Mike said. "I just made up my mind."

"Why law school?" Hank asked.

Mike looked at Hank and for the first time his eyes shifted away and Hank saw a protective, private look cross Mike's face.

"Why not?" Mike asked.

"I don't give a damn what you do. I won't give you reasons why you shouldn't go to law school. I just thought you might have some good reasons for doing it."

"Maybe I do," Mike mused. "Just maybe I do. Anyway what we've got to worry about now is financing me through law school and you through medical school. What are you going to do about finances?"

"Well, if my grades don't drop they tell me I'll get a scholarship which will take care of the tuition," Hank said. "And I'll keep working in the bakery. It doesn't cut into my studies. I've even worked out some wooden braces on the wrapping machine so that I only have to load it with paper every forty-five minutes. I'm all set. What about you?"

"I should get a hashing job, but it takes too much time," Mike said. "I still have a lot of reading I have to do and I don't have much time. I can't take a hashing job."

"What'll you do? Don't kid yourself, Mike. You can't get through law school like this. You'll be up against competition. Most of your competition won't be working on the outside either. You have to get a job, but if it takes too much time you'd better give up law school until you've got some money saved."

"Christ, I'll worry about law school when I get to it," Mike said. "Right now I'm worrying about this year; what I'm going to eat, how often, and how? Five minutes after that I'll start to worry about getting through law school."

Something flitted through Mike's mind; elusive, vague, suggestive somehow of a cashmere sweater and a look of well-being. He could not fasten it down.

"Maybe you could get a job at the bakery," Hank said. "They've been getting more business and they may put on another person on the wrapping machine."

The impressions going through Mike's mind slipped together and in a quick moment of recollection a name crossed his mind: Connie Burton. She was the girl who had been in the experiment. She had worn a cashmere sweater. Somehow she looked expensive, groomed, as if she had money. Mike made up his mind.

"Thanks, Hank, but I think I'll try a few other things first," Mike said. "O.K.?"

"Sure. I don't care what you do, just so you do something."

Mike looked around at the room again; the books, the bits of smeared food, the dust. He liked it. The cottage had been a good place. Idly he put his foot out and blocked the passage of one of the streams of ants. They hesitated, milled in microscopic confusion, waved their bits of cracker in the air. Then cautiously they began to move around his foot, following in the general direction indicated by a few fast-scurrying scouts. Mike raised his foot and slapped it down directly on a cluster of the ants. He stood up.

"I'll do something," he said. "I don't know what, but it'll be something."

CHAPTER 7

Young Love

MIKE LOOKED UP Connie Burton's phone number in the University directory and called her. At first she said that she did not remember him, but then he reminded her of the experiment. He talked to her for fifteen minutes and then asked her for a date. She hesitated and accepted.

He borrowed a car and took her out to Rossotti's beer garden back in the Stanford foothills. Mike bought two quarts of Acme beer, four hard-boiled eggs and a bag of potato chips and they carried them out to the tables alongside the stream. It was late afternoon and the beige-colored hills were turning a light pink. In the meadow a fraternity was having a pledge party and the muted, beery shouts floated over the live oaks and were finally lost in the sound of the stream.

Connie told Mike she was from St. Helena. Her family owned a winery there and she had gone East to prep school. She was studying sociology and she wanted to go into social work or politics when she graduated.

"My folks think I'm an awful radical," Connie said. "I'm a New Dealer and they think that's awful."

"My father thinks I'm pretty far gone too," Mike said.

"Why are parents so conservative?" Connie asked.

She peeled the shell off an egg, sprinkled it with salt. She bit into it and smiled up at him with a little piece of yolk clinging to her chin.

"My father's not conservative," Mike said. "He thinks I'm awful

because I'm not out throwing up the barricades in the street or leading
an insurrection in Washington or joining the Abraham Lincoln Bri-
gade in Spain."

"Really?" Connie asked. She was not sure he was serious.

"Really."

Her eyes were suddenly respectful. She asked him some questions
about politics. He said he did not know the answers.

She's a good average girl in looks, Mike thought. Not too bright.
Not too dumb. Probably doesn't have many dates. She's got money
though.

When they had finished the beer and eggs they walked over to the
edge of the stream. Mike threw one of the bottles out into the water
and they watched it float jerkily away, bumping against rocks and
almost hanging up on the grass that grew in the stream bed. It got
colder and a mist came off the stream in thin tendrils that dissolved
quickly.

On the way back to the campus Mike asked her for another date and
she accepted. She told him that she had a Mercury coupé and they could
go out in that if Mike didn't mind.

Mike took her out four times. The fifth time he took her to the
cottage. It was early in the evening and Hank was working at the
bakery. Mike had bought a gallon of port wine and it was resting on
the table. He had washed out the only two glasses in the cottage and
dried them off carefully with Kleenex and they were placed neatly
beside the big gallon bottle.

"This is a cute little place, Mike," Connie said when they walked in.
"I thought it would be real run down and dirty, but it's cute."

Mike unscrewed the cap on the wine and poured port into both of
the glasses. He handed Connie one. The dusty odor of the room was
cut by the heavy, sweet smell of the wine. Connie sat down in one of
the chairs.

Mike studied her as they talked. She was attractive without being in
the least beautiful or unusual. She had regular features and her figure
was good. Her hair was the best thing about her. It had a sheen that
came from much brushing and it curled up slightly when it reached her
shoulders.

Connie tasted the wine and wrinkled her nose.

"I don't like wine very much," she said. "We have so much of it
at home."

"I've got some whisky," Mike said.

He reached under the bed and pulled out the half case of Old Taylor they had stolen from the hotel. He opened a bottle and poured two inches of whisky into Connie's glass and added some water from the tap.

She took the glass and swallowed half of it in one gulp. At once her mouth narrowed and she blew softly. Her eyes watered and she fidgeted with the handkerchief in her hand. She smiled thinly.

Mike waited until she had had two drinks and then he changed the conversation.

"I understand that you're one of the big liberals on campus," he said.

"What do you mean by liberal?" Connie asked.

"Big interest in the Young Democrats, take subscriptions to *PM* and *The New Republic*, leader in the drive to get Negroes admitted to Stanford. That sort of thing."

"If that's being a liberal, I guess I'm a liberal."

"Why are you interested in all that stuff?" Mike asked.

"Oh, it's hard to say just right out," Connie said and she sipped at her drink. "I believe in economic and social justice and so I try to help those people that can't help themselves."

"Help them do what?"

"Help them get justice," Connie said. "The things they are entitled to."

"How do you know what justice is?" Mike asked. "Maybe justice is each person getting what he is able to get. Maybe the Negroes don't get in Stanford because they don't deserve to."

On the side of Connie's face that Mike could see a small spot of pink started to glow. She drank the rest of the glass and held the glass out to Mike to fill.

"I've heard about your views," Connie said. "I heard what you did to Mardikan. You're a reactionary, Mike. Just a plain reactionary."

Her voice trembled slightly.

"What does that mean? To be a reactionary?"

"It means that you are opposed to everything liberal and progressive," she said. "It means that you want to go back to something that existed a long time ago. To feudalism or something like that."

"I don't want to go back to anything. All I want to do is to understand what is happening now."

Connie hesitated.

"You don't believe in progress," she said finally. "You look at the

Negro today and you see him discriminated against, living in slums, undernourished and, of course, he has a high crime rate so you say that the high crime rate is proof that he should stay in the slums and be discriminated against."

Mike sat up straight and stared at the girl. There was something curious about the girl. She strung set phrases and sentences together, as neatly as a child might string a variety of beads and objects on a string and then hold them up to see if they were beautiful.

Mike looked down at his glass. He swished the deep red wine around. Dark particles, the infinitely small debris of wine, swirled at the bottom of the glass. Mike shook his head.

"I didn't say anything like that," Mike said. "I just asked a question: what is justice for the Negroes? I don't know the answer. I don't really even care very much. All I want to do is to see the Negro, or anyone for that matter, just exactly the way he really is. I don't care about uplifting him or educating him or changing him. Why should I worry about that?"

"Because we are all our brother's keeper," Connie said. "No society is any stronger than its weakest link. We should do what is best for the greatest number."

She hesitated, stared uncertainly at Mike. She reached for the Old Taylor bottle and poured a small trickle into her glass. Carefully, keeping the bottle under control, she filled her glass almost a third full.

Mike realized that she was not holding up the string of phrases and sentences to see if they were beautiful; she was holding them up for protection. O.K., you're through the guard, Mike, he told himself. Go easy now.

He wished he had not drunk so much of the port. It was a warm pool in his stomach; blurring the edges of everything, making him limp and agreeable, slowing his reactions. He carefully composed himself.

"We're interested in different things, Connie," he said. "You're interested in how we ought to act toward others. I'm not. I'm just interested in people the way they are."

"But you ought to have sympathy. You ought to feel for people."

"I do sometimes," Mike said. He hesitated and thought quickly. He felt as if he were at the outer edge of a secret; pushing against the last thin barrier to a dark understanding.

Easy now, he told himself. Now is the time to go very, very easily. Make her speak first.

"But Mike, if you don't have sympathy, if you don't like people and they don't like you . . ." She hesitated and her voice dropped to a whisper. "Then you're alone, Mike. By yourself. Alone."

He was through. His breath came easily. He had broken through. Partially, but not completely, he yielded to the warm glow of the port.

"But you're alone anyway," he said. "Whatever you do you're alone. Sympathy doesn't have anything to do with it. You're alone whatever you do. Look at an executive in a big company that's done a good job for fifteen years. One mistake and he starts to drop. The company just stands aside and lets him drop. If he's tough maybe he can claw his way back on top again, hanging on by his fingernails. But if he isn't, no one gives a damn. He just keeps dropping until he drops right out of sight. All by himself, with maybe his wife and kids staring at him, he keeps dropping. No one raises a hand to help him."

"Someone is always around to help, Mike," Connie said. She stared at him over the edge of her glass. "Someone. Maybe . . ."

"No one. My God, Connie, look at the thousands of organizations that have grown up in the last generation just to take care of people no one will take care of anymore. Juvenile homes, homes for unmarried mothers, insane asylums, homes for TB patients. All the things that a family used to do are now done by some government agency. Don't you see: no one gives a damn. You're alone. Everyone is. Look at old people. Every home used to have a couple of old people in it; aunts, grandfathers, old uncles. Now everyone scrambles around and gets old people into a home for the senile. Anything, but just get them out of the house. Get 'em out of sight. Somewhere else."

Connie's lips had pulled back slightly from her teeth as Mike talked. When he paused she threw her head back and drank off the rest of the whisky and water.

"Not my family," she said. "They wouldn't do that."

Her voice was a whisper.

"Don't kid yourself, Connie. Just assume that you had a mental breakdown and the Dean of Women sent you home to St. Helena. How long do you think your family would keep you around? About as long as it would take them to get a psychiatrist to have you committed to Agnew. They'd do anything to get you out of sight. Any family would."

"Not my family," Connie whispered.

Her hand reached for the bottle. The neck of the bottle chittered against the glass as she poured. She looked up and smiled brightly.

"Say you just went home, Connie, after you graduated. Say you just went home and stayed there. Lots of girls used to do that. They became old-maid aunts and fitted into the family and they were sometimes even pretty valuable members of the family. Think you could do that now? Your mother would be embarrassed because you weren't married and she'd suggest that you go see a marriage counselor or go down to San Francisco and get a job. She'd make you do something; anything. But you couldn't just sit around. She'd want you to see one of those social workers. Really she wouldn't care what you did just so you didn't sit around the house and remind them that you were different than the other girls. Isn't that right?"

She was still looking at him over her glass. Through the brown clear drink her chin looked sagging and uncertain. She closed her eyes for a moment and when she opened them Mike knew that she believed him.

"Maybe you're right," she said.

"I didn't mean it personally, Connie," Mike said. "I just wanted to illustrate a point. Once you see the point things aren't really so bad. God, in a sense the system is beautiful. It takes all of the individuals and measures them, shifts them around, tests them, puts them in a new slot and finally they wind up where they belong. The system peels each person like he is an onion. It rubs off all the unimportant layers; the family, education, culture, good teeth, fine smile, nice vocabulary. It gets right down to the core. And at the core is just the skill and toughness of the individual. The system measures that and then it puts him where he belongs. Oh, sometimes it makes a mistake. A rich idiot can sit on a board of directors . . . but not forever. Sooner or later there is a shifting around and someone else has the idiot's money and he's out in the street wondering what happened. If he's an idiot he'll wind up with the idiots. If he's good and tough he'll wind up with the other good and tough people. The unskilled people get the unskilled jobs; the tough people get ahead and the soft people get stepped on; the bright people do the bright work and the dull people do the dull work."

"It's awful," Connie said.

Mike gestured with his hands. It was a fluttering, intricate gesture that indicated movement and complexity.

"It's awful, but it's wonderful too," he said. "That great big disorderly system, carefully grinding away at everybody. Everybody gets worn away at the same rate. Everybody gets the finish taken off . . ."

"Shut up, Mike," Connie said. "Get me another drink. This bottle is empty."

He went under the bed and dug out another bottle. When he handed her the drink he noticed that she was shivering; just slightly, an almost invisible twitching of her shoulders. Along her arms was a fine weltering of gooseflesh.

"They say your sorority is going to build a new house," Mike said.

Connie told him eagerly about the new house. Then they talked about the football team. Connie began to laugh and the color returned to her cheeks. It was eleven o'clock when she went into the bathroom.

"I could drink the ocean tonight," she said when she came out. She saw the empty whisky bottle and picked it up. Cleverly, like a comedy drunk, she put the bottle to her mouth and threw her head back. Her tongue went up the narrow neck of the bottle, was squeezed white and pink as it reached for the few drops of whisky still left in the bottle. When she pulled the bottle away her tongue came out of the bottle with a popping noise.

She turned toward Mike. He walked toward her and they came together softly. He put one hand around her waist and tilted her face up with the other. He felt her hand dig into his shoulder and he heard the bottle fall to the floor.

Her lips were soft, a surprise. He ran his tongue over the inner flesh of her lips and her mouth opened.

He lifted his head away. She stood with her head tilted back in surprise. A streak of whisky ran from the corner of her mouth. Across her forehead there was a faint pattern of sweat.

Mike wiped the whisky from her chin and kissed her again. This time, as if she had learned everything in thirty seconds, her body came expertly against his, her tongue worked across his lips. The soft flesh between her thighs moved across his leg. She was the one that pushed away.

"Sit down," she said. "On the bed."

She turned off all the lights except a study lamp on one of the desks. She walked back and stood in front of him and her face was hard. She kicked her shoes off and pulled her skirt up over her knees. She had fine long legs and delicate feet. She took off a garter belt and her stockings hissed down her skin as she pulled them off.

She walked over to him and he stood up and kissed her. She put her head close to his neck and began to talk very rapidly and softly.

"My father is funny," she said, so rapidly that Mike could barely understand. "He samples the grapes and the wine all day long and his lips get purple. Almost like a woman's. Maybe he is a little drunk all the time. He picks at the grapes and spits out the seeds. And he drinks wine all day long. One day, when I was thirteen, he stopped me out in the vines and put his hand over my breast, like that," and she took Mike's hand and put it over her breast. "And he said that someday a boy would probably try to do that to me and that if he ever heard of it he would kill the boy. Then he kissed me. His lips all moist and purple and smelling of grapes and claret. I never forgot it."

Under his hand Mike felt her nipple harden and press against his hand. She pushed him backward onto the bed and then stepped away.

She pulled the skirt up again, this time to her waist and her neat untrimmed shorts cut into the round flesh of her hips. She undulated slowly; almost as if she were doing a strange unlearned dance, her free hand occasionally running across the roundness of her stomach. She watched Mike tensely and finally she reached down and stepped out of her shorts.

"All right," Mike said and his voice was sharp.

"All right?" she said and smiled. She walked toward him eagerly.

For the rest of that year Connie loaned Mike money. She loaned it to him in small amounts that finally totaled six hundred and forty dollars.

Connie also insisted that Mike stop swearing. She corrected his grammar and Mike did not object.

CHAPTER 8

"Ungrateful, Voluble, Dissemblers . . ."

$\mathcal{T}$HE WINDOWS of Professor Moon's office opened onto an arched passageway. Across the scalloped strip of shade was the massive, soft sandstone mass of the Quad. The palm trees gave it a tawny, desertlike look. Professor Moon could see a Japanese gardener arranging a sprinkler. The gardener put the hose down carefully in a square of lawn and as he backed away the sprinkler turned slowly and then more quickly, throwing out glittering streams of water. The spray washed the dust off the leaves of grass and they shone with a brilliant green. In the corners of the square the grass remained brown and dry. When the water hit the sandstone it steamed a few seconds until it had cooled the stone.

It was merely warm in Professor Moon's office, but he knew that the Quad and the corridors around it were very hot. As he looked out the open window the sound of the sprinkler, the whir of distant automobile tires passing over soft tar and the trembling of heat waves had a hypnotic effect. With an effort he took his eyes away from the window and looked at the papers in his hands. They were his lecture notes, and for a moment, as his eyes readjusted to the dimness of his office, the words looked Oriental and distorted. His forehead wrinkled as he focused his eyes.

"On the battlefield the flowing-haired Achaians and the Trojans were throwing stones and arrows zissed through the air. Then Agamemnon, king of men, went between the two arrays, in the space where the rank of chariots were drawn up facing one another," he read. With a precise copperplate hand he changed the first sentence to read, "Like a cloud, stones and arrows soared between the Achaians and the Trojans."

Professor Moon was a lazy man, but he prided himself on changing his lectures each time he gave them. Sometimes the changes were not extensive, but always changes were made. It was a part of his reputation, just as his discovery of obscure French and Swedish and Italian poets was a part of his reputation. Professor Moon did not expect to be a great or distinguished professor. He was too fastidious for that. To be distinguished was to be vulgar and the inevitable price of popularity was a cheapening of quality. Whenever one of his discoveries among the poets of Europe had become popular Professor Moon had quickly dropped the person from his lectures and conversations. His standards were high and he did not therefore regret that he had such a small following. Indeed he experienced a tiny, intense thrill of excitement each time he went to his first lecture and saw only six or eight people. The smallness of his following; their minute, careful, almost adoring attention; the obscurity of his references; their look of appreciation when he delivered a jeweled or obscure phrase; all of these were signs to Professor Moon of fidelity and quality.

His followers were almost all girls and most of them came to Stanford from Catholic preparatory schools. Although he was profoundly anti-clerical and most of the girls in his classes had long ago renounced Catholicism, he and they were convinced that only the rigors of a Catholic eduation could provide the preparation for the type of intellectual exertion that students must make under Professor Moon's direction. Only those who had endured the doctrinaire training of nuns could appreciate that Boethius made St. Thomas clear; that Berdyaev contained all of the mysteries of Lenin and Stalin's political behavior; that the vulgarities of Kant were made meaningful by the works of Moritz Lazarus. Professor Moon was only thirty-five, but already he was engaged in writing a book which he had entitled *The Daemons of History* and which was to be a history of the little-known, anonymous. but critical people who in the interstices of history had really formed the ideas which less gifted, but more distinguished men had made popular. The book was slow work and Professor Moon smiled wistfully when asked about its progress. He had no optimism as to when it would be finished. His following was convinced the work would be published posthumously and they shared a peculiar pride because of this knowledge.

Professor Moon looked up from his lecture notes and caught sight of two figures walking across the Quad. The glare of the sun was so bright that the two figures were black and featureless, edged by light. As the spectral figures walked into the shade of the corridor they regained their identity and Professor Moon could see that one of them was Mike Freesmith and the other was Hank Moore. He looked back down at his lecture notes and hoped the boys would walk by his office. In a moment, however, there was a knock on his door. Professor Moon hesitated only long enough to put his lecture notes in a drawer, take out a small book on Hugo of Saint-Victor's, *Summa Sententiarum,* and then he called softly, "Come in."

"Hello, Mike; hello, Hank," he said as they came in. "Sit down. To what do I owe the honor of this visit?"

"Just passing by and thought you might be in," Mike said. "Have you got a minute?"

"A minute? Lots of minutes. As Milton said, 'Immovable, infix'd and frozen round, Periods of time,' and I have plenty of them to spare," Professor Moon said. "A much overrated poet," he muttered almost to himself and smiled at his visitors.

Mike sat down in a chair across the room and put his feet up on an empty bookshelf. He was wearing blue jeans and moccasins and a T-shirt. Hank stood beside the door, leaning against the wall.

"I heard your radio lecture the other night," Mike said. "It was pretty good. 'Good Men and Bad Taste,' that was a good title."

"Yes," Professor Moon said. "Not much to it, you know. Doubt if they'll ever ask me to do it again."

He had been invited to give one in a series of radio lectures by university professors on whatever subject the speaker wished to discuss. Most of the other speakers had attempted to give a popular version of their specialty. But Professor Moon had resolved to keep the same standards he employed in the classroom; indeed, he made the lecture somewhat more difficult. It had been heavy with allusions to little-known artists, poets, and writers; the sentences had been models of difficult, precise language. The station manager had blinked at him in astonishment when he was through and this had rewarded Professor Moon for his labors.

"A few things you said I didn't understand," Mike said. Professor Moon watched Mike's legs. Mike's blue jeans were tight and the muscles of his calves bulged solidly and then flattened as he pushed himself back and forth in a short arc. "You said that everyone had good taste, but that modern society had corrupted the natural good taste that every man possesses. Wasn't that it?"

"Yes, that was it. The argument was a bit complex, but that was the essence of it," Professor Moon said. He was vaguely irritated by the way Mike simplified the discussion; it was almost as if the boy wanted to take away the elegance of words, to reduce them to hard, flat statements.

"Well, you don't really believe that, do you?" Mike said.

Professor Moon looked sharply away from Mike's legs, over Mike's face, and then down at the book in front of him.

"Of course I do," he said.

"Why?"

"There is a good deal of evidence that when people have not been told what to like or their taste has not been corrupted they will choose the most beautiful thing in a completely natural way. Primitive tribes, for example, will prefer Beethoven to boogie-woogie if you give them a chance to express a preference."

"But it doesn't prove anything. What does it mean to say that an isolated, natural individual likes Beethoven more than boogie-woogie? I remember in the lecture you said that almost everyone at birth has a sense of color that is as good as Van Gogh's."

"But the society corrupts the natural capacity for good taste," Professor Moon said.

"That's the point," Mike said. "Everyone, everyplace, lives in some sort of a society. There are no isolated, natural individuals. Everyone lives in a group. What difference does it make if everyone has natural equipment as good as Van Gogh's? The minute they're born it starts to change; the group bangs it around, alters it, modifies, corrupts. By the time a kid is three years old his color appreciation is as good as the group around him. And most of the time that's pretty awful."

"The taste of the group doesn't have to be bad," Professor Moon said. "There is no reason why the society has to brutalize the individual. What I mean is that there are real standards of beauty and the society could help the individual to see these clearly if the society were properly organized. Why does a society have to insist upon bad taste? Why can't it insist upon good taste? That's the point, Mike. If it's true that simple and unsophisticated people have good taste, why can't society just let that taste develop instead of insisting that everyone have very, very bad taste?"

Mike leaned back in his chair and looked at the ceiling. The sunlight outside was bright and clear, but it was so broken and diffused by the dull sandstone walls, the dusty grass and patches of shade that it entered the office as a golden haze. The light shifted and moved; was made tangible by motes that hung motionless in the still air. A beam of light fell on Mike's bare arm and surrounded each hair with a minute glow. Professor Moon watched Mike's hand curl into a fist and he flinched. But Mike only tapped his kneecap gently with the fist.

"But there aren't any simple unsophisticated people around any more," Mike said. "Maybe every person has the potential to become a Michelangelo, the nerves, eyes, color sense, imagination. If you say so I'll believe it. But the fact is that they don't all become Michelangelos. The great mass of the people just don't care about taste or beauty or whatever you want to call it. Look, the mass of people don't even determine what popular taste is. Do you think the mass of the people determine what kind of beautiful cars they are going to buy? Hell no. A little group of men is busy right now in Detroit deciding what we are going to like and admire in new cars ten years from now. If it's beetle shaped and squat and dripping chrome, why in 1949 we'll stand around and admire it and go in debt to buy one. But we don't determine what is beautiful or ugly. All we do is wait to be told what is beautiful in cars and then fight like hell to buy one."

"You're right, of course," Professor Moon said. "Popular taste is incredibly bad now, but that is because it had to be weaned away from a sense of taste and beauty that was once almost perfect. Whenever the awful hand of industrialism and commerce has touched anything it has become tawdry and distorted."

"Do you really believe that?" Mike asked.

"Of course. That's why I'm partly communist and partly Catholic. The communist is right in de-emphasizing private property. If the mass of people weren't driven to own property, to blindly acquire more and more, they could be interested in what is beautiful and tasteful. If private property were eliminated then the natural law of the Catholics would make sense. Either doctrine by itself is senseless, but if private property were eliminated, then Catholicism would make sense."

Professor Moon looked anxiously at Mike. He had a nagging doubt that he sounded childish or sentimental when he talked to Mike. He wanted very much to sound convincing.

"It narrows down to two issues," Hank said. Mike and Professor Moon swung their heads around to look at him and he flushed and spoke very rapidly. "One, does each individual really have the natural

capacity that Professor Moon thinks he has? Second, if each individual
does have a high natural capacity why doesn't he develop it?"

"O.K., I'll buy that," Mike said. "I think people may have the natural
capacity. Probably you can make a statesman out of a kid born in the
slums if you start soon enough and work hard enough. So it comes
down to the second question. Why don't these wonderful individuals
live up to their potential? Everyone agrees they don't. Professor Moon,
John Locke, Thomas Hobbes, everyone. They all look around and think
the men they see are pathetic, inadequate, scared, shameful."

"Right," Professor Moon said crisply. "It's obvious that men don't
live up to their capacity. In my radio lecture I tried to indicate why.
I stated that individuals don't live up to their potential because the
society corrupts them. Change the society and the individuals can live
more fully."

"No, it's more than that," Mike said, speaking very slowly. He sat
up in his chair, took his feet off the desk. "It's not the society. It's
something inside of people. Maybe they've got all the potential for
good inside, but they've also got something else inside of them too."

"Like what?" Hank asked.

"Like a feeling they'd like to bitch everything up," Mike said. "Like
a feeling they'd like to break something up even if they can see it's
good. It's hard to say it. Look, prize fights are more expensive than
symphony concerts. And everyone is always telling everybody else that
they ought to like concerts more than prize fights; their teachers, the
newspapers, the radios. And everyone is always telling them that prize
fighting is cruel and anti-social and vulgar. So why do more people go
to prize fights than go to concerts? I'm not sure. But I've got a hunch."

"I've got a hunch too," Professor Moon said. "The hunch is that
there are more fight arenas around than there are symphony halls."

He laughed, but Mike looked at him without smiling, almost as if
he did not hear.

"No, that's not it," Mike said, going slowly, feeling his way. "It's
like they know that they don't want the best thing. They want something else . . . they want the thing that isn't best. Because it isn't the
best, because they've been told that they shouldn't want it they want it.
Oh, not all of them. Some little quiet guys go to the opera and hate it,
but they do it because they think they should. And some people, a
very few, actually prefer the opera to the prize fight."

Mike paused. Hank and Professor Moon were watching him. He
was embarrassed. He walked over and looked out the window, watching
the distant whirling of the sprinklers.

"Well, now, Mike," Professor Moon said. "You have a good healthy interest in the way people actually behave and I must confess that you see such behavior with much more clarity than most young people. But certainly it is important to see that people are motivated by other things than just envy."

"I didn't mean just envy," Mike said defensively. "I didn't say it the way I wanted."

"But that's what you said," Professor Moon went on. He felt more secure now.

Mike swung around and looked at Professor Moon. He put his hands in the pockets of his blue jeans and stood with his legs apart.

"Mike is a little intoxicated with history and psychology," Hank said. "He gets things mixed up and they come out in queer ways."

Mike knew that Hank was trying to take him off the hook. He grinned and stepped into the center of the room.

"Professor Moon understands about queer ways," Mike said. Professor Moon's smile vanished abruptly. "He is tolerant about queer ways."

Mike stood with his shoulders hunched belligerently. Professor Moon looked sharply away from Mike, ran his eyes over the rows of books. His forehead was very pale and his lips were pressed together.

"Let's go, Mike," Hank said. "We've got to get going."

Professor Moon looked up and his face was collapsed and formless, his lower lip struggling to regain its shape. The only firm thing in his face was a tear that glittered sharply in each eye. He automatically waved to them and his face creased in the smile which he gave students leaving his office. As Mike and Hank walked by the window of his office they could hear him sniffling and they knew without looking that he had his head down on the desk.

They walked by the Japanese gardener and stepped out of the shade of the passageway into the gathered, yellow, intense heat of the Quad. The heat flowed from the stones of the buildings, gathered in pools of dead air that smelled of scorched cement, burnt palm leaves and an utter absence of moisture. It was an aseptic, crisp hotness. They walked through it as if it were water; slowed by the density of it; feeling their nostrils distend as if searching for air. Drops of sweat popped out on their foreheads and were pulled into the dry atmosphere and in a few minutes their faces were powdered by small particles of dried salt.

"Hot day. Really hot day," Mike said. "I like hot days."

Hank did not reply. Their feet scraped over the stones of the Quad and the sound floated over the dead scorched air and came back rounded and plump off the thick walls. They walked by a small circle of palm

trees and brilliant summer flowers. Above them the bright mosaic work
of the chapel glittered.

"You son of a bitch," Hank said. "You had to let him know that you
know he is a queer. Is that the only reason you stopped by his office?"

"No," Mike said.

"He's a quiet little guy. He's a good teacher. He doesn't bother anyone. Why did you say that to him?"

"Why not?" Mike asked.

"Why not? Is that an answer?" Hank asked savagely. "You go in
and hurt someone and I ask you why and you say 'why not.' Even if he
is a queer what's wrong with that?"

"Nothing's wrong with it," Mike said and he was grinning. "And if
nothing's wrong with it why not talk about it? Maybe it's just like having the mumps or going to the movies. Maybe Moon likes to talk
about it."

"Shut up."

"I don't get it. Being queer is all right, we say. Maybe it's better
than being normal. Maybe it's being superior. But we can't talk about
this fine thing. It's very bad to mention to a queer that he possesses
this fine thing."

"That's not why you said it; to be nice and conversational," Hank said
wearily. "You said it to hurt him. You said it for the same reason that
you talk tough to Mardikan and Connie. You want to see if you can
break through and find something that a person is scared of. You like
to find the soft spot and then press it hard, drive your finger into it.
O.K., forget it. I just don't want to hear it any more."

They came to the end of the Quad. There was a water fountain in
one of the columns and Mike stopped for a drink. When he finished
he ran the stream of water over his face and stood up. The water ran
into his T-shirt, turned the thin cotton a wet gray color. He turned
around and looked down the Quad; almost straight into the sun.

"Sit down, Hank," Mike said. "I want to talk."

They sat down on the hot cement, full in the sun. The smell of hot
asphalt came faintly off the surface of the Quad.

"Go ahead, talk," Hank said.

"You're wrong about me wanting to hurt Moon. I don't care one
way or the other about him. I don't care if he's happy or miserable."

"Well, why did you say it then?"

"It's hard to say it just right. But I didn't do it to hurt him. I said
it to see what he was scared of. I found out he's scared of being a

queer. Maybe it's possible to be a queer and not be scared of it, but I had to find out. That's why I pushed him. I didn't want to hurt him though."

"Why did you want to find out what he's scared of?" Hank asked. He looked sideways at Mike.

Mike was staring down the Quad, his eyes narrowed against the sun.

"I'm not sure," Mike said slowly. "To test a theory, I guess. To see if there are any exceptions; to find if there are any guys that aren't afraid of something. It's like an itch, Hank. I see a guy like Moon or one of the rich kids on the Row. Or even some bright little character in class who seems to have it made. I just start to itch with curiosity when I see a guy with a perfect little world, everything consistent, everything balanced . . . the guy happy in the middle of the world. I don't believe in it. I have to see if it's real."

"And is it?"

"No. It never is. Everybody is always scared of something. After a while you get good at finding out what it is. Sometimes I can find out what it is without pushing very hard. Sometimes the guy doesn't even know what I'm doing. Sometimes you have to push harder . . . like with Moon. But I don't do it to make the guy miserable. That's not it."

Hank felt something relax inside of him. He knew Mike was telling the truth. They sat quietly in the sun for a while. The heat made black dots crawl before their eyes and the sharp lines of the buildings quivered, broke, slowly reshaped. A dog trotted into the far end of the Quad, stood black and perfect and diminished, swung its head to study the emptiness and quiet. The dog's tongue dripped. After a few seconds it trotted back into the shade and disappeared.

"Why do you want to know something like that, Mike?" Hank asked. "What difference does it make if people are scared?"

"I don't know. It's just important to me. That's all," Mike said. Behind his eyes his skull felt empty; filled only with the crawling black dots and a sort of warm redness. He did not know where his words were coming from. They seemed to come just from his lungs and lips; as if his mind were being short-circuited. "You're interested in one thing, I'm interested in another. You're brain-clever, Hank. It's part of being a Jew. You're reasonable and logical and calm. Like something was chilled out of you. I think a different way."

Mike looked away from the Quad. Between his feet he could see the asphalt surface of the Quad. Little bright pieces of stone embedded in old soft asphalt. The little pieces of stone seemed very far away and

Mike put his hand down; reached for what seemed an endless distance until his knuckle rested against one of the stones. He pushed against it until he felt a slight pain and he once again felt anchored to the earth; released from the heat and brilliance of the sun.

"In six weeks we'll graduate, Hank, and I've only learned two things and one of them I knew before I got here," Mike said. "At first I thought there was a lot more and I kept reading all the books, listening to the lectures, trying to find out what the other things were. I really got confused. Even when I was getting A's in all my courses I was confused. They didn't make sense. Neither did the books. It was all crazy. You couldn't add up all the books and get agreement. I soaked it all in and coughed it back up for the examinations, but it didn't make sense. But if I just stuck to two things, then the whole thing made sense."

"They must be pretty terrific things," Hank said. "What are they?"

"They're kind of like principles," Mike said slowly. "Like things I know are true . . . or at least I haven't seen anything that proves them wrong. Maybe I'm wrong and I don't care if you believe me or not, but I'll tell you what they are. The two principles are the only things that make sense out of all the lousy lectures in economics and politics and philosophy and history. The first principle is that everyone is scared."

"We can call that the Principle of Fear, eh?" Hank said.

"I don't care what you call it. That's as good a name as any: The Fear Principle. The second principle is that everyone hates. Call it the Hate Principle if you want. I've never given them a name."

"Fear and hate sound pretty much the same thing to me," Hank said.

"But they're not," Mike said. He felt excited, as if he were at the edge of a discovery. "Take a family. A kid might hate his mother, but he doesn't fear her. Or take a big businessman. He might hate his workers, but he might not fear them. Or the workers might fear him and think he is a pretty good guy, even like him."

"It doesn't explain anything, Mike," Hank said. "It sounds impressive, but what does it mean?"

"Well, take something like a revolution. Take the French Revolution. All of a sudden the streets of Paris are full of a bunch of people who are willing to kill the king, slaughter one another, change everything. Marx takes a look at it and says it was just one economic class trying to overthrow another. A regular historian looks at it and says it was a fight for power between the Jacobins and the Royalists and the Babouvists and a lot of other groups. Someone else looks at it and says it was the triumph of the Enlightenment, the inevitable result of the spread of rationality. Christ, there are thousands of books on it. Each one giving a slightly different reason. But they don't add up; they don't make sense."

"And your two principles do make sense?" Hank asked.

"Maybe they do. I'm not sure. But just take a look at the heads that were being carried around on the tips of pikes during the Revolution. At first they were the princes and the landlords and the mayors. The mob chopped their heads off and put them on pikes because everyone hates the people in charge. I don't know why, but they do. Then after this has gone on for a while the people who made the revolution, the real revolutionaries, decide that things have gone far enough and tell the people to stop. Then a strange thing happens. They discover that the people hate them, too. They find out that overnight the people can transfer their hate from the old regime to the new regime. That's what they mean when they say that old revolutionaries always die first. The successful revolutionaries are the ones that are able to make the people transform their hatred into direct action. But then orders; execute opposition; pass edicts; take over. They wind up with a guy like Napoleon . . . the most precise contradiction of the revolution. And they love him. Because now they're looking for a way to escape their fear. The hate is pushed below the surface; now they're scared. And because Napoleon will take over, because he'll ease their fears, they rush to die in his armies, freeze in Russia, burn in Africa, starve along-side of every road in Europe . . . with a great big glow of pride and love in their eyes as they stare at the Little Corporal riding off without them. Jesus!"

Mike stopped. He pressed his knuckle against the sharp stone. He looked sideways at Hank.

A bell rang, sharp and glasslike clear, peculiarly distinct in the hot air. People came from classes and moved slowly down the covered passageways. Two nuns stepped into the Quad, hesitated and then scurried across the hot cement. Their small black shoes twinkled in the sun, their heavy black habits swayed provocatively. Hank waited until the Quad was still again.

"What about the Russian Revolution?" he asked. "They didn't kill the revolutionaries there."

"That was different," Mike said. "They hated the Czar and the Germans and their landowners and just about everyone else. Christ, at first they didn't even know who to kill. They went around shooting everybody; they discover that hate is indiscriminate. The people just hate. And so for a few days the heads of the revolutionaries appear on the pikes."

"Of course, there are some people who revolt on rational grounds," Hank said. "Tom Paine and Jefferson and . . ."

"Sure they do. And they are the ones that are always knocked off first. They start the revolution and then they are either killed or pushed aside and someone else takes over."

"Nice situation," Hank said. "What stops everyone from killing everyone else until just one guy is left?"

"Fear. The second principle. The Fear Principle," Mike said. "They've even got a name for it. The *thermidor:* the revolutionary July. After a while fear sets in. Then everyone starts looking around for some way to end the fighting. Not because they're tired of it or feel ashamed or the hate is gone. But because they're fearful. Fearful that they won't get food, fearful that they might be invaded, fearful that their property might be taken away, fearful that they might be the next ones to get the guillotine. It happens in every revolution. In a spasm of fear they strangle the revolutionaries and then they start to look desperately for authority. They turn to someone like Robespierre or Babeuf. Exactly the sort of tough, dominant guys that they thought they were getting rid of when they made the revolution. Guys that are willing to act tough; Bolsheviks, Mensheviks, soldiers, sailors, mayors, policemen, everybody. But then a guy came along with a spike beard and hard gray eyes and he knew how to hate and to fear. And they turned the revolution over to him. Not because they loved him, Hank, but because he could control the fear and the hatred. One day he would tell them who to hate . . . work out a nice slogan for it. The next day he would give them something to fear . . . the Cheka or the army. So he sat on top of the situation; opening the spill-gates of fear one day and hate the next. Hank, make no mistake about it. There is one thing that the masses know: real authority. And a real authority is someone who can satisfy their desire to hate and their fear. A good authority works the two of them together. He plays on 'em like they're an organ. He pulls out the stop labeled Hate and they run screaming through the street shooting up landlords and shopkeepers. Then the next day he pulls out the Fear stop and lets them see that if they're not careful he'll have the Cheka or the GPU chewing their ass. He sits at the console and gives 'em what he thinks they need; a little fear today, a little hate tomorrow. Some days he gives 'em both. And they stand together and shiver and think he's the greatest guy in the world and love him."

"But they don't like that crap, Mike," Hank said. "They hate it. The Russians hate it."

"The hell they do," Mike said. "They love it. We'd like to believe all that stuff they write about loving Lenin and adoring Stalin is written by a bunch of frauds in Moscow. But we're wrong. The Russians love it. One day they get the 'hate' theme and they all start sending in secret letters on the manager of their collective. The next day they get the 'fear' theme and they start looking over their shoulder scared pissless that the manager might have a brother in the Cheka. But the big thing is that they like it; it gives a kind of crazy tension and shape to each day. The fear and the hate complement one another; fold into one another. They feel complete, filled up, whole."

"Sometimes people go along for a long time without seeming to me to be very fearful or very hateful," Hank said. "Like right here in America. Right now."

"Take another look, Hank," Mike said. "Sometimes it's hard to see. Sometimes because everyone is well fed and no one is too high above anyone else the hate and fear come into balance. But they're there. Do you think Roosevelt talks about Wall Street bankers because he really believes they want to dominate the country? Of course not. He does it because they're easy to hate. Same with the businessmen. They don't really think Roosevelt is trying to socialize the country or that he's a Commie. They just sense that people are scared of socialism or communism. So that's what they say: Roosevelt is a socialist or communist or both."

"It's just not enough to explain everything that happens, Mike," Hank said. "I wouldn't get excited about it."

"I'm not excited," Mike said. "I'm just trying to find things out. Maybe there's a pattern to things. Look at politics. You can see the hate principle working out. If you have the best ruler in the world, doing the best possible job for everyone, he still gets kicked out after a while. Not because he's bad or evil or inefficient, but because the hatred just starts welling up."

"Mike, how do you know this stuff?" Hank said. He stirred on the warm concrete; suddenly itched with restlessness. "You sound crazy."

"I feel it. That's how I know it. I sound crazy because people are crazy. The only way you can describe it accurately is to sound crazy. This is a senseless, irritational, unorganized, inarticulate thing, Hank. Maybe the craziness is the only orderly thing about it. Maybe if you understand the craziness you understand the whole thing."

"O.K., O.K., Mike," Hank said. "I'm not interested in changing your mind. But why aren't you interested in doing something that will improve the process? Assume that you're right. Why don't you try and change it? Make it better?"

"Why?" Mike asked. "Change it to what? Maybe I'd change it and it would be worse than it is now. Everyone wants to change things; make them better. Hitler, Mussolini, Stalin, Roosevelt. Father Coughlin, the Pope, trade union leaders. Think they'll make things any better? Maybe so, but I doubt it. Anyway, I don't know how I want things changed. I just want to live in the world the way it is now."

"You're probably right," Hank said wearily. He reached down to the warm asphalt surface, tried to scrape a few pieces of gravel together. He managed only to get three small pieces of stone. He poured them from one hand to the other. They were hot against his palms. "Every tyrant in the world has thought he was doing good. Matter of fact some of the worst tyrants are the boys who get the idea that God is on their side. But, Mike, what's the alternative? Is everything good? Do you give up trying to find out what is right just because a lot of people have been mistaken about it before?"

"You don't worry about what's good," Mike said. "Maybe there isn't any such thing as good. And when you start to worry about that you get like Moon and all the thousands of birds like him in the world: politicians, messiahs, bureaucrats, prophets. They start worrying about what's good and what's bad and pretty soon all alone and in isolation they've built a perfect little world of what ought to be. It's like one of those clocks you see inside a glass dome; all of the beautiful wheels and gears whirring and clicking together and lifting little levers and moving other things. In that private little world you can cut out anything you don't like, you can make everything match. And then these poor bastards turn to the world and announce that they've got a new system, a new morality, universe, a new interpretation. And nobody even listens. Nobody cares. See, Hank, I don't care about these guys and their little worlds. Sometimes they even do good. But I'm interested in something else. I'm interested in what is actually happening."

"You can say that again," Hank said. He stood up and threw the three pebbles in his hand far out into the Quad. He pounded his hands against his pants. He was unbearably nervous, anxious to go. "Let's get going."

Far across the Quad the shadows were starting to lengthen and there was the first breath of chill. When they stood up they were dizzy for a moment from the heat and the sudden rush of blood through their veins. They started to walk.

"I told Connie I'd meet her by the bookstore at five o'clock," Mike said. "What time is it?"

"Quarter to five."

"I better get going. You want to come along? We're going up to the City tonight to hear a speech. Come on along."

"Who's going to talk?"

"Cromwell. John Cromwell," Mike said.

"You going in Connie's car?" Hank asked.

"Sure. Do you want us to go on the train just because I don't have a car?"

"O.K., O.K. Only someday I want to see you buy a tankful of gas for that car. The only time you give it back to her is when it's out of gas."

"She gets a fair return on her investment," Mike said and grinned. "A very fair return."

They left the Quad and walked into the shade of the oak trees. They saw Connie's car in front of the bookstore. By the time they reached the car evening had fallen and suddenly it was much cooler. They shivered as they walked toward the car.

CHAPTER 9

Vox Populi, Vox Dei

Iᴛ ᴡᴀs ᴅᴀʀᴋ when they arrived in San Francisco. Mike drove slowly out to North Beach and found the square in which the speech was to be given.

"It's only seven," he said. "The speech probably won't start until eight. Let's get something to eat."

"Let's have spaghetti," Hank said. "North Beach is supposed to be good on spaghetti. How about that restaurant over there?"

They parked the car and walked across to the restaurant. The square was big, stony and almost empty. There were a few patches of grass protected by low wire fences, but the wire was kicked loose and hung down in loops. The grass was thin and brown. A group of Italian men stood in the middle of one of the grass plots, smoking rat-tail black cigars and talking.

Around the square the street lights made weak puddles of light. Most of the buildings had small businesses on the ground floor: salami factories, wine dealers, bars, a travel office and warehouses. The upper floors were apartments, most of which had small iron balconies.

Women stood on the balconies. They were fat, petulant, irritated with the work of preparing the evening meal. Children stood behind them, waving moist pieces of bread. The faces of the women softened as they sniffed the cool air off the Bay. Most of them wore dirty chiffon dresses that gave their bulky bodies a wispy, fragile quality.

In the middle of the square was a statue of Garibaldi. It was an equestrian statue and the huge bronze horse and rider rose so high into the night that all one could see was the pawing hoofs of the horse and a huge booted foot stuck into stirrups. Occasionally a pigeon flew down to the base of the statue, picked through the litter of peanut shells and then soared back up into the blackness again.

Mike led the way into the restaurant and sat down at a table in front of the large flyspecked window that overlooked the Garibaldi statue.

"How about some wine?" Mike asked.

"See if they have Chianti," Connie suggested.

"We'll have three orders of spaghetti with meat sauce and two bottles of dago red," Mike said to the waiter.

The waiter turned and walked toward the kitchen.

"Mike, they don't like to hear the word 'dago,'" Connie said. "It's like 'nigger' or 'kike.' You shouldn't use the word."

"Hey, waiter," Mike called.

The waiter turned away from the kitchen and walked over. He was a young man with a small round belly and a mustache.

"Do you mind people calling you 'dago'?" Mike asked.

"Hell, no," the waiter said. "Dago, wop, ginny; they're all the same to me. I'm a dago, ain't I? Why should I care?"

"Damned if I know," Mike said. "I just wanted to find out."

The waiter looked down at Connie, ran his eye over her arms and the swell of her bosom, studied her clothes. He grinned at Mike.

"She's worried, eh?" he asked.

"That's right," Mike said.

The waiter turned his hands up in puzzlement and winked at Mike. Connie looked down at her hands. The waiter walked over to a sideboard and picked up two bottles of wine and began to polish three glasses.

"See. He doesn't care," Mike said. "Where do you get those crazy ideas, Connie?" He grinned at her.

"All right, Mike, skip it," Connie said. "I just don't like the word. That's all."

The waiter brought the wine and Mike filled their glasses. It was a bitter wine with a thin biting taste. A black residue floated in the bottom of the glasses.

The waiter brought three large plates of spaghetti and meat sauce. In the center of the table he placed a wicker basket full of big chunks of sour-dough bread and he gave each of them a small white dish with a pat of butter. Mike bent his head over the plate, twirled the spaghetti with his fork and began to eat. Pieces of spaghetti dropped from his lips and with a piece of bread he pushed them onto his next forkful. He finished half of the plate before he paused. Connie was looking at him.

"All right. I'll be a good boy and watch my manners," he said.

He sat up and began to eat more slowly, taking smaller bites. Connie began to eat. Hank, without talking, finished his plate and asked the waiter to bring a second helping.

They were almost finished when a white panel truck with loudspeakers on top came down the street, lurched over the curb and drove into the square. It stopped between the restaurant and the Garibaldi statue. Two men got out and opened the rear door of the truck. They took out a portable platform and put it just beneath the window of the restaurant. They hauled spools of black wire from the truck and unloaded a microphone.

Out of the darkness, flitting through the pools of light, children gathered silently. They looked in the back of the truck, played with the wire, talked softly in Italian.

"For Christ sake get away," one of the men said. "Keep back until we get the equipment set up."

The children paid no attention.

"Who's this Cromwell, Mike?" Hank asked.

Hank was eating the bread left in the wicker basket. He did it unthinkingly, by habit.

"Just a talker," Mike said. "He's a lawyer, but he makes speeches all over the state. I've heard him a few times down in L.A. and once up here."

"Is he in politics?" Hank asked.

"In a way, I guess. He's run for office a few times and was a Congressman for a while. But he isn't a regular politician if that's what you mean."

The waiter brought another basket of bread and Hank reached for a piece, crumbled it into chunks and threw them in his mouth.

"What does he live on?" Connie asked.

"He's rich. Comes from a real old California family. They say he has a fortune. That's one reason these Italians will come out to hear him; because he's a Cromwell and has money."

"I still don't get it," Hank said. "What does he talk about?"

"It varies," Mike said. "Once I heard him talk on unemployment; another time he talked on trade with Japan. Different things."

"Why?" Hank asked. "What's the point?"

"I'm not sure what the point is," Mike said. He paused and looked out the window. "Sometimes I think he just likes to talk. Other times I think he really feels about things. You'll see. It's funny. Wait till you see him."

Outside in the square one of the men picked up a microphone, plugged it into a black wire and mounted it on a stand. He spoke into it gently.

"Testing . . . one . . . two . . . three . . . testing," a huge magnified voice said.

He whistled and an earsplitting shard of sound crashed through the square. The man stepped back and smiled.

"It's O.K., Jamie," he said. "Turn the volume down a bit."

In the warm air the voice was enormous. The words floated like sluggish balloons, keeping their shape until they reached the buildings and then fractured into smaller sounds. People appeared in the windows of the apartments; men in undershirts, children, old women. Almost at once people began to drift across the square, made a scattered thin line around the Garibaldi statue.

"We'll just sit right here," Mike said. "We can hear everything and get a good look at the crowd."

"Good," Connie said. "Standing up makes my feet ache."

"I still don't get it," Hank said. The breadbasket was empty and his fingers ran crablike over the wicker strands, found a few crumbs. "Does Cromwell belong to a political party? Or is he trying to start one? Or what?"

"I don't know," Mike said impatiently. "I told you that. I've heard he's a Democrat, but he never mentions political parties. You'll see. He just doesn't sound like a politician. Someone told me that he wants to be governor of the state, but he never mentions it."

The loudspeakers on top of the truck were connected to a record player. The two soundmen put records on the turntable and then sat on the fenders of the truck and smoked cigarettes.

> *Green eyes, those soft and limpid green eyes,*
> *Your eyes that promise sweet nights,*
> *Give my soul a longing, a search for love divine.*

As the song floated over the square the children stopped playing. They gathered around the truck and stared up at the big white speakers. One of the boys, about four years old, stepped out from the crowd of children. He was a stocky boy, with black thick hair and strong legs. He closed his eyes romantically, held his arms out as if they were around a partner and began to mimic a couple dancing. He had a slight subdued smile on his face; as if he were about to burst into laughter. The children cheered. In the faint light the boy looked dwarfish, like a full-grown person imperfectly viewed.

Someone put a foot out and the boy tripped. He stumbled to his knees, his eyes popped open and he roared with laughter. He got to his feet and lunged at the boy who had tripped him.

The crowd started to thicken. Women filled up the shaky green benches that lined the edge of the park, holding limp babies in their arms. The air was turning blue-white with cigar smoke. Men stepped out of nearby bars. Most of them wore black hats and their shirts were buttoned up to the top button, but they wore no ties.

An old gray Cadillac came around the corner, worked through the people in the street and drove over the curb. Finally it came to a halt in front of the restaurant. The driver got out of the front seat and opened the rear door. A woman got out. As she stepped from the car she lifted her hand, but not quickly enough to conceal the purple splash of a birthmark down the left side of her face. It started under her eye and like a vivid welt, furry in texture, spread down her cheek. With a practiced, expert gesture she lit a cigarette and held it so the birthmark was covered. She turned and walked up the stairs to the restaurant. As she turned her profile came into view. She had a perfect cameo profile, with flawless skin, a flaring nose and a beautiful rounded chin. She had a superb figure.

"Who's she?" Connie breathed; her voice admiring, but her lips drawn back slightly, as if by disgust. "She's beautiful. I mean really beautiful . . . except for that thing."

"I don't know for sure," Mike said. "She's his secretary or something. She's not his wife. She's always with him. Her name is Clara."

Mike looked through the window into the car. Cromwell sat in the back seat, the light from the window falling directly on him. He was a big man with lanky legs and long arms. He looked about fifty years old, but it was hard to tell. He might have been much older, but it was impossible that he could be younger than that. He had a hat pushed back on his head and the tanned angularity of his face showed. He scratched savagely at his armpit and looked out at the crowd. He turned suddenly, stepped out of the car and came into the restaurant.

When he stepped into the restaurant he stopped and looked for the woman. He was wearing an expensive suit that was almost ruined. The seams were stretched so that the threads showed, buttons dangled, a pocket was torn in one corner, the shoulder pads had slipped. The zipper on his fly was stuck partly open. The suit was covered with tobacco ash that fell in a light gray mist whenever he moved.

"Clara, where's Leo?" he asked. He scratched at his thigh and the motion pulled his pants leg up. A sock dangled around his ankle. "Christ, that's just no crowd at all. Leo said they'd have a mob. Where is he?"

"He said he'd meet us here," Clara said. "We're a little early."

Cromwell looked angrily around the room, stared for a moment at Mike's table and then, quite suddenly, he relaxed. He stopped scratching and he walked over to the small bar and asked the bartender to make him an Irish coffee.

"Make it just right," Cromwell said. "Two ounces of Bushmill's, half teaspoon of sugar, big slug of whipped cream."

Leo came in. He was a big, worried-looking man. He was wearing a collarless shirt fastened at the top by a gold collar button that gleamed deep from the fat of his neck. A small group of men stood outside the restaurant window and looked in.

"Hi, John," Leo said. "You're a little early. The crowd will be bigger a little later. It's a bad night. St. Mary's is having a bazaar, couple of other things going on. But there'll be more people before you start."

Cromwell did not say anything. He took a taste of the Irish coffee, looked up with a smear of whipped cream on his upper lip. Then satisfied with the taste he drank it off in two large gulps. He wiped his mouth on his sleeve.

"What else is going on?" Cromwell asked. "Here, have a cigar," he said before Leo could reply. He held out a handful of cigars. Leo took one, bit off the end and lit it with relief.

"Good cigar," Leo said, letting the smoke float out of the corner of his mouth.

"Baloney," Cromwell said sourly. "They're awful, but I'm used to 'em. What else is going on tonight?"

He was taut again, his long fingers picking at the back of his neck, then scratching his ribs. Occasionally he held his hands quietly over his chest as if he hoped in that way to keep them quiet. Then in a few seconds they started to move again.

Leo looked pained.

"Well, the North Beach Civic Club is having a steak and beer party tonight," Leo said. "They've got money, you know. Free steak and beer. That'll draw some of the people away."

"Clara, remind me to give the Civic Club a call on Monday,"

Cromwell said. He stood for a moment, staring through the window at the crowd, one finger carefully scratching the lobe of his left ear. He turned and looked at Leo. "Leo, you should have told me earlier. You made a mistake."

"I know, Mr. Cromwell. I know I did," Leo said quickly. He shifted his feet. "It just couldn't be helped."

"Anything can be helped, Leo," Cromwell said severely. "Whenever you get into a jam like this let me know. I can do something about it."

"I know you can, Mr. Cromwell," Leo said and his face relaxed. "I'm sorry. It won't happen again."

"Well, let's go out and get going," Cromwell said. He turned toward the door.

"Fine, fine, Mr. Cromwell," Leo said. "I want you to meet the members of our executive committee who organized the meeting tonight."

The little group of men outside the window had drifted into the restaurant and they stood by the door, smiling at Cromwell.

Leo walked over to the men and started to introduce them.

"I don't want to meet them, Leo," Cromwell said. He ran his eyes over the group. "They were supposed to do a job and they didn't do it. We don't have anything to talk over. When they show me that they can do a job we'll have something to talk about. Introduce me to them then."

He walked by the group of men. They stared after him. Their faces twisted with anger. Leo's face was gaunt with surprise. He walked out into the square and the men slowly followed him. Clara got up and walked out. She was smiling.

"I can tell you one thing," Hank said as the restaurant became silent. "That guy will never be a politician. He loses friends faster than anyone I ever saw."

"Wait. Just wait," Mike said. He looked out the window.

Cromwell walked to the platform and stepped to the microphone. He looked out over the square. He shot his cuffs, reached into his vest pocket and took out a small paper bag of Sen-Sen. He shook a few pieces into his hand and threw them into his mouth. He stared calmly out over the crowd, thoughtfully sucked at the Sen-Sen. He reached down with one hand and dug his fingers into his buttocks, scratched hard. Someone in the crowd laughed and the laughter spread, rolled over the square. Cromwell looked up in surprise.

"He looks like Charlie Chaplin," Connie said. "All that scratching and jerking. Mike, he's just hopeless."

Mike did not reply. Standing in the weak light Cromwell's figure was caught in sharp outline and he did look antic; half serious. There was something elaborately portentous in the way he scratched himself, the deliberate motions of sucking the Sen-Sen.

Mike replied, finally, to Connie without taking his eyes from Cromwell.

"Look, Connie, imagine that you're one of those wops out there. You've heard of the Cromwells. You've heard that they own the biggest bank of San Francisco and rice fields around Sacramento and, in general, they're loaded. You come out to hear Cromwell because you've heard about all the money and power. And you see Cromwell scratching his butt and picking at his ear. Suddenly he's like someone you know; he's like your father or uncle or grandfather. Scratching, worried, messy looking. Would it make you like him or loathe him or . . ."

Mike stopped talking, for Cromwell had put his hands into his pockets and stepped forward to the microphone.

"Si è fatto un gravissimo errore e voi ne siete i responsabili," Cromwell said in perfect Italian.

His voice thundered out over the square. He pointed a finger at the crowd. His voice was mocking.

"Yes, a great injustice has been done," he said in English. "And you, all of you, are to blame."

The laughter of the crowd was chopped off. An old man took the butt of a cigar out of his mouth, stared slack-jawed at Cromwell. In the back of the square a pregnant woman slowly stood up on one of the benches, her pear-shaped silhouette caught in the light.

"I know, I know. You're happy, you go to work, you get enough to eat," Cromwell said. "Sheeplike, ignorant and happy you go along your way. Well, you've been duped. While you drank your wine and ate your spaghetti something was taken away from you, you were cheated. *Vox populi, vox Dei.* That's what the Romans used to say. The voice of the people is the voice of God. Your ancestors said that. And they meant it. But not you. Not anymore. Now you're content to let someone else do everything for you. And they cheated you. While you were looking at your plate of spaghetti or guzzling your wine it happened."

Cromwell stopped and mauled his ear with his closed fist. The

crowd stirred restlessly. A murmur of anger came from the rear of
the crowd. The sounds that came out of the loudspeakers were like
strands; almost like lashes, making the crowd shuffle forward in
protest.

A woman stood in the front row. She was middle-aged and dressed
in a thin black coat that she held tightly about her body. Her upper
lip was dark with hair and she held her mouth in a suspicious pout.
Her gray-streaked hair was dirty. She stared at Cromwell with outraged eyes, her face livid with hostility.

"What, you ask? What has happened?" Cromwell went on. "What
did we miss while we were sleeping off a binge? Well, friends, let
me tell you that while you were going on your comfortable way here
in San Francisco our president, consulting no one, working in secret,
gave fifty destroyers to Great Britain. Now think for a moment how
much of our national treasure, our wealth, the sweat of our own
American men, the tons of our steel, the hundreds of our cannon,
went into those fifty destroyers. Were you consulted when these
millions of dollars were given away? Don't make me laugh."

The crowd stirred. Their faces were blank, confused, uncertain.
The gaunt woman in the first row looked over her shoulder, stared
at the crowd and then turned her angry eyes back on Cromwell.

"You weren't consulted on this gift of destroyers to Great Britain
and there are a lot of other things that you are not being consulted
on," Cromwell said. He leaned forward, his voice dropped slightly.
"I am told, by people who had better remain unnamed, for their own
protection, but I can assure you that they are reliable. I am told by
these people that even more monstrous deals are being negotiated
at this very moment. More of the treasure of America is being given
away, more of our ships and planes and tanks and munitions are being
given to a nation which got itself into a war and now wants us to
bail them out. And do you know where those destroyers will operate?
They will operate in the Mediterranean, they will roam the length
of Italy, sinking innocent fishing boats, denying movement of legitimate cargo in and out of Italy."

Cromwell paused, scratched behind his ear. This time no one
laughed. The faces in the crowd were losing their indefinite look.

"And in our papers, friends, do you ever hear a mention of Il Duce?
Do you ever hear a mention of the man who has cleared the swamp
lands of Italy, reunited a divided people, forged the will of a nation
into unity? Of course not."

"What is he trying to do?" Hank asked. "Tell them that Mussolini is a nice guy? The dirty bastard."

The words from the loudspeaker came distinctly into the restaurant, and were made round and distinct; as if the square were a sounding board.

"Mike, he's insulting them," Connie said. "I've never heard anyone insult a crowd like that. They hate him. You can see it in their faces."

Mike waved his hand at Connie to be quiet. Without looking away from Cromwell he answered her.

"Wait until he finishes before you make up your mind," Mike said. "All the regular politicians never try to offend anyone, but Cromwell always starts out by insulting the audience. I can't figure it out, but it works. Wait a while."

"Friends, why are you so hopeless against these termites who infiltrate our government, against those small gnawing animals who chew away at our independence and freedom?" Cromwell said. "Why do you sit back and let clean Italian youths get killed with American steel in a war in which we are not involved? Because you are lazy. Because you are not interested. Because you are bored."

Cromwell paused, took the package of Sen-Sen out of his vest pocket, popped a handful of the small black bits into his mouth. Over the loudspeakers came a moist sucking sound. Cromwell carefully put the package back in his pocket.

"He's crude, Mike. Really crude," Connie said. "Just plain offensive."

"Sure, sure," Mike said impatiently. "You're not telling me something I don't know. But maybe they like him that way."

The woman in the front row had released her grip on her coat. She was wearing a dirty dress. Her thin breasts hung limply under the cloth, her nipples making two dents in the cloth. Her mouth opened and her small white teeth, separated by wide gaps, gleamed. She was mumbling and her lips moved as Cromwell talked.

Cromwell's voice thundered over the square, broke and came echoing back. The sound came from all sides, harsh and critical, heavy with scorn.

The sound battered the crowd together. Isolated, unneighborly, mostly strangers, they huddled together in their antagonism to Cromwell, pushed forward into a tight interlocked crescent around the Garibaldi statue. When Cromwell's finger jabbed at them the crowd flinched and then drew closer together.

Once a person at the fringes of the crowd started to leave and even took a few steps away. Then as if caught between the fierce magnetisms of anger, curiosity and fear the person wavered; his face contorted and became indecisive. Then the sound drove him back into the crowd; he shoved fiercely in, fought to the warm huddled middle of the people.

"Why do they stay and take it?" Mike asked in wonderment. "Why don't they go?"

He looked at Connie, searching for the answer.

Connie did not answer. She was crouched forward in her chair, her eyes glittering, utterly absorbed.

"He's awful. He's really awful," she said and she was unaware that her face was taut with curiosity. Unconsciously she whispered. "Why don't we go?"

"Friends, maybe you are right to be bored by all this," Cromwell said. "Right now we are going through an evil cycle of history. Behind our public leaders, the big politicians, a Satanic group of fanatics, the real leaders, are determined to see that the cycle runs its dire course. Things are going to be done that we know nothing of; we are going to be manipulated; we are going to be used. Things like the free gift of our destroyers to the British are going to be repeated and repeated. Some of them you will hear about; more of them you will not hear about. And you will not hear about them for a simple reason: it is dangerous to talk about them. They don't want them talked about. Why, in this audience tonight there are people noting down what I say and sending it along to the enemies of our people."

The crowd shifted, nervously. The gaunt woman looked sharply over her shoulder, stared bitterly into the crowd.

"That son of a bitch is a demagogue," Hank said. "He's a fraud. I'm leaving."

"Go ahead, leave," Mike said.

Hank got up and walked out of the restaurant. He turned down the side of the square and disappeared.

The crowd mumbled in a broken collective voice. They crept closer to the statue of Garibaldi and a buzz of anger rose in the warm air. Cromwell stared out over their heads.

"Maybe it's hopeless," he said and now his voice was weary. "Maybe we are opposed by forces too evil and too powerful. But we must still fight back. It is the job of Christian Americans to fight back.

We must find our enemies, pick them up by the scruff of their neck and hold them up to public view; the way a housewife holds up a rat before she smashes it against a rock."

Then, at that moment, the crowd changed. They had been united in their hatred of Cromwell. He had come as a stranger and frightened them. Agreement welled in their faces, rubbed out some of their dissimilarities, made them suddenly a wedgelike, solid community. Primitive and breathless they hung at the edge of violence, hating Cromwell.

Then, at the sound of weariness in his voice, they changed. For a tiny, poised, balanced moment the whole square was silent. Then they changed. The hate was still there; palpable in the air, as solid as fog. But now it was directed at Cromwell's enemies. As if the weariness in his voice had opened some gate in every person their hatred flowed in a different direction.

The crowd knew it at once. They stared at one another dazedly, uncertain of the change. They took courage as they saw it in the faces of others. A growl came from the crowd; a growl that was protective of Cromwell; a sound that threatened his enemies.

"Bene, bene," said a few voices and then the rest of them took it up. *"Bene, bene."*

And yet, mixed in their anger, blended in their fury was a thin fundamental hesitation. For Cromwell had not yet forgiven everything. His bony finger was still accusing. There was still a distance between all of them and Cromwell. They did not separate. Instead they huddled closer.

The children stood rigid in front of the crowd. They bent forward with excitement. Their lips moved as Cromwell talked. When he said "evil" they repeated the word in a quiet chorus; playing with it the way children will, extracting by repetition some secret knowledge from the word, teasing it into a new and deeper meaning. And they did the same with other words he used, knowing by some infantile instinct which words to take.

The woman in the front row was now rigid with excitement. She waved her hand in the air and in one corner of her mouth saliva gathered, ran unnoticed down her chin and dropped to the ground in gobbets.

Cromwell went on, his voice soaring powerfully out into the square. The voice was full and complete and heavy with assurance.

He went on talking for twenty minutes. The executive committee which had been standing sullenly behind the platform melted into the crowd and began to shout "*Bene, bene*" with the others.

Then, quite suddenly, Cromwell stopped. He was through and he stepped away from the platform. The crowd hesitated a moment and then applauded. The woman in the front row stood raptly, her head cocked sideways, staring after Cromwell. In each eye she had a tear. Her lower lip trembled and she looked at Cromwell with an expression that was a mixture of regret, anger and love.

Then the crowd pressed up around Cromwell. He shook hands with everyone who wished to, but he did it in a cold, austere and formal manner.

"Let's go," Mike said to Connie. "It's over."

They stood up and walked out of the restaurant, moved around the edge of the crowd and then walked to Connie's car.

CHAPTER 10

On Muscatel and Nerve
and Life and Death

CONNIE AND MIKE drove back slowly. They drove past the bocci ball houses, the pizza restaurants, the clots of old Italian men standing on corners and all wearing fedoras, the salami factories, the sourdough bakeries. They stopped at a coffee shop and had a glass of hot chocolate with brandy foamed into it and they ate a plate of small bitter green olives. They got back in the car and drove around the foot of Telegraph Hill and along the Embarcadero. They drove past the empty piers, the big quiet warehouses and they stopped and watched as a knot of longshoremen worked one ship under floodlights.

The booms swung back and forth, the winches clanked, and the thin cables whined up out of the hold with a clutch of cargo at the bitter end. The apparatus was black and spidery, and the men served it efficiently and quietly. Occasionally there was a flash of a cargo hook, a voice was raised, but most of the time it was utterly quiet and the men hardly spoke.

High above the piers was the curve of the Bay Bridge. The automobile ramps sparkled with headlights. The cables hung tautly between the great cement piers. High above the bridge the red aircraft warning lights blinked on and off. A streetcar moved across the lower level and gave off a grinding, harsh, metallic noise.

Connie walked to the edge of the pier and looked down at the water. Oil slicks smeared the water in great iridescent curls and loops.

The water gave off a salty, oily smell as it swished among the pilings, moved by the passage of unseen ships.

"Let's go," Mike said. "We have to be back by two o'clock or you'll get a lockout."

As they walked back down the pier one of the cranes swung a single case of scotch out of the hold. A checker carefully turned away; then, as deliberately as a person breaking an egg, the case dropped sharply on the pier. There was a tinkling sound as the bottles broke and then the case was lifted a few feet from the surface of the pier. A man shoved a big tub under the case and the whisky trickled into it. The checker turned around.

"One case of scotch broken by a winch failure," he shouted and made a notation on his board.

From the deck of the ship came a single laugh. When the trickle of scotch thinned out the winchman let the case smash once more on the dock, the remaining bottles were smashed and he raised the case over the tub again.

"All right, let's go," Connie said. "But let's go someplace for a drink first. I don't want to go right back to Stanford."

They got in the car and Mike headed back across Market.

"Where do you want your drink?" he asked.

"Anyplace," Connie said and hesitated. Then she went on. "Someplace where there are just men. Not a cute cocktail bar. Someplace that's real. You know what I mean."

Mike turned up Mission Street. He stopped in front of a bar.

The bar had once had an imitation log-cabin front, but now the brown exterior of the logs had fallen off in strips and a white, powdery composition spilled out onto the sidewalk. Above the door a neon light spelled out "Last Chance." Several men leaned against the imitation logs, watching a drunk try to get to his feet and applauded his attempts to stand up. He crawled around a splash of vomit, stared thoughtfully down at his hands and pushed almost to his feet and then collapsed sideways with a crumbling boneless motion.

Mike and Connie walked inside. It was dark and Mike saw a row of men seated at the bar. They were drinking beer or tumbler glasses of wine. Three tables along the wall were empty. Mike and Connie sat at one of the tables. Mike walked over to the bar and ordered two beers.

"I wanted a scotch and soda," Connie said when he brought it back.

"Sure you did, but they don't have scotch in here. Bourbon maybe, but they don't sell a drink of bourbon a week across the bar. If these men drink bourbon they buy a half-pint bottle and drink it in the street to save money and then come in here and nurse along a beer or a glass of wine."

"They don't look very violent," Connie said looking at the almost silent line of men at the bar.

"They're happy enough," Mike said. "They just don't talk very much. Mostly they just sit."

Two men at the end of the bar began to argue. One of the men raised his voice in a petulant whine.

"It's alfalfa. I know it's alfalfa," he said. He swung his arm around to include the other men at the bar. "Isn't alfalfa the biggest cash crop in California? Isn't it?"

"It's oranges," the other man said.

The men at the bar ignored the argument, stared down at their glasses, looked into the dirty mirror behind the bar, stacked and re-stacked their change on the bar.

"Everybody thinks it's oranges, but it's alfalfa. God damn, I know it's alfalfa. You're stupid, Sweeney. God damn you're stupid. Really stupid."

Sweeney said something like "You can't say that to me," but it came out a squashed, mangled sentence. He pushed back his stool and hit the other man. The men at the bar swung around to watch; their faces coming to life.

The fight was almost soundless. The two men staggered toward one another, barely able to keep their balance and as one man's hand hit the elbow or wrist of the other the man would stumble sideways, trying desperately for balance. Even when there was a solid blow it lit with a strange weakness as the other man's body curved away. Like a fantastical slow-motion ballet the two men pawed at one another in the half-light; stumbling and falling, sliding down the walls, colliding occasionally and then staggering back, their arms waving with a slow wildness. Sweeney backed off, carefully assumed a boxing stance. He jabbed the air with his left hand and with his right thumb brushed his nose and snorted through his nostrils. His face lost its boozy softness and became hard. He narrowed his eyes and began to shuffle toward the other man. The other man watched in fascination, his arms by his side, impressed by this new decisive-ness. As Sweeney drew back his right arm to strike, the man fell sideways onto a chair, but Sweeney continued like a machine that once started could not alter its motion. There was nothing in front of Sweeney except the bare wall, but deliberately and with great force he hit it. Everyone in the room heard the crisp crackling sound as several bones in Sweeney's hand broke. Sweeney wheeled around, his face gone soft again and twisted by a sudden confusion. He closed in on the other man, but the decisiveness was gone.

They slipped in puddles of beer and then recovering bumped aimlessly into one another, recoiled and assumed offensive boxing postures, but the opportunity was passed. Enraged they stared across the room at one another and then came together, extravagantly weaving and feinting. The fight had no definite end. People stopped looking at it. It became shadowy and unreal and at some point it expired and the two drunks stood shoulder to shoulder breathing heavily, forgetful of what had started the fight.

"Not too savage a fight, eh?" Mike asked.

Connie giggled.

"It was funny. Not like the fights you see in the movies. I expected to hear the crack of fist against jaw. This was just funny."

A man sitting in the middle of the bar swung around and looked at Mike and Connie. He stood up and walked over. He walked steadily, but when he leaned over the table they could see that he was drunk.

"College kids, eh?" he said. "Out slumming. Mind if I have a seat?"

"No. Sit down," Mike said.

The man's eyes had white triangles of sleep in each corner, his beard showed blue-black through his skin, his collar was brown with dirt. Like a thin yellow spiderweb a pattern of old dried vomit was spread over the shoulder of his suit. The suit itself was expensive, but very dirty.

"I'm a college man," he said. His voice was clear and he spoke slowly, bringing each word up deliberately from the well of his consciousness. "Dartmouth '32." He glanced shyly at them. "I know you don't believe me. What does it matter? I don't care if you believe me."

Mike did not say anything so Connie said, "We believe you."

The man ignored her and went on talking. He talked with determination, with his eyes fixed on the strings of bubbles that rose from Mike's glass of beer. His voice was friendly, but inflexible, as if he did not want to be interrupted.

"You think it's smart to come down here and watch a bunch of broken-down bums paw one another. Sociology of the drunk, sociology of the whore, sociology of the misfit. You'll go back to that little cotton-batting world of yours and tell the other kids all about life on Skid Row. You've met 'em, or at least you've seen the backs of all those drunks. Oh, you'll be smart. But you miss the whole point of the thing." He lifted his eyes from the beer and looked at them. "The point is that you think these people are misfits. You think being a drunk or a whore or a drifter is eccentric. But let me tell you friends that it's the only sensible thing in a society as rotten as ours. When a society is as bad as our society is today the only thing to do is to sit drunk all day at a bar and talk. Or become a whore if you are a woman." He waved in the direction of the bar. "Those men over there; they are the only people left who think with their hearts instead of their pocketbooks. These men are individuals, understand? They're not like the great big stupid mass that keeps electing a bastard like Roosevelt time after time." He paused and his face became angry, as if he had recalled something unpleasant. Then he brightened. "They come into a bar like this and order their beer and drink it and talk a little bit to the other drunks. Not trying to make friends, not trying to hustle business, not frantic. They're relaxed, see? They make sense too. Kind of a hazy, obscured sense, but more sense than anyone else."

"Can you remember the good sense the next morning?" Mike asked.

"No. Why should you have to? Look, boy, the truth is too delicate to last for long. By the next morning it's gone. That's the surest sign it was the truth. If you believe something is true and you write it in a book and it becomes a habit of the people you have all the evidence you need that it is not true or that it is unimportant. But at the bar, hunched over the stool, drinking three beers an hour day in and day out and eating a few hard-boiled eggs and maybe a hot dog, that is where you hear the truth." He hesitated a moment as if a new thought had occurred to him. "You know I've got a constitution like a horse." He pounded his chest. "Good lungs, good legs, good arms. I was a 220 man in college. Ran on the relay team that held the world's record for the half mile. And I'm as fit as when I ran in the '32 Olympics."

"What is your name, mister?" Mike asked.

"Allbright, Jack Allbright. You don't believe me. I'll show you." He reached in his pocket for his wallet. He brought the wallet out and laid it on the table and then stopped. "I don't care if you believe

me or not. Why should I try to prove anything to you? What difference does it make?" He laughed delightedly, but he proceeded
to take out a card and some pictures of himself in shorts and T-shirt,
his face contorted, breaking a tape with his chest. He rummaged
around in one of the compartments of the wallet and took out a
Phi Beta Kappa key on a fine gold chain. He pushed all of it over
toward Mike.

Mike remembered the name. The relay team had broken the world's
record and he could remember the faces of the men in the pages of
the Los Angeles *Times*.

"You don't have to prove anything to me," Mike said. "I believe
you." He pushed the heap of credentials back with the golden key
glittering on top, but Allbright did not pick them up. "You want
a drink?" Mike asked.

"Of course. Larry," he yelled to the bar tender, "bring us three
beers." He turned back to Connie and Mike. "I only drink beer.
That is after the first three or four days of a bat. At first I drink
whisky to get me up on the level I want to maintain, then I coast
along on beer. You know, that's the real secret of being a drunk.
Those people that are always passing out, stumbling around. They
aren't real drunks. They drink too much too fast and they don't
really like being drunk; they don't understand it. The secret is to
get just enough booze into your system so you're not sick and still
not sober. Then you glide along on that amount. You have to calculate how much alcohol your system is burning up and then replace
that. Once you have yourself really boozed up it is surprising how
little it takes. I calculate for myself; I've got a high metabolic rate,
that is about three beers an hour. But most people when they get
tight feel so good that they think that more will make them feel
better, and they take some more and they get sick or pass out." He
stopped and laughed. "I talk a lot don't I? That's all right; people
should talk more. They don't want us to talk. Those people in
Washington and New York don't want us to talk, they just want
us to read the crap they put in the papers. They're afraid we'll talk
and discover what they're doing to us. Get married, screw your
heads off, have big families, they say, but don't talk. Just read our
newspapers, read what we write for you. Work eight hours a day,
raise a family so Roosevelt can get their ass shot off in a war. Well,
not me. I come down here and talk. I find things out."

"Are you married?" Mike asked.

"It's funny," the man said ignoring Mike's question, "when I get drunk I never think of running off to a woman, I never think of sex. It's kind of pure asceticism; the only kind of anchorite we have today is the real, systematic drunk. It's a calling." He paused. "What did you say?"

"I asked if you were married."

"Sure I'm married. Got a fine wife and three kids . . . all boys. Pillar of the community. Wife from a rich San Francisco family. Look, I'm a respectable man. I could go up to the Palace Hotel or the St. Francis and walk in the men's bar and I would know half the people there. They would all be friends of mine. Dull, silly bastards though. I wouldn't want to see them. They hate me, I hate them." He paused a moment, a look of recollection went over his face. "I fooled them all. They all thought I married the girl for her money and that she married me for my body. They were right that far. But I beat 'em at their own game. I borrowed twenty thousand from my wife's father. Went into the stock and bond business. Aimed at the small buyer, delivered sales in beautiful envelopes by motorcycle messenger. I've got business all over San Francisco and the Peninsula. God, how it grieves my wife to see her name on cheap, loud little motorcycles. You ever seen one? Allbright is painted on the side-car."

Mike had seen dozens of them.

"Oh, I've made lots of money and they all hate me for it. I don't give a damn. Every few months I go on a bat; come down here and get drunk and then wander around talking to people like those men at the bar. Look, I could do anything. I could be a successful politician, a writer, a businessman, a flyer. But hell with it. Them and their lousy world. All I want to do is just to be left alone and have the chance to talk with people like those over at the bar."

Connie's eyes glowed with admiration. Mike looked at her and then back at Allbright.

"You're talking to the wrong people, friend," Mike said. "We'd like to be in the world you're running away from."

"Not me. I wouldn't," Connie said. "If I were a man I'd do just what you're doing, Mr. Allbright. Really I would."

"I just wanted to come over and puncture your balloon," Allbright said. "I saw you were college kids thinking you were doing something daring and I wanted to give you the other side. I'll go back to my buddies now. Back to that snug world of the alcoholic." He did not stand up. "It surprises you to hear a drunk talk about drunkenness, doesn't it? You think I ought to be ashamed of it. But it's a calling, a dedication. And I'm dedicated to it. When I get drunk I practice it twenty-four hours a day. Never have to sleep, hardly eat anything. Just drink my three beers an hour and talk with my friends. I'm not apologizing for it; I'm proud of it.

"I'll tell you what it's like," he went on. "It's like one of those motion pictures you see of people underwater; everything is slowed down and wavy, big black figures that look dangerous turn out to be nothing but harmless little fish. And everything has its edges softened, turned green and soft." He picked up his glass of beer, held it up before them. "All of that comes out of this glass. That god damned miserable world of Montgomery Street and Pacific Heights and stocks and bonds and a clinging bitchy wife and snot-nosed kids are all washed away by the bubbling beer. It's all gone. All of that dirty rotten system." He smiled benignly at Connie and Mike. He poked his finger into the glass of beer, held the wet finger up in the air. "Here is the only reality left in a god damn phony world." He put the finger in his mouth and licked it clean.

"You're right," Connie said. "You've got more courage than most of us. The rest of us are all wrapped up in habits and mores and customs. We're frightened. We just go along doing what we are told and never stop to take a hard look at our lives or at our culture."

She said it like a prepared speech that a person might prepare for a college recitation, but her eyes were liquid with intensity.

"You're right," Allbright said and his face broke out in a grin. "You're absolutely right." With his hand he rubbed at a corner of his eye, disturbed the triangle of white sleep so that it came to rest on the bridge of his nose. He gulped the rest of the beer down and ordered another round.

"See, I could be a success if I wanted to," he went on. "But not on their terms. That's not being a success, that's being a god damned slave. I've escaped them; they can't catch me in their lousy system." His voice went crafty. "And if they push me too far, or if the booze starts to wear out or my kidneys or bladder give out there's always a way out."

"There is?" Connie asked.

"Sure there is," he said and his voice swooped up in triumph. "I'll just step off the Golden Gate Bridge and end it all. It's as simple as that. Or as complicated as that. You're not really free unless you have the courage to take your life . . . if you know you have that courage then you can live a free life. I mean a really free life."

Connie's eyes glowed with admiration. She licked her lips.

"You shouldn't talk like that," she said. "You have so much to contribute."

"Contribute? Contribute to who?" Allbright asked. "My wife who is a crazy bitch, my kids who don't have a clue to what is going to happen to them, my lousy father-in-law? Larry, bring us another round. And make mine a muscatel boilermaker." He looked at Mike. "When I talk my metabolic rate goes up. Have to stoke away more booze to keep the alcohol content up. That's the art, see . . . just keeping the alcohol level at the right place."

"Yes, you told us that before," Mike said.

Allbright looked slyly at Mike and when Mike stared back at him he winked. When the waiter brought the drinks Allbright took a gulp out of his glass of beer and then poured the glass of muscatel in the beer. The heavy wine swirled redly through the yellow bubbles of the beer. Allbright mixed it with his finger until the glass was an even pink color.

"Connie, we have to go," Mike said.

"Right now?" Connie asked.

"Right now."

"Where are you going?" Allbright asked.

"Down the Peninsula to Palo Alto," Mike said.

"I'll go with you," Allbright said. He raised his hand as if to stop a protest. "Now don't get me wrong. I'm no bore. I'll just ride along with you and when I get to Palo Alto I'll visit some friends. I've got friends all over. Couple of nice bars down there where I know everybody. I'll spend a day or two down there. You won't be stuck with me. That's what you thought, eh?" he pointed a gleeful finger at Mike and chuckled. "Well, you're wrong I just want a ride. I don't give a damn where I go. Booze is my friend, understand? I don't care where I wind up. Don't worry about money either. I've got plenty." He took out his wallet and showed them a sheaf of twenty-dollar bills.

Allbright got up and went to the bar. He ordered another muscatel boilermaker and drank it off. When he came back his walk was unsteady, as he sat down his hand pawed the air in slight searching jerks as he felt for the chair.

"O.K. Let's go," Allbright said.

"This is fun," Connie said.

They went out and got in Connie's car and Mike drove. As they

drove along Allbright told them about how he had broken training
during the '32 Olympics and wound up with half of the relay team
in a Mexican whorehouse in Tijuana. The coach found them and
drove them back to Los Angeles with their heads hanging out of the
car, changed into running clothes and broke the world record.

Suddenly, through the haze of beer and wine, something came to
Mike. It was at the very edge of his mind, it lacked words, but it
was sharp and clear cut. Somehow the idea would give part of the
final answer, would shape-up confusion. He looked over at Allbright
and Connie. He licked his lips and when he came to Tenth Street
he turned right and went out Van Ness instead of heading for the
Bayshore.

"First world record, betcha, that was ever broken under the influence
of alcohol," Allbright said. "Betcha. But it was fun."

"All that honor at an early age is probably what made it possible
for you to rise above the clamor of the crowd now," Mike said.
"You've been on top and you know how little it means."

Connie looked sharply at Mike. He stared back at her and what
he had to do became sharper. He felt uncertain, at the edge of a
great risk. His stomach knotted.

"That's it," Allbright said. "That is absolutely it. I've been on
top of their god damned world. I know that all those honors and
laurel wreaths and gold watches and newspaper clippings don't mean
a damned thing." Allbright twisted his head and looked at Mike.
"Mike, that was very clever of you to see that. You're all right, Mike."

Mike drove slowly for a few more blocks. Connie looked out the
window and then turned to Mike, her face questioning. Mike knew
he could wait no longer.

"Allbright, you're a liar," Mike said softly. "A god damned drunken
liar. I don't believe a thing you've said."

Allbright's head jerked sideways and he stared across at Connie,
then at Mike for a moment. Then stiffly he grinned.

"I don't care if you believe me or not," Allbright said. "What difference does it make to me?"

"Don't talk to him like that, Mike," Connie said.

"All that crap about being a Phi Beta Kappa and being an Olympic
champ and running a stock and bond business," Mike said softly,
turning the words over carefully on his tongue. "All that was crap.
Anyone can buy a Phi Beta Kappa key in a pawn shop and have an
identification card made up in any penny arcade that says you are

Jack Allbright and then all you have to do is look up his records in an old newspaper and no one can ever tell the difference."

"Mike, shut up," Connie said. "Also watch where you drive. You're almost to the Golden Gate turnoff. You're going the wrong way."

The two men ignored her.

"A year or two ago, Mike, I would have cared," Allbright said. "But now it doesn't bother me a bit. I don't care if you believe me or not." He grinned out the window, hummed a tune under his breath. After a second he dug his wallet out of his pocket, pawed through the contents. "But just to show you, Mike, here is a solid gold ticket admitting me to any athletic contest that Dartmouth ever plays. Is that proof?" He handed the shining flat piece of gold over to Mike.

Mike looked at it quickly and threw it back on Allbright's lap.

"Don't be silly, Allbright," Mike said. "You could have one of those made up as easily as not. Why, Jesus, any jeweler would make you one if you had the money. Who are you trying to kid?"

"No one, damn it," Allbright said. The grin was gone from his face and his eyes were trying to focus. "I don't care if you believe me or not." His voice shook very slightly, however. "You're like the rest of them out there." His hand smeared over the window, taking in the entire world outside the automobile. "You don't bother me, though. What do I care if you believe me or not. What difference does it make?"

"And all that crap about going to the Palace Hotel and being welcomed with open arms," Mike went on, talking very softly. "Look, Allbright, every bum in the Last Chance would tell you the same thing if you asked him . . . big man once . . . disgusted with it all . . . rummies are the only good people . . . anything to keep them from facing the fact that they can't resist that awful temptation in the morning to ease the headache and stomachache and heartache by pouring a glass or two of beer into their belly. Every rummie has the same story, Allbright."

"Yes, sure, maybe so. Maybe they do, but I'm different," Allbright said and his voice was becoming shrill. "I've really got the money, I really was a champ, I've really got the motorcycles with my name on them." Allbright's hands ran over his clothing as if he were searching for some absolute means of identification. "I don't care what the rest of the rummies say. I tell you that I'm telling the truth."

"Sure, sure," Mike said, his voice heavy with disbelief.

"Don't talk to him like that," Connie said again.

The car started up the soaring concrete ramps that led to the Golden Gate Bridge approach. The traffic thickened as cars swept in off the various approaches, melted into a stream of cars. The fog lights made everyone's skin turn yellow and coarse; in some peculiar cosmetic fashion seemed to underline every facial gesture.

Connie jerked her head, stared at Mike and her eyes were already bulging, as if she sensed what would come. Mike fought down the doubt, kept his voice steady.

"And the biggest lie, the easiest one, is all that crap about committing suicide when this hard world gets too much for you," Mike said. "You've just heard about Schopenhauer someplace and use that as a smart little argument to entertain yourself and the other rummies."

"You're wrong. That's the part I believe the most," Allbright said. He leaned forward to see across Connie and his face was working, lips quivering. "That's what I really believe."

"Prove it," Mike said softly.

They came to the toll plaza, Mike paid and they drove on.

There was a sudden stillness in the car, broken only by the whirr of tires on the concrete of the bridge. The other cars pulled away from them and they were moving by themselves. The red cables of the bridge came thickly down out of the high fog, the supporting wires hung tautly and the blackness below the bridge was so solid, so endless, so deep that it seemed to hold up the structure.

"Prove it?" Allbright asked. He grinned fiercely, defiantly and then, as if some inner thought had gripped him, his face went smooth and flat. "How?" he said in a distant voice.

"The only way you can prove something like that is by doing it," Mike said. "There are some questions which only allow of one answer. This is one. There is only one way to prove it." Mike paused for a moment and then went on in a more jovial tone. "When I think of all that crap you were handing out in that bar. God, I have to laugh. You were really a kick. Tap any one of those rummies on the shoulder and ask him to talk and he would have given just the same kind of a song and dance that you did."

"I don't know about them," Allbright said in a voice that would have been a scream if it had not been so shrill and thin. "But I wasn't lying. I was telling the truth."

"Mike, will you stop this?" Connie said and her voice was pleading.

In the bar Allbright's face had been round, fattening, relaxed and soft. Now it seemed as if the flesh had melted from his face. His cheekbones stood out, his jaw muscles were taut. Under the yellow light there was something skull-like and gaunt about him. As they moved toward the center of the bridge the fog began to thicken. The bridge appeared insubstantial, tattered by white fog. Far away the blobs of rear lights wavered and grew dim. Their car was alone, suspended in the fog.

"I don't have to prove that I'm not afraid to commit suicide," Allbright said. "If I know it inside," and he tapped his chest, "that is enough." On his forehead small yellow lumps appeared, shook as the car moved and then resolved themselves into drops of sweat as they dropped off his chin.

"Sure, sure," Mike said and he laughed.

"I'll prove it, god damn it," Allbright shouted.

Mike jammed on the brakes and the car stopped. The next wave of cars had not yet approached. They were alone.

"O.K.," Mike said. He turned the engine off.

In a sudden silence they could hear drops of water falling from the superstructure of the bridge They hit with a sharp resonant sound. A lower, more basic, massive sound came from below where the ocean pushed against the cement casements of the bridge, sighed through the kelp, came with a muffled sound against the rocks. Connie was sitting with her head back and her fists pressed against her eyes making a tiny gurgling sound of fear deep in her throat.

Allbright ran his hand across the glass window and left long smears of sweat. He pressed his face against the window and stared out. "O.K.?" he asked and stepped out of the car. Connie took her hands away from her eyes.

Allbright put his hands on the low railing. He looked back at Mike and then climbed over the rail, turned and faced the car, holding tightly to the railing with his hands. Behind him there were the blurred misty lights of ships in the bay.

"See, I told you I wasn't afraid," Allbright said. He laughed shrilly and started to climb back over the railing onto the bridge. He hesitated a moment and hung with one hand, with the easy grace of an athlete. Then he threw his leg over the railing and started to climb back.

"What does that prove?" Mike asked.

"It proves I would do it if I wanted to," Allbright said.

"It proves nothing," Mike said.

Allbright hesitated with one leg over the railing, his face suddenly working like that of a small child on the edge of crying. It was a look of despair. Slowly he put his leg back on the outside of the railing. Mike looked across Connie at Allbright. A spatter of condensed drops came down out of the night.

"Come on, rummie," Mike said. "Get back in the car. We'll drive you back to the Last Chance."

Allbright stared very hard at the open door of the automobile, as if they were at the end of a far tunnel. His tongue ran over his lips once. Then he crouched down, let his hands go and with his legs gave himself a powerful push. His body sailed away into the night, neatly poised like that of a diver, the fingers and toes pointed.

Mike started the car. He looked over at Connie. She was coiled up on the seat. Her eyes bulged and her throat and lips worked spasmodically as if she were screaming, but no sound came from her lips. Silently, desperately, she was being hysterical.

CHAPTER 11

The Pacific, 1942

*T*HE WAR started at a very precise moment in time. It did not start at the moment when Lieutenant Commander Teretsuka of the Imperial Japanese Navy wheeled his plane over Oahu and looked down at the beautiful green, black and white geometry of Pearl Harbor. It did not start when he began his long, chattering power glide toward Battleship Row and the earth rearranged itself below him and the hills fell away. It began when the U.S.S. *Arizona* grew from a speck and filled the middle distance and then dominated the world and Lieutenant Commander Teretsuka pressed the button on his stick. The steel toggles on the torpedo jerked apart. The great shiny cylinder fell away from the plane and curved toward the water. The plane bounced upward as it was released of the load.

The war was well begun as he looked over his shoulder and with a great surging ecstasy saw the explosion as the torpedo hit the side of the U.S.S. *Arizona.* The towers on the battleship jerked suddenly; guns and lockers and fragments of steel and chunks of men gushed upward into the sky; turning clumsily at first and then forming a huge flowerlike pattern and descending slowly to earth. Lieutenant Commander Teretsuka looked at the pink and black cloud and was gripped by a pleasure that was almost too much to accommodate.

Then it ended for Lieutenant Commander Teretsuka, for he let his plane go too low in the pleasure of watching the flower of steel and fire and he crashed into the pineapple fields in the hills beyond Pearl

Harbor. The crash tore his head off and sent it rolling among the almost ripe pineapples and his head lay there with a toothy grin, his eyes locked open. When they came to look at the wreck of his plane they hardly noticed his head for it looked very much like the pineapples. Pineapples have a thatch like hair on top and when they are ripening they are almost the color of skin, especially if the skin is yellow and Asiatic. But the big red ants that crawled among the pineapples knew. They tried his head once or twice and found it not sweet and then after that they split their columns as they went past his head and by some fundamental and oceanic discipline none of them sampled the head again as they went by.

Of all the men that died in the war this man was the luckiest. He died in certain victory, without the mud and sweat of the war, as a hero of his people, without doubts, beyond despair, with a picture of Nagoya and a sweet slant-eyed girl in his wallet, with a venereal chancre almost healed on his thigh, as an officer in the Imperial Japanese Navy. Probably as his head separated from its third vertebra and flew through the air with the severed blood vessels redly pumping there was a split beautiful second in which he was aware of his luck and as his head bumped through the pineapples he must have been almost satisfied. But in any case the head stopped rolling and stared up at the beautiful blue sky above Oahu, which at this season of the year is ringed around with white packed clouds of an incredible purity.

Back in the States, by a lemminglike instinct, the anonymous faces, by the millions, began to appear in front of recruiting offices and draft boards. While mothers pressed whitely against sofas and held handkerchiefs drenched in spirits of ammonia against their noses, the young anonymous faces fell into lines. They thought that the lines led to something like Paree filled with lascivious girls who weren't afraid to try a new position, or lines of jolly young men swinging down a road and singing a song and standing shoulder to shoulder as they marched toward a frightened enemy. Some thought the line led to the seat of a plane that careened through the sky alone and met the enemy in single combat or the bridge of a destroyer with a fur-lined collar against your neck and a sextant in your hand.

Some thought the lines led to the inside of a big hulking tank with a huge gun that swung ominously in a circle and was controlled by cool, collected men riding on leather seats. Some, a very few, were afraid that the lines led to death.

The lines passed through the recruiting offices and the draft boards. The civilian clothes were shucked off and khaki clothes put on and, somehow, the men in the lines looked smaller, more identical. The lines thickened. The men from all over America began to push across the country; into boot camps, AA schools, tank schools, radar schools, sound schools, language schools, obstacle courses, short-arm inspections, rifle inspections, teeth inspections, yard-bird details, mess-cook details, officer-club details, and details. The huge system ground away at them. They responded to bugles, bo'sun whistles, loudspeakers, sergeant's voices, notices on bulletin boards, general quarters alarms, air raid alarms, warning whistles, "hands off your cocks, pull up your socks," "now hear this," reveille, retreat, fifteen copies of mimeographed orders.

They left their barracks in platoons, and their camps in companies, and the lines spilled onto the trains and buses in regiments and brigades. By some senseless and enormous magnetism they were attracted to the two seaboards. The lines thickened and grew until they were the size of divisions and corps and armies and they went onto the ships in that manner.

The men hung their faces from windows or pressed them against portholes: the white pimply faces of men who had once been fry-cooks and turned ham and brown pads of pancakes in pools of hot grease; men who had been mechanics and whose fingers had never been free of dirt before; the bland faces of insurance office clerks who, late at night, secretly sewed tucks into their rough jackets so that the cloth hung in clever swoops down from stuffed shoulders to trim waists; farm-boys, cow-boys, bell-boys, college-boys, pin-boys and boys. And occasionally a man.

But as the lines whirled by there was something very much the same about them. It was as if the machine that stamped out the identical mess trays and the identical salutes and identical clothes had also taken a lick at the men. The old men looked younger and the boys looked like men so that there was an agelessness about all of them. The starchy diet made for a roundness of face in all of them. The situation made for an identical look of suspicion. The system made them walk and stand the same. When seen in a line they looked like the same man endlessly reproduced, each waiting with an identical degree of patience to be told to march again.

So, too late, they learned that the lines really led to Fort Ord, Quantico, Camp Roberts, San Diego, Corpus Christi, Fort Bragg, Maxwell Field, Newport, and after that to North Africa, Oahu, London,

and India. The lines also led to D–Day, H–Hour, M–Minute, S–Second
and Guadalcanal, Iwo Jima, Omaha Beach, Cassino, Tarawa and, always, Blue Beach and Red Beach. The lines also led to dysentery,
jungle rot, gun-shot wounds in the head, fungus in the ear, athlete's
foot, the trots, a sulfa cure for clap, malaria, elephantiasis, and con-
stipation. Occasionally the lines led to hot babes in Sydney who knew
no new position, cold babes in London that did, the Pink House in
Nouméa, a gig-gig in some Filipino shack, the great profligate screwing on Rennell Island, the restrained and modest screwing on Princes
Street in Edinburgh, and the happy love in the Statler Hotel, Washington, D.C. The lines also led to mountains of paper work, ALNAVS,
revised Tables of Organization, changes in manuals, promotions, de-
motions, alterations in design of the 105 howitzer or 40 mm. or the
operation of a steam system.

Sometimes the lines led to the wild second when the soldier could
see panic in the second lieutenant's face and knew that the whole
thing could be organized just so far and it was all about to come
apart; or a second of marvelous clarity when the man in front of a
skirmish line turned around with a slow regretful look on his face and
like a gray expanding worm his brains bulged out of a black precise
hole in his forehead and blood ran from his ears; or the moment when
a Betty slices down out of a beautiful Solomon sky and like a black
lovely mote grows in size and cuts through the white puffs of clouds,
getting so large that it covers the horizon and then crashes into the
ship.

Very occasionally, much less often than you would expect, the lines
led to a grave in coral so porous that the smaller crabs snuggle in
with you; or a grave in the steel compartment of a sunken ship where
your bones slowly shed their flesh and float in the water to be moved
only by tiny eddies of the sea; or a grave on the beach at Guadalcanal
where they put you in a long trench with fifty other men and a
Tennessee Negro smoking a cigar drives a bulldozer which neatly
pushes sand over the whole lot of you; or a grave in the rusty red
carcass of a tank.

One thing to which all the lines led was boredom and the men and
boys learned to subdivide and measure the boredom and by their ingenuity to reduce it to manageable fragments. On a hot day a drop of
sweat falls from a sailor's jaw and drops to the deck. As it sizzles on the
hot iron he wonders how much of his kidneys and brain and muscle
and genitals and intestines the drop of sweat contains and his mind

spins off on the pointless conjecture for an hour. Even after the drop of sweat is a ring of whitish salt he is still tracing out the fantastic mathematics. That was one way to subdivide the boredom.

Another was gambling. Shooting craps in the crew's quarters against a bulkhead with someone holding a battlelamp up for a light and the dice spinning so small and white that it was like looking down a microscope at them. Or poker in the officers' club for white chips that cost five bucks apiece. All the gambling had one thing in common: the grinding, luxurious, wonderful hatred that everyone felt when the winner put out his hand to rake in the winnings. The smothering feeling of losing was almost as satisfying as the wild sensation of winning.

Another way to cut the boredom was to eat. The Quartermaster Corps thinks the soldiers got fat because the food was high in calories, but they were wrong. They got fat because eating is a way to pass the time. They ate hamburgers, meat loaf, sweet corn, dried eggs, canned bacon, evaporated milk, thick slices of bread, canned butter, black coffee, pork chops, K-rations, canned hash, french toast, horse cock, canned turkey, green beans, white beans, kidney beans, jam. During the midwatch they brought up fried sandwiches made of peanut butter and canned ham. On leave they went to the U.S.O. and ate doughnuts, sugared, glazed and coconut, and drank coffee. During the day they drank Coca-Cola, ate salami sandwiches and potato chips. Before, in every war, men had starved to death, but in this war no one was hungry; their eyes bulged from eating. In the Solomons they used to stack the boxes of food so high that the bottom couple layers would disappear into the mud. The soldiers hated the cooks for a reason: they were the only men they depended on.

And so the long lines led into the gray mists of boredom and the fattening foods, and, very occasionally, death. The lines moved like many-legged worms, senselessly, planlessly, formlessly.

CHAPTER 12

In the Sunshine and Under Grapes

Behind the low adobe house of the Burtons' was a stretch of very green lawn. The vineyards began just at the far edge of the lawn. The Italian and Mexican workmen had built a bower at the edge of the vineyard and trained the live vines over the structure. Clumps of grapes hung down into the bower; great dusty purple grapes, bursting at the stem with juice and each grape nourishing a small cloud of flies.

Connie and Mike were married in St. Helena in the summer of 1942. They were married in the bower with the guests standing behind them on the lawn. The Episcopalian minister was a short fat man and he said the ceremony in a dreamy voice, listening with his head cocked as if someone else were performing the ceremony. From an inner patio came the sound of corks popping out of champagne bottles.

Mike was wearing an ensign's uniform and Hank stood beside him in a rented white dinner jacket and black pants with a strip down the side. Hank was drunk, but Mike was the only one who knew. Hank got up at six that morning and went to the patio where champagne was cooling in big tubs of ice and brought back three bottles. By noon he had drunk all three of them.

Behind Connie Mr. Burton was standing. His lips were stained purple and this made his teeth very white by contrast. He was wearing a very white linen suit and he wavered slightly in the heat.

Mike raised his eyes from the minister's face and looked out past the bower. The vineyard climbed steeply up a hill that shimmered in heat, was twisted by heatwaves. Around the main root of each vine was a heap of brown stones that collected heat during the day and kept the ground warm during the night. Toward the brow of the hill the families of the Mexican and Italian workers stood, looking down on the ceremony. Beyond them a single great white cloud slowly changed form, like marble suddenly become liquid.

The minister, finishing the last words of the ceremony, smiled at Mike and Connie. As Mike turned to kiss Connie he had an elongated, squeezed-off view of Mrs. Burton. She was a big woman, expensively dressed. She was bent forward, her dry eyes peering intently over her handkerchief, waiting for Mike to kiss Connie. Then, as Mike pressed his lips against Connie's mouth, the rigid, mutely protesting figure of Mrs. Burton vanished.

The guests moved through the patio, drinking cold champagne from the Burton winery. At a large table smoked turkeys and king salmon were being sliced onto plates.

"I'm sorry your family couldn't be here," Mrs. Burton said to Mike.

"Me too," Mike said. "But I told you they wouldn't be interested. I sent them all invitations, but they didn't come. I told you they wouldn't."

Mrs. Burton smiled thinly and turned away.

When Connie had written her parents about her engagement they had asked Mike to visit them for a weekend. The first afternoon they had gone for a walk to a cave where some of the wine was stored for aging.

Mr. Burton had walked briskly through the vineyard. He was a startlingly handsome man with a very narrow waist and big shoulders. His fingers plucked at the vines, came away with a grape and he popped the dripping pulp into his mouth as he held the dusty skin in his fingers. He chewed the grapes carefully and spit the seeds out only when he had made some comment on the quality of the grape.

"Pinot noir grape," he had said. "Best grape in the world. Makes a fine rich wine. These are getting a little thin, though. Probably because the summer's not as hot as it should be."

Mr. Burton drank wine all day long. He started with a little glass of claret before breakfast and then, for the rest of the day, he drank constantly. He drank his own wines and those of his competitors. He drank wines from France and Germany and Italy. With each fresh wine he made some remark, but Mike soon realized that this was a sort of ritual that he expected of himself and Mr. Burton nor anyone else really paid any attention to the comments. The remarks were made to justify the drinking. No one expected them to make sense, especially by afternoon.

When they went into the cave Mrs. Burton turned on a switch. A line of weak electric bulbs went on. The necks of thousands of bottles gleamed. Along one wall a line of casks gave off a vinegary, sour smell.

"These are excellent wines," Mrs. Burton said. "They're good for a reason. Good grapes, good heredity and good care. Best grapes in the world, the result of thousands of generations of breeding."

Connie walked over and stood beside Mike. She whispered into his ear.

"She's going to give you a lecture on good blood now, darling," Connie said. "Don't be angry. Just listen patiently and then forget it."

"In humans it's the same thing," Mrs. Burton said. "Good blood and good environment. That's what counts."

Mr. Burton wandered over to one of the casks. With a pipette he drew off a glass of wine and sipping it, muttered something. "Coming along fine. Good body, bit raw yet, but developing . . ." was all that Mike could catch. Nobody listened to him.

"Yes, Mother," Connie said. "We heard you. Let's go back to the house. We're supposed to play tennis this afternoon."

"You can spare a few minutes, Constance," Mrs. Burton said. "After all, if you're going to be married there's nothing more important than what we're discussing. Nothing. Absolutely nothing."

Mr. Burton came out from a shadow with a bottle in his hand.

"One of our best years," he said. "Won't be perfect for another eighteen months, but then it'll be the best in California." He cracked the bottle against a post and it shattered. A jet of wine shot back over his arm, stained his jacket a soft purple. "Smell it. Generations of skill and breeding in that bottle. Wonderful, eh? Go ahead, taste it."

"Don't, Father," Connie said. "He'll cut his lips on the glass."

"What's the matter, Mike?" Mr. Burton asked. "Don't you like good wine?"

"I don't know about breeding and good environment," Mike said. "Not a thing. But I know something about you. I know that both of you came from good old California families who left you a lot of money. And I know that neither one of you has earned a cent in your life. You even lose a couple thousand dollars a year on this vineyard. And I know that you run the vineyard because it's fashionable and you can play like the country squire and his lady. And I also know that you run a winery so that you can have a good excuse to lap up a couple of gallons of wine every day."

Mr. Burton was standing beside one of the weak lights and he was staring at Mike. He seemed lost in admiration for what Mike was saying. He smiled faintly. The wine bottle hung at his side, dripping wine onto his pants and shoes. Mrs. Burton had stepped back into a shadow and all Mike could see of her was her fingers which knotted together, untwisted and then tore a handkerchief to pieces.

"My family's nothing," Mike went on. "I don't know what their blood is like. If I had to guess I'd guess it's pretty bad. I know something about environment. I was raised in a bad one. So that answers your questions, Mrs. Burton. No blood, no environment."

"It doesn't matter, Mother," Connie said. "Those things aren't important. Really they aren't. Mike can do things."

"I believe that," Mr. Burton said. He stepped away from the light and his lean face, the purple lips, the slightly bloodshot eyes, lost their distinctness. "I believe Mike's going to be all right."

The handkerchief in Mrs. Burton's hands came apart with a slight rasping sound.

Mike and Connie turned and walked out of the cave into a warm spring day.

Looking now into Mrs. Burton's face as she greeted the guests and shook hands and directed the servants to pour champagne, Mike knew she would never forgive him for that day in the cave. He also knew that it did not matter.

"Here's to you, Mike," Hank said. He was carrying a bottle of champagne in one hand and he poured a little into his glass after each sip. He did not look the least bit drunk. "Here's to old Mike who clawed his way up out of the laboring masses into the middle class. Old Mike, the upward mobile. Old Mike, the go-getter."

Mrs. Burton came back and stood beside Mike and Connie.

"Where do you go now, Mr. Moore?" she asked. "On to medical school?"

"On to medical school," Hank said. "The Army is sending me to medical school and has assumed the fullest responsibility for my immediate future." He poured his glass full, sipped at it.

"That will be exciting," Connie said.

Hank looked at her and ignored what she had said.

"Let's don't talk about me," Hank said. "Let's drink to Mike, the upward mobile, and Connie, his wife."

"Mike the what?" Mrs. Burton asked.

"It's a joke, Mother," Connie said.

"Boy, is it a joke," Hank said and laughed. "It's really a joke."

He held the champagne bottle up and it was empty. He threw it casually into the bushes. Mrs. Burton winced.

"What're you grinning for, Mike?" Hank asked. "You aren't supposed to grin."

"Just grinning," Mike said. "Can't a man grin?"

Hank patted Mike on the shoulder and then turned and started to search for a full bottle of champagne.

CHAPTER 13

"Our Forces Suffered Light Losses . . . "

THE DESTROYER was three miles off the island. In the darkness the island was a long humped line of black. Occasionally, far up the mountains, a light flickered from a native village, but at once it vanished as the blackness rushed in; solidly, like a liquid.

During the day, however, the island was different and made up of many things. The parakeets made slashing colored lines across the green of the jungle as they flew in short screeching flights; there was the endless tin humping of Quonset huts; there were the brown carcasses of wrecked planes. During the day the roads gave off curls of dust, forming a brown atmosphere which ended only at the white strip of sand which edged the island. During the day men stepped out of the dust, stood on the beach and looked out over the sea and the ships. Then the men turned back and disappeared into the brown haze; Sea Bees, Marines, fliers, Negroes, Californians, soldiers, generals, Mexicans, Okies and natives.

The destroyer moved across the sea as if it were going through smooth black oil. The screw kicked up a ball of foam that glowed solid and phosphorescent. From the bow of the destroyer a wave broke on each side and expanded away in two narrow bright lines. One of the lines shattered on the island. The other stretched away with a simple perfection to the horizon, where it vanished but did not end.

The destroyer stayed to seaward of the transports and cargo ships that were unloading. The sound gear pinged endlessly, sending shrill blocks of sound through the water and making a biting echo on the bridge.

In a cabin directly below the bridge Mike was sleeping. Drops of sweat swelled up on the sides of his chest, joined together and ran in trickles over his ribs and left a trail of itch on his skin.

Mike was dreaming. It was an old and familiar dream. He was very young and he was wearing knickers and holding a sock cap in his hand. He was standing before a shiny glass window. In raised black letters across the window were the words, "Home-Made Sausage. See It Made." Inside the shop a fat girl was seated on a stool before a gleaming porcelain table. Her cheeks glowed and she had a delicate fringe of blond hair on her upper lip. She had an enormous bosom which hung, ponderous and warm, under the crisp cloth of her uniform.

The girl smiled at Mike and shook her head at the five thin smears his hand made on the window. She turned to her table and deftly arranged a long wet glistening tube of skin. She put the tube to a nozzle that extended from a large machine. Gray meat flecked with red spots poured suddenly into the tube. The skin jerked and snapped on the table, writhed as the sausage filled it. In a few seconds the tube was full and was stretched to shiny thinness. Water bubbles popped out and as the meat continued to shove into the tube the skin slowly stretched and the bubbles grew larger. The girl took the skin from the nozzle and a jet of meat shot out on the porcelain table and the machine stopped operating. Casually the girl took the long taut sausage and began to twist it into short links.

Feet scuffled on the deck above Mike's head and he woke up. He lay still for a moment. His body came into contact with the wet sheet only at his heels, buttocks and head. Each muscle was stiff and contracted, each toe curled tightly, each finger was huge and separate. As the ship heaved slightly he felt his viscera roll softly. The general quarters buzzer went off and Mike came out of his bunk in a lunge.

Mike stuck his feet in his shoes, pulled on his life jacket and went up the ladder. The moon was just coming up over the island. In the haze of dust it was heavy and distorted and yellow, but he knew that in a few minutes it would push into the cleaner atmosphere and become smaller and more remote and glow with a clean austere light. The water between the destroyer and the island caught up the yellow reflection in a single broad band of gleaming water.

As Mike walked to his battle station on the wing of the bridge the wind changed slightly and brought the heavy odor of the jungle across the water. It smelled of old rotted trees which never died, but shed a green excrescence which slid to the ground and mixed with leaves and vines. It smelled of ancient mud that bubbled with the gases of decay. And it smelled of newer smells also: gasoline, spoiled cans of C-ration, the reek of slit trenches, cordite, grease covered metal. The smell puzzled Mike. There was something familiar, nostalgic, well known about the smell. But he could not remember what.

"What's up, Captain?" Mike asked.

The captain was a small neat shadow on the other wing.

"I don't know," Captain Dunbridge said. "Dog Cactus came up on the TBS with a six-bandit raid, but nothing shows on our screen. Of course nothing ever shows on that damned screen of ours except grass and friendly strikes."

"What we need is a good radar repairman," Mike said.

Captain Dunbridge grunted. Then he hummed and sang a line, "The world is waiting for good repairmen." He stopped suddenly and snarled at the helmsman, "For Christ's sake keep on two four oh. Your wake looks like a snake."

"Steady on two four oh, sir," the helmsman said. The helmsman's voice was defensive.

"Balls," the captain said. "Somewhere around two four oh, you mean."

Mike liked the captain and he was the only officer on the ship who did. Captain Dunbridge was a small, cocky Annapolis man. He was utterly sure about everything in the Navy. He navigated beautifully, knew every linkage in the 5"–38, understood every line in the engine and boiler rooms. He respected every tradition in the Navy. And he did all this with a sort of grace and sureness that was mortally offensive to everyone. Even to other Annapolis men.

The TBS speaker hummed and then crackled into words. "Dog Cactus to all ships and stations. Condition Red. I repeat. The condition is red."

A report came up from CIC that there were two bogies on the screen, closing fast, but coming so low they were mostly lost in the grass at the bottom of the screen.

"Talker, pass the word to the gun crews to keep a sharp lookout for planes on the starboard side," Captain Dunbridge said.

The talker spoke into the sound-powered phones. The destroyer slid in closer to the transports and Mike could see the intricate superstructure of the transports silhouetted against the yellow loom of the moon. All the boats from the transports had run into the beach and the ships were utterly silent. Occasionally a helmeted head moved on one of the ships and high in the masts the radar antennas spun soundlessly.

They all heard them at the same time. They sounded tiny and far-away, but the sound was foreign and dangerous and they knew they were Japanese. They simply sounded different from the P–38's and B–24's. The sound became snarling and loud, as if they were rushing down an empty tunnel toward the ship. Mike felt the air in his lungs grow hot and he put a finger to his face and at the feel of flesh upon flesh he could suddenly breathe easily again. The noise of the planes grew louder and Mike knew they were rushing down the path of moon-light which silhouetted the transports. He looked out to seaward and could see nothing. A 20-mm. started to spark, sending out a short stream of incandescent balls, then stopped uncertainly. Then the whole maga-zine traced out a long, beautifully wavering line.

"Silly bastard," Mike said. "Probably an LCI that got panicky."

At the same time he felt relief at seeing the tracers from the 20-mm. They gave a definition to the blackness of the night, announced that the fight had begun, were a sign that one could fight back.

Suddenly two thin lines of exhaust flame became visible. At the same time, the planes started to take form out of the darkness. There were two of them, moving like shadows, very close to the water. They came slowly, their lines and shape utterly foreign. The transports started to fire. The 40-mm.'s made straight hot lines across the sky and then they were crisscrossed by the countless smaller tracers from the 20-mm.'s. The tracers all converged just behind and below the target. The planes seemed to be riding the stream of fire directly toward the transports.

A black object detached itself from the leading plane and slipped into the water, leaving a white wreath on the smooth surface. Almost at once the object began to trail a finger of gleaming phosphorus. The torpedo straightened out and headed toward a transport. The plane pushed blackly on toward the ship, a wing delicately tipped the fore-mast of the transport and quite suddenly it started to tumble. It slowed down and moved in absurd wounded flight. It touched the water and bounced into the air and bits of material flew from it like torn-out feathers. Then as it bounced across the water it burst into a gigantic solid ball of flame. For a few seconds it looked like a huge flower, with a black skeleton in the center.

Mike remembered the torpedo and turned back in time to see it hit. It hit aft on the transport and he felt a shock as the underwater explo-sion crystallized the water for a brief second. Then the destroyer shivered. From the stern of the transport a thick bright column started to rise slowly. In its yellow solidity Mike saw a machine gun mount, an ammunition locker and a man. They all turned slowly in black, perfect outline. As it reached its peak all of the light went out of the column and it collapsed into the ocean.

Then the air blast from the explosion hit the destroyer in a solid invisible wave. Mike felt himself pushed hard against the bulkhead and a row of rivets was moulded against his back. A signalman with his back to the explosion was forced to his knees and as he looked over his shoulder in surprise his movement was suddenly accelerated. The man's face mushed soundlessly into the steel deck. The blast wave passed and Mike stepped away from the bulkhead. The signalman pushed himself up and his face had a soft grinning look. A tiny stream of blood ran like black mucus from his nose. He started to say something to Mike, but he only bubbled and then a white tooth came out of the mess of his mouth and fell to the deck. He suddenly was articulate.

"God damn," he said. "God damn, but that happened fast."

He walked past Mike onto the bridge. Mike felt a sharp rage at the two planes. He hoped the second one had been hit, but he could not see it and its sound was already remote and faraway. He felt a futile, hopeless, formless anger.

"Mr. Freesmith, organize the rescue party," Captain Dunbridge said. The captain was giving orders to the helmsman. Between orders he gave instructions to Mike.

"Take the rescue party to the fan-tail. Ease your helm. Stop the starboard engine. Back one third on the port engine," he said sharply. "The fan-tail is closer to the water. Put over Jacobs ladders and nets. Also some rubber rafts if you can."

Already the transport angled up into the air. There was a ripping sound as some object tore loose and crashed down the tilted deck. A growing circle of fire burned around the sinking end of the ship. The crackling of burning oil and the crash of falling objects were the only sounds. The small bright eye of an Aldis lamp started to blink from the bridge of the transport.

" 'Send boats' is what they're sending, Captain," one of the signalmen said.

"We don't have any boats," the captain said. "We'll come in close and pick up survivors."

The destroyer, swinging in a wide beautiful circle, headed away from the transport. As Mike ran back toward the fan-tail he heard the cap-

tain give the order to stop all engines. The rescue party assembled on
the fan-tail, watched as the stern of the destroyer swung around and
finally pointed straight at the transport.

"He's going to back down on them," Mike said. He felt a flash of
admiration for the captain. "Put over cargo nets and Jacobs ladders.
Don't take off your life jackets. Don't go into the water unless you
get orders."

Slowly the destroyer backed down on the transport, bearing precisely
on the circle of burning oil. When they were fifty yards away Mike
felt the engines stop and silently they slid toward the transport. He
thinks of everything, Mike thought. He even got enough way on so
that we will come up to them without our screws turning over.

Mike hung over the side and suddenly he could see dozens of heads
floating on the water. As if by a signal the mouths in the heads opened.
Mike could see the white flashing teeth, the gaping, huge mouths, the
glint of wide eyes. What the men shouted was senseless and chaotic;
strangely irrelevant.

"Me. Me. Me, I'm married," a head with a chief's cap shouted.
"Married and two kids." He roared the words in a steady monotone
and his voice was unexcited, but his eyes bulged from his head and
glittered with queer lights.

"First. Me first. Broken leg," a head, with black oil covering everything except the eyes and mouth, yelled. "First, first, first." The voice
was savage with determination.

These were the only voices Mike could make out, but he realized that
each man in the water was shouting out his justification, his claim to be
taken out of the water first. The sound was more urgent among the men
at the rear who were closest to the burning oil. Mike knew that most
of the men were in shock and this accounted for their peculiar immobility.

"We ought to go in the water after them, Mr. Freesmith," a chief in
Mike's rescue party said. "They're not going to be able to get to the
ladders and nets."

"Shut up," Mike said. "Nobody goes into the water until we see if
that fire is going to spread. If the ship starts going down the suction
will pull everyone in the water down with it."

"The captain says to get the lead out of your ass and get the survivors aboard," the talker said. Mike jerked his head around. Under his
huge domed helmet the talker was not smiling and Mike knew this was
exactly what the captain had said.

"Tell him they won't swim to the ladders," Mike said.

The talker spoke into the phones. Then he looked up.

"Captain says to get 'em moving. Any way you know how," he said. "But get going."

Mike looked back at the water. A few feet behind the chief was a very young boy. He was shaking his head in quick negative motions as if he were denying something. One side of his face had a crusted black look to it. He was not looking up at the ship and each time he shook his head his face dipped in the water and came up glistening.

That god damn captain, Mike thought. Get them moving how? Dirty bastard.

"That kid out there, the one shaking his head. He isn't going to last much longer," a voice said at Mike's elbow. Mike turned and saw it was Wilson, a fat middle-aged carpenter in the rescue party. "I'll go in after him."

"The hell you will," Mike shouted. "You want to make a damned dead hero of yourself?"

He turned back and saw that the boy's head was moving only slightly. Mike put his leg over the wire stay and turned to the rescue crew.

"I'll get 'em moving toward the ship," he said. "Don't any of you come over until I give the word."

He turned and dove into the water. The kapok jacket kept him from going deep. As he started to swim he saw that he still had his wristwatch on and he cursed. Now that he was level with them the sound was deafening and incredibly confusing.

The boy was even younger than he had looked from the ship. The water around him was perfectly flat and a queer phosphorescent light loomed up from the bottom. Half of the boy's face was in the water and the eye that was under water was open and staring, exactly like the eye above water. The eyes moved slowly and stared at Mike. Mike reached over and pushed the boy straight in his life jacket.

Water gushed out of the boy's mouth and he spoke very deliberately.

"Look, sir, this isn't my fault. I saw the fucking plane, but my gun wouldn't train. And I'm one of the best gunners on the ship, sir," he said in an apologetic voice. Mike realized the boy could see the bars on his shirt.

Mike reached out and grasped the boy's hand and started to swim with him toward the destroyer. The boy's hand slipped away with a soft lubricated feeling. Holding up his hand he saw that it was filled with black horny material. The boy's hand was pink and naked looking and from the slick raw flesh small drops of suppuration were running down the fingers. The hand had been flash-burned to a crisp and Mike had stripped off the burnt skin. The boy looked at his pink fingers and made a whimpering sound. Mike shook his hand violently, snapping the matter from his fingers.

"Try the other hand," the boy said and brought it up from the water.

The hand looked normal with white callouses and brown skin. Mike took it and started to tow the boy toward the destroyer. As he went past the chief he hesitated and then yelled.

"All right, Chief, get going over to the fan-tail or you'll drown out here. Get going."

He hauled the boy to the nearest Jacobs ladder. He started to shove the boy up the ladder. As if by a signal the other men in the water started to swim toward the destroyer. The shouting stopped abruptly. None of the men broke the water with their hands. They surged forward the way a dog swims, with no splash, heads bent forward, necks stretched, eyes bulging. They came like a swarm of lemmings; silently, uniformly, swiftly. Mike saw the eyes of the first man and knew that he saw neither him nor the boy, but only the strands of the Jacobs ladder, the round dark rungs of wood that led up the side of the destroyer to safety. The vanguard of silently swimming men reached the Jacobs ladder. They swarmed over Mike and the boy. Mike felt fingernails dig into his face, shallow rapid breaths hissed across his face, feet dug into his hips and then his back and finally his face.

Mike slashed out with his free hand.

"Take it easy," he yelled. "You'll kill one another. Let me get this boy on the ladder."

The men kept coming. Mike was forced underwater. He kicked himself sideways and came up a few yards away from the Jacobs ladder, still holding on to the boy.

Mike stared for a moment at the stream of heads. They looked disembodied and self-propelled. The heads thickened around the foot of the Jacobs ladder and then sleek, oil-covered bodies reared up out of the water, clawed at the ladder, silently fought upward. Like a long multiple-linked organism the stream of men spilled out onto the deck of the destroyer.

"Dirty bastards," Mike said aloud. "Dirty scared bastards. If you'd slow down we'd save you all."

He had been furiously angry when the first man crawled over him. Now, watching them, he felt a numb sort of pity for the anonymous, quiet, frenzied men. They were reduced to raw nerve, to burnt muscle, to a simple urge to exist. He knew that any of them would have calmly, quietly, desperately drowned him if that were the price of gaining the ladder.

Mike swam around to the stern of the destroyer and saw an empty ladder dangling. He shouted and faces appeared over the railing. He put the boy's hands on the first rung and easily, as if he were uninjured, the boy swarmed up the ladder and disappeared over the railing.

"Freesmith, are there any more survivors out there?" the captain shouted from the fan-tail. "Get 'em all. Every damned one. You're doing a fine job. You'll get a medal for this."

Medal your ass, Mike thought. He felt an intense anger and wanted to swear back at the captain. He looked sideways again and watched the stream of men moving toward the ladder. The stream was moving slower, for it was made up of men who were injured or deep in shock. Occasionally one of the heads would stop and the men behind pushed over it, smashed it aside and under and continued toward the ladder.

"I'll check 'em, Captain," Mike shouted.

"But watch out for the transport, Freesmith," the captain yelled. "It's going to go under. Don't get caught in the suction."

Mike looked at the transport. The oil burned in a tight circle around the ship and it was tilted almost straight up into the air. Everything that could had torn loose. The ship hung silently.

Mike swam toward the ship, paralleling the stream of heads. Not a head turned to look at him and the only sound was the sharp intake of breath, so harsh and flat that it sounded like a chorus of hisses.

Mike swam to within a few feet of the burning oil and stopped. He knew that the oil might spread or he might be pulled under by the suction, but he was so angry with the captain that he felt no sense of danger. As he looked at the ship his teeth chattered with rage and he kept muttering senseless words to himself. He knew they were real words, but he did not know what they were. Deep in his mind, like a tiny crystal of logic, he knew he was in some sort of shock himself; that he was not reacting normally. He watched the ship slide slowly into the water, inching slowly downward. At the very edge of the burning water there were a few motionless heads and Mike touched one of them. The head fell limply to one side and a pair of blue eyes looked lifelessly at him and then the face buried itself in the water.

"Dirty shit of a captain," Mike said. "Dirty lousy bastard. Get a medal for survivors. Me get a medal for survivors."

Then he saw a huge pot-bellied chief on the transport hanging to what had once been a horizontal railing. The chief was staring down

at the ring of burning water and his fat lips worked, pulled back to
expose big white teeth. Mike knew the chief was so frightened of the
flames that he would hang on to the railing and go under with the
ship before jumping into the water.

"Chief," Mike shouted and the man's head snapped up and looked
out at Mike. "Jump into the water. Swim under water until you are
clear of the flames."

He licked his lips and glanced from Mike to the flames. Then the
ship settled for a few feet in one swift rush and the chief's shoes were
within a yard of the flames. Like a great overfed monkey he shinnied
up the railing, his face expressionless.

"Look, I'll show you how," Mike shouted.

The chief looked down and Mike dove under the water and came
up in the flames and threw his arms sideways. The burning oil was
pushed away from him and for a few seconds he was in a circle of clear
water. Then the burning oil poured back and Mike went under and
came up again, throwing his arms violently to make enough splash to
throw back the flames.

This time the chief jumped directly on Mike. Mike felt strong
fingers grasp his head and the breath was smashed out of his lungs.
The impact carried them both under the water. Frantically Mike kicked
with his legs and stroked with his arms. His eyes were open and he
could see the orange tint in the water and knew they were still under
the burning oil. For a moment he thought of tearing the chief's hands
free, but he went on swimming. The chief's great body was clamped
onto him and his swimming motions seemed utterly futile. But in a few
seconds the orangish tint faded and Mike stopped swimming. They
came to the surface, a few feet free of the flames.

The chief's eyes were wide open and he stared at Mike. Oil and salt
water gushed out of his mouth. His lips formed words.

"The suction?" he said.

"Start swimming and we'll get away from it," Mike said.

"Can't swim."

Mike wanted to smash him in the face, but instead he told him to
roll over on his back. Obediently he rolled over and his great khaki-
covered belly stuck up out of the water. Mike grabbed him by the hair.
Swimming on his back Mike felt a sharp pang of pleasure as he yanked
the chief's hair and heard him moan softly.

Mike saw the transport go down. It went swiftly, without a sound
and there was no suction. A circle of oil still burned on the water.

Mike towed the chief over to the Jacobs ladder. Around the foot of the ladder there was an almost perfect semicircle of heads. They were tilted at various angles and seemed to be staring at the silver circle of the moon. They looked as if they were listening for some great submarine sound that would never come.

Mike pushed between two heads and they swirled away, rolling loosely, almost good-naturedly. He put the chief's hands on the bottom rung and watched the huge bulk of the man become agile and alive. The chief went up the ladder without an effort and flowed over the railing onto the fan-tail.

Along the railing the crew looked down at Mike. In the thin pure light of the moon and the flickering of the oil flames Mike saw admiration on their faces.

"I don't think there are any more men alive out there, Mr. Freesmith," one of them said.

Mike looked back over the ocean. There was just the circle of fire, an oil slick and the heads.

"Pass me a line and I'll tie it to the bodies," Mike called.

"That'll take a long time, Mr. Freesmith," a boatswain's mate said.

"Pass the line," Mike said.

"Aye, aye, sir," the man said. In a few seconds a line came coiling over the side, fell precisely at Mike's right hand.

"Freesmith, what are you doing out there?" the captain yelled through the loudspeaker. "Get back aboard. We've got a sonar contact about two thousand yards away. Have to get moving."

"I'm going to pick up the bodies, Captain," Mike said. "I'll pass a line around their chests and we can recover most of them."

Floating on his back Mike felt at home. Somehow he was reminded of the days at Palos Verdes and the great curling lips of the combers and he felt at ease; sure of himself for the first time since he had been in uniform. He was not really interested in recovering the bodies, but he did not want to come out of the water. He wanted to stay in the ocean, swim slowly back and forth in a medium he knew absolutely and surely. The thick scum of oil made swimming harder, but it was still pleasurable. If anything happened he could swim to the black hump of the island. He felt safer here than aboard the ship; oddly disconnected with the steel hull that had been his home and prison for over a year. He was reluctant to enter it again.

"Get back aboard ship," the captain said. "Let the bodies go."

"Fuck you, Captain," Mike said. "I'm going after the bodies."

"What did you say, Freesmith?" the captain said in a sharp startled voice that boomed out over the ocean.

The crew had heard Mike's words and they started to laugh, almost hysterically, as he replied.

"I said, Captain, we better get the bodies," Mike said. "COMSOPAC has an order out on that. The desirability of collecting all bodies after an action; good morale element; commanders to make all reasonable efforts; include as a figure in action reports; basis for commendation."

"O.K., O.K., Freesmith," the captain said uncertainly. "Take a turn around each body so they're all attached to a single line. If we have to get under way we'll come back for you."

Mike started to swim toward the closest body. Far below he heard the ocean tremble and knew something had exploded in the hulk of the transport. His arms rose and fell in the water, the drops turned to brilliance by the oil. He swam a breast stroke to keep his face out of the oil and he could see the whole bright surface of the ocean; the distant dark blobs of transports and AKA's, the perfect cone shape of Savo, the incredible whiteness of the tropical clouds, the sheen of the oil, the grayness of the ocean.

The first body was covered with so much oil that the head was only a tarry knob. Mike ran the line under the armpits, tied it with a half-hitch and moved toward the next body.

Behind him there was a shout from the destroyer.

"We're getting underway, Mr. Freesmith," the bosun shouted. "Submarine contact. I've attached the line to a cork float and it'll unreel as you pull it. We'll come back for you. You're being set toward the 'Canal by a two-knot current. Stay close to the slick."

Mike waved his hand. He floated on his back and watched the destroyer get underway. A streak of foam stretched out from the stern and for a few seconds the ship remained motionless. Then silently it began to move, with an impossible slowness. Under the stern a ball of foam grew and shattered the surface and in a few more seconds the destroyer was cutting through the water. It went without effort or sound or light. The sharp bow cut through the slick and with pleasure Mike watched it carve through the thick oil, heel over in a sharp turn and rush out into Sea-Lark Channel.

An hour later the destroyer returned. Mike was resting at the edge of the slick, treading water. Reaching into the slick, like a huge-beaded necklace, was a line of bodies. They bobbed and twisted in the water whenever he tugged at the line.

For a few moments Mike had thought of towing the string of bodies to the island, but had given it up.

The destroyer came to a smooth stop a few yards away. Mike threw the end of the line over the railing and then climbed up a Jacobs ladder.

"Sorry we took so long, Freesmith," the captain said. "I think the soundman got a bounced echo off the hulk of the transport or a thermal layer. Anyway it wasn't a submarine. Also took longer because the ship is crowded with survivors."

"How are they?" Mike asked.

Two seamen were swabbing Mike down with gasoline to get the oil off. The gasoline hurt on his shoulders and arms.

"Pretty bad," the captain said and his voice was puzzled and somewhat resentful. "Even with the doctor and the corpsmen working on them six have already died. Nothing wrong with them. They just turn white and die."

"I'll go help out," Mike said.

The captain sighed and walked back toward the bridge.

Mike walked forward to the wardroom. He opened the inner door and stood for a moment, blinking in the bright light.

The table had been converted into an operating table. Three naked men were stretched out on it. Oil and blood ran off the green baize and covered the deck. Wounded men sat hunched up against the bulkheads, their legs under their chins, watching Dr. Martin and two corpsmen. In one corner there were some blankets with legs sticking out.

Mike walked over to the table.

"Can I help, Doc?" he asked.

Dr. Martin had a cigar in his mouth. It was unlit and he held it so tightly that his lips drew back, showing the moist pink inner surface, and from the corner of his mouth a trickle of brown tobacco juice ran down his jaw. His white smock was streaked with blood, oily fingermarks, bits of hair, pieces of thread. He looked fiercely at Mike.

"Sure you can help, get the hell out of here."

"Tell me what to do and I'll do it," Mike said.

"Get out," Martin said. He lifted his head and watched two seamen bring in another injured man. They held him by his legs and arms and the man's body sagged between them.

"He just collapsed back in the crew's quarters, Doctor," one of them said. The man's eyes were open, but his face was chalk white and his lips were a bright blue.

"Swell. And you're helping him out," the doctor said bitterly. "You lifted him up like he was a sack of potatoes so that if he has any internal injuries you will kill him for sure. That's swell. Thanks. We need more patients." He turned back to the man on the table and said between his teeth, "Put him on the deck. Mr. Freesmith here will give him a shot of morphine. The man is in shock. If the morphine works and you wrap him up he has a little chance of living. Not much, but a little."

The two seamen gently placed the man on the deck and backed out of the room.

"Where's the morphine?" Mike asked.

Martin waved his hand at the table.

"On the table. Everything in this god damn ship's medical locker is on that table. Just grab for what you want."

Mike looked at the table. It was covered with a thick, hardening layer of blood and black oil. On top of the layer floated a debris: broken capsules, bits of black thread still attached to short curved needles, strips of white bandage, little bags of sulfa powder, empty bottles of plasma, shining surgical instruments, alcohol bottles, discarded rubber gloves, fragments of flesh with hair protruding from them, a few teeth with bloody roots still attached.

The ship lurched and the three men on the table slid sideways. Martin and the two corpsmen stopped working and pulled the men back into position.

"And the captain has to go fight some Japs in the midst of all this," Martin said through his cigar. "He's already killed two men by the crazy way he jerks this ship around. See that corpsman over there," he said and pointed at the youngest corpsman. "He's already done four operations tonight that should only be done by a doctor and a specialist and they all came off all right, but once the ship lurched and he put a scalpel through an aorta."

Mike saw the morphine syrettes and picked one up. He picked off the plastic cap, pushed the plunger. A white liquid oozed from the needle. He walked over to the man the two seamen had brought in. He jabbed the needle into the man's arm and squeezed the tube of morphine empty. He picked up a blanket and wrapped it around the man. The man was stony cold and stiff, but his tongue worked in his mouth, sending saliva out between his lips, and his eyes followed Mike.

Mike worked for a half hour and then, suddenly, they were through with the worst cases. Martin began to walk around the room and check over the patients.

Mike walked over to the corner where the legs were sticking out from the blankets. He lifted up one edge. The boy with the burnt hand and the chief were there. The boy's hand, pink and delicate looking, was placed on his chest. Beside him the huge distended body of the chief was stiff.

Mike looked up and caught Martin's eye.

"Both dead?" he asked.

"Dead as doornails," Martin said. "The boy of burns, the chief of shock and, maybe, heart failure. When they came walking in here I knew they didn't have a chance."

Mike dropped the edge of the blanket.

He left the wardroom and went out on deck. In a few minutes his eyes adjusted and he could see the long line of the island, the black shape of ships. He looked around and saw the big round slick from the transport, glittering on the water.

How could the two of them die so easily, he thought? Could I have died so easily?

He felt no fear because he might have died. But, suddenly, he felt a terrible anxiety. It ripped at him like a gnawing animal in his guts. It was so sudden, so intense, that he could not phrase the feeling. His fingers tightened on the railing.

What if I died before I knew anything for sure? he thought. What if I died before I knew about me . . . and all of them? His hand moved and took in all the world outside himself. What if I died and never knew what it was all about? Never knew if I was right about a single thing?

The words did not drive the anxiety down; it stayed there relentless and hard. He was sure that it did not come from a fear of his own death. But because he could not understand it, could not master it, he told himself that this was why he was afraid. It was a thin comfort, but a comfort. But the gnaw was still there.

They gave Mike a Silver Star in Nouméa. An admiral came out from COMSOPAC and pinned the medal on his chest. The crew was drawn up at attention, flags were flying and sea gulls whirled in the air. As the admiral read the citation Mike was astounded to see tears in the old man's eyes.

"You did a very fine thing, young man," he said in a husky voice. "Staying in the water to recover bodies was especially outstanding. Sharks, burning oil, enemy submarine. Real courage, young man, and a high regard for your fellow man."

Mike started to say something for he was startled by the words. But he realized it was hopeless. He saluted.

CHAPTER 14

"No Rust of Superstition"

THE SPIRE of the cathedral of Nouméa holds its black cross against the tropical sky with a stony arrogance. The cathedral is built of huge yellow sandstone blocks. The blocks are rough and uneven from the picks and chisels of the quarrymen. The soft stone absorbs water out of the ground and during the rainy season the moisture line creeps up, black and wet, as high as one's eye. But as one looks up the side of the cathedral the surface seems to change. The gouges in the blocks become invisible, the cement disappears and the stone starts to flatten out and look machined, rubbed, almost polished. Finally the upper spire becomes a slippery golden spike of stone, thinning to a point and then suddenly breaking out into the sharp angles of the cross.

The only break in the stone of the cathedral is the patinaed windows of colored glass, which are punched through the thick walls at irregular intervals. The windows of the cathedral look north toward the tree-covered hills of New Caledonia. To the south they face the deep blue water of the South Pacific where a long jagged reef is decorated with the hulks of ships, and a tall lighthouse, striped like a barber's pole, marks the entrance to the passage. The windows gaze out like dull medieval eyes, disapproving of the blue sea, the yellow hot sky, the piled up green richness of the jungle. For all but a few minutes of the day the windows stare out with a calm flatness. However, in the early morning the rays of the sun are flat and cool and penetrate the stone sockets. For a few restless seconds the windows flash brilliant stabs of light. The sun pushes higher into the sky and the windows again become dull eyes, the cathedral is once more made of wet, bruised, cheap blocks of sandstone carelessly put together.

Mike was leaning against the stone wall that surrounded the courtyard, his head bent back, trying to look up the side of the cathedral. When he threw his head back he brought his hand to his naval officer's cap; deliberate and unnecessary for the cap clung tightly to his head. He spread his legs out carefully and braced himself solidly against the stone wall.

With his head bent back the spire of the cathedral seemed to be expanding away into the sky, pushing the sharp angles of the cross into the thin blueness so that it became smaller as he looked. His Adam's apple pressed tightly against the taut skin of his throat and he could feel the stone wall irritating his back. Reluctantly, he brought his head down and stared at the dark water line on the side of the church. The expanding spire tore the church out of proportion, drawing it thin and tall, and it was a pleasant sensation. It was as if he were standing still and very stable and the church was being distorted and changed in front of his eyes.

Mike muttered, "I oughta go in and pay a visit. Even if I'm not a Catholic. But I'm scared."

He looked at the black hole of the door and could smell a faint inviting odor made up of burnt candles, incense, old books, perfume, and sweat. He licked his lips and looked away.

In a minute, he said to himself, in a minute I'll go in.

He turned and with his hands braced against the wall looked down at the town of Nouméa spread out below the cathedral. Far down to the right, almost alongside the harbor, he could see the Hotel Pacifique which had been turned into an officer's club. Even from here, almost a quarter of a mile, he could hear the voices singing, confused and tattered, and without identifying the tune he knew they were singing "Bless 'Em All." In some part of his mind he could see them clearly, standing in circles with sweat pouring from their bodies and making big circles of dark moisture underneath their arms and eating wetly into their caps. They would sing for hours, their voices getting hoarser until the song was a rasping caricature, each man singing whatever he wanted and the circle swaying dangerously as the officers got drunker. Then when it was dark and the bar closed they would stagger out into the streets of Nouméa, looking for women. Still singing wisps of the song, but driven by something more urgent than alcohol or camaraderie, so that they finally gave up the pretense of singing and cursed and made fevered plans. The alcohol and the desire would run out at the same time and finally they would all end up at the Fleet Landing, waiting with red eyes and pounding headaches for their boats. They would stand silently, the whiskey-smelling sweat drying on their backs, like sad bulls. Occasionally they would look at one another with shy embarrassed glances.

Not me, not tonight, Mike said to himself. No more hunting around for those Javanese women in the villages outside of town. Not me.

He turned around and looked at the cathedral, gazed for a moment at the black inviting maw of the entrance and then quickly turned away, thinking again of the last visit to the Javanese village. He looked almost straight into the sun and the blinding light burst against his eyeballs and somehow jogged his memory loose, so that the recollection was very strong and clear, a spinning black dot of memory in the midst of a sunburst of brilliance . . .

. . . six of them had left the club drunk, and piled into a jeep.

"The pussy is located in the Javanese villages," Jack Brannon said in his high, shrill southern voice. "I have researched and discovered that pussy is found there in fine and great quantities Two miles out toward Anse Vata, turn left, stop by a clump of coconut trees. Gentlemen, let us proceed."

The Javanese village was built of tiny wooden shacks made out of old K-ration cases that were roofed over with flattened tin cans. A stink, strong as acid, rose from the ground. Small ageless men sat on their heels in front of the houses, watching with almond eyes as the American officers came down the street, stumbling and laughing.

Brannon knew where to go and he took them to the largest shack at the end of the street and swept them into the room with a gesture of southern gallantry.

"Bring on the girls," he called and his voice was slightly hoarse, the shrill edge gone. "My friends want entertainment. Where is the pussy?" Brannon giggled.

From behind a burlap curtain at the back of the shack an old woman peered out. She grinned at them with black teeth. In a few minutes she pushed a young girl out of the door.

The girl was small, even for a Javanese, but she walked with oil-packed hips and wore a tightly wrapped skirt and a jacket. Doll-like she stared at them for a moment and then took off her jacket so that they could see her perfect small breasts with faintly pink nipples. She smiled and there was a look of idiot concupiscence on her face; a sort of infantile lust. She began to move her hands in an elaborate dance; the fingers spread far apart, the wrists twisting rigidly, the long arms slowly weaving back and forth in front of her body. Her knees bent sharply and she shuffled woodenly sideways. The stiff ritual movements of the dance seemed to emphasize the overripe richness of her body, the provocative roundness of her hips, the softness of her breasts. From behind her fingers she smiled at them.

They stared at her, hardly watching the delicate unfolding of the dance, but only aware of the perfection of the tiny body, the strange impression of wantonness about the girl.

"Old lady, where is the rest of the pussy?" Brannon roared. "We want more women."

The other men did not take their eyes from the girl. The old woman stuck her head out the door and signaled that there was only one girl that night.

Like a wave the six men moved toward the girl, grabbing for her. She continued to dance until the first man reached her, a grin of delight on her soft full face. They all reached her at once and forgot they were friends, and began to fight and knee and kick at one another, struggling to get the girl first.

"God damn," the old woman said. "One at a time. Just one at a time. All possible."

They shivered and stopped fighting and stood still; breathing through their nostrils; their eyes red. And they waited their turn listening to the girl's rich throaty laugh roll out from the back room . . .

. . . not tonight, Mike said aloud. Reluctantly he pushed himself around and looked again at the cathedral.

"I oughta go in," he said aloud. "I'll feel better if I do. Later I'll feel much better about it."

He licked his lips again, shuffled his feet. He stared again at the entrance, anxious about what was inside.

He started to walk toward the cathedral door and suddenly a priest was standing in the door, looking out. Mike remembered in sudden confusion that there was something you had to do when you passed a Catholic priest. He did not know what it was and wondered desperately what his Catholic friends would do in such a situation.

Mike was confused by the priest and turned away, afraid again to go in the cathedral. He wondered dully why he had ever come up the hill; what had led him on such a God-damned silly chase. Then he remembered that he had seen the spire of the cathedral from the officer's club in the Hotel Pacifique. He had been listening to a Marine major talk and he could see the glistening spire, thin, delicate, sharp against the sky. He had stared at it as the Marine talked and in his mind's eye had filled in the unseen shape of the cathedral.

Mike thought again of the major's story. The major's face slid across his mind, blurring his vision . . .

. . . his face was incredibly young with a mustache of coarse blond hairs and eyes that were a little watery from whiskey. He talked in an eager, flat voice.

"Jesus knows how long they'd been pushing through the jungle like that, but it must have been at least two days, ever since the fight around the Tenaru. My patrol turned them up and we followed the two of 'em for an hour just to see what would happen to them.

"This little dinky Jap bastard was carrying the big one in his arms. I could see right away that the big one was wounded in the legs because his feet were hanging over the little guy's arms and one of his shoes pointed up in the air and the other pointed straight into the ground. Yeah, and I guess they were bleeding a little, just a few drops off the toe that was toward the ground. But we couldn't figure out what was wrong with the little Jappo. Every once in a while the little guy would stumble and the two Nips would fall down. The big guy would start to call directions to him in Japanese and the little runt would crawl around feeling with his hands for the big one."

The major spread his hands apart and waved them in arcs over the table.

"The big guy would scream and curse the little guy and finally the little runt would crawl over the big guy. Then he'd pick the big guy up and they'd start off down the trail again. You see, the big Jap couldn't walk and the little Jap had been blinded. So between the two of them they were trying to get back to the Jap area."

The young blond face looked around the table, making sure they understood. He grinned and for some reason the others grinned back at him.

"Jesus, those birds have bowed legs naturally, but with that load this little bastard's legs were so bent he was almost walking on his knees. He'd stagger back and forth, bouncing off the trees and stumbling around in the bush. With the big guy all this time banging him on the head and cussing him out."

The major made zigzagging motions with his finger through the scum of beer on the table.

"We followed 'em for about an hour and then I finally told the boys to finish them off. One of the boys stepped out on the trail and yelled to them and, by God, they both just about pissed their pants right there. The big Jap looked back and then he started to shriek at the little Jap and you should have seen that Nip take off. He started running down the trail like a deer with the big Jap telling him when to jump over logs and vines and damned if he didn't get going so fast they almost got away. He was going so good at the last there that I began to think the little one wasn't blind afer all. Our BAR man finally stopped them with one burst."

The major cocked his arms into a rifle position and sighted along them, making an expert clicking sound with his tongue.

"The little guy was blind all right. He had his head wrapped up in one of his khaki leggins and there were two spots of blood where his eyes should have been. But Jesus, he was a tough character."

The major looked down at the glasses on the table, quiet for a moment, and then looked up grinning at the other officers . . .

. . . Mike turned around and saw that the priest had vanished from the doorway. He walked slowly toward the open door.

The doors were thin and covered with shiny varnish, but the locks were huge chunks of iron that looked heavy enough to rip the flimsy doors from their hinges. Mike passed through the doorway and stood for a few seconds in the dim vestibule. There were two small benches, covered with red velvet which had been worn to white threads in the middle and only around the edges remained thick and soft and red. There were two faded pictures on the wall, which had crinkled and shrunk in their frames. The colors had thinned out into a smearing of browns and yellows. In one there was still a faint ring of thorns visible and a blurred face underneath it. The drops of blood that fell away from the ring of thorns were dark and fresh as if they had been freshened over and over again.

Mike walked across the vestibule into the hall of the cathedral. As he passed the font he caught a faint, stagnant odor as if all the hands that had dipped into the font had each left a tiny smell behind.

Inside it was brighter but still so dim it was difficult to see the length of the cathedral. The windows muted the rich hot sunlight into dull laminated bands of light, in which countless motes swarmed in clouds. The dull bands of light were just sufficient to see the hulk of the altar and the long rows of pews. The statues along the walls leaned out into the room, only their white plaster faces visible. The light caught the white cheeks and the fullness of the lips so that the statues took on a leering look.

Suddenly Mike was aware of a small boy sitting in one of the pews. The boy stared over at Mike; picked at his nose, found something and wiped it on the bottom of the pew. At the front of the cathedral Mike could see a thick shadow caught in the loom of the candles and realized it must be the boy's mother. Mike stood uneasily a moment, not sure what to do. In the coolness of the cathedral he waited for something to happen, for some change to occur within his head or his heart. He closed his eyes.

"God help me," he whispered softly. "I'm scared I might get killed. I'm scared." He hesitated a moment. "Give me a sign."

He waited miserably a moment more. He ran his tongue over his teeth and they felt large and solid and ended any possibility of a revelation. He opened his eyes.

The boy was standing in front of him, staring upward into Mike's face.

"Gom, gom," the boy whispered. "Chewing gom, chom." He held out his hand.

Mike shook his head. The boy's lip lifted in a sneer. Mike hated him and had an impulse to slap him.

The woman turned from the bank of candles and with a moist sniffle walked quickly back down the aisle. As she reached the boy her arm shot out, her hand fastened on the boy's shoulder like a claw, and without breaking her stride she continued down the aisle. Her fat corseted body creaked as she walked and she gave Mike a look of suspicion.

Mike waited a few minutes, hoping the bands of light would soften or that the figures would lose their agate-hard eyes and chalky faces and become something else. He started back up the aisle and as he went out the door the tropical sunlight fell hot and solid across his eyes. He walked to the edge of the courtyard and leaned against the stone wall to look down upon the town of Nouméa. The boy and his mother were out of sight.

Mike looked around and was angry. He glared at the cathedral. He reached in his back pocket and took out a half-pint bottle of Black and White Scotch which he had bought from a sailor off an English destroyer. He opened it and drank off half the bottle.

He turned toward the entrance of the cathedral. A young priest in a long black habit stood on the steps, making a clucking sound with his tongue and shaking his head at Mike. The priest's face was fat and round with a youthful blandness. The skin along his chin was stretched and pink as if he had just shaved. His neck went down into the habit with two small rolls of fat left behind and bulging over the white collar. He raised his hand in a graceful, Christlike gesture.

"Not on the ground of Jesus, my son," he said in a fine deep voice. "Do not let us make a café of the consecrated ground."

His hand dropped to his chest where the other joined it and he locked his fingers together so tightly that they puffed out red against the whiteness of his hands. He looked down solemnly at Mike.

Mike looked away from the priest, down at his shoes, studying the mud that had splashed up on his shoes in an even line. He looked up again and the priest was still standing on the steps and Mike could see the long falling lines of his skirt pressed flat and black. Suddenly Mike felt the pores of his chest and shoulders popping and his shirt became sticky against his flesh. Where the excitement had been a few minutes before there was now a hot core of ferocity. The ferocity was automatic and complete, as a flicked-on switch will flood a room with sudden light, packing every corner, every angle and leaving no shadows, no dark spots.

"Go to hell, God damn you," Mike shouted. "You and your God-damned fake church. Getting me up here and letting me shuffle around like something was going to happen. I just came because I was scared; that was the only reason. Just scared of getting killed or wounded maybe." Mike felt excited and, somehow, liberated. "I just did it because people in books are always going into churches and having things happen to them. Well, nothing happened to me in your God-damned church. Nothing, do you understand? I don't owe you a damned thing."

The priest's fat face contorted with surprise.

Mike drew his arm back carefully, snapped it forward and the little green bottle left his hand and cut through the air toward the priest. The bottle sailing through the air gave Mike a sudden delighted feeling.

At the last second the priest jumped aside in a great awkward spring. Even while he was in the air his face became red and angry and his large thin mouth was forming words. The bottle smashed against the yellow stone of the cathedral. The glass fragments sprayed into a heap and Mike watched as the dark smear of Scotch ran in moist tendrils down the side of the wall. He turned his head slowly and looked again at the priest.

"*Oiseau de merde*," the young priest hissed at Mike. His face was contorted in sharp lines so that it no longer looked fat. His eyes bulged until they popped ludicrously, the blue iris standing out wildly. The coloring of his chin had disappeared in the red that crawled from his cheeks. It was as if a mask had been clamped on his face; a mask with deep lines and a thin angry austerity. It was a different face, strained and gaunt.

Mike looked at him with a long focusing stare. The hot core of ferocity had disappeared, leaving him curiously relieved. This day would be like any of the other days, he realized, another day stacked on the heap of empty days.

"*Oiseau de merde, oiseau de merde,*" the priest hissed.

He was rigid with excitement. The words beat in the air like a pattern, repeated until they became a profane chant. To the chant the priest made a slow recessional, feeling his way backward up the steps until he had almost disappeared in the gloom of the vestibule. His fine deep voice continued to hiss out faintly from the dark. It stopped suddenly in the middle of a sentence and the white face started to loom up out of the darkness as he walked again toward Mike. His face became visible as he pushed out into the sunlight. Putting one hand against the frame of the door, he looked steadily down at Mike.

"The English of this is 'shit-bird,'" he said in a careful voice. "You are a son of a shit-bird. Understand?"

Mike nodded his head and the priest's face dropped the hard mask and the fat jovial lines reappeared; he seemed almost happy again. With a satisfied look on his face he turned and walked into the darkness of the cathedral with big steps. The day was gone now, Mike thought. Gone with all the other identical, rounded, eventless days. The day would pack neatly against the other days, like another saucer added to a huge stack. It would become another twenty-four hours of time that flowed through his mind and which only his wrist watch chopped into any pattern.

He plunged through the gateway and started down the hill. His knees were relaxed and loose so that as he went down the steep hill he seemed to be swarming down the path of cement. He rushed past the houses he had seen from the hill and noted with a curious inverted pleasure that although they had looked clean and spacious from the cathedral, actually they were crowded and dirty, with streams of murky water running from them. As the hill became steeper his knees snapped and jolted as his limp body rushed down the slope. The houses and small green trees whirled by pleasantly, and he felt as if the snapping, whipping legs and the limp body had nothing to do with his eyes and mind which looked at the trees and houses casually.

"Hell with all of 'em," he said as he ran. "The church is just like anything else. Just exactly, precisely, identically the same. And that priest," he said with loathing. "Like all the rest; every single one . . . the priest and everybody else. All of 'em."

He was running now, his arms weaving through the air in wild balancing movements. He sped past a fat woman and one of his waving hands tipped a bulky package protruding from her arms, ripping the package and sending small yellow carrots in a shower, skidding along the sidewalk. He felt he should stop to pick them up, but now it was more difficult to regain control over his legs which were rushing him down the hill. He shouted a sympathetic word to the fat woman over his shoulder.

The houses blended in a streak of doors and open windows and startled faces. In some miraculous way his timing and muscular control had become razor-fine, exact, split-second. His speeding legs missed the small fireplugs, the sprawling children, the slippery stream of water, the occasional street light. He ran smoothly past people walking up the hill, everything flashed by in blobs and whirls and it exhilarated him because it was so easy and effortless.

Suddenly he burst out into the park at the foot of the hill. The tempo of his speeding legs slowed down and his arms stopped the wild balancing movements. For a moment it was difficult to walk slowly; he felt earthbound and sluggish after the running. But as he began to walk across the thin grass of the park, watching the crowds of idle sailors and soldiers, he grinned and felt a secret satisfaction as if he had eliminated some last tiny gnawing of doubt.

CHAPTER 15

The Pacific, 1945

To the shrill young yells of countless second lieutenants and the whirling of mimeograph machines, the shuffling lines were pulled through San Francisco, San Diego and Seattle. They were loaded into DC–4's, AKA's, APC's, DD's, CL's, Liberty ships and Victory ships.

Sometimes the smooth routine would be interrupted and then like a rupture in the shining skin of a sausage the men would pour out into San Francisco and the other towns. For a few wild and lost hours they would invade the penny arcades and shoot toy machine guns or go to the whorehouses where sweating middle-aged women would wriggle automatically and pat the young boys on top of the head. Late at night they stuffed food into their intoxicated throats, smashed the hamburgers and french fries and sweet coffee and beer into their heaving stomachs. Then, as the lemming instinct reasserted itself and as the liquor wore off, they would ride buses, hitchhike, hire cabs, steal cars, walk, ride double on motorcycle back to the camps and receiving ships where they could fall back into the lines.

As the lines pushed across the Pacific they spread out into huge thick waves. The waves of men pushed across the islands and over the seas and through the air. Between them and the enemy they kept a huge spongy barrier. The barrier was made up of flights of PBY's and B–24's, stacks of carrier planes, mountains of C-rations, hummocks of cigarettes, tons of sixteen-inch shells, screens of destroyers, banks of neatly wrapped bandages and haystacks of morphine syrettes. The barrier was also made up of heaps of barbed wire, fleets of repair ships, floating dry docks, refrigerators full of whole blood, flasks of yellow plasma, U.S.O. shows, Red Cross canteens, stacks of books. By cautious and infinitely careful maneuver the protective barrier was kept between the Americans and the enemy.

Sometimes the barrier was made up of subtle unseen things. Things like the ghostly ping of the sonar gear as it echoed through the water, probing for the enemy. Or like the strange stabbings of the radar gear which reproduced on a black scope the luminous worms which were enemy ships and airplanes. Or the IFF gear which mechanically and endlessly sent out a signal, "identify friend or foe." Or the "Fox schedule" which filled the air of the world with a ceaseless pattern of dots and dashes and which, like a bodyless intelligence, directed the movements of the long anonymous lines of men.

Only at a few times and in a few spots did the lines of khaki become separated from their protective barrier. When it did the edge of the khaki wave suddenly exploded in bloody sticky froth. Then Marines screamed insanely on reefs a quarter mile at sea and their broken bodies sank reluctantly into the water. Then soldiers watched objects like rocks soar out of the jungle at them and lie sputtering at their feet for a moment until the objects exploded and sent hot grenade fragments shredding through kidneys, muscle and eyeballs. Then enemy task forces maneuvered through the blackest night, probing one another with radar, and, finally cutting the night with slow-traveling projectiles which smashed steel ships into indecent hulks. Then men in a B–24 watched a Messerschmitt knife sharply through the sky, roll slowly on its side and then suddenly the leading edge of the Messerschmitt wing would crackle with fire and the machine gun slugs would tear the bomber to pieces and with a giant whoosh of gasoline burning it would be gone — with nothing left but falling shreds.

Most of the time the great mobile protective barrier of equipment and organization was there, but when it wore thin or disappeared the pimply faced fry-cooks, the truck drivers, the insurance clerks, the college boys and the men all stood beside their guns and watched Japanese swarm in hopping bowlegged crowds toward them or stared at German tanks which moved fast across a grey landscape. Some of the men stayed and held their fingers down on the trigger or dropped the shell in the mortar or trained the gun, but others stood perfectly still, caught in the ecstasy of complete and absolute fear.

The B–29 streaked down the long runway barely stirring up a swirl of dust off the face of the clean concrete and finally lifted into the golden California air. The plane flew over the hump of the ocean to Hawaii and here it overtook the most backward part of the khaki wave. Here men were living an almost normal life with highballs and almost white girls and almost good whisky and almost normal weather. The plane fueled and the crew ate Spam sandwiches and gulped ice water. The plane streaked down another clean aseptic runway and headed for Johnston Island and then touched at Kwajalein, Guam and finally Saipan. The B–29 flew over the stretched-out middle part of the khaki wave where men sweated over typewriters and stacked boxes and painted ships and scraped tennis courts at officers' clubs and made showers out of tin cans. Here was where the khaki and material wave was the thickest; where the gear was heaped in mountains and armies of men slowly loaded, shifted, loaded, unloaded and reloaded the mountains of equipment. This was equidistant between the normality of the rear and the madness of the forward unprotected fringe. And because the pressures here were the most equal the men were the unhappiest.

The B–29 passed over the backward part of the wave and got almost to the edges where the bloody froth was exploding and surging again. But the plane stopped short of the fringe and waited for a few days.

Two weeks before, a cruiser had left San Francisco and crawled across the ocean. Ahead of it pushed three destroyers that paced and tracked and doubled back in a scientifically determined erraticness. The tropic sea was hot and flat and only the horizon looked hazy and soft with puffed clouds. On the cruiser a special Marine guard stood endlessly in front of a locked up compartment. The Marines stood stone-faced on watch and when relieved laughed carelessly at the questions of the sailors to hide the fact that they too did not know what they were guarding.

Finally, days after the plane had landed at Saipan, the cruiser anchored in the harbor at Guam. Now, suddenly, the ship was covered with cheerful young scientists in new unwrinkled khakis. They were able to pass through the cordon of Marines. These men knew nothing of military courtesy or relative ranks and they pushed captains and colonels aside to fondle the boxes and behind their glasses their eyes glistened moistly and their voices rose in sharp strained instructions as the boxes were lowered over the side. The scientists climbed on the trucks with the boxes and hugged them occasionally in a curious excess of excitement. They clapped one another on the shoulders and usual cautious barriers between them were melted for a while. On the cruiser the sailors and Marines watched the excited scientists take the boxes and crates away.

"Well, Jesus Christ, they're only boxes," one said.

Yeah, Jesus Christ, the rest of the crew thought before they began to spray the ship with salt water and clean up again.

In due time the eager scientists assembled the contents of the boxes into a long metal capsule of censored length and breadth and censored weight. They deposited it beside the airfield and the young fliers stopped eating their Spam sandwiches, and drinking powdered lemonade and whisky and brought their plane up close to the long dun-colored capsule. They were languid and calm, uninterested as the scientists hovered about the bored ordnance men who trundled the capsule out to the plane and finally snuggled it up into the belly of the B–29. And there the sperm and ova of the new thing lay; separated by a few inches of lead, but firmly planted in the stomach of the plane with her four 2200-horsepower engines and lead-computing sights, and stabilizers, and pressurized cabins and masses of instruments.

The young scientists retired to the edge of the runway and squatted on their heels. A few of them climbed into a second B–29. The first plane turned slowly, aimed itself down the runway and with a long smooth roar was finally airborne. The second plane followed it. The two planes turned north and, switching to automatic, began the flight for Japan.

The world wheeled by under the plane; the sea, an occasional speck of an island, once a task force and finally the perfect lip of the horizon was smeared and then they saw the edge of Japan rising out of the ocean. There was fog over the first target and so, without the people below knowing, with a godly indifference, the plane turned and made for another city. The city came to shape in the bombardier's sight. Far away and microscopic he saw the thin black squares, the parks, the broad line of the river. The bombardier's fingers worked the knobs; wind drift, plane speed, real wind, etc. His sights were not strong enough to see people so that when he squeezed the button and let the capsule fall away in a long slanting spin he only hoped that it would fall exactly in the middle of the mosaic of lines and blocks. He put on the thick black glasses given him by the scientists and pressed against a window of the plane. The two planes were shaken as if a massive tuning fork were vibrating inside of them. Through the thick black lens a flicker of light penetrated.

Below the airplane the tiny particles had come together in a rupturing of heat and light. The light burnt hot on Japanese bodies. Some of the Japanese were killed in the old way by flying stones and bashing their heads against walls or being buried in collapsing walls. But many were killed in a new strange way and simply stood and died gasping for air like landed fish. In a fraction of a second people grew huge blisters on their faces and hands. In some people the marrow of their bones dried suddenly and produced no more corpuscles so that later they died from a cold or a cut finger. But there was the comfort of enormity about it, the solace of common disaster, the stability of ignorance. The shattered burnt bodies nursed crisper, more broken bodies in a nightmare of pus-filled eyes, skinless hands, dust-filled skies and a scarcity of water.

Lines of people walked by looking as if they had been dipped in slime that had hardened slowly. "Look, they are in lines again," an old man, squatting by the road, said. Others took up the cry. "Look, lines again. They walk in correct lines," and suddenly all the wounded people felt better.

"Good stuff," the crewman of the plane remarked. They took off their dark glasses and began to tend the plane again. "Mighty good stuff. New stuff, eh?"

The young scientists were pressed against the windows, their black glasses off and their eyes startled and childlike. They watched the shattered cloud of dust around the ground, heaving and swirling in brown waves. Suddenly out of the brown murk a pure white column climbed clean and untarnished into the sky. At fifteen thousand feet it suddenly spurted a pure and lovely mushroom further into the sky. It was as clean and solid as marble, clear against the blue of the sky.

The youngest of the scientists felt his breath stop and a queer exultation seized him. He dug his fingers against the sides of the plane for support and his body was caught in a slow grinding orgasm as the perfect column split the sky. Minutes later when the wind had begun to shatter the sides of the column and the mushroom was starting to lose its sharp clarity, he pushed himself away from the side of the plane as if every muscle in his body had been broken and hurried back to the tiny lavatory at the rear of the plane.

Then, by some widespread and common agreement, the endless lines and waves of men hesitated and paused and stopped fighting. The rest of it was all done by words spoken by diplomats and statesmen. No one was ready for it.

Now the huge brown wave of equipment and khaki started to roll backward, starting slowly and then gradually speeding up, like a wide-lensed camera suddenly beginning to run in reverse. The wave left behind it a rusty iron fringe; the keen cutting edge began to corrode and rot. There were tanks slowly turning red, quonset huts overrun by jungle, stacks of rotting food in which a few pot-bellied natives and slim dashing parakeets picked, beer cans melting into the mud. The long white strips of airfields grew a fuzz of green that thickened and then finally swallowed the asphalt and cement completely. The temporary docks rotted and sank into the ocean. The only orderly thing left in the rich tropical chaos was the trim rows of white crosses, row on row, marvelously neat and well laid out.

The men and boys making up the great wave went backward through the whole process, but somehow the system worked poorly in reverse, the men changed back slowly and reluctantly. They went through the reception centers, and separation centers and interviews and were handed their manila envelopes and turned loose. They put on flannel suits, corduroys, overalls, blue business suits, sport coats, truck driver uniforms, but in all of them there was the great sameness. The same-ness did not come from fighting for even the men who sat on their buttocks for the entire war with their feet on a desk had it. Cooks, telephone operators, control tower men, transport pilots, radarmen, sig-nalmen, they all had it It was a way of holding the head and opening the mouth to bitch and looking at women and filling out papers and jealously guarding tiny areas of privilege and part of it was a childish petulance and part of it was getting old too fast and part of it was the loneliness that men feel in a mob. But no man could tell another about the sameness and it took weeks and months for it to disappear. Maybe the sameness disappeared when they stopped eating the same starchy food that gave them plump faces or when they stopped march-ing in column when they walked alone. But somehow the great same-ness did vanish, somehow all the men began to function on their own nerves and brains again and in each man there was a day when he realized that the sameness was gone and, at last, the wheel had come full round.

CHAPTER 16

End of the Invisible Hand

THE CITRUS BUILDING was one of the oldest office buildings in Los Angeles. By the Depression it had grown decrepit and grimy. It was noisy with the burr of dentists' drills and it stunk from the cigars of cheap lawyers. The iron grill elevators moved slowly up and down. The operators gradually stopped wearing uniforms and rolled their sleeves up and smoked while they worked. The ledges of the building were whitened by the droppings of the plump stately pigeons. Rents dropped. But during the 1930's the town started moving west and tall sleek apartment buildings went up around the Citrus Building. Wilshire Boulevard became a fashionable and glittering street and the Citrus Building had an entrance on Wilshire. After the war a group of realtors bought and redecorated it. It was painted black and gold. The pigeons remained but their droppings were carefully washed away. On the top of the building a great orange turned slowly and its green brass leaves were ten feet long. The new elevators went smoothly and quickly. It became the most fashionable business address in Los Angeles.

On the twelfth floor Mike Freesmith looked out a window. A single sea gull was suspended outside. It was motionless, frozen by some invisible pressure of winds. Behind it, scaled down the sky, were four other gulls. They were all motionless.

Must be a storm at sea, Mike thought. It's the only thing that brings the gulls in. Usually there are only pigeons outside the building.

The gull had its pink withered feet tucked up beneath its belly. It closed a leathery lid over the single eye that Mike could see. The small feathers along the trailing edge of its wings shivered as the wind molded past the gull's body.

"Would you like me to read back the last line?" Libby Matson said behind him.

Mike was suddenly irritated. He rapped his knuckle on the window. The gull's eye snapped wide, it turned on its back and planed downward, away from the building. The other gulls broke their static formation and laced whitely through the sky in great swoops. Their wings, however, did not move.

"Read it back, Libby."

"The letter is to Ashton in Calexico. The last sentence reads, 'You should realize that the firm of Cromwell and Freesmith is not necessarily interested in having you form the businessmen of Calexico into an active group to bring the new highway through your town. Our client only desires that the wishes of the business community of Calexico be communicated to the Senate Interim Committee on Highways.'"

"All right. Add this: 'Attached you will find a draft statement which your business community might wish to send to the Interim Committee. If your people change the statement in any substantial way we should like to be informed before it is sent to the Interim Committee.' Put in the 'sincerely yours' and the rest, Libby."

"Yes, sir."

"Is Mr. Cromwell in yet?" Mike asked.

"No, but Clara said he would be in later this morning."

"Does he have a hangover?"

Libby looked pained. She ran her unpainted thumbnail over the coil of wire that held the shorthand notebook together.

"Clara didn't say," she said.

"Well, ask her," Mike said. "Or if you don't want to ask her, send her in here and I'll ask her."

Libby smiled with relief and left the room.

She's a good girl, Mike thought. Loyal and bright, but too timid. Mike had picked her very carefully for the job as his personal secretary. Her husband was an electrician and Mike had, at once, gotten him a job with the City doing electrical inspections. It meant that her husband had to be placed ahead of a number of civil service candidates. Mike had also gotten her mother, who was blind in one eye, a small pension from the state after persuading a few people in Sacramento that the old woman had only twenty per cent vision. Mike had made it plain to Libby that both of these favors were illegal. He also made it plain to her that he did not want her to get pregnant and leave him without a secretary. Libby had agreed and she was one of the most diligent workers in the law firm of Cromwell and Freesmith.

The door opened and Clara came in. As usual she had a cigarette in her fingers and she held it so that the smoke floated by her cheek and obscured the lividness of the birthmark. She wore a simple black dress that made her look older. But when she sat down she turned her head and Mike could see the exquisite line of her profile; the fine nose, the deep pit of her eye, the molding of her cheek bone.

"Is John going to be in this morning?" Mike asked.

"Yes. Around eleven."

"Good. I want him to go to lunch with the gang from the Board of Equalization."

"Look, Mike, he shouldn't go. That crowd always drinks too much and it just means that Cromwell will get drunk again," Clara said. "He's already got a hangover. He shouldn't go."

"John's a big boy now, Clara," Mike said. "He knows whether or not he should drink. Anyway, it doesn't make any difference if he does. No one can tell when he's drunk. It just makes him calmer."

"But he hates it. You know that. God, Mike, he suffers afterwards. He can't work. He feels guilty."

"He has to go to lunch with these people, Clara. They're important. Do you know how many liquor licenses there are in this state? About forty thousand. And the people who hold those licenses do pretty much what the Board members want them to do. They control a lot of votes."

"I don't care how many votes they control. It's not worth getting Cromwell drunk again. Being governor is not that important, Mike. Don't kid yourself. If he has to go through all this to become governor it just isn't worth it."

She turned her face straight toward him and her large brown eyes glittered. Then she remembered and she turned her head slightly so that the birthmark was out of sight, but she was still angry.

Does she really think other people get him drunk? Mike thought. Doesn't she realize he's a drunk on his own? No one forces him to drink. He forces himself.

Clara puzzled him. She did everything for Cromwell, wrote his speeches, kept his appointments, made his phone calls, cured his hangovers, brushed his clothes; everything. And then, two or three times a year, she disappeared from the office. Once Mike had gone to her apartment looking for her. She had opened the door, peered at Mike and then opened the door further. She was naked and behind her on the sofa was a man with a glass in his hand. His bellboy uniform was draped over a chair; his eyes were drunken, startled and the least bit frightened. Clara was sober; sober with an eeriness that made the hair rise on Mike's neck. Go away, she said and closed the door. Before the door closed the bellboy raised his head, focused on Mike and grinned. It was the odd strained look of an animal that is being experimented with; being studied; watched.

Mike looked at Clara's profile as she sat across from him in the office. That beautiful, ivory-etched profile had been in bed with almost every man in the office and a lot outside the office: office boys, salesmen, messengers, Western Union boys and men she met casually at parties.

"John wants to be governor, Clara," Mike said softly. "If he doesn't I'd better know about it."

Clara opened her mouth to speak and then paused. She put her hand down and looked at Mike full-face and he could see the soft purple blemish.

I'm the only person she does that with, Mike thought. As if it doesn't matter whether or not I see it.

"All right, Mike," Clara said and she was smiling thinly. "Who's going to be at the lunch?"

"Libby's got the list. She'll give it to you. Make sure he butters up Kelly. Kelly is the most important man on the Board."

"I'll pick it up," Clara said. She walked to the door and turned around. "Can Cromwell get the governorship, Mike? I mean really. Not just cocktail talk, but can he really get it?"

"He can get it," Mike said.

"But his name isn't in the papers," she said. "And he doesn't have much power in the party. When does he start to win friends and influence people?"

"I've told you before," Mike said patiently. "It doesn't make a bit of difference what the papers say. Not now. Later it will mean a lot."

The doorknob turned in Clara's hand and Cromwell came into the office. He was wearing a gray gabardine suit and a new straw hat. The hat was neat and crisp and contrasted with his suit. The suit was wrinkled and twisted; it knotted around his shoulders and pulled the sleeves back so that his wrists showed. The lapel had a black charred spot as if a match had gone out on it.

Cromwell stood in the doorway, sucking on a cigar. His eyes were bloodshot.

"Discussing the campaign strategy again?" he asked.

"Yes," Mike said.

"I've thought about it, Mike," Cromwell said. "We have to get more publicity. After all, it's the people that elect you in this state. If we don't get on the radio, TV, in the newspapers, they won't know who we are."

"We've been over it before," Mike said. "You don't need publicity now. That comes later. Right now you have to persuade the Democrats at their pre-primary convention to endorse you. Get the pre-primary endorsement and you'll be a cinch in the primary. In fact the Democrats won't have anyone else to vote for; you'll be the only Democrat on the ballot. When the general election comes up you'll need publicity. Not a lot, just a little in the right places. Christ, John, I've told you all this before. Right now if you get your head up too high everyone will be trying to chop it off."

"No, Mike. You have to get to the people," Cromwell said. He walked over and sat on Mike's desk. Mike could smell the faint sweet odor of gin. "If the people are for you, then the leaders have to take you." He paused and his bloodshot eyes watered slightly. His voice became pleading. "Mike, that's what I do best; talk to the people. That's what I should be doing. Clara'll tell you that. Remember, Clara, that time in Placerville? Those lumbermen were wild for me."

He looked out the window and his face softened with the recollection. Mike looked at Clara. She did not evade his glance and for a moment they stared directly into one another's eyes.

"I think Mike's right, Cromwell," she said.

Why does she always call him Cromwell? Mike thought. And why does she hate me so much? He almost grinned.

The door opened and Libby walked in.

"Your appointment with Mr. Blenner is in ten minutes," she said. "Here's his file. Mrs. Freesmith wants you to call her. Also there's a letter from Dr. Moore."

She put the letter and a file on his desk.

Clara and Cromwell left the office. Libby went out after them. Mike opened the letter from Hank. A check fell out on the desk.

The letter was written on the letterhead of the Los Angeles County Hospital.

"I don't need the money, Mike," the letter said. "Thanks anyway. I keep telling you that interning at County is luxury after medical school. I get room and board and fifty bucks a month. When things get too bad I swipe some absolute alcohol and distilled water from the storeroom and mix myself a stiff drink. It was good of you to send the check, but I just don't need it. In short, I'm set up. Again thanks.

"How about going for a swim some day soon? They say the waves are really humping this year."

Mike laughed and threw the letter in the wastebasket. He tore the check up. He picked up the file labeled "Aaron Blenner."

It was full of the usual stuff. Date of birth: 1895. Location: Minsk, Russia. Schooling: no record. Family background: no record. Religion: Jew. Clubs: none. Charities: Mount Sinai Hospital, National Jewish Fund, numerous Jewish groups. In the file there were also a number of sheets with just a single paragraph on them. The sheets were not signed and they bore no identifying marks. Mike picked up one of them:

"Informant states that Aaron Blenner has been subjected extensive investigation Bureau of Internal Revenue. All results negative. Evidence that Blenner has used some of wholly owned companies to finance escape of refugee Jews from Germany, but nothing definite. Indirectly Blenner owns controlling interest in two French and one Portuguese import-export firms."

Mike leafed through the sheets and picked out one labeled "Political Activity."

"No known political affiliation. No active political participation. Not carried as registered voter on rolls. No political contributions on record."

The buzzer under his desk sounded. Mike put the file in a drawer. The door opened and Blenner walked in. A woman walked in with him.

"Hello, Mr. Freesmith," Blenner said. "This is my daughter, Georgia." He walked a few steps into the room and sat down quietly.

Blenner was a tiny pear-shaped man. He held a derby hat in his lap and occasionally he brushed the nap of the hat lightly. He wore very small black shoes that had a careful dull polish. His feet did not quite touch the floor and he swung them back and forth. His hands were normal size and against the black material of the derby they seemed large and out of proportion. His face, except for the eyes, had an innocent quality. His large jaw did not look as if he had ever been shaved. His eyes were small and bright. They looked exactly like Italian olives: small, hard, glistening.

His daughter was quite tall. She was wearing a cashmere coat. When she sat down she looked out the window. She was about twenty years old.

"Mr. Freesmith, for some years I have been in the motion picture business," Blenner said.

"Yes, I know that," Mike said.

"Recently I have felt that the motion picture business was getting in a bad way. High costs, television, foreign films, and a number of other things. A very complex situation. I won't bore you with the details." He paused and closed his eyes. He went on talking. "For some time I have been thinking of various forms of new enterprises. I have decided that land is the best form of investment."

Mike waited for him to go on, but he said nothing. The office became silent except for the kaaing of the gulls, the muted staccato of the typewriters in the outer office and the faraway sound of traffic. Mike waited.

"I don't know anything about land," Mike said at last.

Blenner opened one eye. The moist hard eye stared at the ceiling.

"I do," Blenner said. "Land, farm land, is the best thing."

"Why?" Mike asked.

Blenner closed his eye.

"I'm an old man. It takes me a little time to get to the point," Blenner said and smiled. He had no accent and he spoke very slowly; very precisely. "Let me tell you about old-time business, Mr. Freesmith. When I was a boy business was pure competition. The most efficient business drove the least efficient out of business. Everyone thought this was good. Inefficiency was always punished: it disappeared. Efficiency was rewarded: it made a profit. It got more and more of the market. I like that idea and I did pretty well under those rules."

"So I have heard," Mike said.

Blenner opened his eye again and smiled at Mike. Then he closed his eye.

"But businessmen didn't like competition, Mr. Freesmith," he said. "They were frightened of going bankrupt or failing or being driven out of business. Even the men who were successful became afraid they might be ruined. Publicly they still sounded brave and courageous, but privately they were frightened. So they asked to be protected by the government. They asked to be socialized."

"The business community asked to be socialized?" Mike asked.

"That surprises you. But it is the truth. Oh, the businessmen did not use the word 'socialism.' They asked for regulation, elimination of unfair competition, for subsidies, for protective tariffs, for government support of mortgages, for cheap money, for control of the stock market and thousands of other little things. No one of these things was socialism. But together, all added up, they meant the end of competition. Without saying it, the businessmen killed competition and got security. Do you know that if someone sells a bottle of whisky for less than his competitor in California he can be punished by law?"

"Yes," Mike said softly. "I know that."

"Today there is no competition and because there is no competition the rewards have been narrowed down. Few people fail, but also everyone makes much less." Blenner paused and looked at the ceiling again. "Understand, Mr. Freesmith, I don't object to this. People can do whatever they want. I'm not a crusader. I don't want to change anything."

"What do you want?" Mike asked.

"Just to know the rules," Blenner said. With his eyes closed he smiled. "And then to do the best thing under the rules. See, I liked the rules of the old game. It seemed to me that there was a kind of hard justice about the most inefficient producer being always forced out of the game. But then they changed the rules. Not much, just a little. They asked that the inefficient producer be protected. It took a little time for me to realize that this made it a new game. You see, Mr. Freesmith, I'm an old-fashioned person."

He laughed; a clear trilling laugh, a sound of pure joy.

"Now that you know the new rules, what do you want to do?" Mike asked.

"I want to play inside the rules and make the best profit possible," Blenner said. "That's all. Just make the best legitimate profit that can be made."

"I still don't see why you came to me," Mike said.

"Because I want to go into farming," Blenner said.

Mike said nothing because he could think of nothing to say.

"You see, under the new rules farming or just owning agricultural land is the best investment you can have," Blenner went on. "Strange things have happened, Mr. Freesmith. Thirty years ago the farmers were in a bad way. They started to elect congressmen and senators and governors who would help them. First, they asked for cheap farm loans and then they asked for a guaranteed price and then they asked for a regulated market. Finally they got all of that. Finally they got it to the point where the farmer could actually get paid for producing nothing." Blenner opened his eye, rolled it in wonder. "Imagine that! Imagine being paid for producing nothing. Just for promising not to produce corn or wheat or cotton you get paid. The farmers are the winners under the new rules. It's impossible for them to lose."

"But a lot of farmers still go broke," Mike said uncertainly.

"You're right. It's incredible, but they do. They're the ones who buy new Cadillacs with their winter wheat or build a big new house or buy two tractors when they only need one. Those are the ones who go broke. It's hard to do it, but some people manage. Some people just work at being fools. Even with everything designed to prevent them from going broke they go broke. But it doesn't happen often, Mr. Freesmith. And then you have to remember that the farmers who do go broke don't have capital. I'll have capital."

"I'm not an expert on farming, Mr. Blenner, but it was my impression that the government supports were designed to help the small farmer," Mike said.

Blenner sat up straight in his chair and opened both of his eyes. His large white hands caressed the smooth nap of the derby hat. He smiled a withered, slight smile at Mike.

"I came to see you for two reasons, Mr. Freesmith," Blenner said and his voice was slower, more precise. "First, because they tell me that you are a clear-sighted person and you learn new things very fast. And secondly they tell me that you aren't committed to anyone; no political party or company or individual."

Blenner paused, but this time Mike did not speak and the silence grew long. The girl turned and looked carefully at Mike. Finally Blenner spoke.

"You could do two things for me, Mr. Freesmith," Blenner said and his voice was subtly reproving. "First, you could learn something about farm lands in California. How much they cost, what they could grow, that sort of thing."

"I'm not interested," Mike said. "I don't know anything about farm lands and don't want to."

"And the second thing you could do is have the agricultural laws changed," Blenner said, ignoring Mike's remark. "Not a lot. Nothing illegal. But just enough so the big landowner would get the same treatment from the government as the small landowner. That's all."

"I don't want to be a lobbyist," Mike said.

Mike picked up a folder, tapped it on the desk. He hoped they would leave.

Blenner looked at the folder, smiled and closed his eyes again.

"I don't want you to become a lobbyist," Blenner said softly and this time there was something cold in his voice and Mike knew he was being warned. "It just occurred to me that if your colleague, Mr. Cromwell, became governor of the state he would be in a good position to help out."

Mike looked at Blenner's daughter. Her lips were slightly open as if she were surprised at Mike. It was a curious expression; mostly admiration, but also something of fright. Mike looked at Blenner and now the small, well-tailored, neat, poised man looked powerful and ominous; almost reptilian.

"Maybe you had better talk to Mr. Cromwell," Mike said. "I didn't know he wanted to be governor."

"I understand that he takes your advice on such matters," Blenner said and again his voice was warning. He took an envelope out of his coat pocket and tapped it against his fingernails. "I'll be frank with you. This envelope contains a very brief report. The report indicates under what circumstances Mr. Cromwell could be elected governor of California. The report states that he has a following among a number of small groups in California. He is weak among Democratic leaders, but if he could get the nomination and all other things were equal he would win."

"What if all other things were not equal?" Mike said.

Mike said it protectively, to gain time. For the back of his throat had suddenly gone dry. He sensed that Blenner had the secret, had stumbled upon it somehow. Go slowly now, cautiously, easy, Mike said to himself.

"Can you think of many things that money could not make equal?" Blenner asked. "If Cromwell had ample money that would equalize things, wouldn't it?"

"It would help," Mike said. "But why don't you talk to one of the big people in the Democratic Party? You know there are a number of other people who are considered to be much better risks for the governorship than Cromwell."

"That's why I don't want them," Blenner said. "A good risk always pays a low profit. I'd rather take a risk . . . maybe the rewards would be larger." Blenner opened one eye and with that single eye he regarded Mike as an equal, was completely frank, open. "And besides, the prominent candidates are already committed to other people. I would not like that."

You son of a bitch, you lizard-looking, ugly dwarf, Mike thought. You've figured it all out. It took me years to work it out and you come in here with the whole thing down in a white envelope.

Rage rose in Mike, hot as a fever. But he forced himself to calmness.

"Who wrote the report?" Mike said.

"My son."

"Politics is complicated," Mike said. "It's easy to make mistakes. Things don't work out neatly."

"I know that," Blenner said. "But I don't act on bad advice and I'm prepared for things to be difficult. You can take care of the difficult things. I'll supply the money and whatever influence I have. We would not need to sign an agreement or anything like that. We would merely trust one another."

"I'll talk it over with Mr. Cromwell," Mike said.

"Fine. You do that," Blenner said.

He jumped out of his chair, stuck the derby on his head. He shook hands with Mike and his hand was cool, firm and uncomfortably strong. His daughter followed him to the door. He turned.

"You ought to get out and look at some farm lands," Blenner said. "Start to get the feel of the thing. Then you could talk things over with my son. You won't be seeing much of me anyway."

"I'd like to go along with him," the daughter said suddenly. "I know the country around Los Angeles. I'd like to do it."

Blenner looked at his daughter and his eyes were utterly bored. He shrugged his shoulders and looked at Mike.

"I'll give you a call," Mike said. "If we decide to do it I'll buzz you."

The girl smiled and then quickly followed her father out of the office. Mike noticed that she limped slightly.

CHAPTER 17

The Ocean and the Desert

GEORGIA BLENNER called Mike four days later.

"I've found some farming land," she said. Her voice was cool and unexcited. "Would you like to go look at it? I've arranged to pick up an agricultural expert from the University to give us some advice. Could you go this afternoon?"

"I can get free, but I don't want an expert along."

"Why not?"

"All an expert can do is tell you what worked in the past. They're always too conservative. Always hedging; afraid they'll hurt their reputation. The time for experts is later."

Georgia laughed.

"All right," she said. "We won't take the expert. Can you meet me at Karl's Drive-in on Wilshire . . . out by Westwood? Around one-thirty?"

"Sure. I'll be there," Mike said.

When he put the phone down he leaned back in his chair. He hadn't talked to Cromwell about Blenner's proposal. He knew he would not. He also knew that he would go along with Blenner.

It isn't the money, Mike thought. We can win without Blenner's money. But it was the crazy idea about going into farming. It was a little fishhook of curiosity that sunk into his flesh; a curious little gnaw of interest.

She was sitting in the drive-in drinking coffee when he drove up.

She saw him through the plate-glass window and walked out to meet
him. She was tall and she walked with a peculiar gait. It gave her
a coltish, angular appearance, although she had very full breasts and
round hips. She opened the door and got in the car.

"The land is out in the San Fernando Valley," she said. "Why don't
you drive out Wilshire to the coast and then over Tujunga to the
valley?"

"It's shorter to go over Sepulveda," Mike said.

"I know that. But I like to drive along the ocean. It's warmer
too." She turned and looked at him. She had a large mouth with fine
white teeth. When she smiled she brought her lips quickly back
over her teeth, with the curious sharpness that little girls have when
they wear braces. Her hair was very black and cut short. Her skin
was white; the sort of white that never tans, although she had a
pattern of freckles across her nose. "I'm cold most of the time. I
had polio when I was a kid and although the doctors say it's impossible I've been cold ever since. I like the sun."

That explains her gait, Mike thought. She never recovered from
the polio. She must be a little paralyzed.

They did not speak as they went through the heavy traffic around
Westwood. They drove by the big new Robinson store and the sleek
modern apartment houses of Westwood. The traffic moved in great
slooping rushes from one signal to another, like a flight of orderly
birds. The fast drivers slid in and out, jockeyed for position and
between each signal gained a place or two. As they went up the
hills of Westwood they could see other platoons of cars ahead of
them, marked off by signal lights, moving rhythmically up the soaring
strip of highway.

They went through Westwood Village, past the golf range which
was crowded with people driving balls. On the other side of the
highway was the Veterans' Cemetery and behind the hedges the little
white crosses, broken by an occasional Star of David, ran in perfectly
straight lines until they shattered against a hillside.

They stopped at a light and Mike watched a little group of veterans
walk out from among the palm trees that bordered the Veterans'
Hospital and stand on the curb. One of them was wearing a bathrobe
and slippers. His bathrobe was open and the sun splintered on the
gray wiry hair on his chest. The neck of a bottle showed in the
pocket of the bathrobe. They were all slightly drunk and they stared
brazenly, defiantly at the cars.

"How they hate dying in Southern California," Georgia said.

Mike looked around, startled. His eyes went over the veterans, swept up the long reach of green lawn, glanced at the other cars. His face was blank.

"Who hates to die in Southern California?" he asked.

"Those veterans," Georgia said. "That little bunch of them standing there. See the one with the bottle in his bathrobe pocket? He wants to shock the people going by in their new cars and they don't even look at him. He's mad."

The veteran in the bathrobe saw them looking at him and grinned crookedly. He pulled the bottle out of his pocket and unscrewed the top. He put it to his mouth, his eyes glaring at them. When he threw his head back the cords in his neck drew the red wrinkled flesh tight. He looked like a person who had once been very fat and now hated being skinny.

The signal changed and their platoon of cars picked up speed; in a collective spasm they rushed toward the next signal.

"How do you know they hate it here?" Mike asked.

"How do you know anything? I guess by looking at them. I think the sunshine and palm trees and salt air frustrates them. When you're dying you ought to be in a cold, dreary climate. It would make it easier. They ought to build the veterans' hospitals in the mountains and out on the deserts . . . where it's lonely and bleak. It must be hard to sit around in the sun and watch people going by in sport shirts and know you're going to die."

She paused, looking quickly at Mike and then went on. "When I was little and read all the adventure books I used to think it would be easier to die in the freezing Arctic like Scott and those people. It must be easier to die in a harsh climate, a cruel place. This is a terrible place to die."

"I never thought about it before," Mike said slowly. "I've been by this hospital a thousand times and I never noticed them. That's funny, isn't it?"

"Not many people do notice them, I guess," Georgia said. "After a while they become just like the palm trees or fire hydrants. You just don't see the individuals anymore."

At the next stop signal Mike looked over at Georgia. She was sitting very straight in the seat, looking out the window. She glanced quickly from one object to another. He guessed that she was twenty-two years old.

The land in San Fernando was owned by two polite Japs. They said the land was really not for sale and then, with much embarrassment and sucking of teeth, said that it could be had for $10,000 per acre. They all walked out and looked at the land.

The land was very black and rich. It was planted in spring onions and the tiny light green spikes were laid out in long even rows. The earth between the rows was soft and recently turned. A Japanese woman and a boy were irrigating and the water ran down the rows in long thin streams.

"This isn't what we want," Mike said. "They think we want it for subdividing and so they jack the price up."

His voice was irritated and he spoke directly to the Japanese. They grinned and ducked their heads. Georgia blushed.

On the way back to Los Angeles Mike drove to the top of Mount Wilson. It was a clear day with the smog blown out to sea. Below them was all of Los Angeles.

The older part of the city was dun-colored, neat and made soft by trees. Crawling out of the older city, like parasites abandoning a decrepit and useless host, were the new subdivisions. Close-packed, identical, shining-new, glittering with paint and new grass the subdivisions flowed down toward the sea and around the blackened spikes of the abandoned oil derricks of Signal Hill. They moved, in a welter of two-bedroom one-bath globs, toward Pomona and Whittier and devoured the orange trees as they went. In the Hollywood Hills and in the slopes behind Burbank the land was scarred by raw new roads and the units were bigger and sparkled with polished glass and redwood. Only occasionally was there an open and orderly stretch of green where crops were growing.

"Now all this is hopeless," Mike said restlessly, sweeping his hand to include the whole area from the mountains to the sea. "It's too crowded. Pretty soon it will all be subdivided. It's too expensive for farming. We have to get farther out."

"Farther out?"

"Yes, farther out. Out where the land hasn't been worked over. Where you are the first person to get to it. I don't know where, but not around here." With a sharp cut of his hands he rejected the city, the houses, the whole bright saucer of land. "You have to get something that's new; where you're the first one."

Georgia glanced at him and there was interest in her face. Mike put his hands down and stopped talking. They looked out over the city for another minute.

"All right, let's go," Georgia said. "I'll find out about Imperial Valley, the desert, all those places. I understand."

Two days later they drove to Imperial Valley. Hank went along. Mike knew it was his day off and insisted that Hank go with them. As soon as Hank got in the back seat of the car he fell asleep.

He fell asleep sitting up. His chin fell forward slightly, but he sat straight and stiff, as if he had just closed his eyes for a moment. Mike could see his head in the rear-view mirror. Hank was thinner and the hair above his ears was streaked with gray. He had a bone-and-gristle leanness that indicated he would never get fat. Oddly, the freckles still stood out on his nose and added to his bleached-out, tense look.

The highway was new and broad and neat. It was eight lanes wide and was divided down the center by a strip of grass. The lanes were made of poured concrete, six inches thick. The shoulders were made of black asphalt and were bordered by a strip of gray gravel. The trees close to the highway were stifled by the gasoline fumes and their skinny limbs were as leafless as bones.

The highway rolled across the countryside without mercy. It cut through hills in great raw gashes and swept on concrete bridges across the rivers. It cut through mountains in long tunnels lined with white tile and gleaming with lights. Occasionally from the new highway the old twisting road could be seen and the remains of the towns that had lined the old road. The towns held up their french-fried almond signs and antique signs and date shops and chinchilla ranches to the abandoned empty strip of asphalt, while the dirty windows in the back brooded malignantly over the new highway.

Mike held the Cadillac steady at seventy-five miles an hour. The car poured into a long beautiful curve and there was the faint rasp of rubber. Hank opened his eyes, lifted his head and looked out the window.

"Miss Blenner, do you spend all your time driving around with Mike looking for farm land?" Hank asked. "Or do you do something else?"

Georgia turned around and looked at Hank. She smiled.

"Sometimes I go to U.C.L.A. and take a course. I never finish them, but I start a lot of them. Ceramics, creative writing, history; things like that."

"Why don't you finish?"

"Sometimes because they get boring. Take sculpturing. They show you a nude girl and tell you to sculp her. But first you have to learn about armatures and keeping clay wet and plaster and anatomy and sculpturing theory. Someplace along the line I always get bored and give it up. I feel bad about it, but I never finish the courses. And then there's the family."

"What about the family?"

"The family is just more interesting than the courses. So I get to thinking of the family and it's more interesting than ceramics and I go home."

"Do you have a big family?"

"No. Not really. Just Father and Morrie, my brother. But there are always a lot of people around. Fund raisers for Israel Bonds or producers from New York or broken-down comedians who want Father to finance a new picture for them. The house is full of them."

Something about the girl disturbed Hank. She seemed to lack a dimension, a quality. For one thing she was not careful enough. She said everything she thought. When she answered a question she thought for a moment, but not to protect herself or to be careful. She paused the way a child will pause, so that she could give a complete answer. Then she said everything. Some instinct of protection, some device of insulation or caution was missing in the girl. Really, Hank thought, it's that she's exposed. No protections.

They drove past the turn-off for Palm Springs and Thousand Palms and came to the long rows of date trees. The dates were tiny and green against the brown of the trees. At Coachella it began to get hot and in the valley hundreds of Mexicans walked down the rows of melons. Like huge clever ants they hurried down the rows, rapping with a knuckle on the melons, picking only the ripest. The melons gathered in huge yellow mounds along the road.

"They say only Mexicans can tell a ripe melon in the field," Mike said. "They can tell by the smell or the feel or something. Put an Irishman out there and he'd pick all the wrong melons. But a Mexican, even a little Mexican kid, never makes a mistake . . . always picks the ripe ones and leaves the green ones."

Hank moved over to the window and looked out at the fields with new interest.

"That's why all the big farmers encourage the wet-backs to come over from Mexico," he said. "So they'll have a supply of pickers who can smell out a ripe melon. I read somewhere that some of these Mexicans will be deported by the immigration people six or eight times during a harvest season. And they just keep coming back for more."

They left the fields and went past the white glittering emptiness of the Salton Sea and the endless stretching away of alkali flats.

Every few miles there was a little town. They were all alike. Each one had a restaurant, a few bars, a truck-fueling station with a few semis parked around it. There was a garage with a big tow truck ready to go, the hook hanging free. At the outskirts of every town there was always a great ugly heap of wrecked and abandoned cars. The Model-T's and old Chevvies were on the bottom of the heap, turning rusty and stripped almost bare, reduced to a carcass. On top of them were the layers of newer cars; Oldsmobiles, Buicks, Chryslers, Mercurys. Some were squashed up into oddly shortened and twisted bodies; others were jerked lengthways. The guts of the cars; the cushions, steering wheels, wires, rubber mats and mirrors spilled down the side of the heap. On some of the newer wrecks the blood still showed on the wind-shields and the rust was just beginning to eat away the fresh chrome of the bumpers.

"So now you don't sculp or go to school or anything else except go along to see your daddy's investment is protected?" Hank asked as if they had been talking about it all along.

Mike laughed. Georgia turned with a smile on her face, but then she saw Hank's tight unsmiling face and a bruised, confused look appeared around her eyes.

She knows I meant it to hurt, Hank thought. He was sorry at once. The girl had no defenses, it was pointless to attack.

"That's not the reason I'm along," she said carefully, slowly. "I just want to see what happens. See, Hank, we're Jews and we're in motion pictures and those two things make people scared of politics. At home everyone gets nervous when politics come up. They're afraid the government will censor the movies or pass legislation against Jews or something like that. Politics always seemed distant and very bad and confusing." She shrugged her shoulders, despairing of her words. "So I came along."

"You hang around Mike and you'll learn a lot about politics," Hank said and his voice was not mocking. Then he paused and too swiftly his voice became harsh. "Jesus, Mike, you're not really going to run that bum Cromwell for governor? He doesn't have a chance. And if he does he shouldn't."

Georgia looked startled and then interested and Hank felt a quick relief. She had not detected his clumsy shift away from her.

The rest of the way into Brawley they talked about Cromwell's chances. Mike nodded his head and grinned, but he did not say how he thought Cromwell could win.

In Brawley they talked to a real estate agent. He was a lean, sunburned, friendly man. He had an office, but he liked to do business in his air-conditioned Cadillac. He leaned back in his seat, yawned as the air-conditioner hummed quietly. He had shown them all the land that was for sale.

"Well, that's the situation around here," he said. "Nobody really wants to sell. Maybe later if farm prices drop a bit they will. But not right now. Oh, you could get land if you wanted to go high for it. Eight or ten thousand an acre. But, God, with what they're getting for honeydews and casabas in L.A. everyone is making a fortune."

"What if there's a depression?" Mike asked. He was irritated, restless.

"Then watch 'em run," the real estate agent said. "None of these people are really farmers. They're just like the old prospectors. Come in, skim off the surface gold and leave before you have to get down to the low grade ore. None of 'em want to put in fertilizer or really build up the land, they just want to skim the cream."

"O.K., let's go," Mike said. "This isn't what we're looking for."

Later, as they drove back toward Los Angeles, Mike was silent. He did not speak until they reached the Morongo Valley turnoff.

"I don't know anything about farm land, but I don't want to get into anything like Imperial Valley," he said.

"I knew it," Hank said. "As soon as I saw those big melons and those solid red tomatoes and the nice straight rows in Imperial I knew Mike wouldn't be interested. Too easy."

Georgia looked from Hank to Mike. Mike was grinning. His teeth were held together, his eyes narrowed. He fumbled in his pocket for a cigar, slipped off the cellophane. His teeth separated and he put the cigar into the corner of his mouth, bit down with the big heavy teeth, closed his lips. He did not light the cigar for ten minutes.

They turned east and drove past the Bouillon Mountains and the Sheep Hole Mountains. They went past the dry bed of Bristol Lake, through Bagdad and into the white, searing desert below Rasor. Mike parked the car on top of a low bluff and they got out. The sagebrush had vanished and the ground was covered with a few greasewood trees, some dwarfed yuccas, cholla cactus, and occasionally the great spiny figure of a giant saguaro. There was not a building in sight. Only the straight, narrowing strip of grease-soaked road. They stood silently and looked at it.

"It's impossible, Mike," Georgia said. "Nothing could grow here."

"It could if you had water," Mike said.

Hank watched them from the back seat of the car.

At their feet a gridiron-tailed lizard came up out of the sand. His tongue flicked wildly and suddenly he saw them and dove into the sand. He was gone instantly, leaving only a tiny cloud of dust where he had disappeared. In a few seconds he popped up a yard away and then dove under the sand again.

"But there isn't any water," Georgia said.

Mike walked back to the car and took out a map. It was labeled "Irrigation System Map of California." He pointed to a large irregular blank spot on the map.

"That's where we are," he said. "Right in the middle of nothing. The land here is cheap. We could get it for almost nothing. All it needs is water. And the state could put water in here if it wanted."

He pointed at a thick line which marked the Los Angeles Aqueduct. It ran black and promising across the map, far above the land on which they were standing.

"All you'd have to do is to run an irrigation canal from that aqueduct and this land would be as rich as Imperial Valley," he said. His voice was tense. "Then you'd have something, Georgia. And it'd be new; brand new. Something you carved out of nothing. Better than taking over something that's already there."

In the middle distance a big, ugly, splayfooted jack rabbit went in great bounds. His ears stood straight up as he went over some fourpodspurge. Then he disappeared; instantly as if he had been swallowed by the hot sand.

"Could this land grow anything?" Georgia said doubtfully.

"Anything. Bring water in and it'll grow alfalfa, cotton, celery, any damned thing," Mike said. "Georgia, this is like a great big natural hothouse here. There are months when the temperature is over a hundred. And some days the humidity is absolute zero. Bring water in and you'd have tomatoes as big as . . ." he paused, searched for the right word, could not find it and moved his hands to make a globe as big as a watermelon, ". . . really big, huge. Anything would grow."

Georgia looked slowly around the desert, to the burning edge of the horizon, over the shimmering dunes.

Hank saw the excitement start across her face. She looked from the blue hulk of the mountains, across the stretch of sand and burnt earth and her eyes glittered. She can see it already, Hank thought. An irrigation canal, rows of lettuce, enormous sweet melons, everything ordered and won.

Mike kicked the sand. She watched him. It was not a casual kick. It was hard, deliberate, done with meaning. He kicked again and the sand sprayed away from his foot and fell in a shapeless heap. Mike grinned.

Georgia's excitement deepened. She knew it was not her own excitement. It was something borrowed from Mike. It was a paler, more austere, thinner version of what he felt, but it was still important and big. She knew, suddenly, that her perceptions were more diminished than Mike's and she was aware of the larger, harder things that he felt. As if Mike were an instrument through which she could gather impressions of things that she would not otherwise perceive.

And she sensed something of what Mike was unable to transmit to her. She knew that he did not care about the fruit and vegetables and trees and greenness that would come from the desert. She knew that what he wanted was to fight the white still sand, to cut the hot dead surface with bright strips of water, to rip it with tractors, to make it yield. When that was done he would no longer be interested. She understood why he had not wanted to buy land that was already worked or easy to develop.

She understood why he did not need an expert, not for the farm land or anything else. He went at a problem directly, like a physical assault, reaching for the heart of it. Then he reordered the whole thing, reshaped it, made it his. He did not want an expert around to take the edge off the victory. She was certain that he was right about the desert and the water.

Dimly she knew that her own excitement lacked something powerful and violent that Mike felt. But what she did feel was sufficient to make her tense, expectant, excited.

"Let's go and call Morrie, my brother," Georgia said. "He can find out if this land is for sale and how much it costs. Are you sure we could get the water in here?"

Mike grinned at her and nodded his head. He threw the butt of the cigar into a cholla and it caught on the spikes. A thin blue spiral of smoke rose in the hot still air; foreign, different from everything else, it was like a sign of domination. Mike turned and got in the car.

On the way back to Los Angeles they stopped at a drive-in outside of Barstow. It was a huge red and gold affair, built in a great clump of eucalyptus trees. It was late afternoon when they stopped. Mike and Hank went inside.

The carhops were all girls and they wore cowboy outfits with red pants that tucked into white cowboy boots. Their jackets were cut short and buttoned tightly in front. Two inches of flesh showed between the pants and the jacket. The pants were very tight.

Most of the cars were filled with Mexicans, six or seven in each car. The trays fastened to the windows were filled with beer bottles. The Mexicans pressed their faces against the windows and watched the carhops. From one of the cars came the sound of singing in Spanish.

"You look busy," Georgia said when the carhop gave her a menu.

"Usual Saturday night crowd," the girl said. Her face was heavily made up, as if she were a starlet getting ready to go on a set. Her hair was a bright peroxide blond. "They're mostly Mexicans. They bring 'em up to do the stoop labor. They can't get in the regular bars in town so they all chip in and buy a car together and spend Saturday night in the drive-ins." She looked around quickly and leaned forward. "Fact is, honey, they're all horny. They just like to see a girl's ass wobble is all. It's these outfits. The boss orders them from one of those fancy places in Hollywood. They cost a hundred and seventy-five bucks each and they fit across your ass so tight that it feels like a girdle. The boss does it because it brings in the Mexican trade. He only hires blondes because he says they like blondes better. I had to dye my hair. I'd be sore except that the Mexicans always leave big tips." She smiled and touched her hair softly. "What're you gonna have? Hamburger's good here."

"Three hamburgers and three beers," Georgia said.

Hank and Mike came out and got in the car.

"Mike, if everything goes all right who will work the farm?" Georgia asked. "Mexicans? Like the men in those cars?"

Mike glanced at the other cars. The Mexicans stared out, their brown faces gently sweating, their mouths open and singing softly. The leaves flickered, moved by a sudden breeze, and the faces became more distinct in the green light.

The peroxided carhop went to the closest car and picked up the empty bottles.

"You can't just sit here," she said in a hard voice. "You have to have something on your tray."

She tapped her booted foot on the asphalt. The Mexicans talked in Spanish. They ordered another round of beers. When the carhop turned around she winked at Georgia.

"Sure, we'll use Mexicans or whoever can do the work," Mike said.

"Maybe we can use machines for most of it. But there aren't any machines invented that will pick things like lettuce or melons or artichokes. So we'll use Mexicans I guess."

"Have you made any plans for them?" Georgia asked. "I mean for their families? Like housing facilities, laundries, that sort of thing."

"Now, Georgia, don't go getting sentimental," Hank said. "Don't expect Mike to elect a governor, bring in irrigation, raise the biggest crops in the world and also take care of the Mexicans. Not old Mike, not old Mike the big wheeler and dealer."

Mike looked at both of them uncomprehendingly.

"That's right," he said. "You can't plan for people. They come or they don't. If they don't come you raise your wages."

"Maybe we should plan something for them," Georgia said. "I'll talk to Morrie about it."

"No you won't talk to Morrie about it," Mike said. "That's one thing you can't plan. You can plan roads and irrigation and parity prices, but you can't plan for people. They're not like a road, for example. Any engineer can tell you what is the best topping and how much rolling and scraping a road needs. But you can't do that for people. You don't plan for them. You just make them an offer and see if they take it or not."

The carhop brought them the beer and hamburgers. They ate quickly. Before they were finished the Mexicans in the next car had finished their beers. Their tooted their horn for the carhop. When she took the tray from their car there were three one-dollar bills on it. As she walked back to the drive-in, she held the tray low so Georgia could see the size of the tip.

Mike paid their bill and they swung out on the road that led to Los Angeles.

CHAPTER 18

Memories

On THE TABLE in front of Cromwell was an untouched martini. He could smell its chilled, lemon-scented surface. It was a thin odor and he knew the sensation of thirst and tightness in his chest would be eased when he drank. But he waited. He looked at the Board members; made himself smile.

Kelly put his hand around his old-fashioned glass, started to lift it and then thought of a joke.

"Did you hear the one about the woman who saw the bull outside the kitchen window?" Kelly said. "Well, the woman is mixing bread . . ."

Kelly took his hand away from his glass without drinking and Cromwell felt a sharp disappointment. He did not look down, but he turned the cold thin stem. Saliva gathered around the back of his mouth; dry, cottony flecks that stuck to his teeth. He opened his mouth, worked his lips. Costello, the Mexican, lifted his old-fashioned and took a sip. Cromwell raised his glass and drank half the martini. The cold tasteless liquid flowed through dry passages and into his stomach with a soft stunning sensation. Instantly it was in his blood. His head cleared, a nervousness disappeared, the saliva vanished from his mouth. He bent forward eagerly to hear the rest of Kelly's story.

"And there the woman is, kneading and kneading away at the bread and muttering, 'Damn that husband of mine; never around when I want him,'" Kelly said.

Kelly lifted his hand and smashed it down on the table. They all laughed. Cromwell finished his drink and signaled to the waitress for another round. The Jonathon Club dining room was slowly filling. Cromwell looked at the Board men.

Kelly was the strongest member, he thought. Costello was a Mexican with a bland face and a pattern of smallpox scars across his nose. He claimed to have great influence with the Mexican voters and no one could prove whether he did or didn't. Franwich was a small wiry farmer from Yolo County who hated the liquor interests and received the votes of the prohibitionists around Los Angeles. He was reputed to be the most corrupt member of the Board. Smithies was from the north. He was a huge sprawling man. Buttons, belts and suspenders dug into his flesh like strings that held his baggy shape together. But the flesh edged around its bonds. The suspenders disappeared in fat. The tips of his shirt collar stuck out from a drooping roll of flesh. His mouth was a pink gash among folds of flesh. He had an enormous knowledge of California politics and he was scrupulously honest.

"I remember your father, Cromwell," Kelly said. "I went to San Francisco once to see him. Just before he died. Wanted to get him to invest in a pet project of mine. You were just out of law school then."

"I remember," Cromwell said. "It was your avocado idea."

The other men at the table laughed and Kelly's face tightened up defensively.

"That's right. And it was a hell of a good idea." Kelly said.

Cromwell remembered how shocked his mother had been by Kelly. Cromwell's father had brought Kelly to dinner just once at their home in Atherton and after that his mother had refused to entertain Kelly again.

Kelly came to San Diego from Dublin. He stepped off a ship in San Diego Harbor in 1910 and two weeks later he was in the avocado business. He looked at the crisp green skin of the avocado, tasted its bland rich flesh and it seemed the most exotic and beautiful of fruit. In 1910 avocado trees were used mostly for decoration and only Mexicans and bums ate the fruit. Kelly bought 250 acres of avocados. After working twelve hours a day in a foundry he went out to the grove and tended his trees. On Sundays he worked in the hot dry soil, digging irrigation grooves, hoeing around the trees, trimming the limbs back. He wore out his cheap Dublin tweeds, bought cheap blue denims and wore out three suits before the trees bore fruit.

The fruit came out heavy and green, hanging with a peculiar richness from the thin branches. Kelly used to stand and stare at the trees, lifting the fruit delicately with his stubby fingers, unable to believe that dirt and water and sun could do anything so wonderful. The California sun burned his hands mottled brown and his neck cherry red and wove tiny triangles of bloodshot in the corners of his eyes and he forgot entirely about Dublin and its rain and mist and cold.

But no one wanted the avocados. The Mexicans bought a few and squashed them up with onions and ate them on folded tortillas. And the bums from the harbor drifted out on sunny days and stole avocados and spooned their bellies full and fell asleep beside Kelly's trees. Most of the avocados rotted in great stinking heaps; going soft and flowing together and making a brown-green mound that hummed with flies and gave off a queer sweet smell that was enough to make strangers vomit when they first caught wind of it.

Kelly decided to make cold cream out of the avocados. For months he ground the flesh of the avocados into a thick paste, mixed it with perfume and musk and preservative. But the paste always turned brown and stank. Until one day a druggist told him about a new preservative and he added it to the avocado paste and the paste stayed green and sweet. Then Kelly sold the cold cream from door to door. He sold it in white pots with a little brochure which told women how the oil would rejuvenate the skin of the face and neck and hands. One day something happened and like a breeze the knowledge of avocado cold cream spread all over California and movie stars and housewives and great women were using it. The magazines ran articles showing pictures of Kelly mixing the cold cream and quoting him as saying "It's nature's way to nourish the skin."

A neat little factory grew up beside the grove and Kelly stopped working at the foundry. He bought newspaper ads and the white pots started to carry a gold label. He picked up 2500 acres in Seal Beach and planned to plant it to avocados. He bought a car and had cases of Irish whisky shipped over directly from Dublin. But he still worked in the groves; his head bare and grinning as his face and chest were burnt by the sun. The Mexicans who worked the groves laughed and thought he was crazy; made mad by the sun. He roared and bellowed among the trees, jabbing his shovel at the irrigation canals, softly testing the fruit, kicking the dry rich soil.

Then one night a Hollywood starlet woke up, ran her pink tongue over a cupid-bow mouth made tender by avocado cold cream. She swallowed some of the cold cream. She died the next morning, screaming in agony. Like a dropping breeze the avocado cold cream business vanished although Kelly went from door to door again, arguing and scolding and fighting with the women, telling them that the cold cream was wonderful. He would reach into the pots and scoop out huge fingerfuls of the green paste and eat it to show them it was harmless, but they were not buying.

Kelly went broke trying to save his avocado cold cream. He believed in it fanatically, blindly, with an Irish single-mindedness. He spent money on newspaper ads and he hauled seven different people into court for libeling his product. Finally he lost his original avocado grove when he couldn't meet the mortgage.

In the end it made no difference for they found oil on the land he owned at Seal Beach. With a canny insight he refused to sell the land to Standard or Shell or Richfield or anyone. He held on to it and as the land sprouted derricks and black tank farms he grew rich.

For five years he tried to revive interest in the avocado cold cream business. He poured a million dollars into it. He bought new avocado groves and raised the largest, greenest and richest avocados in California. But women would not use his cold cream and Kelly hated them for their reluctance. Finally avocados became a popular food and Kelly, mollified by this, gave up the cold cream idea.

"Some talk the Democrats might run you for governor, John," Smithies said.

He moved in his chair; his body sighed against its braces; the flesh heaved and shifted. The other Board people looked sharply at Cromwell.

Cromwell let the clean chill of the gin and vermouth pour around his teeth. Five minutes before he had been old and defenseless; aware of aching bones and a shortness of breath. And now they were waiting to see what he would say, their faces expectant. He felt confident, alert.

"With Warren going to the Supreme Court the situation is a little peculiar," Cromwell said.

"This is a hard year to figure out," Smithies said, his eyes half closed. "Maybe a Democrat will have a chance. Not much of a chance, but a chance."

"What about Daigh?" Cromwell asked. "The Republicans will run him, won't they?"

The Board members paused, looked at Smithies.

"They'll run him and he'll get the Republican nomination," Smithies said flatly. It was not a conjecture or a guess or an opinion. It was a fact. They all accepted it.

"How could a Democrat win?" Cromwell said.

The waitress brought their food. Smithies looked down at the breaded veal cutlet, the bread and butter, the string beans. He took one bite and then talked through the food.

"Depends on the Democrat, John," Smithies said. "Now you've got two things in your favor. First, you've got a good name. Everybody knows the Cromwells, even if they don't know you. Second thing is you can speak. You're an orator. That helps."

It helps? Cromwell thought. Is that all it does? I don't believe it. It's everything.

With part of his mind Cromwell listened to Smithies talk, but a part of his mind reached back and uncovered an old memory . . . he had learned to speak at a speech class at Stanford. He was tall and awkward and he hated Stanford. He hated the girls, the fraternities, the dances, the football games, the classes. He was depressed by everything about the university.

In the speech class everyone had to give a short talk. Cromwell watched with dread as his turn approached. When he stood up in front of the class and looked at all the strange hostile faces his mind seemed to fall into fragments, to go to pieces. They were ready to laugh, ready to hoot him out of the room.

His first words came out cracked and strained. They fell senselessly from his lips. The smiles in the class grew broader. Then he felt a wave of anger; an intense and personal hatred for every person in the class. The anger chilled him; ordered his thoughts, calmed him.

He forgot his prepared speech and began to talk very slowly and deliberately. He did not know where the words came from, but they were orderly and sharp. He did not hesitate once.

He talked about the idleness and stupidity and irresponsibility of college students. He reminded them of the beer parties and the careless way in which they squandered the money given to them by their families. He scolded them. He was sure he was ruining himself, but it didn't matter. The anger was like a white spiky growth that kept prodding him. He felt righteous and sustained; even if he were ruined.

Gradually the faces in the class came into focus and then, with a slight shock, he saw that they had stopped smiling. The boys were watching him attentively and one girl had tears in her eyes. The other girls were looking down at their hands or out of the window. Slowly he realized that they were angry, but not with him. They were angry with themselves or the system or something, but not with him. He did not know how he knew this, but he did. His words made them angry and disturbed, but not with him.

Then, recklessly, Cromwell tried something else. He told the class how they could restore good moral standards on the campus. Without anticipating the words or forming a definite argument his words became reassuring, calm, placating. The angry look left their faces and a sort of relief flowed back into the room. Intuitively, beyond words, he sensed that he had destroyed something that held them together; a common pride or bond or knowledge. And surely, as if he had always known how, he wove them back together; stitched up the common injury. Just a word here, an inflection there and the sureness came back to their faces, the confidence returned. And they were grateful to him.

When he stopped there was a moment of silence in the room. Then they did something they had never done before. They began to clap . . .

. . . "The family and the oratory will take you part of the way, John," Smithies was saying. "But not all of the way."

"You'll need money and an organization," Kelly said. "Lots of money."

"How much money?" Cromwell asked.

"About a half million bucks," Kelly said. "And you have to raise it all in a few months between the primary in May and the general election in November. That's a lot of money and not much time."

"What he means is that you have to have most of it lined up before the primary," Costello said.

"I think I could get it from the voters," Cromwell said.

In his mind he had a brief, vivid image of all the little groups he had addressed in the last fifteen years. Their faces rolled past some inner eye; thousands and thousands of them; all alive with enthusiasm; all loyal.

The four Board men laughed.

"Don't kid yourself, John," Smithies said. "You won't get enough from the voters to pay five per cent of your expenses. You have to get the money in big chunks. Five or ten thousand at a crack."

"Not me," Cromwell said. Their laughter irritated him. "I'm not going to sell out to the Montgomery Street and Spring Street boys just to get their money. I'll go right to the people. I don't need the bribes of the big-money boys."

Instantly, in one smooth, simultaneous action the faces of the four Board men went blank. They bent over their plates and began to eat. Cromwell watched Costello push some frijoles into a tortilla, put the tortilla in his mouth and bite. The brown, smooth substance of the frijoles gushed out at one corner of his mouth. It was a stranger's face. Costello's black eyes went over Cromwell as if he were not there.

"We're just friends," Smithies said softly, as if Cromwell were the only person at the table. His mouth opened to receive a spoonful of apple pie and ice cream. Suddenly his eyes had become hard.

Without speaking to Cromwell the other three Board members finished their lunch and left the table. Smithies stayed in his seat and lit a cigar.

"John, you weren't fair to the boys," Smithies said. "They're tender on talk about big money and bribes. Since all this crap about Artie Samish and graft came out, everybody thinks that if you're on the Board you must be taking money under the table from the big-money boys. Hell, John, I don't even know who the big-money boys are." He paused, put a thumb under a suspender and pulled it out. It came away from his moist flesh reluctantly and left a groove in his shirt. "I don't know them, but they're around."

"I didn't mean to insult anyone," Cromwell said. "But I'm damned if I'll change my ideas just to get the big contributions."

"John, you're a strange sort of politician," Smithies said. "You've been around a lot, but not in real politics. You've got to learn that you have two platforms. One is the official platform. That public and your party will talk about it and it will go out to the newspapers and they'll make up a pamphlet on it. The voters don't pay any attention to it, but you have to do it anyway." He paused, pursed his lips and cigar smoke trailed out of his lips, thinned out and exhausted as if most of it had been absorbed by the huge spongelike body. "The second platform is the private one. That's the important one. That's what you'll really do. They're watching, John, to see what your private platform is."

"Who is 'they'?" Cromwell asked.

"Not the voters. 'They' are the people who are interested in offshore oil, highways, gasoline tax."

"Or liquor taxes," Cromwell said bitterly.

"Or liquor taxes," Smithies said blandly. "They won't come and ask you, John. You have to let them know. Just a line in a speech or talking to one of their people over a drink. Take liquor. It's big business. Know how much beer we drink in this state in a year? About twelve million gallons. In a year that'd make a hell of a big pile of beer cans.

And that's only beer. There's whisky, gin, brandy, applejack, wine, scotch, sour-mash, corn, rye, crème de menthe and a lot more. And the whole damn mess is sold a shot or a bottle at a time. Maybe a hundred thousand people in this state making money off of booze." He inhaled the cigar, crisped an inch of the tobacco in a breath. He smiled at Cromwell. "They know you have to attack the liquor interests and booze barons . . . just to get elected. They don't care about that. But they'll be watching, John. Watching to see what you're really going to do about liquor. Beer-truck drivers, brewery workers, bartenders, wholesalers . . . all watching to see. Maybe a hundred thousand altogether. Maybe more."

Smithies let go of his suspender and it snapped back, shrunk its way into the grooved and waiting flesh, almost disappeared. He stood up.

"I haven't made up my mind yet about liquor taxes," Cromwell said.

"Sure, John. You think it over and let me know. I'm not threatening you. You know that. But a lot of people around the state ask us about politics and we have to tell them something. So when you know where you stand you just let me know. We'll get the word around. You can say whatever you want publicly, but we'll get the real word around."

Smithies paid for the lunch and they left the club. They shook hands at the door.

Cromwell started back toward the office. He kept walking until he came to Pershing Square. He listened briefly to a dark lithe man speak on the advantages of Syndicalism and the general strike and noted that he was not holding his audience. He walked past a group of slim boys with penciled eyebrows and shrill voices who were talking to a girl in a bright flowered dress.

"You're a bitch to wear that dress down here," one of the boys said in anger to the girl. The girl smiled and lifted a hand to her hair and Cromwell saw that it was a rough, calloused man's hand and that the hair was a wig.

"You're jealous, Danny, that's your trouble," the girl said. "You hope the cops pick me up for impersonation. You do, you really do. You're just mean, I hate you."

Cromwell went over to a bench and sat down. He stretched his legs out in front of him and closed his eyes. The sun beat down on his face and from his stomach the thin vapors of gin floated to his nose and the back of his mouth.

They're worried, he thought. When the Board of Equalization starts to worry, it must be good. If Mike can just do what he says he can it'll be all right. I'll make it. Mike's all right; don't worry about him. He's got some things I haven't got, some talents and skills. Something about Mike disturbed him and his mind moved away from the subject. With a glycerin ease his thought poured around other thoughts.

The edge of his mind dulled and things slipped liquidly through his head. With a sigh of satisfaction he lifted a set of recollections to the top of his consciousness; let them slide easily through his mind.

They were the memories of the six girls he had seduced before he was married. Over the years he had sharpened the recollections; the acid of time worked at the episodes until they stood out with a cameo-like perfection: each pinkening breast, each exhalation of breath, the twist of a thigh, the feel of hair and flesh and moisture. Each of them became more perfect and distinct the farther they retreated in time. He had forgotten all the other conversations of his youth, but these he could recall exactly; with a weird precision. Disembodied, separate in time and space, perfect by themselves, each episode came back to him.

As the sun beat down on Pershing Square and the pigeons cooed on the statues and shuffled through the peanut shells, Cromwell lay back, with his mouth open, and recalled the old, polished, well-remembered episodes.

The first had been the cook at their summer place at Tahoe. He had been fourteen. The cook was a strong pleasant woman in her forties. Cromwell walked into the laundry room when she was bent over scrubbing. He saw the long bare flesh of her legs and the swell of her buttocks and a fuzz of hair. She turned around with her hands full of wet clothes and stared at him. She knew what he had seen and for a moment she said nothing, then she squeezed the water out of the clothes and as the mass of soft cloth shrank in her hands Cromwell shuddered. With that her face suddenly worked and she put the clothes down. She backed slowly into her room beside the laundry and Cromwell followed her. Without speaking she wiped her hands on her skirt and took her clothes off and revealed a strong firm body with soft breasts. She walked toward him and felt him through his pants and he felt a great stab of pleasure. She helped him out of his clothes and he smelt the White King soap on her hands and the flesh of her fingers was white and puckered and very soft.

On the bed her legs wrapped around him and her hands rubbed his back.

"Oh my god, you're good, boy, really good," she whispered after fifteen minutes and her eyes were misted. "You god damned boss's son you, you're really good. You . . . are . . . really . . . good" and the last words were hissed through her teeth.

Cromwell almost fainted with pleasure.

The second and third and fourth and fifth had been college girls. He had forgotten their names, but he remembered very precisely their legs and breasts. He remembered the hillsides and car seats where the seductions had occurred.

They came out of the blackness of his memory like bubbles rising from a pool; each episode rounded and bright, connected to the next memory with a thin bright strand. Each thing about them was jewel-like in its precision: the vaccination scar on a leg, the sharp intake of breath as contact was made, the smell of perfume and beer, the odor of grass.

"Mr. Cromwell, Mr. Cromwell," a voice said.

Cromwell opened his eyes and for a moment he could not focus because of the sun and all he saw was the tangled pattern of Pershing Square, the whirling pigeons, the palm trees, the sailors, the statue, the azaleas, the limp bodies of old men dozing. Then he saw the face of Riley, the office boy, looking down at him.

"Mr. Freesmith sent me out to look for you, Mr. Cromwell," Riley said. "He says he wants to talk to you."

"What's all the rush?"

"I don't know, sir. He just said he wanted to see you and for me to find you."

Riley's face was marked over with freckles and bruised by a blunt nose and a tough look.

He is, Cromwell thought, just like an ape that has been taught to read and write, but still carries around a jungle suspicion. Cromwell remembered dimly a story of Kafka's about an ape that made a speech to an academy.

He felt a sudden pique at having the sequence of his recollections interrupted. Usually he went ahead with the sequence, giving each episode its proper time and never being rushed. It had become a sort of ritual. If he started he must run through the entire series.

"Just a minute. I'm thinking something out," Cromwell said. "Just wait and I'll walk back to the office with you."

Just before his eyes closed, when his vision was cut to a tiny bright crescent, he saw a hard understanding grin go across Riley's face. He felt a flicker of outrage and then forgot it.

The sixth girl had been Gloria. He had met Gloria on a summer's day in Atherton when the whole San Francisco Peninsula had just been swept clean by summer fog that was burned off by sparkling sun. His mother wanted him to marry Gloria. They met by the tennis courts back of his family's big redwood house. Gloria came out to the tennis courts followed by her four older brothers. She had a long elegant neck and rather large feet that were covered with white tennis shoes. Gloria and her four brothers stood at the side of the tennis court, racquets in their hands, watching Cromwell finishing a game. Like Gloria they were all tall and lean and tanned and Cromwell knew they would be very good tennis players. Also he knew from the look on their faces that they thought he was poor. Cromwell had an awkward, scrambling style, but he won most of the games he played. Cromwell ran far back and with an awkward powerful smash sent the ball back and won the point. But, as he ran over to meet Gloria and her brothers, he could see a look of disapproval on their faces and he knew they disliked the way he played.

Days later he and Gloria were in the hayloft of the old barn on the back of the Atherton estate. They were both lying naked in the hay and the sunlight came with a muted golden color through a small window. The air was full of hay motes and the edges of Gloria's legs and arms glowed softly. There was the soft smell of fresh hay and beneath it the odor of the older rotting hay. Once a horse snorted and kicked a hoof against its stall.

Cromwell looked down at Gloria's body and through the muted, obscured, beautiful air he studied her: from her large shapely feet, up the length of her legs, to the round swelling of her belly, to the small hard breasts with their madder-brown nipples and then her long neck. He could not remember her face, but he could remember her eyes. They opened slowly and looked at him with a cool detached expression.

"I wasn't the first one," he said softly.

"That's right," she replied. "You are not the first." Her eyes looked calmly at him.

"Who were the other ones?" he asked.

"My brothers," she said.

Cromwell leaned up on his elbow. He felt a strange churning sensation in his stomach; a mixture of shock and curiosity and desire. He felt as if he would like to vomit and also as if he would like to again take her strong naked body in his arms.

"Which of your brothers?" he asked and his throat felt congested and his voice shook.

"All of them," she said and her voice had something of defiance in it.

Cromwell stared at her, and her body seemed to merge with the soft strands of hay; to glow like some strange plant which took on the color of its surroundings. The churning sensation in his stomach no longer had anything of shock or disgust. The sensation was of complete concupiscence and excitement. He bent down and ran his tongue over her lips. Her golden arms came out of the hay and went around his body. Five minutes later he looked down into her face. Her eyes were wide, looking at nothing, the cords in her neck were tight. Her face was flat with pleasure.

"Wait, just a minute," she whispered fiercely. "Don't come now. Wait just a minute."

Her hands went behind his buttocks, pulled him up against her. At the same time she reached up and bit his shoulder. Between her teeth there was a fold of his flesh and he could feel her tongue run over it.

Later he had married Gloria. Since the day of their marriage he could not recall what she had looked like before they married. It was as if she had become another woman. And really, in his mind, he considered her to be two women. He never consciously thought of the woman that he was married to. Only of the long-legged, golden-colored girl whose body was half sunk in the hay.

Cromwell opened his eyes and stood up. Riley was still waiting for him.

"All right, Riley, I've worked it out," Cromwell said.

They walked across Pershing Square, turned up Sixth Street and walked toward the Citrus Building. The cars poured down the streets and above the buildings the smog was a thin yellow layer. Behind the huge plate glass windows of an airline office there was a new bas-relief map of California and they stopped a moment and looked at it. From a cornucopia in the rear of the window a flood of real oranges poured across the tiny miniature oil derricks, the model ships at San Pedro, and rolled up to the tiny wrinkled foothills of the Sierras. One orange rested in the curvature of the San Joaquin Valley.

As they turned away from the window Cromwell felt the sun on his shoulders and, suddenly, he was very happy. He began to whistle.

CHAPTER 19

A Tiny Systolic Splash

GEORGIA AND MIKE looked at land around Ojai and Santa Barbara. It was mostly elegant little valleys already planted in oranges and lemons. They went up to Kern County and watched the big earth-movers working miles of rolling land into a perfect flatness so that the water could flow across it. They went up to Salinas and looked at the long light-green rows of lettuce that ran from the highway out to where the fog broke the precise lines. They went to Modesto, Merced and Tulare. They followed the Friant Kern Canal and saw that where it ended the growing ended and the desert took over again. And this was true of the Delta Mendota Canal and the All-American Canal and wherever there was water.

"Morrie wants to talk to you today," Georgia said one morning over the telephone. "He wants to talk about the farm land."

"Good. I'll be out about two this afternoon," Mike said.

There was a pause and then Georgia spoke.

"I have to explain about Morrie," she said. "He's an invalid. He's been in bed for twelve years. He was a classics student in college and then he went to medical school. But he dropped out after his first year and has been in bed ever since." She hesitated and because Mike said nothing she went on. "He's very bright and he helps Father a lot with business. He'll try to be rude, but don't let it upset you. He doesn't really mean anything by it."

"He won't upset me," Mike said.

"No. I guess he won't," Georgia said. She laughed and hung up.

The Blenner home was in Bel-Air. It sat far back on a knoll and was hidden by a row of California wild oak trees. From the street to the house there was a stretch of closely cropped and very green grass.

Georgia was waiting for him in a parking area behind the house. It was very hot and bright and the sun was reflected off the white concrete. She was leaning against the garage, dozing; with the sun full on her face. She opened her eyes as Mike drove in.

She led him around the house along the side of a large kidney-shaped swimming pool. An old and very thin man was lying beside the pool in a pair of shorts. He had a shrunken, pot-bellied body and his flesh was very white and wrinkled. He had a beard that reached almost to the middle of his chest. He lay there, sweating and ancient, his eyes closed against the sun, his nose hawklike.

"That's Grandfather Blenner," Georgia said. "He's a very orthodox Jew. He wants us to eat kosher, but nobody else in the house wants to. It's a long battle. Sometimes we have separate china services for dairy and meat foods and then someone wants sour cream and the servants mix the plates up and Grandfather won't eat off of them. Once he ate for a week from paper plates because he said that washing dishes together in an electric dishwasher mixed the plates."

They went into the huge colonial style house. They walked through french doors into a library. On a leather couch two girls and a boy, all about twelve years old, were seated. They were wearing levis and saddle shoes. Across from them was a small dark man who was teaching them an opening move in chess.

"Now this is the Capablanca opening," the small man said in an intense theatrical voice. He moved a pawn and looked up with startled eyes. "What would you do now?"

The children stared intently at the board.

Georgia led Mike up to the second floor of the house. She stopped at the head of the stairs.

"You won't let him upset you?" she asked. In the dimness of the hall she looked intently at Mike, bent forward slightly to see his face.

"For Christ's sake," Mike said.

"All right, I'm sorry," Georgia said. "He upsets some people; that's all. I'm sorry."

She opened a door and went in. The room was dim. Venetian blinds covered one side of the wall and through the ivory-colored slats horizontal lines of brilliant sunshine cut into the grayness of the room. A large man with a very white face was sitting up in the middle of a

Hollywood bed. His head did not move, but his eyes looked at them, rotating like marbles sunk in suet. On a table beside the bed was an array of medicine bottles. A bottle of yellow and red capsules had spilled over the table and onto the rug. In the midst of the medicine bottles was a plate with a half-empty bottle of Pabst beer, a glass with dried beer scum on it and a plate with the remains of a ham sandwich.

"Hello, you're Freesmith," the man said. "I'm Blenner. Morrie Blenner."

He put out his hand and Mike took it. The hand was soft and puffy and the middle finger was squeezed tightly by a thick band of gold.

"That's right. I'm Freesmith," Mike said. "How did you know?"

"I've heard you described," Morrie said. He looked up at Mike, almost shyly. "I told Father to see you. I know a lot about you."

Georgia sat down in a chair by the head of the bed, but Mike remained standing. Georgia looked intently at Mike, trying to read his reactions.

"Are you sick?" Mike asked flatly.

Morrie's head moved for the first time. He looked up sharply at Mike and then over at Georgia. Georgia smiled rigidly and then looked quickly at Mike. Morrie began to laugh. His lips pulled away from his large white teeth and at first, for a short moment, his laugh had the pure trilling quality that Mike remembered when Mr. Blenner laughed. Then Morrie was laughing so hard that he was soundless. He was almost convulsive. He slowly turned red and then with an act of will he pulled his lips back over his teeth and cut off the laugh. He pointed a white finger at Mike.

"You're the first person who's asked me that in ten years," he said. "Everyone else is afraid to. They just come in and stand around and try to be cheerful. Nobody else has asked me if I'm sick. That's funny."

"All right, nobody else has asked you," Mike said. "But are you sick?"

"It's really something of a mystery," Morrie said. "Wait just a second."

He fumbled in the bed covers and brought up a stethoscope. He fixed the earpieces in his ears and then pulled back his pajamas. His chest was hairless and his breasts were white and protruding, like those of a young girl. He pushed the diaphragm of the stethoscope against the flesh and winced. Georgia watched him move the diaphragm, her face strained.

"It's cold at first," he said and smiled at Mike.

He probed with the stethoscope, his face expectant and then he relaxed against the pillows.

"Now I've found my heart. At first it's very faint, but then it gets more solid. Go ahead, take the earplugs and listen."

"No, I don't want to listen. You tell me what you hear," Mike said.

"You've heard the old story about medical school students," Morrie said. "How they develop the symptoms of whatever disease they're studying. They all think they've got syphilis when they're studying that and hypertension when they're studying that. The symptoms change with each disease they study. Well, I was like that. Except that I kept having the symptoms of one affliction, even when we stopped studying it."

"What was it?" Mike asked.

"Systolic splash," Morrie said. "A leakage of the valves of the heart. It is characterized by a tiny gush of blood that leaks during the systolic pulse of the heart. Eventually the valves get weaker and weaker and finally the blood just rushes through and the heart fails. With the stethoscope you can hear the tiny splashing sound the blood makes as it leaks through the valve. In medical school they described it. I listened to my own heart and could hear it; exactly what they described. A throb, an easing of pressure and then a tiny faraway splash of blood . . . barely audible."

He opened his eyes wide and turned his head up at Mike. Georgia turned and looked up at Mike also. Her face was expectant.

"Trouble was that nobody else could hear it. All the professors tried to catch it. None of them could hear it. But I could. Every time I used the stethoscope I could hear it."

"Can you hear it now?" Mike said.

Morrie looked shyly at Mike.

"Yes, I can hear it now," he said. "The only cure for systolic splash is complete rest. So I came home and decided to rest. I got in bed and I'll stay here until I die or the systolic splash disappears. It's as simple as that."

"You'll stay here until you die," Mike said. He reached over and took one earplug out of Morrie's ear so that Morrie could hear him distinctly. "It's simple. Everyone tells you that you don't have systolic splash. You listen and hear it. Obviously you're only going to accept the evidence of your own ears. And you'll hear the sound of the splash the rest of your life."

"You're pretty logical and clever, Mr. Freesmith," Morrie said. There was no irony in his voice. "You're probably right. After a while a person gets some very weird notions. For example, at medical school they tell you that the heart is a firm strong piece of muscle. If I want to reassure myself I can open a medical book and look at the diagram of a heart. But sitting here, listening to my heart, I know that it's a big quivering bag full of blood. It is covered with a thin glistening layer of material. Oh, damn is it thin. I can feel the blood pushing against it, trying to burst out. And it's much bigger than they told me in medical school. It almost fills your whole chest. A huge delicate bag that squeezes softly and sends the blood out through all the arteries. And almost anything can break the bag of your heart. I don't want to do anything that will injure my heart . . . Nothing, understand? Really, nothing."

Mike looked at Georgia. She was watching him. She was tense, waiting for judgment. Then she smiled at something she saw in his face. They looked down at the huge sprawling loose body in the bed. Mike knew they were thinking the same thing: of how long it had been since the body had been used, how the muscles must have become shrunken and thin and encased in fat. They thought of how carefully the body moved, anxious not to disturb the rhythm of the big pulsing membrane of blood that rested in the chest. The long careful thought-out avoidance of strain and effort. And the eating of ham sandwiches and beer and potato chips and chopped chicken livers and rich spicy foods that had gone into the production of the soft rich fat.

Then Morrie looked up at them and smiled and Mike felt that he knew exactly what they were thinking.

"I know what would get you out of bed," Mike said and he laughed. "If the Blenner family went absolutely broke, if you couldn't afford this house and twenty-four-hour a day nurse service and expensive doctors then it would be simple. You'd have to get out of bed and start to work."

Morrie laughed. His face wrinkled with delight.

"You're very right, Freesmith," he said. "If we went broke I'd have to get out of bed. But we aren't going broke. Not even close to it." He swung open a low cabinet beside his bed. It held a row of files. "There are the key files on all the Blenner enterprises. Right there. I keep an eye on them. I watch everything. For example, the matter Father discussed with you was my idea. I worked it up; did all the research, everything."

"Did you tell him to see me?"

"Yes."

"Why?"

"It's really very simple. I came to the conclusion that the only sure investment in the future would be something which was supported by

the government. I decided on agricultural land. It was a long complicated analysis and I won't bore you with the details. But once that was
decided then the problem was to find some person who could do something about the political picture, could make sure that politics wouldn't
endanger the investment. That called for a person who knew something about politics, could exercise enough control and still wasn't
committed to someone else or to a political party. It narrowed down
to you. You've got a candidate, you're not committed to a political
party and you're not in politics for political reasons."

"Why do you think I'm interested in politics?" Mike asked.

"I don't know. It doesn't matter. I just had to be sure you weren't
committed already. I don't care what else is involved. We just had to
make sure we didn't have a reformer or do-gooder or fanatic in the
political end of the job."

"You're a pretty logical person yourself, Mr. Blenner," Mike said.

"Thank you," Morrie said. He smiled at Mike and Georgia laughed
with pleasure.

"What do you think about the farm land we looked over?" Mike said.
"Georgia has told you all about it."

"You did very well," Morrie said and his voice lost the shy, half-
playful quality and became crisp. His body shifted, the fat rolled under
the sheets and somehow he was sitting erect. "I was worried at first
because you didn't take along an expert, but you were right. I've had
everything checked out. That desert land down around Rasor is the
best. It's cheap and they say it will grow almost anything if you can
get water into it."

"That's the land we liked the best," Georgia said excitedly. "There's
nothing there now, Morrie. Not a thing. Just a strip of road and some
cactus. With water . . ."

"Can we get the water in?" Morrie broke in and said.

"That depends on a lot of things," Mike said.

"But the most important thing is whether or not Cromwell becomes
governor," Morrie said. There was no question in his voice.

"That's right."

"You can manage that," Morrie said. "The thing you need most is
money. We'll give you that." He hesitated and then looked squarely at
Mike. "Maybe you'd show Georgia the political side of it some day?
How you see the campaign, the people, the issues . . . all of that. Then
she could tell me."

Mike shrugged.

"Whenever she wants," he said. "It's not very complicated. I'm not running it like an ordinary campaign. I can explain it to her in an afternoon."

Morrie nodded and suddenly his face looked bored. He picked up the stethoscope and put the plugs in his ear. He probed his chest with the diaphragm, his mouth opened expectantly. Mike and Georgia stood up and left the room.

"I've never heard anyone talk to him like that before," she said when they were in the hallway. "I was scared for a minute, but he liked you."

"What were you scared of?"

"I'm not sure. That he'd have an attack or something. Maybe that his heart couldn't stand it."

Mike laughed.

"He could stand that and a lot more," he said. "There's nothing wrong with his heart."

Georgia looked at him and then away. She did not speak until they were out in the sun again.

"Would you like to drive down to the beach and have a drink?" she said. "Sometimes I take a thermos of martinis and go down to Santa Monica or up toward Malibu."

"O.K. Let's go," Mike said.

When they went by the swimming pool the old man turned slowly over onto his belly without opening his eyes. He left a perfect outline of his body in sweat on the warm concrete.

They drove out Wilshire and the sleekness of the boulevard ended when they got to Santa Monica. The chinchilla ranches, the clothing stores, the hamburger stands, the enchilada restaurants began. Then suddenly they were at the Palisades and the city ended. The road cut down the face of the Palisades in a sharp slanting angle and all they could see was the Pacific and the sky and the long black strip of the Coast Highway.

They drove for ten miles along the coast and then Georgia told him to stop. He parked by a big rock that reached across the beach and into the water. Steps had been cut down the side of the rock and they walked down and out onto the sand. The sand was clean and tide-washed. There was a thin crisp layer of sand across the surface and their feet broke through into the cooler sand beneath. They put a blanket beside the rock and sat down. Mike opened the thermos and poured out two cups of martinis.

Behind them they could still hear the shrill whine of tires on the highway, but all they could see was the ocean and sand. Far out to sea a couple of freighters were moving sluggishly. Close to shore a fishing boat was motionless; behind the boat a round saclike shadow floated in the water and the net was held up by an ellipse of cork floats. In the sky two jet planes were moving. They were visible as two tiny triangles at the point of a long, perfect, growing vapor trail.

"You don't spend much time with your wife," Georgia said. "Does she mind?"

"I don't think so," Mike said. "She never says anything about it. She's busy with the two kids, clubs, clothes . . . that sort of thing."

Mike's voice was not apologetic or protective. He looked at her curiously; as if she had mentioned a subject he had never thought of.

"I like the beach here," Georgia said suddenly. "Part of the reason I like it is because you look out and see the big ocean and the sky, yet just behind you, just a few yards away, is the city. Here the beach means something; it's a boundary; a limit. Once I saw the beach up at Big Sur. It was all lonely and desolate. I didn't like it. Here the beach is exciting."

Mike leaned back against the rock. It was getting dark and the sand was cooling. The fishing boat pulled in its net and he thought that he could see the silvery bodies of the fish pour over the side. The two jets had moved to the edge of the sky and just at the line of blackness they seemed to come together; to merge into one heavy and beautiful vapor trail. The waves came higher on the beach, began to break around the base of the rock.

They sat quietly, not talking, and when they heard the voice it came as a surprise.

"Whatcha doing buddy, trying to pecker the girl?" the voice said. It was a mocking voice, very loud and firm.

Mike pulled his head back and sat up. Four boys were standing in a semicircle behind them. They were all about twenty years old, but the one that spoke was older than the others. He was wearing a soft yellow flannel jacket and gabardine pants. The cuffs were tucked into shiny black Wellington boots. The boy's hair was cut long on the sides and brushed back so that his head looked long and lean, like an Indian's. His hair was very short on top. He had strong hands and muscular shoulders.

"I asked you, mister, if you were trying to pecker this poor girl here in daylight," the boy said. The other boys smiled.

One of them was swinging a toy baseball bat in his hand. It was about twenty inches long and it hung from his wrist by a silver chain.

"He could be arrested for exhibitionism," another boy said. He pronounced the word slowly; with elegance.

Mike looked at them. The boys all looked the same, black hair, Wellington boots, flannel jackets. "Imagine being arrested for exhibitionism and sent up to City Hall. It's not worth it, mister. You should've taken the babe to a motel. Here, maybe I can loan you the money?"

The boy reached in his pocket and jerked his hand around and his eyes opened in mock surprise. The other boys laughed. The boy took his hand out and it was empty.

"What do you want?" Mike asked. "If you don't want anything shove off."

"Oh, gee, mister, don't scare us like that," the boy in the yellow jacket said. "We're friendly boys. Just rat-rat-racketing along in our car . . . taking a look at places like this to keep an eye on public morals. Just cruising, that's all we're doing."

"The girl's morals are all right," Mike said. "You can leave now. She's safe."

The boy in the yellow jacket squatted down comfortably on his heels. He smiled at Mike. The other boy, who had reached in his pocket, walked over to the thermos bottle. His eyes opened wide as he sniffed the cork.

"Why, George, I do declare they were drinking," he said. "This bottle smells like liquor. Imagine him bringing liquor along and giving it to the poor girl. The rascal."

"Put on your coat, Georgia," Mike said. "We're going."

He stood up. Before Georgia could stand up one of the other boys reached into his pants and took out another toy baseball bat. The boy in the yellow jacket looked up and grinned.

"Now don't be in a hurry. Just because we came," he said. "You were planning something with the girl before we came. We don't want that blanket and all that good liquor to go to waste. Why don't you just go ahead and keep up the good work?" The boy spoke precisely and slowly, almost solemnly. But his tongue flicked at the corner of his mouth.

Mike stood still. He looked down and Georgia was staring at the boy.

"Don't mind us," the boy went on. "We'll sort of stand guard. You just go ahead and skin her clothes off and you can pecker her right here on the beach. Then you'll save yourself the motel money and we'll make sure you have privacy."

The boys, unconsciously, all moved forward a step. The boys swung their bats. They looked down at Georgia.

"If you don't we'll persuade you," one of the other boys said. His voice was choked.

The boy in the yellow jacket jerked his head around.

"Shut up, Eddie," he said. "Don't be rude to the man. He appreciates the help we're giving. Why don't you just start in, mister? Just as if we weren't here. Give her a kiss and get her hot and then skin her clothes off. A piece at a time. Her sweater and her skirt and then her brassière . . . oh gosh I forgot girls wear slips, don't they. I'm sorry."

"Listen, buddy, you're getting yourself in trouble," Mike said. His voice was flat and steady. "Why don't you just take your boys and clear off the beach?"

"Oh, gosh, you've got it all wrong, mister," the boy said. "We want to help you. You've probably been trying to get into that girl for a long time now. We're going to help you out."

"I won't ask you again," Mike said. "Get off the beach."

The boy stayed squatting for a second more. Then he stood up and as he did his face changed. The humorous joking look left his face. He was suddenly, instantaneously, angry and, somehow, it made him look much younger.

"Ya tellin' us to shove eh?" he said. "You and everybody, always tellin' us to shove. Off the beach, off the road, off the Palladium dance floor, off the school grounds, off the sidewalk. Always get off, shove! Awright, big tough guy. Cops ain't around to make us do it. So you do what we say or we'll pound the living piss out of ya. See?" The boy's language changed; the elegance and precision peeled off as if he had been speaking in an artificial voice. "Take 'er clothes off. Take yours off. Then screw her."

The other three boys stood rigid. When they looked at Georgia their faces came undone, went limp and ragged, sagging with excitement.

It was getting dark along the beach and occasionally a car turned on its lights and the faint yellow column of light swung out over the beach. It was still light enough, however, to see the boys.

Mike looked down at Georgia. He could not see her face clearly, but he sensed that she could see him.

"O.K., mister. Just git goin'. Start skinnin' down. Take your clothes off," the boy said. "Then you can help the girl with hers."

"Boy, I'm not going to take my clothes off," Mike said slowly. "The girl isn't going to take her clothes off. There's not going to be a show this afternoon."

The boy looked startled and then puzzled. His face twisted and he looked quickly at the other boys. Then he took out a set of brass knuckles and slowly put them on. He grinned at Mike.

"You a bully, eh? A tough egg," he said softly, with pleasure. "You like to kick people round. Maybe we'll kick you around. Ever see a man worked over with little baseball bats and brass knucks? It's not nice, mister. Now you just start skinnin' down."

"You'd better come after me," Mike said. "I'm not skinning down. Neither is the girl."

He looked down at Georgia. She picked up the thermos bottles and stood up. She held the bottle like a club.

"We'll fight them, Mike," she said in a distinct voice.

The boys looked at one another. The boy in the yellow jacket grinned.

"No. You start up the path," Mike said. He turned to the circle of boys. "All right. Come on in. You were doing the big talking. Why don't you come on in? There's just one guy and a girl. That's all. Nothing to be afraid of."

The semicircle tightened around them. The boys no longer looked young and somewhat overdressed. They crouched forward and in the twilight they looked huge and dark, menacing. Their faces were twisted with excitement. The boy in the flannel jacket took two steps forward, his hand carefully cocked, the brass knuckles gleaming.

Mike's mind slowed down, he watched the boys carefully. Precisely he remembered what the Marine at Nouméa had told him about in-fighting. "There's no man on the face of the earth who can stand a kick in the nuts. An Eskimo, a Russian, a Texan or an African will stop everything and grab their nuts if they get a good kick. It's the first law of in-fighting."

He watched the boys creep in. The two baseball bats were yellow in the half-light and they swung in easy arcs at about shoulder height.

"Me first," the boy in the yellow jacket said. "Let me clip 'im one first. Dirty son of a bitch. Big-mouth bastard. Let me have 'im first."

Georgia threw the thermos bottle at the boy. He put his hands up and the bottle bounced away. For a moment the boy stood straight and unprotected.

Mike aimed and kicked the boy in the groin. His toe hit cartilage

and bone and something very soft. The boy screamed sharply. His
hands shot out in front of him, fingers widespread and grasping. Then
delicately they moved down toward his groin. Mike caught the hand
with the brass knuckles in mid-air, twisted it sideways. The boy's free
hand grabbed his groin, but Mike had his other hand behind his back.

In the dim light the other boys stumbled forward.

"Just a second," Mike said. "I've got his hand behind his back. The
one with the brass knuckles. You take another step forward and I'm
going to break one of his fingers backward over the knuckles. Before
you can get me I'll break every god damned finger on his hand."

The boy in the yellow jacket was still blubbering, but the pain had
eased enough so that he could hear Mike.

"I'm ruined," he said shrilly. "Get me to a hospital. That's what I
need. Christ, I'm ruined. He kicked my nuts off. I can feel one of
'em hanging down my leg."

The boys hesitated. Mike held the boy's hand so that they could see
it. He bent the middle finger backward over the knuckle and the boy
screamed again. But he did not take his other hand away from his
groin.

"All right," Mike said. "We'll just walk up to the highway together.
The three of you first. Me and your buddy second. The girl last. Just
throw your baseball bats on the sand. Right now."

They hesitated and Mike pulled on the boy's finger. The scream
sounded out above the waves, louder than the whir of tires along the
highway. The boys threw their bats down and started up the side of
the rock.

Mike picked up one of the bats, then pushed the boy ahead of him
up the path. When they came out on the highway the night was sliced
by the swift passage of car headlights in the blackness.

Mike let go of the boy. The boy put both of his hands to his groin.
He held himself tenderly and from between his fingers black drops fell.
His eyes were wide with terror.

The other boys took him by the elbows and led him to their car. It
was a cut-down, powerful car with chrome exhaust pipes sticking from
the hood. They eased the boy into the back seat and he screamed as
he sat down. The car shot out onto the highway with a roar.

Mike turned to Georgia. They walked over and got in Mike's car.

Georgia sat forward on the seat with her arms around her knees.
Mike started the car.

"Don't go home, please, Mike," she said. "Drive up the highway.
Up toward Santa Barbara."

Mike drove slowly out onto the highway. He drove past Cliff Rock, past Malibu Beach and then picked up speed when they came to the divided highway. They came to Point Mugu and the highway swung inland. Across the dun-colored salt grass and sand dunes the super-structure of the ships at Port Hueneme broke the last light with a spidery precision. They went through Oxnard and Ventura and they came out on the great swooping highway that follows the curves of the shore. Salt spray blew across the highway. Below Carpinteria the high-way went up abruptly, like an arrow and they came out on the plateau above the ocean. The smell of oranges was strong.

"Can we stop and eat something?" Georgia said. "I'm hungry."

Mike stopped at a seafood restaurant and they had abalone steak. He ordered a bottle of red wine and they were both thirsty. They drank the bottle and ordered another one. When they were finished they drove on toward Santa Barbara. When they passed the first motel on the outskirts of Santa Barbara Georgia looked up.

"Let's stop at a motel," she said. "I don't want to go home tonight."

Mike stopped at a motel that backed up to the ocean. He registered and then drove the car down to one of the neat little cottages. When they went in Georgia turned on the lights and leaned against the bureau. She turned and looked at Mike. Her eyes were very bright and frightened.

"Mike, there are millions of people like those boys, aren't there?" she said. She gestured and took in the world outside the neat motel room. "I never saw them before, but I know that there are millions of them out there."

"Sure. Millions."

"And we're separated from them by just a thin little boundary that anyone can walk across. A few policemen and some laws. That's all the boundary there is. They can walk across anytime they want to." Her eyes were focused rigidly on the wall. "Why don't they just get organ-ized and take over? What holds them back? They could just come walking in anyplace, with their little baseball bats swinging from their wrists. Into homes and schools . . . and everyplace."

"Because they're scared, Georgia," Mike said and his voice was tired. "Because they're scared and because there are guys like me around that know that they're scared. I'm one of 'em, Georgia. I know what they want and why they want it. There are millions of them, you're right. All mad, frustrated, petulant, whining, ugly."

"I never saw them before," Georgia said.

"No. Of course you never saw them before," Mike said. "All you saw was your father and Morrie. They think they're tough and practical, but they're only tough and practical when they're dealing with their own sort. They don't know about those others out there. They don't know that those millions are waiting for some sort of instruction on how to act. And because they don't get instructions, because no one tells them, they act the way they feel. Which is tough and mean. So someone has to tell them how to act; someone has to give instructions and say that you act like so and so and such and such. Morrie can't do it. Your father can't do it. I can't do it. But I can give orders to someone who can. I can tell Cromwell and he can tell them."

"Let's go outside," she said. "Maybe we can walk along the beach."

They went down a steep wooden stairway and came out on the beach. They took off their shoes and left them on the bottom step. The sand was still warm. They walked by a large hotel and the sound of music came from the open windows.

Once Georgia left him and walked down and stood in the shallow water. Then she came back and they continued down the beach. In the deep sand her coltish, almost crippled gait was emphasized.

They went past the hotel and came to a small oval stretch of sand. Georgia sat down. Mike sat down beside her.

Faintly, like an exudation, the cooling ocean gave off the smell of petroleum. It was the thin passing debris left on the surface by the day's passage of tankers.

A faint light came from the sea; a sort of bluish loom that deepened as each wave broke and then receded. The light was good only for close vision, but Mike could see Georgia's features and her fingers clasped around her knees. The light was adequate only for that. If he moved his head back only slightly she blurred and became indistinct.

She lifted her head. In the blue, faint, oceanic light her eyes were invisible except for splinters of light that reflected from the big bony eye sockets. Her head moved and he knew she was looking at him. Her lips parted to talk and then came together silently.

He noticed that his fingertips were trembling against his pants.

"Mike, you're so . . ." she said and paused, her lips open, trying for the correct words. "You're like one of those little glass balls that has artificial snow and a winter scene inside of it. You shake it and the snow swirls around the scene. Except that all one sees of you is the swirling, the snow. All the things are there inside, but I can't get a fingernail into the glass to pry it open. It's all smooth and tough." She licked her lips. "And you don't want anyone inside. You'd fight it;

you'd keep them out." Her voice faltered and Mike felt that she was almost crying.

Mike leaned forward and kissed her. At first he was only aware that there were a few grains of sand caught on her lips. The tiny pieces of sand worked between their lips, like nuclei of irritation. And then from the grains of sand a sensation of raptness went through Mike. He stiffened and was caught in an experience he had never known.

He pushed Georgia back on the sand. He put his hand on her belly and it was round and firm. It felt incredibly feminine. Her mouth opened slightly and he could feel her breath against his tongue.

Dimly, he was aware that her breathing was the rhythm of the ocean; identical with the rise and fall of the waves. He felt caught between the two rhythms; one pressing against his eardrums and the other communicated through his lips. He felt incapable of moving, caught in a luxury of immobility and, on some deep and hidden level, afraid that if he moved he would end it.

Georgia pulled her lips away and sat up. She clasped her knees. Mike felt a huge despair; he was certain that she would deny him.

"Not like this, Mike," she said. "I'll take my clothes off."

He felt a slow surge of relief. She stood up and in the darkness he heard the soft gnash of a zipper, the hissing of cloth over flesh.

When she knelt down beside him he could, in the bluish loom, make out her naked breasts and the swelling of her shoulders. He kissed her on the neck and then ran his hands over her breasts. She breathed into his hair. When he rolled over on top of her, her arms went around him and her hands locked over the small of his neck.

"Mike, I'm not sure of anything," she whispered. "Nothing . . . not anymore. Except one thing . . . I want all of you in me. Not part of you, but the whole man . . . lonely . . . person."

She sighed and seemed to fall away from him.

CHAPTER 20

"A Low But Certain Ground"

*T*wo DAYS later Georgia came to Mike's office.

"You told me you'd tell me about politics today," she said. "Remember?"

"Sure," he said. But he had not and he made no effort to pretend. He grinned at her and then got up from his desk. "Let's go upstairs. That's where the politics takes place."

They took the elevator and went up three floors. They walked down the hall and entered a room with "Computation Room" on the door.

The room was large and bare. In one corner was a table with a Pyrex coffee maker, a stack of paper cups, a box of sugar cubes and a can of condensed milk. Along the other wall was a long low machine. It had a smooth glistening top, thirteen metal pockets and a number of counters on it. The letters I.B.M. appeared on a metal crest. The machine was well rubbed and it hummed. Beside it, on a metal table, were several boxes of cards.

A woman was leaning against the machine. She had the taut, wiry, nervous body of a marathon runner. A cigarette hung from her lower lip. She wore a cheap rabbit-hair sweater. Her breasts were sharp and small and she looked very confident. She looked at them through the cigarette smoke that swirled past her eyes.

Without looking at the machine the woman pressed a button. The humming rose in pitch; took on an eager sound. The woman touched a lever and instantly a stack of cards began to feed from a hopper into the machine. The cards were snapped flat, caught between some rubber belts and flicked into one or another of the thirteen pockets. The stack of cards in the hopper jiggled downward. The pockets, each one balanced on springs, moved downward under the weight of the cards. The cards shot into the metal pockets with a sharp snip of sound that was repeated with incredible speed.

The part of the woman's mouth that was holding the cigarette was half open; caught in a smile of pleasure. Her fingers rested lightly on the machine.

"Here it is," Mike said and waved his hand around the room. "This is the whole thing."

"Where are the men with cigars and the rolls of bribe money?" Georgia asked.

"Later, that comes later," Mike said smiling. "This is the only systematic part of politics. After this stage it's all guess work."

They walked over to the machine. The woman watched them carefully through the cigarette smoke. With a snap the last card vanished into a pocket and at once the machine started to race frantically. The woman pressed a button and the machine was quiet.

"Henri, this is Georgia Blenner," Mike said. "Henri's an expert on IBM machines."

"Hi. Wanna know 'bout the machine, eh?" she asked. She put out a thin calloused hand, stained with nicotine, and shook hands. "I'm really expert on the 101. You know, the electronic statistical machine. I can run this O.K., but I'm really best on the 101. That's really tough."

"Miss Blenner doesn't know anything about the machines," Mike said. "She's not looking for a job."

Henri's face cleared. A soft covert look of hostility vanished and Georgia did not know it had been there until it disappeared.

"Sure, honey. I can tell you all about it. I can run 'em all," Henri said brightly. She lit a fresh cigarette from the butt of the other and threw the butt on the floor. "Christ, I went to that IBM school for a year almost. More 'Think' signs around than you could shake a stick at. They wanted me to hang around and instruct, but I wanted to get out of New York. After I learned the sorter, the ESM and the collator verifying machines I took off for L.A. Where you can grow gardenias in your back yard. Hah."

"Did the last run of cards come in?" Mike asked.

"Just in. Fresh from the offices of Pacific Polling, Incorporated. Or Pac Pol Ink as I call 'em," Henri said.

She took the cover from a box on the table. It was full of rectangular cards. She ran her fingers down the cards with an expert casual motion. They gave off a sharp trilling sound.

"All right. Run them through for the First Question," Mike said.

"Mike, you'd better explain it to me first," Georgia said.

"Sure, sure," Mike said. "I intended to. First, just forget about the Democratic and Republican Parties. This doesn't have anything to do with them. This is just a little operation by Cromwell and Freesmith. All we're trying to do here is see what makes the California voter tick. Later we'll worry about the parties."

Mike walked over to the table and sorted through some documents. Henri leaned forward.

"This is a crazy operation, honey," she said. "I never saw anything like it. Sometimes I think they're nuts."

Georgia smiled at Henri.

"You start with this," Mike said, handing Georgia a blue document. "It's the census abstract plus a lot of other information. Tells you how the population breaks down: how many street cleaners, Negroes, veterans, trade union members, truck drivers, fry cooks, Protestants, Jews, Catholics, foreign born, Okies, doctors and teachers there are. Also how much money they make, the size of their houses, the kind of car they drive, the degree of education, lodges they join and a lot more."

"Then you get your sample," Henri broke in.

"That's right," Mike said. "This abstract describes the Great Beast, the public. Everything we know about it is there. It's what they've been trying to do for centuries; describe the beast. Hobbes' Leviathan, Locke's people, Rousseau's general will; they all took a crack at it and missed. Partly they missed because the Great Beast is changing all the time. Now if we were really scientific we'd go out and snap a picture of the Great Beast, but we can't. It's too expensive and by the time you got to his tail his muzzle would be changed already. So we make up a Little Beast; an animal that's just like the Great Beast, but smaller, diminished. You take what you hope is a good slice of the Great Beast; you include Jews, Protestants, Catholics, poor men, rich men, city dwellers, farmers, plumbers and carpenters. Then you go to Pacific Polling and tell them to go out and find out what the Little Beast looks like."

"They're good," Henri said with admiration. "If your sample includes three Negro, Protestant, non-trade union, pork-chop-eating preachers they'll find 'em . . . or anything you want."

"And in a calm and neutral voice they ask them any question you want," Mike said. "Then they punch the answers into the IBM cards and bring them back here and we run them through the machine. We pay them three dollars for each card. Our sample is made up of three thousand people." He picked up the box of cards and slapped them on the table. "There they are; a Little Beast of three thousand people that's just like the Great Beast . . . we hope."

"Can I see one of the cards?" Georgia said.

Mike handed her a card. It was rectangular and its face was covered with closely printed, black rows of numbers. Some of the numbers had been punched out, leaving tiny slots in the cards. There were no words on the cards.

"Read it for her, Henri," Mike said.

Henri took the card and held it toward the window. She narrowed her eyes and glanced at the pattern of slots.

"Subject is: White. Male. Thirty-four years old. Catholic. Married. Three children. Clerk. Less than four thousand and more than thirty-five hundred a year. No television. In debt."

She handed the card to Georgia. Georgia turned it over.

"Doesn't it have his name?" she asked.

"We don't care what his name is," Mike said. "We just hope that all the other white, male, Catholic, three-kidded, married clerks react the way he does. Oh, not exactly, but within a per cent or two."

"What was the First Question?" Georgia asked.

"The interviewer handed the subject a card with six names on it and asked, 'If these six men were running for governor of California which one would you like to see win?'" Mike said. "Here's a copy of the card."

He handed her a heavy white card with six names on it. They were:

Earl Warren
Wingate Daigh
James Roosevelt
Richard Cutler
John Cromwell
Hiram Johnson

"But Hiram Johnson's dead," Georgia said. "He died years ago."

"That's right," Mike said. "I threw him in just to see how many people would vote for a dead man."

Georgia looked at Mike and she felt a twinge of anxiety, too slight and passing to notice.

"Who did the white, Catholic, married trade unionist pick?" she asked.

"I can tell you without looking," Mike said. "He picked James Roosevelt. Take a hundred low-income Catholics and show them a list like that and they'll pick the name with the strongest Democratic Party associations. So Roosevelt's son, Jimmy, is who they pick."

"Well, check it anyway," Georgia said and there was irritation in her voice. "Maybe this clerk had a mind of his own."

Mike handed the card to Henri. She glanced at it.

"He picked Roosevelt," Henri said. She grinned.

"All right, Henri," Mike said. "Start to run them through. Give me the percentages when you figure them."

She nodded. She put the cards from the box into the hopper and pressed the button. The machine began to purr. She looked down at it with pleasure, moved her fingertips lightly over the quivering surface. Then she touched the lever and the cards began to flick through the machine.

Mike turned and walked over to the window with Georgia. Outside it was bright and clear. Across the air well of the building they could see into a dentist's office. A well-dressed woman, soft and expensive, was lowering herself into the dentist's chair. They could see the dentist's back, his thin neck sticking up out of the white smock, his hands clean and pink.

"This sort of thing isn't very important right now," Mike said. "We won't be able to use it until after the pre-primary Democratic convention."

"What's that?"

"Well, they have cross-filing in this state. A Democrat can file in the Republican primary and vice versa. So both parties have a pre-primary convention to select the man they want for governor. About five hundred Democrats will go to the convention and make the choice. After that is when the information on the cards gets important."

Henri handed him a card. He showed it to Georgia.

"This is the percentage of voters that picked each of the six people on the card," he said.

Warren	35%
Daigh	22%
Roosevelt	18%
Cutler	15%
Cromwell	4%
Johnson	2%

Georgia looked at the card and then up at Mike. She felt a quick, sharp sense of relief and then anger.

"Why, Mike, Cromwell doesn't have a chance," she said. "Only four per cent of the people picked Cromwell."

Father and Morrie think Cromwell has a chance, she thought. And he doesn't. Not a prayer.

"That's right, honey," Henri said. "That's what I told 'em after the first raw tab. He's backing a bum horse. Christ, his man is just a little better than the dead man."

"It could be worse," Mike said. "Much worse."

He grinned and at once the irritation and anger faded in Georgia; she felt wary, cautious.

"Sure it could be worse," Henri said. "Your man could be dead."

She laughed so hard that her eyes watered. Georgia watched Mike. He was bored.

"All right, Henri, run off the results of the Second and Third Questions," Mike said.

Henri turned back to the machine; rearranged the cards.

Mike put the card down on the window sill. He drew a line through three names.

"The voters aren't going to get to vote for all six people," he said. "Johnson's out: he's dead. Warren's out: Supreme Court. Roosevelt is out: he's running for Congress."

The card now read:

Daigh	22%
Cutler	15%
Cromwell	4%

"But Mike, only four per cent of the voters are for Cromwell," Georgia said softly; not confidently, but cautiously, waiting.

"Sure. That's right. But Daigh's a Republican. He'll get the Republican nomination in the primary for sure. Cutler and Cromwell will be going for the Democratic nomination. But only one of them

will be on the primary ballot . . . the one who gets selected by the
five hundred delegates at the pre-primary convention of the Democrats," Mike said.

He spoke as if there were something she should understand. Georgia
shook her head.

"Mike, the Democrats won't pick Cromwell at the pre-primary,"
she said. "They'll pick Cutler. He's got more support, a better chance
in the general election."

"Look, Georgia, there are only five hundred people at the Democratic pre-primary convention. They'll go for Cromwell. And when
they go for him he'll be the only Democrat in the primary."

"But why, Mike? Why would they go for Cromwell?"

"Because there are only five hundred of them and a group of people
that small is pretty easy to influence," Mike said. His voice fell away,
was more cautious. "The pre-primary convention will be in Fresno
in March. Why don't you come up and see what happens?"

"I will," Georgia said. "Look, Mike, I'm not trying to be dumb,
but even if Cromwell does get the Democratic endorsement how will
he beat Daigh? My God, Daigh's a big man in this state. I've even
heard of him. And nobody knows Cromwell. Look at your own statistics. He's just a little more popular than a man who's been dead for
years."

"O.K. Forget about the pre-primary. Assume that Cromwell wins
the Democratic nomination and Daigh wins the Republican nomination. Then they run off in the November election. All right?" He
stepped over to the table and picked up the box of cards which
Henri had just finished running through the machine again. He put
the box on the window sill and opened it. "Now here's your Little
Beast; a diminished tiny copy of the Great Beast. Just the same
except there's only three thousand of him here instead of five million . . . but just the same. Makes the same noises, barks the same,
scared of the same thing, same markings, same gait."

Mike ran his fingers over the cards and Georgia noticed, with
surprise, that his fingers were trembling. Somehow she was embarrassed. She looked across at the dentist's office. The chair and its
chromium and steel appliances glittered in the sun; water bubbled
from a spigot. The dentist stood with a hypodermic in his hand,
a drop of liquid hung at the sharp point of the needle, with his left
hand he made a placating, distracting gesture. The woman looked
sideways and instantly his right hand darted forward, disappeared
in the woman's mouth. The woman's shoes jerked suddenly and her

arms went rigid. The dentist pulled the empty hypodermic from her mouth.

"Go on, Mike," Georgia said.

"A funny thing happens after the primary . . . after the Republican and Democratic candidates have been chosen," Mike said. His voice was only a shade tense. "Just put 'Republican' after a man's name and he'll get forty-five per cent of the votes. I don't know why, but it happens." Mike lifted out a little less than half of the cards and placed them on the window sill. "And the same with the Democrat. He'll get forty-five per cent of the votes just because he's the Democrat. It doesn't matter if they're crooks, cuckolds, veterans, young, old or a damned thing. Just put the label on and each of them will get forty-five per cent of the vote."

Mike took out almost all of the remaining cards. There was only a thin stack of cards left. The rest were on the sill.

"Why does it happen that way, Mike?" Georgia said.

The dentist stepped away from the woman and a burr in his hand glistened with bright red blood.

"I don't know," Mike said. "I really don't. But they do. It's like an instinct; something that tells them to split up; to divide evenly. Jesus, it's uncanny. The Great Beast splits up into two beasts; almost exactly the same size. It always happens."

Georgia looked away from the dentist's window, down at the cards in the box.

"So these cards, the ten per cent left over, they're the ones that really decide the election," Georgia said. "That's it, isn't it, Mike? You just forget about the rest . . . the ninety per cent who are going to vote Democrat or Republican and you concentrate on the ten per cent. That's right, isn't it? They're the ones you try to attract to your candidate?"

"Not attract," Mike said. He grinned. "That's not the way it works. The ten per cent that's undecided is scared. So you scare them into voting for your man. See, that's what nobody knew before. They didn't know why the undecided voter was undecided. But I found out. He's undecided because he's scared."

"And that's what the Second and Third Questions are about?" Georgia asked. "That's it, isn't it?"

"That's right. That's absolutely right," Mike said.

He went back to the table and picked up some papers that Henri had just finished.

"Here's the Second Question," Mike said. He threw the paper on the sill. "Usually the polls just ask who's going to win. But I asked a couple of extra questions."

"What's the Second Question?"

"The Second Question is: 'In general, what sort of things do you worry about?' That's all."

"What did people say?" Georgia asked.

Georgia hesitated. She felt a nag of irritation. She looked out the window again. The woman was sitting up. She opened her mouth and a spill of red liquid gushed from her lips. She smiled wanly at the dentist. His left hand was again reassuring. The right hand fumbled with a new burr; a bright sharp piece of steel.

"I don't know. Communism or the atom bomb or war . . . something like that," she said. "Maybe they're not worried about anything."

"Everybody worries about something," Mike said. "And if they're approached by a neatly dressed interviewer who says their answer will be confidential they blurt it out. Like you. Tell me what you worry about most." He pointed his finger at her. "Go ahead. Don't think. Just say it."

Georgia looked at his finger, at the neat white crescent of his fingernail, the strong bony undulations. She looked over at the machine. It rested quietly.

"I won't tell you."

"All right," Mike said and laughed. "But you had an answer. That's the important thing. Everybody does. And their answers fall into four classes. The first class is what I call 'Economic Worries.' That's for guys who are worrying about payments on the television set or unemployment or the cost of living. The second class is 'International Worries'; like fear of a war, a catastrophe with Russia, reciprocal trade, Red China . . . that sort of thing. The third is 'National Worries.' That's for people worrying about the national debt, Communists in government, politics, that kind of answer. The fourth is 'Personal Worries.'" He grinned and shook his head. "That's for the guy who is worrying about being impotent or his kid getting polio or if the boss likes him or if his clothes look like a hick's. That's the kind of thing you were worrying about. Right?"

"Yes," she said. She did not even feel curiosity. "It was a personal worry."

The dentist took the drill from the woman's mouth and already it was a bright dab of blood.

Georgia looked down at the paper.

Economic Worries	43%
Personal Worries	49%
National Worries	5%
International Worries	3%

"I don't believe it," Georgia said. She stared at the paper. "Only eight per cent of them worry most about war and depression and the atom bomb. The rest are worried about their jobs and themselves. I don't believe it." Mike laughed and she knew he did not believe her. "What can you do with this information?"

"Wait till you look at the Third Question," he said. He put the paper on the sill. "The Third Question was 'What group, in general, do you think is most dangerous to the American way of life?' Any guesses about the results?"

"No," Georgia said. "Not anymore."

"The answers always fall into five categories," Mike said. "Just like clockwork. First, the people who say Big Business or Wall Street or the Bankers or Rockefellers or General Motors. I call that the 'Big Business' category. Second is the 'Trade Union' category. That's obvious . . . anyone who says trade unions or Walter Reuther or John L. Lewis. Third is the 'Communist Conspiracy' category. Fourth is a category you won't like much. It's the 'Jewish Conspiracy' category. That's where you put the people who say the Jews or International Jewry or Bernard Baruch. The fifth group is the 'Religious Conspiracy' . . . people that say the Pope or the Catholics or 'those snotty Episcopalians' or 'those Mormons and all their wives' . . . that sort of thing."

Georgia looked down at the paper.

Big Business	32%
Trade Unions	22%
Communist Conspiracy	11%
Jewish Conspiracy	21%
Religious Conspiracy	14%

"What does it mean, Mike?" she whispered. "How do you make politics out of it?"

"That's the end of the scientific part of it," Mike said. "To make politics out of it you use your common sense, your intuition."

"Sure. But what do you do? How do you use the answers?"

The dentist bent forward and his back tensed. The woman's legs suddenly went rigid, lifted off the footrest. Her hands tightened on the armrests. Then she relaxed. The dentist stood back with a bloody tooth held in heavy forceps. The woman sat up and spit into the bowl. She was very pale. Georgia felt some plug of anxiety pull loose in her mind; she felt almost gay. She was ready for Mike's answer.

"I tell them what to be scared of," Mike said. "It's as simple as that."

He picked up the ten per cent of the cards left in the box. He held them in his hand like a small club and slapped them hard on the window sill. They made a loud cracking sound. Georgia twitched as if she had been hit on the spine.

"Scared?" she asked.

"Sure . . . scared. That's what the rest of them are afraid to do; the politicians, the professors, the clubwomen, the bureaucrats, all of them. They're afraid to ask the questions I asked and if they did they'd be afraid to use the answers. But I'm not. And it's so simple. Most of the voters don't care about politics. They're bored. It's faraway, distant, meaningless. They vote out of habit, because they've been told to vote. And they always vote Democrat or Republican. Everybody knows this, but the more obvious it becomes the more everyone feels that they have to tell the voter that he's smart and has a lot of power . . . that he's important. But the really important ones are the eight or ten per cent that're scared. They're the real independents, the people whose vote can be changed."

"Can you change their vote?" she asked.

"Yes. I can."

She looked at Mike. Then she looked out the window. The dentist's chair was empty. A neat nurse was laying out fresh aseptic linen, shining new tools.

"I want to see you do it, Mike," she said.

He took her arm to lead her out of the room and through the thick soft material of the coat he could feel a slight shivering.

CHAPTER 21

The Convention

$\mathcal{T}$HE ROAD to Fresno was lined with vineyards. Clumps of tiny green grapes hung from the branches. Occasionally a spray rig moved down the rows, the mist drifting from the nozzles in great glittering shreds and making the vines glisten wetly under the sun. Once they passed a winery and saw a railroad tank car backed up to the building. Wine, a huge thick red gush of it, poured from a hose into the tank car and a pink spray rose from the opening; tinctured the air. Far away the hills were green and fresh, but they simmered in the thin heat of early spring. The sunny slopes were already turning brown; very softly and slowly.

"When we get to Fresno, I'm going to get a bottle," Hank said from the back seat. "I need some relaxation. So don't count on me for the convention."

Georgia did not turn around, but Mike nodded.

"Do whatever you want," he said. "I don't give a damn. I just want to get you out of the hospital for a little while."

Hank narrowed his eyes and watched the vines in the distance turn from a green mass into separate vines, separate into rows and then suddenly snap by the window of the car. He was irritated.

"Why don't the Democratic bosses just decide by mail who the candidate will be?" Hank said. "Save the expense of a convention."

"Hankus, you've got bosses on the brain," Mike said. "There aren't bosses anymore in politics. Wait till you see this bunch in Fresno. They aren't bosses."

"Who says there aren't bosses?"

"I say. That's old stuff; Lincoln Steffens stuff. The party boss depended on two things: graft and immigrants. All the immigrants would come trooping into a town; couldn't speak the language and too dumb to find work. So the boss would give them a job wiping blackboards in a public school or a pick-and-shovel job and they give him their votes. With the votes he'd put his people in office and then collect whatever graft was around."

"And I suppose that's all changed?" Hank said ironically.

"Hank, they have machines in Sacramento that would turn up graft money in two minutes. Just take roads. The boss used to let the contract go to his brother or uncle and they'd put in lousy material and overcharge the state. Nobody was the wiser. But now all construction jobs are publicized, bids are solicited, opened publicly and then awarded to the lowest bidder. And the immigrants stopped coming . . . or they started making two-fifty an hour screwing bolts on Fords and they own cottages in the suburbs. No immigrants, no graft, no nothing."

"So nobody gets anything out of politics today?"

"I didn't say that," Mike said. "Hell yes, some people get something out of politics. Take Georgia's daddy. If all goes well he'll benefit. But not by grafting; not by having a boss who's his friend and does him a favor. He'll benefit by changing the law. The law will be changed publicly; out where everyone can see it. That's not graft. That's making something legal that you want to do. Or making something illegal that you don't want done."

Hank saw Mike's grin in the mirror; twisted squat and huge by the distortion in the glass. Georgia looked back at Hank; her face expectant.

Hank started to reply and sensed that it was useless. Not if the laws were changed publicly by the representatives of the people.

"What kind of people come to this convention?" Hank asked.

"Middle-class, college-educated people," Mike said. "Doctors, lawyers, professors . . . maybe a few do-gooding housewives. They're the ones that remember their civic lessons when they grow up: be a doer, an activist . . . work hard and keep politics out of the hands of the bosses. You'll see."

Ahead of them a low-slung truck was moving down the highway.

It was heaped high with freshly picked carrots and a few of the carrots spilled out onto the highway, left a green and orange track behind the truck. Mike rushed down the trail of carrots, exploding them under his tires with a sharp popping sound. Behind the Cadillac the carrots were turned into little mashed heaps of orange fiber. Mike swung around the truck and the highway was clean and unblemished. He went faster.

They came to the big clover-leaf intersection outside of Fresno and ten minutes later they arrived at the Hotel Conquistador. Over the marquee of the hotel was a large cloth sign that said "Welcome Democrats."

When they walked through the lobby they saw a huge blown-up photograph beside one of the lounges. Over the entrance to the lounge a sign said, "Dick Cutler for Governor HDQ'S." The face on the blow-up was round and honest like the face of a very fat child. The picture was so huge, however, that the pores on Cutler's nose, the hairs in his ears and a wart along his chin looked outsized. His face looked as if it were wet.

"That's the competition," Mike said. "He's a big car dealer from San Fernando and he's got lots of money."

Mike had reserved three adjoining rooms for them. When they registered he had their bags sent up and then asked what room Cromwell had.

Only Cromwell and Clara were in the room. Clara was sitting in a chair in the corner. She lit a cigarette, held it in her fingers, her hand cupped over her cheek. She glared at Mike over her knuckles.

"Cutler's already made his move," Cromwell said as the door closed. "His people are giving cocktail parties in every motel in Fresno, they've passed out lapel buttons and you saw that blow-up picture when you came in the lobby. He's going to beat us, Mike."

Cromwell stopped pacing, stood rigidly in one position and scratched his nose. He stared suspiciously at Hank and Georgia and then ignored them.

"Don't worry, John," Mike said. "Things are going to be all right."

"Whadda you mean, all right?" Clara said. "No pins, no cocktail parties, no banners, no placards, no quarter cards, no nothing. And he says don't worry. This isn't a League of Women Voters meeting, Mike. This is the real thing."

Cromwell started to pace again. He searched his pockets for a cigar, could not find one. He picked up a cigarette from a table, stuck it in his mouth. A shred of paper stuck to his mouth. His tongue licked at it.

The cigarette came apart in his mouth, pieces of wet tobacco flecked over his lips. He wiped his mouth harshly. The grains of tobacco were black against the fabric of his sleeve. He dropped the ruined cigarette on the rug and stepped on it.

"It's going to be all right," Mike said. "You just do two things. don't drink too much and don't be seen with Clara." Cromwell wheeled and looked at Mike. His hands trembled across his vest pockets, vainly searching for a cigar. His eyes were angry.

"Listen, Mike, don't go too far," he said. "I'm not . . ."

"At a convention like this people get all concerned about personal morals," Mike said. "Some of them might think that Clara's your mistress. There's been talk about that before."

Clara sat motionless in the chair. She pushed her hand flat against her birthmark, as if it were suddenly hot.

"I'll stay out of sight," Clara said.

"That's a good girl," Mike said. "Now I'm going to go out and scout around a little."

Mike led Hank and Georgia out to the elevator. As they waited for the elevator they heard a door open and Clara came down the corridor. She stopped a few feet from Mike. She carefully looked away from his face.

"Look, Mike. You get him that nomination, understand?" she said. "You said you would. You told him. He left everything to you. Now you get it." Her voice was fierce.

She turned and walked back down the corridor; not waiting for an answer.

"Can you get it for him, Mike?" Hank asked when they were in the elevator.

"Sure, sure. If he'll just do what I say."

"Mike, those Cutler people are awfully well organized," Georgia said doubtfully. "Maybe you should have some cocktail parties and posters . . . things like that. After all it's not a question of money. Father said he'd pay for anything reasonable."

"Look, just leave it to me," Mike said. "These posters and buttons and free drinks don't mean a thing. Everybody does it because they believe they ought to. Nobody knows if it really helps. You just forget about your daddy's money and leave it to me."

They stepped into the lobby and walked over to the Cutler headquarters. The lounge was called the "Room of the Dons" and the walls were hung with thick green gold curtains. Huge pictures showed columns of Spanish Dons on tossing horses moving toward a distant mission. On one of the hangings a huge Catholic monk with a crucifix around his neck was blessing a crowd of Indians who were kneeling at his feet. At one end of the room some tables had been converted into a bar. On other tables were stacks of campaign literature, boxes of shining buttons and quarter-cards with pictures of Cutler on them. The room was crowded with people.

A man walked toward them. He took Mike's hand. Georgia recognized him. It was Cutler.

"Mike, it's good to see you," Cutler said. His face was flushed with excitement. He looked much older than his pictures. His face was wet. "Things are happening, boy. Really moving. I never thought I'd pick up support like this. Really, Mike, I'm as surprised as anyone."

"I'll bet," Mike said and smiled.

"Really, Mike," Cutler said. "Jesus, all the northern counties have already caucused and they're for me . . . Shasta, Alpine, Modoc . . . lots more."

"They're little counties, Dick," Mike said.

"Jesus, we've got two thirds of the delegates to the convention in here. I've already got commitments from over half of the delegates to go for me on the first ballot," Cutler said.

"What do you want me to do, Dick?" Mike asked. "Congratulate you?"

"Quit kidding, Mike," Cutler said. "I've got the nomination for sure." Cutler opened his big red hand, closed it slowly and held the fist up for Mike to examine. "But I'd like to get it on the first ballot and I'd like the party united behind me. So I've been thinking about the lieutenant-governor's spot. Why doesn't Cromwell come in with me on the lieutenant-governor's spot? It'd be a strong ticket. I'll win without him, but I like Cromwell and it's a chance to get party unity."

"Dick, you'd make a good governor," Mike said.

Cutler's tongue came out of his mouth, flicked at the corners of his mouth and a slow grin was suppressed on his lips.

"Don't kid me, Mike," Cutler said. "Cromwell wants the governorship. But he hasn't got the votes. He might just as well face the fact. I'm giving him a chance to be lieutenant-governor. If he doesn't take it, hell with him." The grin went off Cutler's face and he looked carefully about the room, made himself grin again, but when he leaned toward Mike and spoke his words were threatening. "Don't try anything funny, Mike. Let me know before the first session if Cromwell wants a joint ticket. If he doesn't, don't try and foul me up. I'll break your wagon, Mike, if you try and stop me."

Cutler smiled, his automobile salesman's smile, all white teeth and pink skin and the faint odor of Aqua Velva, but the words were tough and hard. Underneath the prosperous fat and the double-breasted suit, Cutler was still muscular and strong. Cutler smiled over Mike's shoulders at delegates and occasionally his hand went up to wave at them. But his other hand was knotted into a ball and was jammed into his pocket.

"Cutler's making a mistake," Hank said in Georgia's ear. "He's getting tough with the wrong guy. When you get tough with Mike it's like giving him permission to ruin you. Did you ever notice that Mike can't get tough with gentle people?"

"No. I never noticed," Georgia said.

She turned and looked at Mike. He was grinning.

"All right, Dick, you've got the votes. You've told me that," Mike said. "But don't try to scare me."

"No one is trying to scare anybody, Mike," Cutler said. Cutler waved at a woman with a big blue and gold "Cutler for Governor" button on her lapel. "But Cromwell is soft, Mike. He's not good on the Communist issue. He's been running around the state for years talking to all those foreign-language groups and Wobblies and the rest. He looks like a radical to a lot of people."

"So did Roosevelt to a lot of people," Mike said.

Cutler hesitated, his tongue flicked again at the corners of his mouth.

"Can I talk in front of your friends here?" Cutler said and glanced at Hank and Georgia.

"Sure. Say anything you want."

"I wasn't going to say anything about it, Mike," Cutler said. "But we've got plenty on Cromwell. We've got sworn affidavits that he spoke to Communists, Syndicalists, radical trade union people. Even anarchists, Mike. Think of that. Maybe you don't know it, Mike, but one of those Italian vineyard workers groups that Cromwell spoke to in the 1930's was an anarchist outfit."

"All Cromwell did was talk to them," Mike said softly.

Hank sighed. Georgia looked at him. He turned his head and whispered to her.

"This Cutler is a sap," he said. "Really a sap. Why doesn't he stop talking? He's just asking for it."

"You know Grover, political editor of the Los Angeles *Post?*" Cutler asked. "Well, he's got a series ready to go attacking Cromwell on this radicalism stuff. The other papers will have to pick it up if the *Post* does, Mike. Look, you better go talk to Cromwell. Tell him he can still run for lieutenant-governor."

A group of women came over and pulled Cutler away. In their midst was a tall calm Negro woman.

Mike turned and winked at Georgia.

"Let's go upstairs," he said. "I want to make a phone call. I'm going to call your brother Morrie."

When they got to the room Mike placed the call to Morrie Blenner with the operator. He whistled as he waited for the call. In a few minutes the call came through.

"How are things going in Fresno, Mr. Freesmith?" Morrie's small precise voice asked. "How is our candidate doing?"

"All right, Morrie," Mike said. "Only one thing can lick him. If he gets over that he'll get the nomination."

"What is it?" the tiny voice on the phone asked.

"A reporter for the Los Angeles *Post* named Grover," Mike said. "He has some articles attacking Cromwell."

"Spell his name please, Mr. Freesmith," Blenner said.

"G-R-O-V-E-R, Robert Grover."

"I'll check it," Morrie said;. "When will they make the nomination?" His words came tiny, jeweled, almost inaudibly to Mike's ear.

"Tomorrow morning," Mike said.

"It will be over by midafternoon tomorrow then?"

"That's right," Mike said. "I'll give you a call when it's over. Don't worry about what you read in the papers. They don't know what's going on. All the reporters think Cutler is a sure bet for the nomination. But they don't know what's happening."

Morrie chuckled.

"I never believe the papers," he said.

The phone clicked dead in Mike's ear. He hung up.

CHAPTER 22

"Bind Not the Madmen . . ."

$\mathcal{M}$IKE woke up. He waited a moment and then put out his hand. Georgia was there. He sat up in bed and called room service. Georgia woke up and reached for a cigarette. Her naked body came up out of the covers and she sat yogi-style.

"Send up a copy of the L.A. *Post* and two grapefruit and a lot of crisp bacon and some buttered toast," Mike said. "You put the butter on the toast. Don't send those hard little chunks of butter. Lots of coffee. O.K.?"

Georgia slid out of bed and stood in front of the mirror. Her figure was far from perfect. Her ribs showed and her wrists and elbows were knobby. Also her legs were too long and the knees showed the effects of being crippled. But her hips were round and firm, the flesh was without a wrinkle and the hipbone was soft and curved. Her breasts were full, but not large, just at the very edge of being lush.

Georgia was showered and dressed by the time Hank knocked on the door. She was putting on her lipstick when he came in. He looked at her without speaking and she flushed.

"Did you see the story in the *Post?*" Hank asked.

"No. Read it to me," Mike called from the bathroom.

"Fresno, March 15. Delegates to the Democratic Pre-Primary Convention in Fresno today were angered by reports that Richard Cutler, candidate for Democratic endorsement for governor at

*the primary, was preparing to blast John Cromwell, also rumored
to be seeking endorsement, as being pro-communist.*

*"Party leaders said that the Cutler charges were based on in-
formation that had long been discredited. It was felt that Cutler's
chances would be endangered by such charges. Cromwell could
not be reached for comment. There was an unconfirmed report
that . . ."*

"O.K. That's enough," Mike said. He came out of the bathroom.
The waiter came in with a large tray and put it on a coffee table.
Mike picked up a piece of toast and put three pieces of bacon on it,
rolled it into a bun and began to eat. "Now that's very helpful of
the *Post* to do that. Who wrote the article?"

Hank looked at the paper.

"Grover. Robert Grover." Hank said. He poured himself a cup of
coffee. "Look, Mike, has Cromwell ever been a Communist?"

"No."

"Then why doesn't he just come out and say so?" Hank asked.
"Just say he doesn't want their support; has never been for them."

"You don't do it that way," Mike said through the toast and bacon.
"See, there are about two thousand Communists in this state."

"Let 'em go to hell," Hank said. "Just count on losing two thousand
votes."

Mike shook his head, chewed on the toast and bacon. He took a
swallow of coffee. Georgia began to eat; not looking up from her
grapefruit.

"You don't get it," Mike said. "The political parties in California
are like two icebergs floating around in the ocean. Most of them
underwater; just a little tip of each one sticking above water. Most
voters won't change parties come what may. They're underwater
and they're happy. At the top, like ants, are the ones that might
change; milling around looking for some reason to jump from one
iceberg to another. I don't know why the icebergs are about the
same size, but they are. Now the trick is to keep them from changing
or to control the change. Or make just the right ants jump from just
the right iceberg at the right time. Control, my boy, that's the answer.
Control."

Mike grinned. Georgia looked up from her grapefruit. Hank
watched her.

"What's all that got to do with the Communists?" Hank asked.

"One thing about a Communist . . . he's a hell of a good worker.

He'll do anything: precinct work, address envelopes, haul people to the polls, ring doorbells, make phone calls. Just as a rule of thumb you can assume that any good worker, in any party, can bring in about fifteen votes . . . he can drag fifteen people up from the bottom of the iceberg and make them jump with him. So multiply fifteen times two thousand and you get thirty thousand votes. That's too many. It might win an election. So Cromwell won't say anything about Communists in this election."

"So Cromwell's going to try for Communist support?" Hank asked.

"I didn't say that, my boy," Mike said. "You don't listen. He just wants to keep them underwater; make sure they don't come out onto the tip of the iceberg and dance around; make people nervous. Don't rock them icebergs, Hank, unless you know what you're doing. That's the art of the politician. The Communists won't support Cromwell whatever he does. What we want to do is just keep 'em neutral."

"Oh, Mike, they couldn't hurt you anyway," Georgia said. "You're just being melodramatic."

Mike shrugged his shoulders. He picked up three more pieces of bacon, rolled them in toast. He sucked the grease from his fingers.

"They could hurt Cromwell if they wanted," Mike said flatly. "Or Cutler or anyone. What would happen if you had two thousand people who went around quietly pulling your quarter-cards down or saying in Jewish delicatessens that they heard Cromwell was anti-Semitic or asking in a Negro liquor store if it were true that Cromwell came from a long line of Mississippi plantation owners? Or say that they came out with a recommendation in the *Daily Worker* for Cromwell . . . the Republicans would smear it all over the state. It would be a real deadly kiss."

Hank watched Mike closely as he talked. Georgia was squeezing the juice out of the grapefruit, watching the spoon intently.

"Mike, aren't you afraid that you or some other guy will calculate things like this and discover you've made a mistake and you've put a Hitler in power?" Hank said. "Look at Germany in 1933. Everyone was trying to play everyone off against everyone else and the result was that Hitler got in."

Georgia hesitated, sat still with the juice dripping from the grapefruit. The spoon filled and then overflowed onto the carpet. She looked down and quickly swallowed the spoonful of juice.

"Sure. It might happen any day," Mike said. "But what of it? Is that bad? Look, Hankus, the first law of politics is: you can't give the people something they don't want. That's true in Russia, Germany, Japan or Timbuctoo. It's true in a dictatorship or a tyranny or a democracy. If the Russian people didn't want Communism it would be over in a week . . . finished, kaput, gone. But they want it; so they get it. So don't worry, Hank. Everything is for the best."

"You know, Mike, for the first time I'm beginning to worry about you," Hank said. "Not a lot, but a little."

Georgia started to say something, but Mike said they had to go to the meeting hall. In the corridor people were moving slowly, talking loud. Several of them had large "Cutler for Governor" buttons on their lapels.

"The Cutler people are organized, Mike," Hank said. "You'd better get moving. I haven't seen a Cromwell sign yet."

"All in good time," Mike said. "That high-pressure stuff can be overdone."

He stopped at a room just outside the entrance to the convention hall. He knocked on the door and it opened. Inside were a half dozen men. They looked like confidential clerks in a bank or stock house; neat, well dressed, modest ties, black shoes. Mike looked at Georgia.

"Keep Hank company," he said. "I'll be out in a few minutes. Got a few things to talk over."

Inside the clerks were writing on pieces of paper with soft lead pencils. They worked quietly, quickly, without smiling. The door closed behind Mike.

"I'm worried," Georgia said. "Mike's so disorganized. Those Cutler people will have all the delegates committed before Cromwell's campaign ever gets rolling."

"Mike's not disorganized," Hank said. "He's beautifully organized. But only on important things. The rest of the things, the unimportant things, he just doesn't care about. If this endorsement is important for Mike he'll be organized. He'll be organized to the last dot."

"He's not very well organized with me," Georgia said. "He's always late for dates, forgets appointments, that sort of thing."

"That's because he's sure of you, Georgia," Hank said. He hesitated a moment and then went on. "He's sure of me too . . . and his wife and Cromwell and Clara. So he doesn't waste any time on us. He concentrates everything on what he feels is important. The thing he's not sure of."

"He doesn't sound like a very nice person," Georgia said.

"But efficient," Hank said. "Mike doesn't worry about everything. He just worries about what's important. Everything else he just forgets, doesn't think of it. Then he concentrates on the few situations or persons that he is not sure about; that are still important." Hank turned and looked directly at Georgia. "Think back. I'll bet there was a time when he devoted a lot of attention to you, when he appeared very organized. And then, after something happened, he pushed you down under."

Georgia stared at him a moment and then realized what he was saying. Her cheeks burned slightly, but she did not drop her eyes.

"You're right," she said. "Until one night at Santa Barbara I had the feeling . . ."

"I don't want to hear about it," Hank said. "I'm not interested in your love life. I just wanted to illustrate a point."

Hank's voice was harsh.

"I'm not sure I'm below the surface now," Georgia said. "I feel . . ."

"You feel you're very prominent in his mind," Hank said. "Well, you're wrong. You're under the surface . . . just as I am. That doesn't mean he can't love you. Maybe he does. Maybe he loves you very much. But he just doesn't waste time on you. It's a wonderful thing about Mike. That's why he can do so much. He's not like the average sharp young executive who gives the impression of being highly organized and spreads equal energies over his wife and kids and business and Rotary Club and college reunion. Not Mike. Mike knows what he has to do. Exactly. He does it. The rest he doesn't worry about."

Inside the hall the "Star-Spangled Banner" sounded. In a moment four American Legionnaires came walking out of the hall. Only their hats and jackets were uniform. Their pants were regular business slacks and they wore natty two-tone sport shoes. The two men with the chrome-covered rifles marched smartly, but the men with the flags were more heavily burdened and they moved slowly as if their feet were tender.

Mike came out of the room across the corridor.

"Let's go on into the hall," he said. "They've just opened the floor to nominations."

They walked in and sat in the rear row. The hall was almost full and several people were moving around the platform. Behind the podium were large pictures of Roosevelt and Truman. A tall fat woman in a mauve suit was standing behind a lectern.

"The chair will recognize Mr. Ernest Eaton," the woman said. "A delegate from the Lassen County delegation."

A tall, almost bald young man stood up. He had small and very shrewd eyes that were lost in a pleasant face. He wore a plaid shirt and his tie was pulled down from an unbuttoned collar. He stood with his hands in his hip pockets.

"Up in Lassen County us Democrats aren't used to big-time political doings," Eaton said. "Mostly we just sit around and talk and try to win a schoolboard election or a few county offices and it's all peanuts, I guess. But we'll learn pretty quick how you do things around here and we'll probably be able to get along." Eaton rocked back on his heels, looked broadly out over the hall. The delegates laughed.

"Eaton is one of Cutler's men," Mike said. "He's been in Lassen County three years and you'd never think he went to Harvard Law School and has twenty thousand a year of inherited money. He picked up that hayseed pose very, very quickly."

"I'm here today to do just one thing," Eaton said. He scratched his head. "That is to place before you the name of a candidate who can win the governorship of California for the Democratic Party in November. He can win for three reasons. First, because he's never been associated with any group or person which has been in the least sympathetic to Communism . . . foreign or domestic. And that's important to California voters."

He paused as a ripple of applause went through the hall.

"Secondly, my candidate is a self-made man. He's met a payroll; he knows the problems of the working man; he knows the problems of business. He doesn't live on inherited wealth or from clipping coupons. He is a man of action," Eaton said. "Thirdly, the person whose name I am going to place in contention has been a lifelong Democrat. He hasn't wavered from party to party; from candidate to candidate. He has always gone right down the line for the Democratic platform and for Democratic candidates." Eaton paused and his big, egglike face creased in a smile. "And that can't be said of all the names you will hear today."

Mike smiled and whispered.

"He means Cromwell," Mike said. "Cutler's really taking out after Cromwell. He's sore because I didn't come around and talk about Cromwell running for lieutenant-governor."

Eaton went on talking, but Mike did not listen. He looked around the hall.

He nudged Hank and pointed at a little group of eight people sitting in the rear of the hall. They were older people and they sat primly in their seats. The women were dressed in cheap dark clothes. The men wore black suits. They sat quietly, listening to Eaton talk. "They're the pension people," Mike said. "They aren't delegates; they're observers. Up from Long Beach probably. They represent the senior citizens, the Ham-and-Eggers, the Townsendites. The pension people send a group to every political meeting in the state. They just sit and watch and then report back what happens. They've got a lot of votes. No one knows for sure, but it's probably a hundred thousand . . . maybe more."

Mike pointed to a small dark Jew who was sitting off by himself. He was a small man and only his eyes, the top of his head and a cigar showed. He studied the tip of his cigar very carefully and then looked up at the ceiling.

"Who is he?" Georgia asked.

"That's Notestein, he's the political agent of the public utility companies," Mike said. "That's not his title and he doesn't even have a position with the utility companies. But he's their man. Lately he's become the political man for the oil companies too. They're starting to worry about the state gas tax getting too high. Oil consumption is starting to go down so the oil people are getting back into politics."

"Who's that big red-faced man?" Hank asked. He pointed at a man sitting in the front row.

"That's Wilson, an AFL man," Mike said. "We won't see much of him. Trade unions don't mean much in this state; not in politics. But we'll see some of the others. Come on, let's get out of here. We'll go up to the room. This will go on for five or ten minutes and then Cutler will give a speech. We can miss all that."

They stood up and walked up the aisle. Hank looked at the rows of identical, round, prosperous faces. They were attentive and alert. They gave off an aroma of Odorono, Aqua Velva, Old Crow, good perfume and tobacco. When they stepped out of the hall at once Hank caught the old, familiar cheap odor of the hotel.

Mike walked over to the little room across the hall and knocked on the door. One of the neat clerkly-looking men opened the door. Mike spoke to him. The man nodded and went into the hall.

When they got to the room Mike took off his coat.

"Call up and order some beer," Mike said. He went to his briefcase and began to haul out documents. Georgia ordered the beer and some chicken sandwiches. Almost at once there was a knock on the door. Mike went over and opened the door.

"Hello, Mr. Appleton, come right on in," Mike said.

Mr. Appleton was a small thin man. He had a long thin neck with red skin, folded like turkey's skin into tough slanting rolls. He looked as if he had once been much fatter and his bones and cartilage had simply shrunk inside the bag of his skin. He had bright glittering eyes, hard with suspicion. His shoes were very shiny and when he sat down he carefully pulled up his pants legs to save the press. His shoes were high. He wore a white shirt, but the points of the collar were tiny and yellow; the kind of yellow that comes from home washing and long careful storage and putting mothballs in linen drawers.

Mr. Appleton was followed by a woman whom he introduced as Mrs. Sweeton. She was formless in a black crepe dress. She wore a long string of coral beads around her neck and they hung to her waist. The beads were large and yellow, like the aged teeth of some large animal. Her fingers never left them alone.

"It's your meeting, Mr. Freesmith," Mr. Appleton said. "You asked for it. So tell us what's on your mind. Mrs. Sweeton and I will talk to any politician that wants to talk to us. We represent the Senior Citizens Clubs of Long Beach, Gardena, Seal Beach, and San Pedro. So what's on your mind?"

"I'm not a politician," Mike said. "I'm just a lawyer."

"That's right, you're just a lawyer," Mr. Appleton said and laughed a dry thin acid laugh. "But maybe you represent a politician. So get on with it."

Mr. Appleton sat with a simple proper arrogance, his back not touching the chair, his feet squarely on the floor. There was something mathematical, precise, clean and unattractive about him.

"How do your people feel about Cutler?" Mike asked.

"Don't know yet. Haven't seen his pension planks yet. Next question?"

"What would you like to see in a platform, Mr. Appleton?" Mike asked.

"You know that. A pension that senior citizens can live on, an act by the legislature that will make pension funds the first obligation on state funds, the administrator of the pension fund to be a friendly person. It's all on the record. We've said it before. We'll say it again. It's all on the record. Next question?"

Mr. Appleton sat calmly in the chair, rigid with confidence.

There was a knock on the door and it swung open. A waiter walked in with a tray on his shoulder.

"Six Pabsts, chicken sandwiches. That right?" the waiter said. He swung the tray down onto a table. Mike pitched him a half dollar.

"Like a bottle of beer or a sandwich, Mr. Appleton?" Mike asked.

"Don't drink," Mr. Appleton replied crisply. "Go right ahead, though. Go right ahead."

"Mrs. Sweeton, excuse me," Mike said. "Would you like a glass of beer or a sandwich?"

Mrs. Sweeton's brown round eyes moved for the first time since she entered the room. She had been sitting quietly, her fat smooth hands manipulating the jagged coral beads. Since the tray came in the room, however, she had been staring out the window. Now her eyes focused on the sandwiches, examined the soft white bread, the green lettuce, the rich mound of potato salad on each plate, the brown heap of potato chips.

As if she were remarking on something novel and unique and quite unrelated, she said, "It's been so long since breakfast," and after a quick look at Mr. Appleton she stared out the window again.

Georgia picked up a plate and passed it to Mrs. Sweeton. Staring out the window, quite obliviously, Mrs. Sweeton took the plate and her soft sure fingers quickly grasped the sandwich and put it to her lips. She turned her head away so that they could not see her take the first bite.

"Would you like me to send out for some tea or milk, Mrs. Sweeton?" Georgia asked.

The gray hair moved quickly and she looked up at Georgia.

"Oh, don't send out for anything. I'll just drink whatever you have here," Mrs. Sweeton said.

She did not look at the glass of beer as Georgia pressed it into her hand. She took a deep drink of the beer and then put a wisp of a handkerchief to her lips to wipe away the foam.

"Go on, Mr. Appleton," Mike said. "You were saying that your aims were all on the record. Do you think Cutler is in agreement with those aims?"

"Can't tell, I said," and his voice was as cool and thin as shredded ice. "If we ever get him on record we'll know what he stands for."

"Your people would not approve him though on what you know now?"

Mr. Appleton brought the tips of his fingers together in what was clearly a gesture of pleasure. "No," he said. "No. We wouldn't approve him or any other pie-in-the-sky, big-bellied lying politician. Not until we saw their platform in black and white. If his pension plank is right we'd support him. But we wouldn't really believe him until we saw the right laws roll out of Sacramento." Mr. Appleton paused a moment. He glanced coolly at Mrs. Sweeton, at the big attractive tray of beer and sandwiches, at the big suite of rooms. "We're not as stupid as we were ten years ago, Mr. Freesmith. And we're a hell of a lot better organized. We don't buy very easily now. We've got a program and we're going to get it. Franklin Roosevelt framed us, Upton Sinclair framed us. But we ain't fools anymore. We're organized."

He stopped abruptly. Like a man who has already said too much. He stopped tapping his fingertips together and twisted his hands together into a mass of thin fingers and white knuckles.

Mrs. Sweeton was frightened and she put the glass of beer down on the table. She continued to nibble at the sandwich. Her teeth worked deftly and minutely at it, wearing it down with nervous small bites so that she chewed incessantly.

"Mr. Appleton, what did you do before you retired?" Mike asked.

"I was a carpenter. Journeyman carpenter. Iowa first and then California. Good one too. Laid three thousand feet of oak flooring in . . ." he stopped slowly and glanced at Mike. "I was a carpenter."

Mike poured a glass full of beer. He did it slowly. He poured the beer down the side of the glass and watched the thin collar of foam climb slowly up the side. He turned the glass upright just as it was perfectly full. He took a bite of a sandwich and then pushed a handful of potato chips in his mouth. The sound of the chips being crushed was the loudest noise in the room. Mike wiped his hand across his mouth and smiled at Mr. Appleton.

"Mr. Appleton, have you got a minute to spare so I can tell you a little story?" Mike asked. "It's a very short story. Very short."

Mr. Appleton's bright birdlike eyes swept over Mike with a look of hard pity. His hands uncurled and he tapped his fingertips together; the five fingers of one hand gently bouncing off the five fingers of the other hand.

"A minute, Mr. Freesmith? I've got lots of minutes," he said and cackled shrilly; a harsh arrogant sound; chickenlike and hard; utterly confident. "Sure. I've got a minute."

"You see, Mr. Appleton, we know a little bit about how our elder
citizens, our senior citizens, were treated in other societies," Mike
said in a soft voice. He looked relaxed and powerless. Sweat marked
his armpits and blotched the front of his shirt. His eyes were half
closed against the heat and the glare of the sun that came in the
venetian blinds. "We know, Mr. Appleton, from anthropology and
sociology that every society tends to protect its most productive members . . . the men and women who can work the hardest, reproduce,
fight wars, invent things, expend energy. In tough times the entire
society will instinctively protect its strongest members. An old
Eskimo will make up his mind one day and wander off into a storm
and die if the food supply gets low enough. He does that because
he knows that if he doesn't the younger people might force him out
into the storm. And so he goes by himself."

"Mr. Freesmith, my people are waiting for me back in the Convention Hall," Mr. Appleton said and his upper lip was drawn thin.
"They want to know what Cromwell stands for. They don't want to
hear horror stories."

"Sure, sure. Just a minute," Mike said. He took another drink of
beer. He put more potato chips in his mouth, crunched them loudly.
"Just hear me out. Let me tell you about one society and the way
it took care of its older people. This was a society that was hard
pressed by its enemies . . . pretty much the way the United States
is today. They began to worry, wonder if they could stand the pressure, argue about how they'd do in a war. They worried about whether
they were strong enough and what they ought to do to keep strong.
What they finally did was have all the citizens take off their clothes
once a year . . . all at the same time. Then they would all gather
naked in the public square and march in front of a committee of wise
men. It was pretty clever really. All the young bucks would see girls
they were interested in and it would become obvious that they were
interested and, even more important, that they were capable of doing
something about it."

Mike paused and looked at Mr. Appleton. Mr. Appleton was looking straight ahead, but his eyes were a deeper color and they had
lost their hard suspicious look. His tongue licked at the corners of
his dry old lips and he almost smiled.

"Round and round the public square they'd march," Mike went on.
"Everyone buck-assed naked. And slowly they'd pair off. The strong
young men would pick the strong young women they liked and the
committee of selection would let them leave the square and wander

off into a grove of trees nearby. Then what would be left would be old people who obviously couldn't do what was necessary. Thin old geezers with skin hanging around their waist and knock-kneed; fat old men with pot bellies and double chins. Old hags; no corsets or girdles to hide them. Just their white old ruined childless flesh for everyone to see. No muscles left; no energy, no nothing. Understand?"

Mr. Appleton was still sitting very straight, but his eyes were unfocused and vague. His face seemed slightly dissolved. He crossed his arms across his chest and rocked back and forth.

"Understand, Mr. Appleton?" Mike asked. "No energy, no nothing?"

Mr. Appleton's eyes roamed around the room and then fastened fiercely on Mike. He nodded savagely.

"Finally the only ones left in the square would be the old people," Mike said. "They'd walk around and around, the old naked men and the old naked women . . . with the committee giving them a cold eye. Waiting to see if the old men still had it in 'em. Or if anyone wanted the old women. The committee didn't say a thing. They didn't do anything. But after a while the old men and women would disappear. They would wander off. Not into the grove but out into the countryside and far away from the town. Out of the society altogether. Gone. Gone forever. Some of the stronger ones became slaves or shepherds, but none of them hung around." Mike paused a minute and took another sip of beer. His teeth, when he bit into the sandwich, looked very white and strong and he looked up with a grin.

Mr. Appleton twisted in his chair. Mrs. Sweeton sobbed distantly and fumbled for the beer glass with her hand. Hank handed it to her and she drank deeply and then wiped off her lips with the back of her hand. There was a smear of mayonnaise on her chin. Mr. Appleton was trying to smile, but his teeth made a thin, chalky sound as they ground together in a desperate effort to keep his chin from gaping and wagging.

"You're . . . you're . . . you're . . . a savage," Mr. Appleton said finally and snapped his mouth shut. Saliva ran from the corner of his mouth and in a bright silvery streak down his chin. He leaned far back in the chair. Suddenly he looked very frail and small; almost childlike. Some thin strong certitude had snapped and his jaw hung open and showed the false pinkness of his dentures and the real pinkness of his tongue.

"No. I'm not savage," Mike said softly. "I'm just trying to tell you the facts of life. The story is true. It happened in Sparta and the man who wrote it down was Lycurgus. Go to the public library and check it out. Read it. It really happened."

"Well, it's uncivilized," Appleton said, but his voice lacked conviction. His tongue clacked softly against his false teeth.

"You have to realize that America's in a crisis today," Mike went on. "Just like Sparta was. Russia is looking down our throat. Pretty soon there's going to be a war. And people will get scared. They'll wonder if we're strong enough to win. And they'll take a cold look at who can help in the fight and who can't. Every society does it, Mr. Appleton. Every single society that's under pressure does exactly that. When we take that cold look we might decide that our senior citizens are a liability; a handicap."

"It's not so," Mrs. Sweeton said. There were tears in her eyes, but her face was not anguished, it was frightened. "No one thinks that in America."

"Look, Mrs. Sweeton," Mike said. "Did you ever hear of euthanasia until recently? Of course not. It's a polite term for murdering people who don't have any good reason for living anymore. Right now euthanasia would only be applied to congenital idiots, incurable cancer and things like that. But let things get really tough; let the battle really begin, and that will change. Someday soon someone is going to suggest that maybe euthanasia be applied to people over a certain age . . . everyone over a certain age would get the works. It's in people's minds already; you can see it stirring around; just waiting to be said. You don't see many young people anymore, but they're talking about it; gnawing away at the idea. Worries 'em. And the word euthanasia keeps popping up."

"You shut up. You're a god damn liar," Mr. Appleton said. He was crouched in the chair, like a tiny defensive monkey. His old splayed carpenter's hands were held out in front of him. "You're lying. That's what you're doing."

"Mike, my God, don't talk like that," Georgia said. She looked at Hank, but he was staring at Mike. Her voice was thin; at the shatter point. "Even if it's true don't say it."

"But it's true," Mike said. "I have to say it. If these people are going into politics they better find out the facts." Mike reached out and shuffled through the papers on the coffee table. He picked up a sheet. "Now, look at this report. It's from UNESCO. It's a survey of what age groups suffered most in Russia and Germany during

World War Two. Do you know that the old people, people over fifty-five, just about disappeared from those two countries? No one knows just how, but they did. They just vanished away. Starved, maybe, or sent off to Siberia or killed from overwork or something. But they're gone. Just as if the Germans and the Russians decided that the old people had to go first."

Mr. Appleton moved his bent, tough carpenter's hands, but no words accompanied them: only a sound like a muted sustained yelp.

"The point is, Mr. Appleton, you don't want to press a society too hard," Mike said. "Those slick young men down in Long Beach that run your organizations tell you you can get anything you want if you just push hard enough. But maybe you'll get more than you bargained for. Maybe America is saving up a surprise to hand you. Maybe you'd better protect yourself."

Mrs. Sweeton stood up as if she were going to leave the room. She stood hesitantly and then Mike looked up at her. He did not smile and for a few moments they looked at one another. Then she saw the sandwiches and the broken look left her face; she went soft with desire. She picked up a sandwich, pushed it savagely into her mouth, roughly jabbed the bits of chicken past her lips. Little bits of lettuce fell unnoticed on her neat black bosom.

"What should we do?" Appleton asked. His voice was thick and mechanical; as if the words were made only by the false teeth.

"The first thing is to forget all that stuff about calling yourselves senior citizens or the deserving elderly or any other term like that," Mike said. "Just face the facts. You're old, marginal, used-up, surplus. All right. How do you protect yourselves?"

Mike picked up a folder. He opened it and spread the paper on the table. The top item was an architect's sketch of what looked like a great sprawling army camp with Quonset huts and barracks neatly arranged in blocks.

"Now the worst problem that old people face is adequate housing," Mike said. "Cromwell is prepared to undertake a state program of old-age camps where everyone past a certain age could have an individual room, adequate food and an issue of clothing. The camps would be out in the country. They would be nicely built. It wouldn't be luxurious, but it would be safe. Now the thing the old people have to do is . . ."

When Mr. Appleton and Mrs. Sweeton looked up their eyes were bright and clear like the eyes of very trusting and loyal children.

They watched Mike's lips move, but they scarcely heard his words. They nodded endlessly.

When the old people left Mike stood up. He walked to the bathroom door. He turned.

Hank spoke very slow, with careful deliberation, reaching measuredly for the words.

"Mike, you dirty, dirty, dirty bastard, you deliberately . . ."

And then he stopped. For a grin was spreading over Mike's face. It was not a hard grin or without pity. But it was certain; absolutely sure.

Mike waited, but Hank did not speak. Mike turned and went into the bathroom.

CHAPTER 23

An Honest Man

THERE WAS a knock on the door and Notestein came in. He wore a large hat that came almost to his ears and hung just over his eyebrows. It was an expensive and subdued hat and he wore an expensive and subdued suit. He took a few steps into the room and stopped, peering out at them. He smiled, almost puckishly; like a person expected to be clownish. Without speaking he took the hat off. The hat was too large, the suit tailored too abundantly as if to show that he could afford plenty of excellent material. His hands manipulated the expensive hat as something to be valued, to be viewed, to be appreciated. He wanted it big. He moved his feet, calling attention to his shoes. They were two-toned, brown and white. The white inserts were made of linen lattice that was worked into the initials T.N. Mike came out of the bathroom and Notestein smiled at him, took a few steps toward Georgia.

"Good morning, Miss Blenner," Notestein said. He held the hat a few inches in front of his belt and turned it slowly with his hands. "'Ve never met, but you I recognize from der picture in society page. Dis man I never met, but it is a pleasure."

"Shake hands with Hank Moore," Mike said. "Hank, this is the only really honest man in California."

Notestein rolled his eyes modestly.

"He jokes," Notestein said. "California is full mit honest men. Lots I meet every day. An honest man is not so hard to find."

"No, Terence is really honest," Mike said. "He represents all sorts of people on all sorts of things and never has a contract. He just gives his word and says how much it will cost to do a certain thing and he does it. Absolutely trustworthy. Never betrays a confidence."

Notestein sat down. His suit wrinkled and the motion forced the tips of six Bering Ambassadors, in aluminum tubes, out of his breast pocket. He glanced down and picked one out. Neatly and quickly he opened the tube, took out the cigar, threw the debris in the wastebasket, bit off the end of the long cigar and lit it.

"I von't offer you cigar," he said quietly to Hank. "I never giff or accept little giffs. Or big giffs for dat matter. Only exactly vot was agreed. Giffs can be misunderstood. Look, dis crazy investigation in England. A big government man is persecuted because he takes a bottle whisky and a toikey from a friend who vants a license or something. And the toikey only weighed seven pounds. Dey should make toikeys that little? You can nefer tell ven dey'll vant to know if you took any favors from Terence Notestein. Now you can say no. But if you took a cigar form Notestein and someday dey put you on de vitness stand, dey vould keep screaming about dat cigar and vould discover it vas an expensive cigar. Ver der are expensive cigars people vill think der is expensive booze and ver booze is der might be girls and ver girls der might be big money. Now I don't giff you a cigar and you can say no, I never took a ting from Terence Notestein."

Notestein sat quietly while Mike filled the beer glasses again.

"How does the convention look, Terence?" Mike asked. "Think Cutler will get it?"

"Can't tell," Notestein said. "Dese tings are crazy. Cutler looks strong now. But you haven't moved Cromwell. I'll vait and see how you handle Cromwell's nomination. Den I tell you."

"Notestein, you're an old hand at this game," Hank said. "You tell me. Has Cromwell got a chance?"

Notestein rubbed his cheek and then leaned toward Hank with his finger alongside his nose.

"Look, Mr. Moore, just in dis room I tell you someding," he said in a grotesquely loud whisper. "It's like a crazy chess game in vich the pawns get excited and can jump around. Dose delegates are the pawns. Excitable people. Cry easy, laugh easy, easy to make enthusiastic. The queen, king, knight and rooks . . . all sensible pieces, all able to deal with one another. But the pawns get excited, jump from

square to square, advance too fast, retreat too soon, jump crazy sideways. You can't win unless you make the pawns do the right things.
Maybe that's democracy. I don't know. How vould a Hungarian Jew
refugee know?"

Notestein fluttered his fingers and drew a crazy erratic pattern. He
put his hands over his ears and shook his head from side to side,
moaning.

"Your people going to support Cromwell?" Mike asked.

"Not *my* people, Mike," Notestein said. His face was pained. "I
don't control what they do. I just giff advice. But you esk a question,
I giff an answer. Cromwell won't get the support that Cutler gets.
My friends would giff more quickly to Cutler. After da primary dey
giff to both candidates . . . Republican and Democrat. But dey would
giff more to Cutler."

"Why?" Mike asked bluntly.

Notestein looked steadily at Mike.

"Cutler is the more steady man, Mike," Notestein said.

He said it as bluntly as Mike asked it. Hank felt warmness for
Notestein; a quick admiration for his directness. He leaned forward
and whispered to Georgia.

"This guy's tough," he said. "He won't roll over like those old-age
people."

She looked up at Hank and nodded, but he could not tell what
she was thinking. He thought she looked frightened.

"What difference does it make that Cutler's more steady?" Mike
asked.

"Mike, dese are hard times for businessmen. Especially businessmen in the oil business," Notestein said. "All kinds risks. Terrible
risks. What if gas tax goes up another cent or two? Maybe people
stop driving their cars so much. Z . . u . . t . . ," he hissed and drew
his hand across his throat. "End of profits in the oil business. Or what
if the oil companies don't get the offshore oil. Z . . u . . t. Or what
if the mineral exploitation clause is cut out of the tax law. Z . . u . . t.
Profits gone, men out of work, equipment obsolete. Awful business."

"They want to be reassured?" Mike asked.

Notestein smiled. His accent had thinned out; was less consistent;
almost as if he were an American who had learned an accent.

"That's it, Mike. Dey want to be reassured. Also, Mike, just as a
friend, I tell you something else." Notestein paused, bit the soggy
end off his cigar and dropped the moist wad of tobacco in the waste-

basket. He lit the cigar and waited until the tip was a round perfect circle of red. "On this Communist thing, Mike, my friends act like pawns. Crazy, wild, excited. Jist on this one thing. I got a theory why dey act that way. Because dey hated Roosevelt and the New Deal and all that government interference with business and when dey were told it was due to Communist agents it was good to hear. Also, Mike, they are scared. Like everyone else. The atom bomb is too big to worry about from day to day . . . but a Communist. Now dere is something you can hate every day in your life. So dey don't worry about the bomb; dey worry about the Communists. That's my theory, Mike."

"They think Cromwell is a Communist?" Mike asked.

"Of course not," Notestein said quickly. "But look at 'im. Rich son of a rich family, but always out talking to anarchist and radical groups. Always signing petitions to get Tom Mooney out of jail. Always supporting the newest thing."

"Terence, your friends are way off base," Mike said. "They ought to calm down and get reasonable. Cromwell's no Communist. They know that. He talks to all those little groups because, taken together, they've got a lot of votes. A thousand Italian anarchists here, a thousand CIO votes there, five hundred longshoremen in L.A. or San Francisco . . . pretty soon you've got enough people to swing an election. You know that, Terence. You get votes wherever you can; the vegetarians, the Bohemian Club, the churches, the Italians, the Portuguese, the sardine fishermen. Your friends think Cromwell is radical because he talks to those little off-beat groups, but he's always been looking toward an election. All those little chunks of votes are what will put Cromwell in."

"But why not talk to the regular Democrats and Republicans a little?" Notestein asked.

"Because the Democrats will be for him if he gets the nomination," Mike said. "He doesn't have to talk to them. But those little blocs of votes, those are the real difference in this state."

"And Cromwell has influence mit them?" Notestein asked. He smiled at the tip of his cigar.

"Sure."

"Evidence, Mike? What is the evidence?" Notestein asked.

Mike stood up and walked to the table. He picked up a briefcase and turned it upside down. A stream of letters poured out on the carpet.

"Pick any one of them," he said. "Read one."

Notestein bent forward. The tip of his cigar broke away, the ash fell on one of the letters. He picked up the letter carefully, slid the ash off into the wastebasket.

At the top of the letter was a small red and white engraved sailboat. At the left was a list of officers.

"Dear Mr. Cromwell," Notestein read. "The Executive Committee of the Balboa Yacht Club would like to thank you for your efforts in having the Corps of Army Engineers widen the Eslay Channel. As you know this makes it possible for the members of this club to use their boats throughout the entire year. This means, of course, that our seamanship skills, so valuable in time of war, are not allowed to grow rusty . . ." Notestein waved the letter in his hand, "and so forth and so on."

He picked up another letter. It was written on plain white expensive paper with no letterhead.

"Mr. Cromwell," Notestein read. "We have watched your efforts to restrict the import of Italian prunes with very real gratitude. As you know the livelihood of many hundreds of Californians is dependent upon a healthy prune industry. It occurs to us that we might best reward your fine efforts by making a contribution to some charity or other activity of your choosing." Notestein paused and said, "The 'other activity' is underlined. That means political contributions." He went on reading from the letter. "We hope that you will see fit to oppose H.S. Bill 7320 which is now pending before a House Committee in Washington. This bill would allow importations of fruits in years when our native crops fall below a certain level, but it overlooks the fact that we already have a surplus of dried and canned fruit which should be disposed of. This un-American attempt to flood our markets with . . . and so forth."

Notestein picked up a handful of the letters and thumbed through them, only glancing at the letterheads. Hank walked over and stood behind him. Some of the letters could be identified by the objects pictured on the letterhead: briar pipes, a tanker moving through the sea, an orange tree in bloom, a bottle of wine, a tiny bicycle. Others were written on plain parchment paper and bore the heavy uniform type of an electric typewriter. Others were written in longhand. Some were from patriotic societies, chambers of commerce, political-action groups. Notestein shuffled them as if they were cards, muttering under his breath.

Suddenly he snapped the letters straight, neatly arranged them in a pile and dropped them on the floor.

He looked quickly at Mike and then threw his cigar butt into an ash tray. He took out a fresh cigar.

"Very good, Mike," he said when he had the cigar lit. His mouth and lips were bored, but through the cloud of smoke his eyes glittered with interest. "But don't kid yourself. It's not enough to win an election."

"It is enough to win an election," Mike said. "We've made calculations. We know how many people those letters represent. Our figures indicate that with the right kind of a campaign after the primary Cromwell would win."

"May I see those figures?" Notestein asked. "My friends would be interested."

"No. You can't see the figures," Mike said and smiled.

Notestein sighed and leaned back in his chair. He nodded his head. "I know, Mike, I know," he said. "I just thought I'd ask."

Hank noticed that Notestein's language had changed as he spoke. At first he sounded like a newly arrived, harried, nervous Jewish refugee. But gradually the accent and the nervousness had dropped away. Hank realized suddenly that Notestein spoke poorly on purpose. He deliberately played the role of a nervous, grasping, outlandish Jew. He was a kind of antic, overdressed person who would do the difficult and dirty things for his clients that they would not do for themselves. His rich and vulgar clothes were a badge of his competence to do the unsavory things that a gentile executive could not do.

"Mike, my friends will be impressed," Notestein said after a moment of silence. He smiled. "Maybe, even, they will support Cromwell. Not publicly of course, you wouldn't want that. But they would want reassurance on one thing. Just one thing."

"What's that, Terence?" Mike asked.

Notestein looked at Mike and then around at Hank. He smiled and shrugged his shoulders as if what he were going to say was foolish; he shared his sense of preposterousness with them. He was the picture of the pacifier, the middle man, the compromiser.

"The Communist thing, Mike," he said. "They're crazy on that. They worry, worry, worry about that. If Cromwell could just make a little anti-Communist statement. Nothing big or dramatic, just a little thing. They'd feel better." He spoke with no trace of accent.

He stood up and walked to the door. He shrugged in his suit, swaggered slightly. He twisted the big and expensive hat in his hands.

"We'll think about it, Terence," Mike said.

Notestein went out the door. The room was silent for a minute.

"So that's how it's done?" Hank said softly. "So that's how you get a governor elected?"

"I don't know if anyone else does it this way, but this is the way I'm going to do it," Mike said and grinned. "Usually they do it the way those people are doing it down in the convention hall. I'm trying a different way."

"Mike, you're crazy," Hank said. "When Notestein reports back to those oil and utility people they'll just laugh. You haven't got a chance. Why, my God, you haven't even got the Democratic endorsement yet. And nobody knows Cromwell. They won't give money to an unknown person. And those old-age people! Mike, they'll slaughter you. You scared the hell out of them. They'll fight Cromwell like he's poison. I think I'd better go get my bottle of bourbon and start relaxing."

Mike drank the rest of the beer from his glass. He walked over to a drawer and took out a fresh shirt. He peeled off the damp shirt and draped it over a chair. He put the fresh shirt on. He opened the door. The booming sound of applause drifted down the corridor.

"Cutler must be giving his speech," Mike said. He closed the door and leaned against it. He grinned at Hank. "Hank, you're just about fifty years too late. You're like all those people down in the hall. They all think that politics is being nice to people; giving them pensions and cocktails and placards and sugary speeches and never offending anybody."

"You think that the American voter likes to have a candidate that sends a little shiver of fear down his backbone?" Hank asked. "Well, I can tell you he doesn't. He likes a glad-hander, a Jim Farley, a candidate that's old-shoe."

Georgia licked her lips and then spoke slowly.

"Hank's right, Mike," she said. "You scared those pension people. They'll fight you."

Mike buttoned his shirt and began to knot his tie. They saw his grin in the mirror.

"Maybe so, but I doubt it," he said. "Maybe people don't really vote for the guy they like the best. Maybe they vote for the guy they're a little afraid of . . . someone like F.D.R. who was cool and aristocratic. Or Teddy Roosevelt who despised them. Do you think the voters liked Lincoln or Woodrow Wilson or Washington? Were they glad-handers? Don't kid yourselves. They were cold fish. Just a little awesome; not a lot, but a little."

"You're nuts, Mike," Hank said. "For a while you really had me

worried. But now I think you're nuts. You'll see when we get down
on that convention floor. They'll ruin you. But you're all right, Mike.
Now how about buying me that quart of bourbon?"

"Right away," Mike said. "Let's go down to Cromwell's room for
a minute. I have to talk to him. You can call room service from there
and have them send up a bottle. Get the best."

When they went in Cromwell's room Clara was sitting on the sofa.
Cromwell was leaning against the bureau. He had a glass in his hand.
The room smelled faintly of good sour-mash whisky.

"Hail, the big fixer arrives," Cromwell said. "The mastermind comes
to announce the terms of defeat."

"Go easy on the bourbon, John," Mike said. "You have to make
a speech this afternoon."

"Not me, Mike. The will of the Democratic Pre-Primary Convention has been plumbed and I have been found wanting," Cromwell
said. "Alas, they have gone for Cutler."

Mike walked over and picked up the bottle of sour-mash. He held
it up to the window. It was a quarter full.

"Don't give him a lecture on drinking," Clara said. She stared
angrily at Mike.

"Not with the whole damned convention marching around and
cheering for Cutler, don't give me a lecture on abstinence," Cromwell
said. "Now that it's all over don't start to lecture, Mike." Cromwell
hesitated and looked down in the glass. He looked up bewildered.
"God, Mike, they're all for Cutler. Tell me, how did you ever think
we'd win?"

"Calm down, John," Mike said. "Cutler's made his play early and
it's a good one. He oiled everyone up with free liquor and steaks and
confetti. But the votes haven't been cast yet. You're still in the
running."

"Don't kid me, Mike," Cromwell said. "It's all over. Cutler's got
the convention sewed up. I don't feel badly. It's all right. But I just
wonder how you ever thought we had a chance. Come on, Mike.
Let us in on the secret."

"Clara, call up room service and get some coffee," Mike said.
"Look, John, Cutler's trying to do it one way. But there are other
ways."

"Don't kid yourself," Cromwell said and his face worked. "I'm a
good loser. I know when it's all over. And it's all over." He repeated
it, softly, unbelieving. "All over."

"Look, John, you're going to be nominated this afternoon," Mike said. "And you're going to give the speech we worked out. With just one alteration. You're going to attack the Communists."

Cromwell laughed. He looked around for the bottle. It was in Mike's hand. He licked his lips, but he did not reach for it.

"It's all over, Mike," Cromwell said. "Even if it wasn't I wouldn't attack the Communist Party. I believe in all parties having a right to put their program before the people."

"You're not going to attack the Communist Party," Mike said. "You're going to attack a Communist."

"I don't know any Communists."

"I'll tell you about one. You're going to attack him in your speech after you've been nominated."

"I thought you said it wasn't smart to alienate the Communist Party," Hank said. "You said you wanted to keep them neutral."

"It's all in how you do it," Mike said. "Pick the right Communist and even the Communist Party won't care if you attack him. I'll pick the right one." He turned and looked at Cromwell. When he spoke his voice was hard. "O.K., John, snap out of it. You haven't got all day. Right after lunch you'll be nominated and you'll win the nomination. I'm going to give you one more shot of whisky to steady you down. Then you're going to drink some black coffee. Then I'll brief you for the floor. You have to play it just the way I say, understand?"

Cromwell took the bottle and splashed an inch of whisky in his glass. Over the rim of the glass he stared at Mike, his face gray, his nicotine-stained lips biting the edge of the glass. Hope washed across his face. He barely tasted the whisky and put the glass down. He stood up and faced Mike.

"Is there still a chance on the nomination, Mike?" he asked.

Mike nodded.

"What if I don't mention the Communist?"

"You don't have a chance," Mike said.

Cromwell looked at Clara and then at Mike. He stood very still, as if he were listening for a signal. His mouth opened slightly and his eyes watered.

They knew what he was thinking. He was thinking of the years that led to this day. The meetings he had addressed, the countless petty letters, the phone calls, the anonymous hands he had shaken, the innumerable commitments he had made, the thousands of faces that had looked up at him as he spoke. All of this was telescoped into a small, heavy recollection. And he thought of the bottles of grappa he had drunk, the empty bourbon bottles he had dumped into hotel wastebaskets, the fashionable martinis he had drunk on the Peninsula and in Beverly Hills and La Jolla, the endless meals of pizza and fried chicken and potato salad he had eaten before he could speak. Aspirin, dirty sheets, midnight caucuses, newspaper stories, telephones, political throwaways, radio microphones, stacks of precinct lists, ditto machines, billboards . . . he thought of the debris of politics and how much of that debris he had created. He thought of the hangovers, county fairs, trotting races, finance committee meetings, county central committees, endorsements, meeting in hot hotel rooms.

And today was the result. Like a tiny clear drop pressed out of a vast, dirty, heaped-up, chaotic harvest this was the result: this day. The drop trembled before him. He had to move it or it would fall, be gone forever.

He licked his lips.

"What is the Communist's name, Mike?" Cromwell said.

"I'll write it down for you on a piece of paper," Mike said. His voice was empty of exultation or relief, as if he had known what the decision would be. "Now all of you clear out. I have to talk to John about his speech. He has to take a shower, brush his hair, put on a clean shirt. They'll start the afternoon session in a few minutes."

As they went out the waiter arrived with a pitcher of coffee.

CHAPTER 24

"As Men Grow More Alike..."

*T*HE CHAIRWOMAN called the meeting to order. Her orchid was wilted and only the throat of the flower was still purple. Her suit was stained with sweat. The delegates fell silent.

Mike was sitting with Hank and Georgia in the rear row. Behind Mike two men were leaning against the wall. Cutler was sitting near the front of the hall. Cromwell sat in the middle of the auditorium, in a little island of empty seats. He bent forward with his chin on his hands and looked somberly out over the crowd.

"You will recall that the name of Richard Cutler was put in nomination this morning," the chairwoman said.

A wave of applause started. Cutler's head came up out of the crowd and he half stood. He grinned and then, at a loss, made a V-sign with his fingers. The applause deepened.

Cromwell rubbed his eyes and then buried his face in his hands. The chairwoman raised her hand. The applause died.

"The chair now declares the floor open to receive any further nominations for endorsement by the Democratic Party for governor," she said.

There was a sudden silence in the hall. Then a man raised his hand and stood up. He was a short man with a round mouth.

"Madam Chairman, I am Jim Bellows from San Bernardino County," the man said. "The purpose of a political meeting is to ascertain the will and desire of the delegates. It is my feeling that this meeting has

reached unanimity. I say that we are agreed that Dick Cutler is the
man we want for governor. I move that the nominations be closed
and Dick Cutler be made the unanimous choice of this convention."

The hall was very quiet. The delegates looked up at the chairwoman. The chairwoman stared at Bellows for a moment. Then a
look of relief crossed her face. At once the uncertainty vanished from
the faces of the delegates.

A roar went up from the delegates. A few of them stood up in
their seats. The Cutler posters began to wave above the crowd. The
delegates along the aisles spilled out of their seats. The round prosperous faces opened and shouted. A serpentine formed and began to
circle the hall. It grew thicker as people spilled out of their seats.
Noisemakers appeared and long bright streams of confetti floated
loosely above the crowd. At once the temperature in the hall rose
and the faces of the delegates began to sweat. The serpentine grew
and thickened and the noise rose to a bellowing din. Someone began
to sing "Hail, Hail, the Gang's All Here" and the identical mouths
opened and roared out the song. Hands reached out from the serpentine and pulled people into the stamping, shuffling crowd.

A woman darted from the crowd and leaned over Mike. Her face
was perspiring and excited. She shouted something and he shook his
head. At once her face went flat with suspicion and anger. She turned
and threw herself into the crowd; was swallowed up, disappeared.

Mr. Appleton and his group of old people sat in their seats, staring
stonily at the stage. Notestein was slumped down in a seat, studying
the tip of his cigar. Cromwell had his head on his arms. The rest
of the delegates were in the serpentine or milling around Cutler.

The chairwoman smiled down damply on the crowd.

"Mike, they can't do that," Georgia said. "They haven't even heard
Cromwell speak yet. It's not fair."

Mike was slumped down in his seat. He shrugged.

"They can do whatever they want," he said. "That's democracy.
Whatever the majority wants they can have."

"For Christ's sake, Mike, stop them," Hank said. "These people are
on a jag. They don't know what they're doing. Go up and tell the
chairwoman that they have to listen to Cromwell."

"I'm not a delegate," Mike said. "I can't."

"I'm going up and tell her to stop it," Hank said. "This is rotten."
Georgia looked up at him. His thin face was pale.

"Do something, Mike," she said. "If you don't do something Cutler's won. And they haven't even heard Cromwell yet. They won't even listen to him."

Mike looked at her. There was a pitiless, angry tear in each of her eyes. Her jaw was hard. Mike reached up and pulled Hank down by the coat tails.

"Sit down," he said. "Don't do anything rash. The chairwoman won't listen to you anyway. She's one of Cutler's people. She didn't expect the motion for unanimous nomination, but she was glad to hear it. She won't listen to you. Why should she? This is pure democracy, Hankus. The will of the people is being expressed."

"Knock that crap off, Mike," Hank said. "This makes me sick. I hope they clobber Cromwell, but they ought to listen to him first. God damn it, Mike, you can make her stop it. Talk to her."

"Not me. Not when the will of the people is being expressed."

"Mike, look at Cromwell," Georgia said. "This is killing him. You've got to do something."

The empty seats around Cromwell had grown. Somehow he looked smaller; crouched antlike in his seat, remote and protective, trying to shut out the sound of the crowd.

The chairwoman spoke into the microphone. Her words boomed out over the hall, shattered against the crowd and were unheard. Her voice became more shrill. The screaming voice pleaded in enormous sharp sounds and, finally, pried a few groups loose from the serpentine. They stood, their faces flushed, staring up at her. Gradually the serpentine broke up; like a segmented collective animal it broke down. The shouting began to die away. There was a moment when the serpentine trembled and then, in an instant, the noise was gone and the people were all individuals again; separate and personal. Reluctantly they began to walk back toward their seats; their faces still tense with excitement.

"It has been moved that the nomination be closed and this convention unanimously endorse Richard Cutler as Democratic candidate for governor," the chairwoman said. "Is there a second to that motion?"

Several voices shouted "Second" from the floor.

"The motion is now open to discussion," the chairwoman said.

On the far right a tall thin man stood up. He wore a dark suit and a white clerical collar. He had a sharp face and the wide cruel eyes of a child.

"The chair recognizes the Reverend John Seaton from Altadena," the chairwoman said.

Mike turned and signaled to one of the two men standing against the wall. The man bent forward and Mike whispered something to him. The man started down the left aisle.

Seaton stood for a long moment without speaking. His eyes ran over the crowd, stopped briefly on groups that were talking and waited them into silence. When the entire hall was quiet he spoke. The words fell from his lips without changing the severe expression on his face.

"I am curious to see how immoral a political assemblage can become without being aware of the fact," he said bitterly. "We have gathered to hear the various people who wish to represent the Democratic Party at the polls. As I understand it, it is our task to hear all of the candidates and then to select the one we feel best qualified."

He paused briefly and looked at the chairwoman. The delegates stirred in their seats and a murmur of voices protested. There was a brittle hostility in the air.

"We have been given a task to do by a large number of party members," he went on. "That they selected us as delegates indicated their faith in our judgment." He paused and went on in a voice that was suddenly thundering. "And we have betrayed their trust. We have not listened to all of the candidates. We have no way of knowing whether we might not make a better selection. We have acted like excitable children; wild with emotion, swept off our feet. Is this what we were selected to do?"

The delegates were silent. They stared at the Reverend Seaton with an odd intensity. It was the women who reacted first. Female hands flicked at clothes that had become disarranged in the demonstration; elbows were neatly tucked back against bodies; the women sat up straighter. Pieces of Kleenex were passed over moist faces; handkerchiefs were pressed against foreheads. The men watched Reverend Seaton stubbornly, bull-like, impatiently.

"Friends, I do not care who you select as our candidate today," Reverend Seaton said. "We have an abundance of excellent candidates. I have no objection to the name that has been put in nomination. I know it is the name of an honest and God-fearing man. But, friends, we have a duty. And we are not doing that duty. We are indulging in an emotional binge . . ." and he smiled wryly, tolerantly, ". . . and we shall have to suffer an emotional hangover."

There was a sigh of laughter.

The men looked aimlessly around the hall. They looked at the chairwoman, their eyes searched for Cutler, and finally came back to

the tall figure of Reverend Seaton. Most of the men shifted in their
seats, looked down at their hands, fingered the badges on their lapels.
They were impatient to make the nomination; they were angry with
the minister.

Reverend Seaton finished. He stood for a moment and looked at
the crowd. His lips moved as if he were praying. Then he sat down.
The hall was quiet.

A hand went into the air.

"The chair recognizes Mr. Bellows from San Bernardino County,"
the chairwoman said.

Bellows' face was solemn. He turned and looked in the direction
of Reverend Seaton.

"Madam Chairman, I have been deeply moved by what the Reverend Seaton has said," Bellows said. "I now believe that I was mistaken
in my motion. We should instead hear everyone. That is our clear duty.
I was swept off my feet, carried away. I apologize to this group. With
the consent of the person who seconded my motion I shall withdraw
my motion."

The crowd stirred. Several people said they would withdraw their
second. The chairwoman looked confused.

"That's it," Mike whispered. "Cutler's through. The thing a crowd
like this hates worse than anything else is to be foolish. And they
feel foolish now. And Cutler did it. All they needed was a preacher
to tell them and they all start writhing."

Hank looked at Mike, startled. He glanced around at the crowd.
Most of the women were staring at Cutler with hostility. The men
looked dazed and resentful. Cutler started to stand, saw the faces of
the delegates, and slowly sat down.

"The floor is open for further nominations," the chairwoman said.

Reverend Seaton's arm rose.

"I am going to put a name in nomination," he said. "I am going
to put this person in nomination, not because I know him or because
I am his special advocate. I am going to put him in nomination because
he has been much discussed at this convention. There are many of us
who would like to hear him. We must judge his qualifications as we
must judge the qualifications of all who ask our endorsement. For
that reason, and no other, I put in nomination the name of Mr. John
Cromwell."

The hall was silent. The delegates carefully avoided looking at
one another. The Reverend Seaton waited, but no one seconded the

nomination. He looked over the hall and there was a fluttering of heads, a bobbing away, a refusal to meet his eye.

Bellows seconded the nomination.

The delegates turned toward the empty seats surrounding Cromwell. Cromwell's head was still in his hands.

"Mr. Cromwell?" the chairwoman said in a strained voice.

Cromwell lifted his head. He looked coldly at the delegates. His lip curled. He stared for a moment at the chairwoman and she flushed. Her fingers reached for the wilted orchid, slowly picked off small pieces of the flower and dropped them to the floor. Absently one of her feet scratched her leg. Cromwell's big, unruly head swung once more over the crowd. He stood up slowly.

Even in a fresh suit he looked disheveled. As he walked down the aisle his Congress suspenders showed. The cuffs of his shirt stuck out from his suit. They were frayed. His vest pockets were crowded with pens, pencils, bits of paper, cigars. When he came to the stairs he paused for a moment. He put his hands on his hips and then slowly climbed the stairs. He walked across the stage, turned and grasped the lectern with his big knobby hands.

He looked out over the crowd; with contempt and disbelief. He rubbed his hand across his neck.

"There are some things more important than the Democratic Party," Cromwell said in a tired voice. "One thing that is more important than the Democratic Party is common honesty. Another thing is common sense. Common honesty would not let us come to this convention already committed to a candidate." He seemed bored, icily removed. "For the purpose of this convention is to select a candidate. Each of you represents a huge voiceless mass of voters. They have asked you to search out a candidate for them. They have given you a trust. In common honesty you must, I feel, listen to all candidates."

A reflex, a shiver of tension went across the crowd. Cromwell moved his big hands to the front of the lectern, pulled himself forward. He looked unkempt, old-fashioned, pedantic, scornful. They watched him with a queer resisting attention, as if they did not want to hear, but knew they must.

Hank watched the confusion vanish from the faces of the prosperous middle-aged men.

"Common sense would have told you that you had fallen victim to a clever campaign . . . so cleverly planned that you parade around with placards that were printed months ago, glut yourselves on free cocktails and canapés, and then persuade yourselves that your foolishness is spontaneity and enthusiasm," Cromwell said. "I do not care that you are manipulated by people who have laid a clever plot for you. But I am disappointed that your common sense was not outraged."

Heads turned toward Cutler, tense with antagonism. The men, finally, had found a common look and posture: they were angry. A voice cut harshly across the silence.

"Come on, Cromwell. Tell us your program. We don't want a sermon. We can go to church tomorrow," the voice said.

It was the second man who had stood behind Mike. He was now sitting in the middle aisle.

Cromwell waited until the gasp from the crowd had died.

"Friend, you are acting for another candidate," Cromwell said. "That is as it should be. Heckling is part of the American tradition. But tonight I am tired and, I confess, somewhat sick at heart. I feel that this assembly has already expressed its opinion. I do not wish to detract from your unanimity. If your mind is made up I shall step down and most energetically support your selection."

A man stood up. It was Mr. Appleton. He was neat, brushed, and orderly.

"I am not a delegate to this meeting," Mr. Appleton said. "I have no legal right to speak. But I represent a large number of senior citizens from Southern California. I came to this convention as an observer. However, I feel compelled to speak out. I must tell you that the senior citizens of California will be outraged when they hear this. They will be shocked when they discover that a great political party did not listen to all of the candidates. They will be shocked when they discover the amount of money that has been expended on liquor and gaudy buttons at this convention. I say to you that a man like Mr. Cromwell, who has honestly and modestly tried to put his name before you, deserves your attention." He paused and shook his head. "I hope that none of you will feel committed by the free liquor you have consumed or the free meals you have eaten."

Cromwell nodded at Mr. Appleton. He looked over his shoulder at the chairwoman. He was tired.

"Easy now, John," Mike whispered. He watched Cromwell. "Very gently now."

"I don't know, Madam Chairman, whether it is any use for me to speak," Cromwell said. "Perhaps the convention has made up its mind in favor of another person. Perhaps, to save time, I should sit down now."

He locked his hands together on the lectern, in full view of the audience. The long fingers twisted together until the knuckles were white. The chairwoman looked at Cutler and then at the delegates. She tried to read the sentiment in the hall and the confusion showed on her face.

"Why, that's very considerate of you, Mr. Cromwell," the chairwoman said. "The agenda is rather crowded and . . ."

"Railroad, railroad," someone screamed. "Cromwell's being railroaded. Give him a chance to speak. The chairwoman is Cutler's person. Let Cromwell speak. Railroad."

The man who shouted was one of the men Mike had spoken to a few minutes before.

The chairwoman stood paralyzed. Another person jumped up and shouted "Railroad." Suddenly the whole auditorium was on its feet shouting at the chairwoman. "Let him speak. Railroad."

The delegates began to boo. Cutler stood up and the boos deepened. Cutler sat down. The delegates began to stamp their feet.

"Mr. Cromwell will give his speech," the chairwoman shouted into the microphone.

Her voice was heard, but the delegates continued to boo, as if the offense called for further punishment. When Cromwell raised his hands they finally fell silent.

"The first thing I shall do as governor is quite simple," Cromwell said. His voice was still cold, but it was no longer condemning. "I shall end the Communist menace in this state. Oh, I know. Everyone is against Communists these days. But one must do more than merely be against Communists. Words are cheap," and his voice was softly loathing. "But actions are hard. And I intend to act. I intend to do very specific and concrete things."

The delegates were rapt.

"I am going to start with one Communist professor who is infecting the youth of one of our great universities," he said. He reached into his vest pocket and spilled some papers on the lectern. He shuffled among them and the thin rustle of papers came over the microphone. He selected one paper from many. He held the paper up. "On this paper I have the name of a Communist professor. I am not alleging this or suggesting this or hinting this. I am telling you flatly and categorically that this professor is a Communist. And he is teaching the youth of this state." Cromwell paused, bent forward and spoke in a whisper into the microphone. "And I shall give you his name."

He paused and there was a vast exhalation in the hall. He moved the paper and the eyes of the delegates jerked.

"The professor's name is Professor E. T. Moon."

There was a slow collective sigh from the delegates. They did not know Moon, but they knew a decision had been made. They were at the end of one kind of confusion. They clapped and stood up on their seats.

"And this is only the beginning," Cromwell said.

The delegates howled. Someone pressed something into Georgia's hand. It was a cheap white card. Scribbled on it with a pencil were the words "Cromwell for Governor." It was carelessly and quickly printed. It looked spontaneous. Stuck in one corner of the card was a pin. She pinned on the card and noticed that all over the auditorium people were taking off the Cutler buttons and putting on the white Cromwell cards.

The delegates beat one another on the back, pointed at the crude cards, felt somehow that the person next to them had produced the cards.

Once a small group started a serpentine, but Cromwell stared at them and they saw his unsmiling face and abandoned the attempt. They got back on their chairs and applauded.

"All right," Mike said. "Let's get out of here. It's all over. Cromwell will give his speech, but he can say anything. It won't matter. He's won the endorsement."

Mike started to push up the aisle. Hank reached out and grabbed his arm.

"Just a minute, Mike," Hank said. He stepped close to Mike. "Seaton was your man, wasn't he, Mike? You arranged it, didn't you?"

"Sure. That's right."

Hank looked at Mike for a moment. Then he smiled. He reached back and took Georgia's hand and led her through the crowd.

Outside in the corridor Clara was leaning against the wall. She was smiling, but when she saw Mike her eyes hardened like splintered agates. She put the scarred side of her face against the wall. Mike walked over to her.

"Well, we did it," Mike said.

"Sure. You did it. You son of a bitch," Clara whispered.

"Stay away from him today, Clara," Mike said. "Cutler might make trouble. Might try to block John's nomination on grounds of moral turpitude. Stay away."

Through the cigarette smoke her splintered agate eyes looked at Mike. She turned and walked for the elevator.

Mike watched her walk away. He turned and grinned at Hank.

"I'll tell you something else, Hankus," Mike said. "Remember Bellows, the delegate from San Bernardino who made the motion to make Cutler the unanimous choice? Well, he was our man, too."

"And so was the guy who started to yell 'railroad,'" Hank said. "He was your man too, wasn't he?"

"That's right," Mike said. "We needed that little touch to persuade the delegates that Cutler and the chairwoman were trying to take something away from them. Funny thing, Hank, try and take something away from people and all of a sudden that's the thing they want."

Hank looked from Mike to Georgia. For some reason he felt an intense anger with Georgia. He was angered by the blank, unknowing way in which she looked at Mike. He wanted, very badly, to shatter the look; to make her share his sense of outrage.

"And the little cards and pins with Cromwell's name on them?" Hank asked. "Those were your idea too. That's what all those clerks were doing in that room. They were printing out those little cards with soft pencils so that they would look real spontaneous and home-made."

"That's right," Mike said. "The delegates had to feel that Cromwell was their man. The cards helped."

The look on Georgia's face did not change. Hank felt his stomach tighten. Inside the hall Cromwell was speaking and the strong, harsh inflection of his voice carried into the corridor although the words were lost and garbled.

"I'm going to go get my bottle now," Hank said. "I'll see you in the morning."

Georgia started to say something, but he had already turned and was walking away. He did not turn around.

CHAPTER 25

Two Calm Men

Robert Grover, head political reporter for the Los Angeles *Post*, walked down the inner quadrangle of Stanford University. He was forty-two years old, proud of his leanness and tended to dress in very severe double-breasted suits. He was also proud of the fact that no one ever took him to be a reporter. On the city desk they said it was one of his great advantages; that he looked like a bank clerk. No cigars, no hat with a press card stuck in the band, no fast talk, no soft lead pencil and wad of yellow paper, no boozy last-minute reporting. He carried a big old Sheaffer pen in the inner breast pocket of his suit. When he took notes he wrote them in a small black loose-leaf notebook and he took them in shorthand.

Not good to leave Fresno before the convention is over, he thought, but this story is worth it. Mike Freesmith had told him what Cromwell would say in his speech so it didn't matter if he was there or not. This Moon business would be the big story of the convention anyway.

Still he hated to be away from the convention. He liked the rich environment of political conventions. He liked to stand in a crowded room, a glass of ginger ale in his hand, and listen to the boozy loud talk of the politicians and the would-be politicians and the fixers and the people that thought they were fixers.

Because he was completely trustworthy he usually knew more about what was happening at a political meeting than any single participant.

One of the keenest thrills, the thing that made the job worthwhile, was to listen to the boastful, extravagant talk of a politician who did not yet know that his throat had been secretly cut by more powerful people. The fact that he was privy to such information, that he knew who was dangling and who was solid, was the reason that Robert Grover liked political reporting.

He came to a door with "Classics Department" printed on it in faded gold letters. He went into a corridor and saw several closed doors. Each of them had a card thumbtacked to it. He found Professor Moon's office and knocked. There was a rustle of paper from inside the room, the sound of a chair scraping and then a voice called softly, "Come in."

Grover liked Professor Moon at once. He liked the neatness of the office, the absence of ashtrays and cigarette butts, the neat piles of lecture notes on the shelf, the orderliness of card catalogues. He liked the simple black suit that Professor Moon wore. He even liked the way Professor Moon's eyes swam uncertainly behind thick glasses.

"Professor Moon, my name is Robert Grover, political reporter for the Los Angeles *Post*," Grover said. He shook Moon's cool small hand and sat down in the chair that Moon pushed forward.

"You can smoke if you want to," Professor Moon said and he took an ashtray from a drawer and put it at Grover's elbow.

"No thanks. I don't smoke," Grover said.

Professor Moon nodded his head with approval and they smiled at one another with understanding.

"What does the *Post* want of someone like me?" Professor Moon asked. He smiled deprecatingly, but his eyes focused behind the thick lenses and peered sharply at Grover. "I'm just a professor of classics you know. No political expert."

"Just a background story," Grover said. "A sort of think piece. We understand that you are doing some interesting work and the city desk thought it might work up into a good article."

"A political article?" Professor Moon asked. "I don't see how . . ."

"Well, you've done some research on communism and religion and art, haven't you? That sort of thing?"

"Yes, but it doesn't have much to do with modern politics. I don't really think your readers would be interested in my sort of thing."

"Just tell me a little about it," Grover said. "Just describe the work generally."

Professor Moon smiled. He shook his head modestly, deprecatingly, but Grover could see he was flattered. Professor Moon reached in a drawer and took out a thin typewritten manuscript.

"These are the first few chapters of a large work I intend to do on the subject," Professor Moon said. He glanced shyly at Grover. "It's very slow work, you know. There is a tremendous amount of material. These few chapters are based on thousands of pages of notes. The whole work won't be finished for years, I'm afraid. Very difficult subject."

"Why don't you just describe it to me?" Grover said. "In simple language, of course. Just as simply as you can."

"All right, in simple language," Professor Moon said. He was pleased. He leaned back in the chair and held the manuscript in his hand. "I got interested in the subject of property relations through my study of art. I discovered that whenever you have a good and free art you have communal ownership . . . communism, you might call it. And when you have good art and communism you also have a strong religious faith. In the time of the Torah, for example, which regulated the life of the ancient Jews, you find communist ownership and very good art and strong religion. And in primitive Catholicism, in the early days of the church you find that natural law, good art and communal ownership all emerged at the same time. Then I found that whenever private ownership emerges art starts to decay and then, almost inevitably, the religious faith starts to crumble. Now that's it. Put much too simply of course."

"Would that mean that Christianity, primitive Christianity that is, was communistic?" Grover asked.

"That's right," Professor Moon said enthusiastically. "You've caught it. And whenever private ownership emerges the religious faith diminishes."

"What about modern Christianity, Professor Moon? Is it communistic?"

"Not yet," Professor Moon said. He leaned forward, laid the manuscript on the table, smoothed it out. "But it's becoming more communistic. Just look at the Social Encyclicals of Pope Leo the Eleventh. Why they're just full of communist notions of ownership and social relations. And Protestant theology is the same way. It's leaning more and more toward communal ownership. And the more it does the deeper the religious faith."

"Do you think that Communism and Christianity are compatible then?" Grover asked.

Grover took out his notebook. He unscrewed his Sheaffer pen and made a few quick notes in shorthand.

"I've always wished I had learned shorthand," Professor Moon said. "It would save so much time taking notes in the library. Especially from the rare books which you can't remove from the library."

Grover smiled at Professor Moon and nodded.

"I was asking if you thought that modern Communism and Christianity are compatible?" Grover said.

"Oh, yes. Sorry. I don't really know much about modern communism, you know," Professor Moon said doubtfully. "But just speaking off the cuff I'd say that Christianity and communism are having an effect on one another; they tend to soften one another. Maybe if it continues we'll find that the simplicity of the primitive Christians will return and adopt some of the ideas of communism. I never thought about it much . . . the problem of modern-day relations between them."

"Could you tell me your best opinion though?" Grover asked.

"Well, I think they are compatible," Professor Moon said. "Communism and Christianity will probably come together and each adopt the best features of the other and we'll have something like what we had after the fall of the Roman Empire: communist ideas of property, religious enthusiasm and good art."

"Would you say, Professor Moon, that you are a Communist?"

"Of course. I'm a communist. Just as I'm a Catholic. Part Catholic and part communist. That's what I tell my classes," he said. He looked at Grover and then leaned forward confidentially. "It rather shocks them at first. They find it difficult to deal with antinomies."

Grover made notations with his pen. He filled one page with sharp angular marks and turned the notebook over. Just as he looked up again there was a knock on the door.

A young man pushed through the door. He was breathing hard. He stood spraddle-legged. There was a press card stuck in the brim of his hat.

"Is one of you Moon?" the young man asked.

Grover closed his notebook and screwed his pen shut. He stood up.

"I'm Norton from the United Press," the young man said. "John Cromwell has just been endorsed by the Democratic Pre-Primary Convention for governor. In a speech he made this afternoon he stated that you were a Communist."

"Me?" Professor Moon asked.

Professor Moon looked at Grover and his eyes diffused completely behind his glasses. His lips trembled and he seemed to be asking Grover for instructions.

"Yes, you," the United Press man said.

"I don't know who Cromwell is," Professor Moon said. "I've never heard of him."

"What difference does that make?" the United Press man said. "Are you a Communist?"

Professor Moon looked around for Grover, but he was already in the doorway, his hat in his hand. Professor Moon was suddenly defenseless.

"I guess I am a communist," he said. "But a very special kind. A kind of scholarly interest led me . . ."

"Professor Moon, I have to leave," Grover said. "Thank you for your time."

As Grover walked across the Quad two men came loping across the asphalt. He knew they were reporters. He hurried to find a phone.

CHAPTER 26

A Monday Morning Ride

O<small>N</small> M<small>ONDAY</small> morning Hank and Georgia drove back to Los Angeles alone. Mike flew to San Francisco from Fresno. He was meeting with some members of the State Central Committee to talk over Cromwell's campaign.

Georgia was driving. Hank was asleep. When they were just outside of Bakersfield, Hank groaned once and turned over.

"Do you want something to eat, Hank?" she said.

"Sure. What I need is some chili," Hank said. His eyes were bloodshot. He was hung over. They had already stopped three times so that Hank could eat. Each time he wolfed down a sandwich or a piece of pie à la mode and walked back to the car and promptly went to sleep.

"I'll pull in at the next restaurant," Georgia said. "You're the first person I ever saw who wanted to eat when he had a hangover. Most people just want black coffee." Hank said nothing; he stared out at the fields, watched a truck load of pickers jog across a corduroy road. "Where did you go last night?"

"Out. Someplace in Fresno," Hank said. "A couple of bars and then a dance hall. God, I haven't danced for years. I must have danced thirty dances last night. I think I had a good time. I feel good now. As if I had a good time. Maybe I did."

"You're sure you want something to eat?" Georgia asked.

"Yes. I'm sure. I like to eat when I'm hung. Also I like to talk.

I've been sleeping so I wouldn't talk. I get boring. It's funny, I feel miserable physically, but inside I feel sort of weak and purged. Like after you take a cathartic. It makes me want to talk. Just tell me to stop if I get boring or euphoric."

Georgia pulled over and parked by a small restaurant. They went in and Hank ordered a bowl of chili beans. Georgia had a cup of coffee. Hank gulped down the beans and ate three cellophane packets of crackers. He picked up a half dozen packets of the crackers when he left. Georgia continued to drive. Hank munched on the crackers.

"Mike told me that you were going to specialize in psychiatry, but you switched to surgery," Georgia said.

"That's right. There's more money in psychiatry, but I decided that surgery was more interesting."

"Really? I would think psychiatry would be very interesting."

Hank opened another packet of crackers. He ate them before he replied, "I was lying. It is more interesting than surgery. I've never talked it over with anyone, not even Mike. But I don't care now. I went into surgery because I couldn't stand psychiatry."

"Do you really want to talk about it?"

"Sure I want to talk about it," Hank said. He leaned back in the corner of the seat, closed his eyes and talked through the crackers. "I spent three years studying psychiatry, why shouldn't I talk about it? I was the hottest psychiatry intern they had. A real whiz. Super-ego, id, ego, narcissism, insulin shock, Rohrschach test, T.A.T., hydrotherapy, Ménière's Syndrome, hypertonia, ataxia, stuttering, paranoia, negativism, regression, metrazol, hypnogogic reverie, oneirosis . . . Jesus, I knew everything. I was going to be the boy wonder of psychiatry. I was going to save a tortured world . . . ole Hank Moore, all by himself."

He opened his eyes, reached for another packet of crackers. He opened the packet and put two crackers in his mouth.

"Then they gave me my first case," Hank said. "Jesus, I went at it carefully. She was thirty-five years old, married, four kids, a Catholic. I found out everything about her, just the way I'd been taught. Not forcing her, but letting her bring it out. She complained of headaches, walked with a limp, had occasional tinnitus and almost constant scintillating scotoma. . . ."

"What's that?" Georgia asked. "Scintillating scotoma?"

"Bright spots before the eyes," Hank said and laughed. "Silly, eh? But she had more, much more than that. And I put it all down, the

way you're supposed to. Neatly in a notebook. Subject was one of
six siblings. Cruel, dominant father. Beat the kids on Saturday night
before he went out and got drunk. Retiring mother. Subject had
great fear of sex during menarche. Didn't know where babies came
from until she was three months' pregnant. Married a shy linoleum
salesman. Never experienced orgasm. Associated sex with pain, rape,
bleeding. Subject suffered from intense depression, pains in abdomen,
and fear of high places. That's just part of it, just a fraction. I got
it all down, worked it over, slaved on it, consulted with experts, went
through the books, listened endlessly to this fat whining woman talk
and put down every single thing she said."

"What was wrong with her?" Georgia asked.

"I never found out. I gave her the most thorough physical that any
person ever had. Blood count, urinalysis, regular X-rays, barium meal
X-rays, spinal tap, Stanford-Binet I.Q. test, an ataxigraph, campimeter
. . . there was nothing I didn't do to that lady. I thought she might
have Ménière's Syndrome so I tested for sludging of the blood in the
labyrinth of the ear. No results. I discovered she had an enormous
amount of water in her body and she said she ate salt in quantities
. . . half a cupful a day. She heaped it on meat, eggs and potatoes. So
I rushed to Freud and read about the symbolic meaning of salt and
concluded that she was suffering from a suppressed desire for im-
mortality. She was literally trying to pickle herself, make a brine out
of her blood and lymph. So that she could keep that defective, hulking, worn-out body of hers forever. The notebook got bigger and
bigger. They gave me a secretary to transcribe the notes. Everyone
thought it was going to be one of those epic cases; go down in all
the textbooks. Moore's Syndrome they would call it."

"Did you cure her?" Georgia asked.

"Let me finish," Hank said. "I put her on a salt-free diet and nothing
happened except she lost thirty pounds. She just liked salt. She didn't
protest when I put her on the diet. She said the food was a little flat,
but that was all. Matter of fact she didn't mind anything. She'd sit
there, smiling a little anxiously, trying to be co-operative. She said
her headaches were worse at certain times. It took me a month to discover that she had them worse in intercourse. Whenever she felt her
husband tighten up and knew he was having orgasm the headache
would hit; flash through her head like a bullet. So back to the books I
went; Reik, Freud, Carveth, Alexander. Hatred and revenge on Father,
I concluded. Suppressed and emerged physically in the form of a

crashing, instantaneous headache whenever she knew that any man was experiencing pleasure with her body.

"I was sure of the diagnosis, but she didn't respond well to treatment. I probed her about her feelings during intercourse, tried to get her to admit that she hated it. But she would just blush and say, no, she really liked intercourse. In fact she was after her husband all the time for a little extra piece.

"I gave a long wordy diagnosis and everyone smiled and agreed that ole Hank Moore was on his way. Then she jumped off the Arroyo Seco Bridge in Pasadena. I never did find out what was wrong with her. And I gave up psychiatry."

"Why? Every intern must make mistakes at first," Georgia said. "That's what internships are for. So you make your mistakes under supervision."

"I wasn't afraid of making mistakes," Hank said. "But later, after she had committed suicide, I went over my notes. And it all became clear. There was nothing wrong with the woman; not at first. She just wanted to talk to the nice young doctor and it didn't cost her anything and it kept her out of the house. It gave her a nice break. She kept changing the symptoms on me, just to keep my interest up. But at some point the whole thing changed. The more I talked the more she became apprehensive and frightened. And in the end I drove her to the bridge."

"Oh, Hank, that's silly. She must have been way off base before she ever came to you."

"But she wasn't," Hank said. "She just wanted a chance to get out of the house for a few hours a week and she liked to have someone to talk to. But at some point I got the thin end of the wedge into her brain. And every word I said drove it in farther. See, I really drove her to suicide. She was just a normal, whining, fat, bored housewife. And I, Hank the wonder intern, was clever enough to drive her nuts; I got her so worked up that she committed suicide."

"Is surgery better?" Georgia asked.

Hank sat up. He rolled down the window and spat a mouthful of crackers out onto the highway. He rolled the window up.

"I'm sorry," he said. "I'm talking too much. Also I'm trying to be smart and flip. I don't feel that way about it. Really I liked psychiatry, but I just couldn't do it. Too chancy."

"Too chancy?"

"Yes. Too chancy. Too much guesswork. Too much opinion. Too

much wild imagination. Too much of something that I don't have."

"Are you a good surgeon?"

"No. Just average, but I'll get better."

"Well, why did you pick surgery then?"

"Because it's sure. Absolutely, positively sure. If you're a surgeon a cancer specialist brings in a patient and tells you that he's got a patient with a cancer in the cortex of the brain. He makes the diagnosis. It's all his responsibility. All the surgeon does is operate. The other guy takes all the responsibility."

"But that's part of being a doctor," Georgia protested. "You have to be willing to make a diagnosis."

"Not if you're a surgeon. They bring the patient in with the diagnosis already made. All you have to do is operate. They bring him in with his head shaved so close that it gleams like brass. You caliper off the distance, make a mark on the skull . . . it's all exact, precise, with instruments that measure the same thing on every person. No guesswork. You sponge off the skull with alcohol that kills the same kind of germs on every kind of head. You take a scalpel and cut and elevate and reflect a flap of skin. Same size on every head; same place; same problem. You clamp off the blood vessels. They're always in the same position in every person's head. Once in a while one vessel bleeds a little more than most and then you just electro-coagulate it. That's the only difference. Then you cut through the skullbone with a trephine; five holes, each exactly the same. You cut between them with a special stainless-steel wire saw. You elevate the flap of dura and gently explore the brain. And either it's there or it's not. Either you see a little yellow growth spreading across the surface, sending tiny ramifications into the healthy tissue, crowding against the sulci and causing the memory lapse and gradually killing the patient — it's either there or it isn't. If it isn't you back out of the skull, sew the skin back over and the internist was wrong. Not you."

"And if he was right?"

"Then the operating nurse slaps an electric knife in your hand and slowly, gently, holding your breath, sweating, you cut it out. The curious little piece of flesh falls away from the brain, the electric knife seals off the blood vessels and, finally, it's just lying there . . . an ounce or two of crazy flesh. You pick the growth up with a forceps and start backing out. And you feel as good as if you'd done something really important. And no responsibility."

"But somebody has to do the diagnosis, someone has to take the risk."

Hank opened his eyes a slit, glanced down the long shiny hood of the car, down the rushing strip of black asphalt, saw dimly the beetle-like rush of the other cars, the green foliage alongside the highway. He smiled and closed his eyes.

"Sure. Someone has to do it. Let someone do it that likes to take a chance, that likes guessing. I don't like it."

Georgia drove a few more miles without speaking and Hank almost fell asleep.

"Is it worthwhile studying surgery, Hank, if you're not very good at it?"

"Good question. First, I'm not bad at it. I'm just not gifted in the fingers the way some of the surgeons are. But you can improve yourself by practice and so I do that. When I was at medical school I used to practice on old cadavers; the ones that were so sliced up they were about to send them away to wherever they send used-up cadavers. Sometimes I practiced on beef. I never told anyone about that. I'd get a big roast of beef, take it to my apartment, lay out the instruments and practice. Practice at tying knots with two fingers in a deep bloody cut; practice at feeling things with the tips of my fingers; practice at thin cuts ... so thin that a hundred of them wouldn't cut through more than a quarter inch of flesh." Hank waved his hand in the air. "Don't worry. I'm good enough and I'm getting better. I'll be one of the best someday. Not right away, but someday."

Hank opened his eyes again, looked sideways at Georgia. She was looking straight ahead, sitting easily in the seat. The speedometer held exactly at 60, not falling or rising a hair.

"The only thing I saved from psychiatry is a name for what I'm feeling right now," Hank said. "Parorexia."

"What's that?" Georgia asked, laughing.

"Perverted appetite," Hank said. "I'm hungry for something else. Fried eggs. Stop at the next restaurant."

They stopped and Hank ate four fried eggs and some toast. When they got back in the car they drove through the mountain meadows — on top of the Ridge Route. The lupin was turning brown and great patches of the flower marched over the hillsides. In a few places, deep gullies and ravines, there were still streaks of brown winter snow. Trucks crawled up the grade, their wheels barely turning, the diesel smoke hanging motionless in the air.

"You were mad at Mike during the convention, weren't you?" Georgia asked.

"For a little while. Then I got over it. I was really mad about him giving Moon's name to Cromwell. That was a hell of a thing. But last night when I was out on the town I thought it all out. I'm not sore anymore."

"I'm glad. I wouldn't feel good if you were mad at Mike."

"Well, I'm not mad anymore. I figured it doesn't make any difference. The Moon thing won't amount to anything. It'll just blow over. If I really thought that it would hurt Moon any I'd have really given Mike hell . . . made Cromwell retract the statement or something. But it won't matter. Everyone will just forget it. Think it's a political attack and forget it."

"Isn't Professor Moon a Communist?"

"He's not a member of the Communist Party. He's one of those odd balls who likes to startle his students and he's convinced himself that he believes in some special obscure aspects of primitive communism. But he's not a member of the Party. I'll bet he doesn't even know that there is a Communist Party."

"I'm not so sure that everyone is going to forget it, Hank. People are worked up these days about Communism. What if the newspapers pick it up?"

"They won't. Everyone knows that it was just politics. They'll forget about it." Hank leaned back in the seat and yawned. He rubbed his hands across his eyes. "That was a neat job that Mike pulled on the convention. I wonder if any of them realize what happened?"

"What did he do to them, Hank?" Georgia asked. "Why did they all switch so easily from Cutler to Cromwell?"

"Because they were a middle-class crowd," Hank said. "All clever, well-educated people. They all knew about mob psychology and emotionalism and they know it's not nice for respectable people to get too excited. They're stiff with respectability; really proper people. But they all thought that a political convention is different. There you can get excited and yell and parade around and it's all right. You're doing it in the interest of good government, for the state. But then Mike pulled a switch on them. After they had paraded around and acted foolish they sat down; all feeling righteous and spent. And then the minister stands up and gives them hell. Suddenly they're all embarrassed sick. They hated the minister and Cromwell for reminding them of how foolish they'd been. Hell hath no fury like an embarrassed respectable person."

"If they hated the minister and Cromwell why did they go along with them?" Georgia asked.

"Because they couldn't admit they hated the people that scolded them," Hank said. "They had to turn their hatred on the guy that made fools out of them . . . and that guy was Cutler. And the cards helped. They looked spontaneous, homemade, crude. Not like Cutler's slick, high-powered buttons and posters and photographs. Everyone thought the person next to him had scribbled out the cards. So they turned on Cutler, tore off his buttons and put on the hand-written cards for Cromwell. That was pretty clever of Mike. Really clever."

"Mike was right," Georgia said. "The problem is not so much to get them to like your candidate as to persuade them to hate the other candidate."

"Sure, he was right for a little group like a convention," Hank said. "But it's just a trick. You couldn't pull it on the whole voting public."

Georgia glanced at Hank and her face was relieved; almost smiling. "But why can't Mike work a couple of tricks and win the election?"

"Because you can't manipulate five million people the way you manipulate a few hundred people that are all gathered together in one hall. The mass of voters is just too big. That's their protection from people like Mike. Just their great big bulk makes them difficult to persuade and handle. Wait until Mike starts trying to manipulate five million people. Then you'll see. He'll get smothered. And it's a damn good thing."

"That's funny, Hank, I just don't see Mike being wrong on this. I'd like to see him lose. But I don't think he will."

The relief was still there on her face, but she wanted more assurance.

"Well, he's going to lose the primary. If the Republicans run Daigh he will take both nominations in the primary. My God, Georgia, nobody even knows who Cromwell is. He's just a man with some inherited money who likes to talk to people. He's good at it. In a way he's superb. But he'll never be governor."

They came to the Santa Paula cutoff. A huge gas station glittered at the intersection. A single great truck came powerfully down Highway 126 and swung into the traffic. From the hills above Chatsworth they could see an occasional glimpse of the sprawling geometry of Los Angeles.

"But Mike's so sure he can do it," Georgia said.

"He could be sure and still be wrong," Hank said.

"Maybe," Georgia said.

They came to Sepulveda and swung right. They went past the

glittering expanse of the reservoir and then, far ahead of them, the first traffic light blinked red. The flicking, fast-moving, atomized cars slowed down, formed into bunches. Tamely they moved into Los Angeles.

Hank waited for a few moments. He closed his eyes and leaned back in the corner of the seat.

"Georgia, why do you hang around with Mike?" he asked and his voice was tough and determined. "Nothing can come out of it. There's nothing in it for you."

The car spurted forward, whined down the road. Hank had a brief flash of memory: he remembered the time when he was taking the pulse of a man after a long diagnosis. Hank told the man he had incurable cancer and at once the pulse grew thick, enormous, thudding; as if the artery would burst under his fingers.

"Why do you hang around Mike?" Georgia asked.

"Because I've known him for a long time and I like him," Hank said. "I don't know why, but I do. I like him and there's something curious, attractive about him. I keep thinking if I hang around I'll find out some answer that will make the whole thing sensible." How can I tell her, he thought? He felt dull, used up. "With you it's different. You want something he can't give."

"I'm not sure, Hank," Georgia said and her voice was only a whisper; almost frightened. "At first I thought it was because he was so certain; always sure of everything. No doubts. No hesitations. But now I've changed. It's different. I think I make it too complicated. Maybe it's just as simple as the fact that I . . ." She paused. "Just as simple as . . ."

"Don't talk about it," Hank said harshly, quickly. He was suddenly desperate not to have her say it. He wanted, with a dead anxiousness, not to have her uncover herself; to speak the final words. "Shut up."

He opened his eyes. She was looking straight down the highway, her eyes distended. On her arms the flesh was puckered and he realized that she was shivering slightly; almost invisibly.

CHAPTER 27

Election Year

$\mathcal{T}$HE CALIFORNIA GOLD had been there for ages. It was washed down out of the hills in shining flakes that gathered at the bottom of river beds. Sometimes it came down in dull and tiny pieces as big as peas. Once or twice, no one knows how, it stayed in the hills in chunks as big as a boulder; heavy enough to make a man's arms strain when he tried to lift it. And heavy enough to make him scream with joy when he hefted it.

They took it out first with iron pans. Three handfuls of black sand, wash it with river water, let the black silt sluice over the edges. Then tilt and tip, wash again and again and again. And finally the streak at the bottom: thin, yellow and heavy. Scrape it, along with the black mud, into the leather bag and to assay.

Later came surface diggings, wet diggings, crude flumes, cradles, riffles, tailings, leads, coyotes and each of them took some gold and left the land unchanged.

But then they came with hydraulic gear. They came into the counties of Plumas and Placer and Eldorado with the big squat pumps, the long lengths of pipe and the sharp lawyers who bought "hosing rights." From the end of the monitor came a hard bright gush of water. The water hissed against the startled land. It cut around rocks, chewed up adobe, lacerated hills, chewed through roots and old lava. The land resisted for a few hours. And then it turned into thin coffee-colored slop and poured slowly down the hillsides, into the ravines, down to the river beds and finally into the mouth of the big machines.

The sharp young mountains were worn smooth. They turned into brown hills, laced with gullies and ravines. And the hills became mounds of soft leached-out dirt. And if the gold persisted the mountain became a hole in the ground.

The dredges came last. They were huge, ugly, black and created their own world. The dredges floated on water. The continuous belt of scoops dug up the earth in front of the dredge and threw the exhausted and goldless waste out behind. Each dredge moved its pond across the countryside, ignoring the old stream beds, chewing into pastures, flat land, through small hills, up valleys. The land they moved was ruined, covered with smooth round rocks that had been underground for a million years. After the dredge nothing could grow or did. Highways were built across the desolation, but that was all.

When the gold was gone the dredges died. They died where the gold ended; the barges rotting in the artificial lakes, the pipes turning red with rust, the scoops hanging like useless claws on an iron dinosaur. The incongruous, unbelievable wreck took only ten years to rot and disappear, but the land behind them was gone forever.

"What we need is reforestation," they said. And they said it in Nevada City, Eldorado, Yankee Jim's, Grass Valley, Gold Run, Sierra City and elsewhere. "And the state should pay for it."

At first only the resort owners and lumbermen said it and they said it for the purposes of simple greed. Then the rotary clubs and chambers of commerce and the bankers said it. And pretty soon the Catholic priests, the Protestant ministers, the Grange and newspaper editors began to say it.

One day it had a slogan: "Restore the Land."

And that day it became political and a bill was introduced named "# 1090: A Bill to Provide for Reforestation in Certain Counties of Northern California." And soon after it became a political plank in the party platforms.

It is a long low building built of concrete and covered with gray paint. It is surrounded by shrubs and neat lawns and behind the building is a farm with cows and barns and pigs. The land in front of the building drops slowly to the sea and in the far distance one can see the faint smudged outline of Point Buchon, the sandy spits over which the Pacific breaks, the deep green lines of windbreak eucalyptus trees.

From the building no one watches the view for it is an insane asylum and everyone inside is too busy. A middle-aged woman sits rigidly on a stool, her jaw tight, her eyes abstracted, passionately busy defending a dark inner privacy, locked in a catatonic rigidity which absorbs all her energy. She is oblivious even when her mouth is opened, the rubber tube is stuck in, and the warm soup funneled into her stomach.

In a small room a man masturbates endlessly, childlessly, fondly. Once his hands were strapped so that he could not touch himself and with an infantile ingenuity he rubbed himself with the heel of his right foot and when this was strapped tight he rubbed the inside of his thighs together and they saw it was hopeless and freed his hands.

In a common room a thin bony man talks fervently to a large, fattish, slack-jawed man.

"And just when I had the well ready to come in and the oil people were making offers from New York they framed me and stuck me in here," the thin man says, his eyes gleaming with paranoia, black with suspicion.

"Shame, awful shame," the fat man says. He shakes his head and the skin of his jaw, pebbled by paresis, trembles.

"And under that well is the god damnedest, biggest pool of oil ever seen. Reaches for miles, big and shiny, biggest pool in the world," the thin man says. Then suddenly crafty. "But I've got a plan. Can't keep a good man down."

They smile at one another; a tiny community of two; isolated against the rest of the asylum; perfectly matched by their diseases; their afflictions enfolded and complemented within one another.

The less afflicted work on the farm. With nightmarish slowness they pitch hay, watching each yellow curl of hay fall on the pile, turning with scarecrow awkwardness. They stumble across the barnyard, smiling dimly, doing the rote and hard-learned tasks with a minute precision. The overalls hang from them, shred on nails and boards, and the naked skin shows through and they still continue the convoluted, elaborate ritual of the farm. Occasionally, very occasionally, through the dullness comes a sense of outrage and there are fights. Slow, shambling fights; like drowning bears fighting under water; hands pawing one another; teeth biting fingers; a pulling of ears and a welling of tears in the eyes.

The Visiting Committee comes once a year. Three psychiatrists, two educators, three businessmen, one housewife and a retired army officer. They inspect the kitchen, made bright for the occasion. The housewife tastes the spaghetti and meat balls and, as the superintendent hangs nervously on the fringes of the group, she asks how much milk the inmates get per day.

The Committee walks through the wards and rooms. They look at hydrocephalics, microcephalics, paranoiacs, schizophrenics, paretics and Mongolian idiots. They watch a fifteen-year-old girl snap her fingers, slap her right fist into her left fist, pause fifteen seconds and repeat the gesture. Her fingers are covered with thick callouses from the snapping and the palm of her left fist is a huge swollen pad of callous.

They came to the large common room, reserved for the good and sober cases, for the patients who are co-operative. They paused and smiled out over the room and a few fragmented, disorderly, crooked smiles came back at them.

Then the housewife sees it: the dark, shiny tendril of blood flowing across the floor. They rush forward and see that it comes from a rocking chair in which the body of the middle-aged catatonic woman rests.

A paranoiac cheerfully reconstructed it for them. The woman had suddenly, after years of immobility, moved her head, peered shrewdly around the room and walked over to a desk. She picked up a pencil, walked back to the rocking chair and sat down. As a few of the interested patients watched she hacked her wrist open with the pencil, chopping fiercely at the tendons and flesh and then, when she had opened an artery, sat back with a smile in the chair. They had watched passively as the blood flowed from her hand, gathered in a pool and ran across the floor and the smile on the woman's face went thinner and tighter until at last it was a thin pale snarl and the woman was dead.

"She should have been in a private isolated room. By herself," the housewife said and looked with horror at the superintendent.

So the Visiting Committee recommended that the legislature appropriate an additional $26,000 for the asylum. The budget read:

    For construction of six private rooms....................$23,500
    For one FTE, hospital attendant............................... 2,500

The legislative auditor recommended that the request be denied. The Budget Committee of the legislature concurred. The two lines were stricken from the budget.

But the housewife on the Visiting Committee was the wife of the publisher of the San Francisco *Dispatch,* a great crusading paper. Pictures appeared in the *Dispatch* of the inmates huddling in common rooms. Stories were written by reporters. And, as a result, the official Democratic Party platform included, "Adequate budgetary provision for the care and rehabilitation of patients in State mental institutions."

The State of California has an agency that makes building loans to veterans. Under the provisions of the original act the state will make a loan, at a low rate of interest, to a veteran to construct a home.

In Sacramento the applications for veteran loans are processed by machines, almost entirely. But not entirely. For at some point humans look over the forms, check them for accuracy and either approve or disapprove on the basis of the calculations which the machines have made. The individuals fix their initials to the lower left-hand corner of the forms, just below their decision. It is as neat and mechanical an operation as one could hope for.

One of the persons who affixed his initials to the bottom of the application forms was Michael Garrity. Fifty-four years old, a Republican, a Catholic, two years of work at Santa Clara University, before he flunked out, a high blood pressure, five kids, a longing for beer, a flaccid wife, an eater of chocolates, the owner of three shiny-pants suits, a tic in his jowl, that, mostly, was Michael Garrity.

One day Michael Garrity received a case of Old Taylor whisky and five cases of Budweiser beer from Sharp's Liquor Store. They were delivered to his door and he thought it was a marvelous mistake and drank all of the beer and half of the whisky in two weeks. Shrewdly, sharply, primitively, he reasoned that he had done nothing criminal . . . any man could drink up booze delivered to his door . . . he hadn't done anything wrong. For two weeks he enjoyed his hangovers, made sweeter by the knowledge that they were acquired at someone else's expense.

Then Mr. Dante Ignazio appeared at his desk. Mr. Ignazio had gone to Santa Clara with Michael Garrity, but Mr. Ignazio had gone on to graduate and then went into big-scale contracting in Santa Clara Valley. He tore down prune trees and put up houses and he prospered exceedingly. He prospered until the spring of Election Year when the recession set in. Then, maddeningly, surprisingly, malignantly, buyers no longer had the down payment or did not want to put it down. They did not have enough money to qualify for the FHA loans and too few of them were veterans.

For three weeks Mr. Ignazio's fortunes dangled in the balance. The houses did not sell; the liens poured in; the blank-faced men from the banks walked curiously about the empty project. Then Mr. Ignazio went to see his classmate, Michael Garrity.

"Here are fifty applications of people who want to buy houses on my Santa Clara tract," Mr. Ignazio said. "That is, they will buy them if they can qualify for the veterans' loan and avoid the big down payment they have to make on FHA ordinary bank loans. Christ, Mike, why does the government jack up the down so high?"

Michael grinned sympathetically. They both looked out the windows, down the tree-lined streets of Sacramento glittering in the sunlight.

"Sure, Iggy," Michael said. "I'll expedite them. If they're veterans we'll get them through."

"But that's the point, Mike," Mr. Ignazio said softly. "They're not veterans."

"Then it's hopeless, Iggy. Really hopeless."

"Nothing's hopeless, Mike," Mr. Ignazio said and his voice turned regretful, but under the voice, lost in its Italian softness was a hint of steel. "I thought, Mike, when I sent you that case of Old Taylor and the beer that you understood that. Didn't you read the note? If you read the note and didn't send the liquor back, Mike, I think it's a little dishonest."

"What note?" Michael Garrity asked.

He looked across at Mr. Ignazio and he knew that they both understood that there was no note with the liquor. But he also knew that it did not matter. The Old Taylor was floating in his blood stream, had gone to fat around his middle. He had belched the Budweiser for two weeks, had floated euphorically on the windfall of booze, had gotten fat on the whole mess of it. Dimly Michael Garrity perceived that he had been bribed and that he had accepted; that literally the bribe had become a part of his body. Metaphysically, he was one with it; there was no way he could ever rid himself of it again. Bitterly he recalled the lectures by Brother Cooley at Santa Clara on the nature of sin and willfulness and gluttony. He knew that he had sinned; that the initialing of the forms would be a lesser sin and that, dimly, inarticulately, dumbly, he knew that the larger sin authorized the lesser.

He looked up at Mr. Ignazio, suddenly shy with the enormity of what he was doing.

"All right, Iggy, I'll do it," he said.

And that night Mr. Ignazio had Sharp's Liquor Store send Michael Garrity three more cases of Budweiser and another case of Old Taylor. The head clerk at Sharp's was a lean and very sharp Mexican boy, who was passionately devoted to the Democratic Party and he thought for a few days about the probity of a private contractor sending liquor to a state employee in the housing division. Then he went to the office of a lawyer who was high in the councils of the Democratic Party and told his story. The lawyer's eyes gleamed, he patted the Mexican on the back and lifted his phone.

Three days later the newspapers carried headlines. "Graft Charged in State Housing," "Housing Official Says Bribe Charges 'Politics,'" "Attorney General Says Indictments Will Issue," "Democrats Charge Corruption in Veterans Housing."

Michael Garrity left his five children and his flaccid wife and his beery tastes and began an elaborate habituation of jails and lockups that ended finally when he was sentenced to five years in San Quentin.

That spring the matter of graft in state offices became a political issue.

And in these ways, and many others, the issues of Election Year unfolded. They were known by manifestoes, resolutions, newspaper editorials, handbills, polls and television and radio.

The issues were made public by the leaders of the Spanish vote, the German vote, the Italian vote, the realtors vote, the Japanese vote, the oil vote, the orange vote, the lemon vote, the walnut vote, the radical vote, the conservative vote, the socialist vote, the golf-club vote, the Montgomery Street vote, the Spring Street vote, the South of Market vote, the Negro vote, the rural vote, the urban vote, and others.

And nobody listened.

The political parties went into dull, self-conscious action. Like a common, harmless, little-noticed weed the party apparatus worked throughout the state. At the ends of the apparatus, like tiny hairlike projections, were the precinct clubs. The weed stirred and held teas, rallies, debates, fund-raising bazaars, and issued statements. Some of the branches of the weed were tobacco stained and bourbon nourished and flourished. Some were bright with summer chiffon dresses and warm bosoms and were nourished on tea and Scotch shortbread and operated in Beverly Hills and the Marina. Some of the hairlike projections were stiff with doctrine and lived in an atmosphere of books, lectures, crew cuts and undergraduate enthusiasm at UCLA, Stanford and Berkeley. The swaying, barely moving tips of the weed were linked by thicker branches to the clubs, county committees and the higher branches.

The political weed stirred in the state, unnoticed and quiet. It talked to itself and ate itself and influenced no one.

And in the interstices of the weed, in the black private earth between the growth, never public, were the things that nourished the weed and kept it barely alive.

There was, for example, Ben Adams, a coffee-colored Negro, with a knobby head, neat small ears and a voice smooth and unctuous from singing in the Baptist choir. In his eighteenth year he walked down Central Avenue in Los Angeles and listened to a speaker standing on the back of a big red Chevvy truck. The speaker reminded the audience of what the Democrats and F.D.R. had done for the Negro and the Democratic platform for an FEPC and his voice soared with enthusiasm for the natural identity between the Negro and the Democratic Party. And as Ben Adams looked at the black, brown, creamy, brown and tan faces and as he watched them nod agreement somewhere inside his head a tiny worm of hatred stirred, a feeling that he was not like them, a wish to be unlike them and different. And quietly, very privately, Ben Adams became a Republican and when he was twenty-one he voted Republican. Of course, without telling anyone and belonging all the time to the Central Avenue Young Democratic Club and even selling tickets to the barbecues and dances.

And there was Joe Wilson of Burlingame, San Francisco Peninsula, who was once Jere Wilzweski of Pittsburgh. He had come from Pittsburgh to demonstrate a new muddling process at the Bethlehem plant in South San Francisco. He had stayed and been promoted and one day even gotten a white-collar job and then, during the expansion of the war, he became an executive. The Wilzweskis moved down the Peninsula to Burlingame and one of the things they discovered was that everyone in the block, all of the barbecue-pit owners, the mechanical-lawnmower owners, the Chrysler and Mercury owners, the commuters, the Peninsulates, the *Fortune*-reading people, were Republican. And so the Wilzweskis quietly changed their registration and put a Dewey sticker on their car and eagerly said harsh things about Truman and, finally, even began to reconstruct their memory of Roosevelt and remembered him as socialist, father of much-marrying children, fomenter of discontent, upsetter of the peace, and heard and believed that Eleanor had never loved him.

And there was Enos Deer, father of three, milk-truck driver, Mason, champion bowler in the Dairy-Bakery-Poultry League, owner of a Ford, a vacationer at Yosemite Park for two weeks of each year, a twenty-year resident of San Bernardino. He had never known a politician and he hated them all. He voted Democratic because his father had once winked at him and said, "Can't tell, Enos, what would happen if you stepped inside the booth, pulled the curtain behind you, and voted for a Republican. You, son, you vote Democratic." And Enos did.

And there was Alden Ethridge, chief clerk at Pacific Mutual Life Insurance in Los Angeles. He was a Christian Scientist, had never taken a drink in his life, wore cheap clothes that looked somehow like those tailormade for insurance executives, subscribed to the *Saturday Review,* married Esther who was thin and faintly aristocratic looking because of her leanness, had no children, started fourteen International Correspondence School courses and never finished one, read books on "Salesmanship," drove a Plymouth, was a seaman in the Navy in World War II for three months and then obtained a medical discharge because of asthma, belonged to Book-of-the-Month. When he was first employed by Pacific Mutual he heard a vice-president say, "If we ever get him out, him and Harry Hopkins and Ickes and the rest of those socialist bastards, if we do that we'll have prosperity in this country again. We'll have businessmen in power. We'll have common sense in Washington. But we won't because too many of the common people vote Democratic."

And Alden Ethridge squared his thin shoulders, put a determined tough grin on his sallow city pale face and voted Republican and never again thought of politics. Except when it occurred to him that he was most uncommon.

The billboards went up throughout the state. Big red and white signs with men ten feet tall on them and, occasionally, the faces of their families. Each billboard cost $80 a month. The throwaways, costing only three for a penny, began to circulate. The mailing pieces went out. Newspaper space was bought. Television time was purchased for $450 per half hour. From parts of the political weed rumors and information flowed and died before they got far.

And nobody listened. Dimly, vaguely, offhandedly they made up their minds. In a casual or antic or sullen or irritated or happy or euphoric mood they arose and went to vote. Five million of them. Their moods and intentions collided, coincided, reciprocated, canceled out and strengthened. Mysteriously, intuitively, by some strange combative instinct, they divided almost equally. With a rubber stamp and ballot they waged primitive war on one another and themselves. Although they could give reasons and words why they did what they did, they did not really know. But the liquor stores closed, the flags waved in front of fire houses and schools, the precinct lists were nailed to trees and the voting was done.

John Cromwell won the Democratic nomination for governor in the May primary. He was little known and Daigh, the Republican, was famous. Cromwell did not wage a big and public campaign. There was some little surprise when Cromwell won the nomination by 102,000 votes. Some gamblers had taken odds that Daigh would win both nominations in the primary.

Mike was not one of those who was surprised. He had told Georgia that Cromwell would win by at least 100,000 votes and less than 112,000.

The betting odds were four to one, however, that Daigh would beat Cromwell in the general election in November.

Ten days before the primary election Professor Moon resigned from Stanford University. The university officials did not force him out; no official reprimand was made. But he felt soiled; unpleasantly contemporary; somehow ruined.

CHAPTER 28

Talk in a Delicatessen

COUNTY HOSPITAL is built on a low hill. Originally it had been surrounded by stockyards and meat packing plants. Outside of the ring of meat packing buildings there was a welter of cheap apartment houses. In these houses lived Negroes and mixed families: Filipinos married to white girls, Negro women married to white men, brown men married to light brown women and combinations that found it difficult to find housing in other parts of the city. Also, the area was thick with butchers, itinerant farm laborers, railwaymen's hotels and miscellaneous unemployed. It was productive of cripples, syphilitics, amputations, industrial accidents, maimings, tuberculosis, stab wounds, drunkenness, flea infestations, pink eye, and all manner of contagious disease. The civic fathers had thought it wise to put the hospital close to the source of its patients.

In recent years the stockyards had moved out. The long sleek lines of the freeways cut across and above the area, not disturbing the buildings. Below the curving perfection of the freeways the apartment houses grew grimmer, more populated and older.

Georgia turned the Jaguar off the Pasadena Freeway and started down into the tangle of streets that surrounded County Hospital.

As she parked in front of the hospital an ambulance came down a ramp, its siren clanging. A young intern, a cigarette in his mouth, smiled at her as the ambulance went by. Georgia walked into the reception room of the hospital.

"I'd like to talk to Dr. Moore," she told the receptionist.

"Dr. Henry Moore," the girl said and her fingers plugged in a phone line.

In five minutes Hank walked into the reception room. He was wearing a tight white skullcap and a long white apron. His arms were bare to the elbow. In the exact middle of the apron there was a spot of fresh blood, the size of a quarter.

"Hello, Hank," Georgia said. "I'm sorry to disturb you at the hospital. Mike wanted you to have lunch with us. He has to meet Notestein to talk over the election and he thought you'd be interested. He said he'd give you a good lunch."

"I'm not sure I can get away," Hank said. "I'm just finishing surgery and I've got a few more ward cases."

She noticed that he held his arms in front of his body, away from the apron, the fingers drooping. His fingers were white and scrubbed looking. They gave off a faint aseptic odor.

"Don't come if it's too much trouble," she said. "There's always another day."

"Oh, hell. I can ask Johnson to take the ward cases. I've put in three eighteen-hour days in a row. I could stand a break. And a good lunch. I'll be back in ten minutes."

A half hour later they were driving out the Hollywood Freeway. Hank drove and he slid the car easily from one gear to another, watching the RPM indicator.

The freeway clogged up with cars and as the r.p.m.'s dropped Hank slid the shift silently into third. With a growl the car slowed down twenty miles an hour and started to feel its way through the other cars.

"What did you think of the primary?" Georgia asked.

"I didn't like it."

"Did you vote for Cromwell?"

Hank looked across at her and his face was puzzled, uncertain.

"No. I voted for Daigh."

"Did you think Cromwell could win the Democratic nomination?"

"I thought he was going to be smothered," Hank said. "I thought Daigh would win both nominations. I still don't understand how Cromwell won."

"Maybe Mike's right, Hank," Georgia said. "Maybe he's right and we're just sentimental."

Hank nosed the Jaguar up to within a few inches of the car ahead, pressed down on the accelerator and turned to the outer lane. The car poured into a narrow space, roared by the other cars and was in the clear. A mile ahead was another covey of cars and Hank bore down on them doing seventy miles an hour.

"It was just an accident, a fluke," Hank said. "Mike had nothing to do with it. You can't manipulate five million people. Anyway, Cromwell will get licked in the general election."

"But what if he's right? What if people really do vote out of fear and hatred?" Georgia said, and her voice was urgent, she pressed Hank for an answer.

"Georgia, don't make it more complicated than it is," Hank said slowly. "There are some things you don't do even if you know they'll work. Let me tell you about an experiment they do in rat psychology. You put the rat on a grid floor that you can charge with electricity by tripping a switch. You start out by giving the rat a hell of a shock. He's so scared his eyes bulge out of his head. Then you start to make him do a lot of things a rat doesn't do naturally: walk on his hind legs, drink too much water, eat until he ruptures his stomach, copulate between satiation. Each time he hesitates you give him a shock. Pretty soon you can get him to do anything . . . he just sees you reaching for the switch and he'll do anything, unnatural things, things that hurt. He'll walk on his hind legs, drink until he vomits, copulate until he's unconscious, doing everything like a mad animal."

"Well, maybe Mike's right then," Georgia said. "If a rat acts that way out of fear, maybe . . ." She licked her lips.

"No. He's wrong. Christ, of course he can get people to act like the rats . . . and just out of fear. But you shouldn't do it. Because after a while the rat stops being a rat. He becomes a sub-rat, pure muscle-raw reflex, brute reactions. And humans would become the same way: hysterical with fear, trying to anticipate when the shock is coming, bundles of raw protective muscle. But they wouldn't be human anymore. They'd be something else." He paused. He shook his head in confusion. His voice was tired when he spoke. "And you can't do that to people. I don't know why, but you can't. If it's possible, you shouldn't do it. Because it makes them something less than human. It's just that simple. That's the only reason I know."

"What you're saying is that there are some things you shouldn't do even if it's possible to do them," Georgia said, her voice questioning. "But why does Mike do them, then?"

"Because he's got certitude," Hank said. "He's absolutely sure of himself; completely confident; utterly assured. I don't know how he got that way, but he did. And when that happens some barrier is gone. Everybody else knows there's a line you can't cross, but not Mike."

"If he would just be wrong once," Georgia said. "Just once. Just one mistake."

She pounded the door of the car with frantic, soft blows.

Hank looked at her and did not speak again until they reached the delicatessen.

Mike and Notestein were sitting in one of the booths. Mike had a turkey leg and a heap of stuffed eggs on his plate. Notestein had an untouched pastrami sandwich on his plate. They were both drinking German beer.

"Terence, you remember Dr. Moore and Miss Blenner from Fresno," Mike said.

Notestein stood up and shook hands. He was wearing an outlandish sport coat. The shoulders were overstuffed and it dropped to a narrow waist. It was only when Notestein sat down that Hank realized that the material was an exquisite Shetland fabric; soft and handwoven.

"Tell the waitress what you want," Mike said. "We had to start. Terence has got an appointment with his friends. Have some chopped chicken livers and turkey. That's the best here. The stuffed eggs are terrible, they've got anchovies in them. But I like anchovies . . . You won't."

Hank and Georgia ordered.

"What did you think of the primary?" Hank asked Notestein.

"Me? Me, I liked it. Big victory for my friend Mike," Notestein said. "Good things for my friends delight me. I'm happy when my friends are happy."

"His business friends didn't like it, though," Mike said and grinned. "They thought it was a fluke. They tell Terence Cromwell won't win in the general. They tell him Cromwell will get clobbered."

"No, no, Mike, they don't say it like that," Notestein said. His face was pained. "They're interested. They think Cromwell made a nice race in the primary. But they have some doubts." He looked quickly at Hank and then signaled to the waitress. "Cocktails for everyone, miss. Everyone deserves a good drink."

"He's trying to get you liquored up," Mike said. "That's part of his job. Get people drunk before you give them the bad news."

Notestein smiled grimly. Nobody ordered a drink, except Notestein.

He ordered a double martini. He waited until the waitress left and turned to Mike.

"You've got it all wrong, Mike," he said. "They like your campaign. But they're just not sure Cromwell can win."

"I've got a theory about your friends," Mike said. "My theory is . . ."

"You and your theories," Hank said. "You have to be careful about theories, Mike. When I was in high school I lived at a boardinghouse and the father of the landlady was blind. He said he was blinded in the war, but his daughter said he had been born blind. Anyway he had cataract growths over his eyes, white as eggshells. He used to sit on the front porch and talk to people as he heard them walk by. He had a theory that he could tell what job a person had by the way he smelled. He'd say you could tell a woman was a librarian because of the smell of book varnish, paste and dust. Or a schoolteacher because of the chalk-dust smell. He could even smell out a plasterer on Sunday because the lime and mortar hung around him."

He paused while the waitress put the double martini on the table. Notestein was watching Hank attentively. He took his eyes away for a second and drank off the martini.

"Go on. Tell us the rest," Notestein said.

"This blind man used to bet he could identify the passersby. He even said he could tell an old maid because she didn't smell of a man. But one day he bet five bucks and sniffed the next guy that walked by and said he was a bank clerk. But the guy was a carpenter who just happened to spill some of his wife's cologne on his suit before he left," Hank said.

"And there's a moral to the story," Mike said.

"Damned right," Hank said. "Don't believe your theory absolutely, the next smell may be a mistake."

"But if you were blind it would be better than no theory at all, wouldn't it?" Mike asked.

Hank smiled.

"You win, Mike," he said. "Wait till I eat my turkey leg."

Notestein had not eaten anything from his plate.

"Now that was a very good story. It reminds me of something," Notestein said. He hesitated, looked quickly around the restaurant, and then went on. "I was a Hungarian Jew, see? But my family lived in Germany. Everything got mixed up and we wound up in a ghetto. Every few weeks they'd call us into a big auditorium to listen to the latest orders from Berlin. I was young at the time; twenty-five maybe. This Nazi would come in the auditorium to give us the orders. He was short, fat. Looked friendly. But the second he walked in the auditorium you could smell him. It was a funny smell. He'd look down at us and smile, but you knew he didn't mean it because of the smell. It was like there was too much pressure inside of him. Like it popped out and congealed on his skin; a sort of beery, acid smell. Like he hated us so much, despised us so deeply, that he smelled of it. And pretty soon all of us would be sniffing, like dogs when there's danger in the air. Then when he left there would be a new smell. But that would be us. That would be the smell of all of us afraid, our skin crawling, trying to make out what the orders meant, wondering if they applied to us."

Notestein held his finger alongside his nose in a strange European gesture. He looked around him, his eyes wide, watering slightly from the martini. Then his fingers touched the soft material of his sport coat, he looked down suddenly and was embarrassed. He grinned at them. But there was a tough, self-sufficient look on his face.

He's got guts, Hank thought. He's been through the mill. Mike can't scare him. Suddenly, Hank felt better.

"Terence, tell Hank and Georgia what your friends think about the election," Mike said.

Notestein put down his fork.

"Mike misunderstands them," he said. "He thinks they're not friendly. But they're businessmen. They have to calculate. They just can't pour money down a rathole. They don't think Cromwell can beat Daigh. They say Daigh is better known. They say he's got a reputation. They believe that California voters vote for a big reputation, a name, and Daigh's got the name."

"So they don't want to contribute to Cromwell's campaign," Mike added. He grinned.

"They can't, Mike," Notestein said. "They're responsible to a board of directors. They have to account for every penny. They just can't throw money away."

"And they're right," Hank said suddenly. "Cromwell hasn't got a chance. Your friends are smart."

Notestein smiled at Hank. Hank felt a surge of confidence; or relief.

"Well, everyone's in agreement," Mike said. "What about you, Georgia? What do you think?"

"I don't know," she said. "I haven't made up my mind."

"Look, Mike, be reasonable," Notestein said. "Settle for what you've

got. You've managed Cromwell very well. People won't forget it.
It will help your law practice. Don't ask anything more than that."

Mike picked up a salad egg that was flecked with bits of anchovy.
He bit it in half, chewed slowly and then put the other half in his
mouth. He took a swallow of beer.

"You don't deserve to know, Terence," Mike said. "You don't
really deserve to know how Cromwell will win, but I'll tell you. See,
we know a few things about the undecided voters. And they're the
ones that will decide the election . . . like always. We know that they're
the people who are worried about something. So they hold off, don't
make up their mind, keep trying to decide."

"So what, Mike?" Notestein said. "That's old stuff. But how are
you going to find the undecided votes? And what do you do when
you find them?"

"First, you find big groups of people that are worried," Mike said.
"You don't worry about isolated individuals; big clots of worried people."

"Like the old-age people in the primary," Georgia said. "Tell them
about that, Mike."

Mike looked at her and smiled.

"O.K.," Mike said. "You brought it up, so we'll tell Terence about
it. Remember, Terence, in the primary we didn't run much of a
campaign. We did that deliberately. We didn't want a lot of excitement. We just wanted a slow, average primary. Because that brings
out an almost equal number of Democrats and Republicans. Normally
they would tend to favor Daigh because he's better known and if we
hadn't done anything he probably would have won both nominations.
But we did something. We talked to Mr. Appleton, one of the old-age
leaders who, for some reason, seems dedicated to Cromwell. And
very quietly, with no fanfare, we sent each person in the state over
sixty years of age a letter."

"Tell them what the letter said, Mike," Georgia said. She looked at
Hank as she spoke.

"Scared people don't vote for something, they vote against something or somebody," Mike said. "They vote their fears. So the letter,
which was signed by Mr. Appleton, didn't even mention Cromwell.
It just reviewed Daigh's voting record. In the last paragraph it just
raised a doubt . . . a little tiny subtle fear that Daigh might not be for
old-age pensions. That's all. And that's the only thing we did during
the primary campaign. The only thing."

"How do you know the letter did any good?" Hank asked. "People might have voted against Daigh for a thousand reasons."

"Good question," Notestein said. "How do you know the letters worked, Mike?" He looked over the edge of his glass at Mike.

"Because we had a polling service take a sampling of all people over sixty in the state and see how they voted," Mike said. He grinned. "They voted eight to one for Cromwell. And the letter didn't even mention him. It just raised a doubt about Daigh. That's all it did. Raised a doubt that he might not give them a bigger pension or might reduce the pension they're already getting."

Unaccountably, for no reason that he understood, Hank felt a tiny gush of terror somewhere in his mind. Mike had just described a simple political trick and suddenly, inexplicably, the leakage of terror started in Hank's mind. For a wild second he tried to reason the matter out. But it did not make sense. Then he looked at Notestein. Notestein was holding the martini glass against his lip and faintly, almost inaudibly, his teeth were chattering against the glass.

Hank looked down at the white scraped turkey bones on his plate. He turned them over with a fork. Notestein had felt it, too. The terror flowed evenly across Hank's mind; was almost beyond control.

Then it came to Hank. Mike had just proved that he could do it; he had supplied the final piece of evidence. He had proved the point.

"That's not enough," Hank said, without thinking, blindly. "You need more than just the old-age vote. You have to pick up five hundred thousand votes to win in the general."

"That's right," Mike said, and his voice was hard and flat. "And up in an office on the top floor of the Golden State Building, we've got a research staff picking out every group, every locality, every organization that's got something to worry about this year."

"For example?" Notestein said. His eyes were bright and he had taken the glass away from his teeth.

"For example, Buellton," Mike said, "The little town of Buellton. A few restaurants, half dozen motels, a few gift shops. Five hundred people of voting age. They all make their living off the traffic that goes past on Highway 101. It runs right through the town. But the state engineers have a plan to by-pass Buellton. Make a new freeway that runs a mile south of the town. Every person in Buellton thinks it will ruin the town if the highway is moved. So you suggest to them that Daigh wouldn't object if the highway was moved. You don't have to say what Cromwell would do. You just let them know that Daigh favors moving the highway. That's enough. They won't care what

Cromwell stands for. They'll vote against Daigh. And the only person they can vote for is Cromwell."

"How are you going to let them know?" Hank asked.

He was hoping that Mike would not have the answer. But he knew that Mike would. His fingers were trembling and he put them under the table.

"Lots of ways," Mike said. "Maybe you send a liquor salesman into Buellton. You have him mention in a few liquor stores and bars that Daigh is tied up with the asphalt interests and they want the new highway to swing around the town."

"What if Daigh doesn't have an interest in the asphalt business?" Hank asked.

"You think I'm going to say that the liquor salesman should say it, anyway," Mike said. "Well, you're wrong. Because what he says has to be plausible. The people in Buellton might check around. So if Daigh doesn't have an interest in the asphalt industry you look around until you find something he has done or said that indicates he would favor the new highway. Like a vote he cast for a highway appropriations bill four years ago that authorized a highway that by-passed a few towns. There's always something. And you have the liquor salesman say that. That's all you do."

"This takes a lot of money, doesn't it, Mike?" Notestein asked. "To find all these groups and localities with a grievance?"

"That's right. It takes a big research staff. A lot of college graduates in sociology and agriculture and city and regional planning. You don't have to pay them much, but you need a lot of them. About a hundred and fifty thousand dollars worth. And your friends, Terence, haven't contributed a cent toward that fund. Not a cent."

Notestein smiled and it was the same, identical smile, except for one thing: it was fawning.

Hank suddenly had to move. He shifted in his seat and still felt stiff with tension. He saw the waitress pass.

"Bring me some pie," he said. "Apple pie. A la mode. Vanilla ice cream."

When she brought the pie he scooped the entire ball of ice cream into his mouth. It was creamy and sweet. It gushed past his teeth, chilled his throat. It drove back the leakage of terror; his fingers stopped trembling. He looked at Georgia. She was watching Mike.

"That's a lot of money. One hundred and fifty thousand dollars," Notestein said.

"Not when you're sure your man is going to win," Mike said. "Then it's very cheap indeed."

Mike grinned at Notestein. It was a grin that Hank recognized. It was a grin in which Mike's teeth stayed together and the lines around his eyes did not crinkle. It was a grin without humor.

All right, Notestein, Hank thought. Stand by for a ram. Here comes your turn. See how tough you are. You're a big-time operator, you deal with this kind of thing every day. So get ready. Stand by.

"Terence, you're going to have to give your friends an opinion," Mike said. "You're going to have to tell them who's going to be governor."

Notestein put the beer glass down. He reached for his lapels, carefully straightened the coat around his shoulders. He smiled carefully.

"I know, Mike. I know that."

"It's a hell of a job, being an adviser in politics," Mike said. "Guess wrong once and you're through. I know that, Terence. I sympathize."

Notestein's eyes dropped, he hunched forward protectively. Hank felt his stomach tighten. He looked at Mike's strong face, the brown planes of his skin and bone, the white teeth, the familiar hands. Mostly he watched the grin.

"It's always tough, Mike," Notestein said. "I'm used to it."

"You're friends have got a lot at stake," Mike said. "Taxes, offshore oil, railway fares, utility rates. They can't miss. Not even once. And it would be tough for you, Terence. You being a Hungarian and a Jew. They'd say you didn't understand American politics. If Cromwell wins they'd say they made a mistake trusting your judgment."

"But I do understand politics," Notestein said. His voice was wheedling.

Hank watched as Notestein seemed to shrink inside the bulk of his sport coat. Almost as if he were going backward in time, to an older and safer level of existence. Notestein wrung his hands together. He smiled slyly at Mike. His accent thickened and the old European gestures asserted themselves.

"One thing I really understand is politics," Notestein said. He picked his nose. His fingers flicked across his chin as if he were caressing a beard. He cocked his head. His eyes were wide and unfocused with anxiety.

"Sure you do, Terence," Mike said. "But it would still be tough to be wrong on the next governor. You don't have your final papers, Terence. Don't be out of a job when they come up for approval. You have to be self-supporting, remember that."

"But, Mike, what do you give?" Notestein asked and his voice was shrill, feminine, foreign. "They should the money give and you nothing? That's honest? I'd spit, but it's not polite. They need the guarantee. That much money, Mike. That is a lot." He paused and was suddenly abashed. "Spit? That I wouldn't do. Forget that, Mike. As a friend forget that. But what could you give in return for that much money?"

"Nothing, Terence."

"Nothing? Crazy, you've gone crazy."

"I don't care what they do. Tell them whatever you want. If they don't put up the money someone else will."

"Don't rush. I didn't say they would not put up the money. Keep calm," Notestein said. His voice went thin and sharp, scratched at Mike's assurance. "Just something to tell them, Mike. Just something to let them know that much money is well spent. Come on. As a friend. What can I tell them?"

"Tell them that I'll know where the money came from," Mike said. "That's all, Terence."

Notestein stared at Mike for a moment. He slid out of the booth. He started to walk toward the door, shrunken in his suit, the collar pressing against his ears, muttering to himself. He was almost to the door when he turned suddenly. He dashed back and picked up the check.

"My treat," he said. "I treat everybody. Notestein's treat, understand?"

He grinned at them as he took a bill from his wallet and dropped it on the table. He turned and hurried out of the restaurant. Hank watched him through the plate-glass window.

Notestein stood on the curb, watching the traffic pour down Wilshire Boulevard. He moved crabbedly into the traffic. For a moment he was caught in the middle of the street, surrounded by the thundering, swift cars. He looked from side to side and once over his shoulder. His face was white and strained.

Somehow the traffic, the flashing senseless rushing cars reminded Hank of a mob. And something about Notestein's hunched shoulders reminded him of something else. He felt a stab of memory: slight, passing, quickly gone. Something about Notestein reminded him of a day long ago when he had walked beside someone who had an accent. They had walked down an empty street, but it was threatening — and behind them was a menace. He remembered that the person had black, frightened eyes, and he had muttered in German and behind them had been the sound of ominous, tramping feet. They had escaped somehow . . . but that was all he could remember. Then the memory slipped away.

Notestein bolted across the street. He stood for a moment at the edge of a large glittering gas station. He was small and hunched, defensive and ludicrous. Then he saw the green phone booth and he scurried toward it. He closed the green folding door behind him and put his hand in his pocket. It came out full of coins that fell from his hands and glittered as they fell. He lifted the receiver and his fingers shoved a dime in the coin slot.

Hank looked away.

CHAPTER 29

The Dream

SHE WATCHED him on the bed. It was dark and cool in the motel room, but his body was glistening with sweat. The motel was built on an expensive curve on Santa Monica Boulevard and as the cars came into the turn their headlights threw hard bands of light into the room for a brief moment. In the flashes of light she could see him, curled up, knees under his chin. Georgia sat in a chair, in the dark, and watched him sleep.

He's not an easy sleeper, she thought. He grinds his teeth when he sleeps. And that curled-up position is not the way a child sleeps. It was the position a boxer might take when he was felled; unconsciously protective, hands knotted into fists, his breath coming heavily through his nose.

She would not go to sleep for hours now. She never did. She got up from the chair and walked over to the bureau. She fumbled for a cigarette. In the flashing, uncertain darkness she could see her naked body reflected in the mirror. It was a black reflection with only the curves of her hips occasionally turning white as the light shattered into the room.

I wonder if he loves me? she thought. If it weren't for the polio I'd know. I keep thinking I'm awkward; that he sees me limp. Once he said he liked the limp.

She sighed and walked back to the chair by the window. She looked down Santa Monica Boulevard, saw the headlights aim for the window,

grow from tiny dots of light to great roaring circles of brightness that
veered away into the curve just before they hit the motel. She put the
full pack of cigarettes on the arm of her chair. Now that she had
started she knew that would go through the whole pattern, think it all
through again.

First, she thought about Mike's wife. Once, months ago, she had
worried about Connie. She had never seen Connie and Mike never
mentioned her. But Georgia was aware of her; waiting for Mike to
come home; waiting with the children. At first she had wondered
what Connie would be thinking and doing; wondered whether she
was anxious.

And then she came to really disbelieve that Connie existed. Because
Mike never mentioned her and because he was never home and because he did not carry a picture of Connie and the children in his wallet;
because of all these things Connie faded in outline and importance
until finally she was only a name; not a name that really stood for a
person, but merely a name.

But Georgia did not forget the name. For Connie stood for something. She stood for the fact that Mike could utterly, completely, without reservation, put a person out of his memory. Connie meant that
Mike could forget you, could draw away and without the slightest loss
to himself leave you abandoned. Connie stood for a puzzled look in
Mike's eye that meant that he quite literally did not remember you;
that he could, without malice or design, simply force a person below
the surface of importance and recognition and remembrance. And
once below the surface, Georgia sensed that a person could never drive
above it again. Mike did not hate Connie, he was not bored with her,
he was not cruel to her. He simply had forgotten that she existed.
Georgia wondered, dimly, how Connie existed. And whenever she
thought of it she shivered; not for Connie, but for the isolation that
was more ominous and frightening than anything that could happen
to Connie.

Maybe the important question is whether or not I love him, Georgia
thought. Maybe you can never know if he loves you so the important
thing is to know if you love him.

It would be a hard thing to know, she thought. Mike was like a
stone; an attractive, magnetic, powerful stone. A stone that was
vaguely translucent; that you could see into for a few inches and then
it went milky and inscrutable. And around the stone all the little
iron filings gathered, people like herself who did not see anything in

the stone, but could not resist it. When the stone moved they rearranged themselves, shifted positions, made an intricate complex maneuver to get closer to the stone.

Once she had said this to Mike. They were walking through Yosemite Park and they saw a tall white tree with spiky branches beside a huge hulking rock. It was the first windy day of autumn and they saw the tree rub against the rock and the stubby branches splintered off their summer's growth against the flint-hard surface. On the side of the tree that was toward the rock the limbs were stunted, raw, splintered.

"That's us," she said and pointed at the rock and the tree. "I keep splintering against you and I never even scratch your surface. And wherever I touch you I'm all splintered. Look at the rock. There isn't even a scratch on it."

Mike looked at the rock and then at the tree. He nodded and they continued the walk. He did not understand.

Part of the process, part of the inevitable thing that kept her awake, was comparing Mike to the other men she knew. He was not like Morrie. Morrie was like a sponge, a big soft sponge with a diamond-hard core. Mike was not like Harry Amsterdam, her second cousin who had come out from New York one Christmas and taken her to five night clubs, gotten her drunk on champagne, seduced her and then put his head on her lap and cried desperately. And Mike was not like Father. At first she had thought they were alike. They were both calm and decisive and that had deceived her. But as she came to know Mike she realized that her father was a balance of tensions, that his surface calm was due to a careful calculation of pressures, a determination to appear a certain way. With Mike the appearance was the reality: he was not under tension.

No, that was not completely right, she thought. Mike was under tensions. But he did not calculate or worry or scheme. The pressures were from the inside, not from the outside. They were Mike's pressures, his own.

A covey of MG's came down the boulevard. There was a boy and girl in each roadster and a little flag was fastened to the rear of each car. They whirred past, jockeying for position. From a few of the cars came wind-shattered laughs.

Mike woke up and rolled over on his back.

"I was dreaming," he said.

"I didn't know you dreamed."

"I do. For years, ever since the war, it's been the same dream. Exactly and precisely the same dream. I know it like I know the palm of my hand."

"Tell me about it, Mike."

"Why would you want to know about a dream?" he asked sleepily. "That's funny about women. A woman is curious about a man. She wants to pull out everything private, see everything inside of him. And when she does she loves him; when his privacy is gone she loves him. Doesn't matter. I'll tell you about the dream."

He pulled the pillow under his head.

"The dream has no color," he said. "Everything is gray. There is a landscape. Somehow I know it's round and limited, has boundaries. At the edge of the landscape are hills, sharp, angular hills, studded with rocks. On the tops of the hills are trees. The trees are huge and tough like no trees I've ever seen. They're the boundary. In between the hills is a valley and I always walk through that.

"The whole thing, the whole landscape, is held together somehow. It trembles as if it might come apart. The whole thing is like one of those airplane wings that engineers test under stress. When the strain gets great enough the wing starts to vibrate and finally a single little rivet goes or a pucker appears in the foil and the whole thing twists itself to pieces. The landscape is like that: under stress and barely holding itself together.

"I walk through the valley and come onto a street. It's a regular city street. There are dried palm trees hanging over the street and they make a gray thin shade. In front of some of the lots there are 'For Sale' signs. In the scorched grass two cats are fighting. I can hear them hiss, but can't see them. Then one cat backs out of the grass, arched and walking on its nails, spitting into the grass. The other cat comes after it in long oily leaps. They circle around for a few minutes and then one turns and runs.

"The nails of one of them scratch the surface of the landscape. I can see it very clearly . . . a long, very thin rent. Through the rent I can see something whirling and turning, like the circle of burning gas you see around a planet.

"The landscape starts to tremble, wrinkles run out from the tiny rent. Somewhere, far away, up in one of the hills, a tree crashes down and I know that if I don't stop it the whole thing will crumple up, twist, tear itself to pieces. So I run to the rent and patch it together. The material is tough and hard, like a ripped open tin can. My fingers bleed as I try to get it back together. The cats come back, terrified at what they have done. They crouch down and watch me, pleading with their eyes for me to fix the rent. And finally I get it back together. The trembling stops, everything steadies down. And I wake up."

"That's all?" Georgia asked.

"That's all," Mike said. "Not very exciting, is it?"

He looked at her for a moment. He turned over and at once he was asleep. In a few moments his teeth began to grind softly together.

Georgia thought of Hank. Hank never became angry with Mike, but the things that Mike said upset him.

Why did it upset Hank so much? she thought. Mike never forced his ideas on anyone. He just believed some unpleasant things and acted on his beliefs. It was one of the attractive things about Mike. He didn't try to be fashionable or popular or easy. He said just what he thought. Hank exaggerates things, she thought. He worries too much. He's like me.

The next day Georgia asked Morrie the name of a good psychoanalyst. She made an appointment. The psychoanalyst was a German and he was very gentle. He spoke with a very thick accent. She told him Mike's dream. Once or twice he asked her to repeat episodes in the dream, very slowly.

"Are those the same words, the identical words, that your friend used?" he asked her.

"Exactly," she said.

He nodded and she went on. He asked her some questions about Mike's age and his occupation and his family.

"No. It's hopeless," he said. "Oh, I could tell you a few things. A lot of technical things about the dream and what the trees and the hills and the cats mean. But without knowing the man, without having him here, it would not mean anything. I'm sorry."

Georgia thanked him. She handed him an envelope that contained a hundred-dollar bill.

"It is not necessary to pay for such advice," he said. She knew he meant it. She took the envelope back.

"Thank you for your time," she said.

"It's all right," he said.

He led her to the door. As he opened the door to let her pass he put up his hand.

"Just one thing, Miss Blenner," he said. "Just one remark that is really an intuition, a guess, a hunch. Do not attach much weight to it.

Do not figure it as important. But I feel that this man is a very power-ful person and that he is not disturbed. He sounds like a man who is balanced. Almost, although it is very vague, I feel that he is a good person."

"Good?"

"Don't ask what I mean by good. I do not know. Only that I feel it. This person does not have evil intentions. He is independent. Maybe he hurts people, but not deliberately. But do not take this seriously. It is just a guess."

Georgia thanked him and walked out into the street.

CHAPTER 30

"A Power Absolute, Minute, Regular, Provident, and Mild"

"WHAT HAPPENS today?" Hank said to Georgia.

She was driving and they had hardly spoken since she picked him up at the hospital. They were driving through Seal Beach and along the highway the old oil derricks were black and ancient. Underneath the derricks, almost invisible, were small, well-kept engines that turned the pumping arms and took a steady trickle of oil out of the ground.

"Mike's meeting with Notestein's friends," Georgia said. "These are men from the companies that pay Notestein for his political advice. Mike says they won't be the real powerful men . . . they don't like to mess with politics. They'll be bright young executives; men who've handled some rough labor negotiation cases. That sort of person."

"They're crazy," Hank said. "They ought to send out their heavy-weights. They send out their lightweights and the champ will just clean up on them." His voice was bitter.

Georgia picked up speed. They drove along the wide strip of beach that runs from Seal Beach to Balboa. The beach was broad, dirty and untended. Thousands of beer bottles and beer cans stuck up out of the sand and there were blackened holes where wiener-bake fires had been built. They passed the first shack. It was built around an old Buick. Stakes had been driven into the ground and then paper boxes, plywood, newspapers and blankets had been hammered to the stakes. The rear of the Buick stuck out of the shack, like a beast that had been caught in some unsubstantial and improbable trap. A spiral of smoke came out of the shack, was caught by the breeze and blown flat across the highway. Three Mexican children crawled on the hood of the car. At a water hydrant beside the highway an old Mexican woman was filling quart beer cans with water. A little girl staggered back and forth from the hydrant to the shack, a beer bottle in each hand. At the edge of the beach the waves came in fresh and blue and were corroded instantly by tar, seaweed, discarded papers and bits of firewood.

"Morrie says that these people will be tough," Georgia said. "He says they'll probably lick Mike. They're used to dealing with hard people."

Hank snorted. He sat with his head bent forward, held up by his hands. His face was thinner; almost bony.

The road curved away from the beach and suddenly they left the dirty beach and the greasy smoke and the beer cans behind. They came into Balboa and it was bright with high masts, flags, sleek shops, the polished glass of expensive shops.

They picked Mike up at a restaurant and then drove on to Balboa Island. They parked behind a long fence. A sign over the gate said "Sea and Sand."

"It's one of those houses that big corporations buy for their executives for recreation," Mike said. "It's deductible as a business expense. Nice way to give your executives a free vacation."

They walked through the gate. The house was set well back from the white beach that ran down to the bay. It was a long, low modern house with blue-tinted windows in front and a wide porch covered with a bright blue canvas awning. A short pier ran out from the beach and a forty-five-foot sloop was moored there. A barefoot man was polishing brass around the binnacle.

In the middle of the beach a group of women were stretched out around a big umbrella. One of the women saw Mike and she said something. The women rolled over and watched them.

The women were all between thirty-five and forty years old. Most of them had loose pebbled skin around their thighs as if they had dieted recently. The sand around them was dotted with bottles of sun lotion. Their flesh was pink and glistened with oil.

Mike walked toward the porch of the house and Hank and Georgia followed him. A group of men were sitting on the porch. They stood up as Mike approached. He stepped onto the porch.

"I'm Mike Freesmith," he said.

He stood stolidly, his legs apart, somber and citified in his suit. Sand poured in little streams from his shoes and cuffs and fell on the hemp flooring. The men watched him uncertainly and then a man with a mustache stepped forward.

"Yes, yes, yes," he said. "We've been expecting you. This is a great pleasure. We didn't know you were bringing friends."

He raised his hand, anticipating an apology from Mike and ready to wave it away. Mike did not apologize. He did not say anything.

The man with the mustache flushed and then stepped up to Mike.

"My name's Matthieson," he said. "Why don't we go inside and talk? The glare is bad out here."

Mike did not introduce him to Georgia and Hank. They walked in and sat down in a room full of rattan chairs and couches. In one corner was a bar and a Filipino boy in a white jacket. Matthieson put Mike in front of a low table that held a box of Bering cigars, a large ashtray, and a box of matches.

The other men walked in from the porch and sat down. There were eight of them. Matthieson did not introduce them to Mike. Most of them wore hula shirts decorated with flowers, sharks, leis and surfboards. Some of them had on denim pants and some wore shorts. All of them had rounded, but not prominent bellies. Their fat was well controlled.

"How about a drink?" Matthieson asked. Mike took a gin and tonic. Matthieson picked up the box of cigars. "And a cigar."

The box was completely full. Mike looked down at it for a moment. Then he grinned up at Matthieson.

"Can't talk politics without a smoke-filled room, eh?" he said. Matthieson flushed again. He jabbed at the cigars to loosen them. "O.K., I'll take one." Mike took a cigar and lit it.

Matthieson raised his eybrows in the direction of the other men. Obediently three of them stepped forward and took cigars. They sat down and inexpertly began to light them. In a few minutes the room was blue with smoke.

"It was very good of you to come down here to talk to us about California politics, Mr. Freesmith," Matthieson said. Hank had a feeling that Matthieson was the most prominent man in the room, the most promising. He was so promising that he could afford the eccentricity of a mustache. He was that sure of a vice-presidency. "After all, our companies have to live and grow and make a profit in California. So we're interested in everything about California. And especially politics, because this is an election year."

"I didn't come to give you a lecture on California politics," Mike said without taking the cigar from his mouth. "I came to talk to you about John Cromwell's campaign for governor."

His voice was rude and sharp. He looked straight ahead.

Here it comes, Hank thought. You well-nourished, successful, ambitious young executives have got your fingers in the wringer now. You'll come out flattened; squashed out flat.

Hank took a gin and tonic from the Filipino and sat back in his chair. His stomach was tight. He looked around at the young executives. With a quick shock of excitement Hank realized that most of them were smiling. The three who had been dutifully smoking cigars reached forward and ground them out, as if Mike's rudeness had released them from a courtesy. The tentative look was gone from their faces.

They're tough, Hank thought. These boys are really tough. Under those silly hula shirts and Bermuda shorts are some very tough characters. These boys are on the make. Maybe they can handle Mike.

"O.K., tell us about Cromwell's campaign," Matthieson said. "Can he win?"

"I thought Notestein told you that already," Mike said. "I told him how we were going to win."

"Who's Notestein?" a man with sunburned knees said. His face was blank. He looked at Matthieson.

"Oh, he was a sort of consultant to some of the vice-presidents interested in this political situation," Matthieson said in a low, quick voice.

"What do you mean 'was'?" Mike asked.

"They let him go a few days ago," Matthieson said. "The senior vice-presidents felt that his judgment wasn't all that it should be in this sort of thing. You know, he's a foreigner. A German Jew, something like that. He really doesn't understand California politics too well."

That's two, Hank thought. First Moon and now Notestein. He remembered Notestein's hurried, frenzied, panicked scurry across Santa Monica Boulevard; his shoulders hunched, his body shrunken in the sport coat. Notestein knew it would happen then; knew he was caught.

Matthieson's face was not apologetic or defensive. And Hank pushed away the memory of Notestein's hunched and fearful body and hoped that Matthieson's face would not change.

"That was a mistake," Mike said. "Notestein was a good person. He understood California politics."

"That was a decision that our people felt competent to make," Matthieson said. He changed the subject. "Maybe you could tell us what you told Mr. Notestein."

"No. I won't tell you that." Mike said. "I told Notestein and he told your bosses. They decided to fire him because they didn't believe what he said." Mike paused and grinned at them. "So if you go back and tell them the same thing maybe they'll fire you."

Matthieson smiled. There was no humor in his smile and no fear.

"Maybe you should just tell us what Cromwell wants to do if he becomes governor," Matthieson said.

Mike looked around the room at the young executives. He moved the cigar into the corner of his mouth; a quick expert motion of strong teeth and lips. He bit the cigar hard and for a few seconds he did not speak. He just looked at the men.

He's sore, Hank thought. He's angry because they fired Notestein.

"Cromwell will do what's necessary to stay in office," Mike said.

"That's no help, friend," the man with the sunburned knees said. "That could mean anything."

Mike turned his head and stared at the man. Then he grinned.

"Well, take your case, just as an example," Mike said. "Your name is Johnstone and you're public relations director for Cortez Agriculture Corporation. Twelve thousand acres in Imperial, seven thousand in San Joaquin, a few ranches around Salinas. Lettuce, sugar beets, some cotton, lots of beef. You're a subsidiary of a New Jersey holding corporation and you pay wages that are eight cents an hour less than most other big farming outfits."

"That's right, friend," the man said. "You've got me tagged."

But he's not scared, Hank thought and he felt assured. This is different from Fresno. This is different from a scared Hungarian Jew. This is power, money, experience. This is organization.

"And every trade union and agricultural worker in California hates your guts," Mike said. "So maybe Cromwell introduces a bill making the minimum wage for agricultural workers one buck an hour." He took the cigar out of his mouth, looked at the moist end. "Or maybe he introduces a bill saying that corporations owned by out-of-state people have to pay a special tax . . . say five dollars a year for every person they employ."

"We'd block it in the legislature," Johnstone said. "We've got friends there."

"So the bill would lose," Mike said very softly. The Filipino had stopped stirring a pitcher of martinis; as if he had received a signal.

"The bill would lose the first time Cromwell submitted it. But just by submitting it, just by attacking Cortez Corporation, he'd pick up a hundred thousand votes among agricultural workers."

Johnstone smiled and leaned back in his chair.

"But most agricultural workers don't vote," Johnstone said. "They move around the state too much to establish the minimum time for residence requirements."

"You're so stupid," Mike said. "Don't you see the next step? Do I have to tell you? Cromwell would introduce a bill providing that agricultural workers didn't have to meet the residence requirements. That if they lived all year round in California that would be enough." He stuck the cigar in his teeth, clamped down on it and spoke harshly. "And the legislature would have to pass that. Because it's democratic, it extends suffrage, it would be popular. And then, Johnstone, Cromwell would have you by the short hair."

Johnstone stopped smiling. He leaned forward and put his hands over his sunburned knees. He looked at Matthieson.

"There's no sense getting emotional," Matthieson said quickly. "A hundred thousand votes isn't going to get Cromwell in office or keep him there. You know that."

Mike grinned and did not answer. He puffed on the cigar.

Matthieson went on to say that wages were higher in California than in most other western states; that the workers were loyal to their companies; that everyone in business had to make a profit.

Mike said nothing. Hank felt the sharp pleasant edge of his gin and tonic vanish. He looked around at the young executives. He hoped the drink had dulled his perception. But he knew it had not. Their toughness was dissolving. Their faces suddenly were covert, protective, sly. The toughness was still there, but it was shattered.

Mike stood up, ignored Matthieson's words. He walked over to the big tinted window and looked across the channel. The room became quiet.

"Outside that window, right across the channel, Los Angeles County begins," Mike said. "Four million voters. Incompetent, restless, discontented. They're the political bosses. You'd like to think that F.D.R. was the political boss that punished the hell out of you for twenty years. But you're wrong. It was those people across the channel. He sensed what they would allow him to do. They gave him permission. And with ninety-five per cent of the newspapers against him, with all of the good and responsible people hating his guts, with all the big money against him he won . . . four times."

Matthieson cleared his throat. He looked confused; as if he did not know how the conversation had gotten sidetracked.

"What's that got to do with the governor of California?" Matthieson asked.

"Maybe a lot, maybe a lot," Mike said with satisfaction. "The boss is out there. In the big cities, towns, farms, trade union halls, beer parlors. Millions of him. But the governor is their executive and, if he's really good he can take all that antagonism and resentment out there and channel it through the legislature, the committees, commissions, research groups, the legislative auditor, federal bureaus and a thousand others. And he can make it expend itself that way. So that when it comes up to the surface again it's tamed and manageable. Or, if he wants, he can give the great big restless mass a kick in the ass. And when they turn around he can point his finger at you and say you did it. You, Wall Street, the big boys, the plutocrats. What you want, gentlemen, for governor, is a man that will not point the finger at you."

They saw what it had to do with the governor of California. They looked out the tinted windows, across the pink scented backs of their wives, through the rigging of the yacht, and beyond that was The City. And in The City were the People. Millions of them. On the faces of the young executives was the sudden knowledge of how slight was their protection against the People. The yacht, the beach house, the cool executive offices, the clean children, the maid, the second car, the precious incredibly wonderful sense of being "in" . . . all this was separated from the brutish, pawing, powerful hands of the masses by the thinnest, most translucent, most narrow of barriers. They had taken it all for granted, but now, by some subtle appreciation of Mike's words they realized how slight was their protection, how easily the barrier could be ripped aside and the People could come pouring in.

On their faces was a sudden wonderment that it had not happened before; that all of the things that separated them from the People had not maddened the People into action; had not teased the jealous, tortured, restless Masses into revenge. And when they looked away from the Balboa Hills that protected them from Los Angeles and glanced at Mike they were different men. They knew he could push his finger against the barrier and it would open and let all of this pour in on them. And they wondered why it had not happened before.

"Assume that Cromwell could win," Matthieson said. "What would he want from us? If he thinks we're going to finance a whole damned campaign he's crazy, we won't."

Matthieson's voice was firm, under control, but Hank was not deceived. They were defeated. Old habits of control and negotiating still remained; the retreat would be orderly; it would not be a rout. But Mike had won. No one in the room was in any doubt about that.

Inside of Hank something collapsed blackly and softly; formed a small hard knob of despair in his mind. Some insulating, protective illusion was gone and he knew that some sort of decision had been made. He knew the last defense had crumbled.

"Mike, I have to go," Hank said. He stood up. The men diminished, fell away into a tinted blue-green shadow, the gin and tonic roared in Hank's head. Then everything took shape again. They were gaping at him; not in surprise, but in relief. "Have an operation in the city. Just have time to make it back."

"I'll go with him," Georgia said. They stood up and walked out of the room. They heard Mike's voice rise, start to outline the terms.

As they went by the umbrella the women looked up. Their faces were resentful, flushed, too pink. The talks had taken too long; it was late for lunch; and, dimly, they sensed that their husbands had lost. As if the smell of defeat had drifted across the porch, down the steps, delicately across the sand and to their sensitive nostrils. They watched Hank and Georgia dully.

Neither of them spoke as they drove out of Balboa Beach, past the dirty beer-can studded beach, through Seal Beach and up onto the Harbor Freeway. Then Georgia spoke.

"I don't understand what he wants from them," she said. "Father said he would give all the money that was necessary. He said he would underwrite all the expenses. Then Cromwell wouldn't be obligated to a lot of other people."

The brakes on the car screeched. Hank pulled over to the side of the road, parked on the soft shoulder.

"Did your father really say that to Mike?" Hank asked.

"Yes. He's made arrangements for Mike to have all the money he needs."

"Are you sure Mike has plenty of money?" Hank asked. "Be sure, Georgia. Are you absolutely sure?"

"I'm absolutely sure. I checked it with Morrie. Mike has all the money he needs."

Hank licked his lips, his lean face seemed gaunt. He started the car and moved slowly with the traffic.

"It means Mike's gone over the edge," Hank said. "He didn't talk to them because he needed money. He talked to them because he wanted them to know that Mike Freesmith was a big tough guy. That he had power. That he could beat them. He doesn't need their money, but he needs their surrender . . . he needs to see that frightened look in their eyes. He'll win without their money. But because they resisted him he had to show them. He knew they were opposed to him; he knew they had power; they were tough. And so he went out and beat them. And he didn't have to."

He looked over at Georgia. For a moment she stared at him and then she knew he was right. Her lips worked as if she might laugh; her fine white teeth showed. But she did not laugh. An anguished sound came from her lips. She bit her knuckles to hold it back. In a few moments she could speak.

"That was the last chance, Hank," she said. "They were the last ones that could stop him. They were confident and they had power. I was sure they'd stop him. And he just had to be stopped once. Just once he had to be beat and then he could be resisted. But they couldn't," she said. She closed her eyes. "Hank, did you see the look on their faces when he talked? He made them feel that there were four million Mike Freesmiths out there in Los Angeles County; four million hard, tough people waiting to get at them. And they knew that Mike was the only person that stood between them and the four million. He broke them, Hank. Just as if he had picked them up and broken their backs across his knee." She opened her eyes and looked across her knuckles at Hank. "Now what happens, Hank?"

"I don't know," Hank said. "Now we try, I guess. Can you stop him?"

"I don't think so, Hank," she said. "He won't stop because of anything I do. If I threaten to leave him he'll laugh. Maybe a month ago if Father had withdrawn his money it would be a threat. But not now. Now he's past that. He doesn't need Father's money. See, Hank, it doesn't make any difference now whether Mike is right or not about how people act in politics. He's persuaded enough people that they act in a certain way . . . and now, they're acting the way he believes they do."

"I don't know if I can stop him, now," Hank said. "Maybe no one can."

He picked up speed. The car rushed down the freeway; like a corpuscle caught in a rushing, busy artery, swept along by thousands of other corpuscles, they rushed toward the great roaring viscera of the City.

CHAPTER 31

The Last Green Hump

$\mathcal{T}$HE OCTOBER STORM waves came thundering in. In the far distance they were blue, heavy and innocent. But as each wave reached the shallows it turned green, its huge bulk rose into the air, it turned a concave face toward the beach. There was a moment when the wave seemed frozen, motionless. It stiffened and along its back appeared short, striated lines of power, like muscles tightened. It was sleek and smooth with force. Then a line of white spume, as solid as cream, appeared along the top of the wave and it curled forward. With a crash the whole wave broke. The green mass was gone and the wave disappeared and was replaced by a huge white seething wall of foam that roared in to the shore.

The waves piled in without pause. They were the edge of a storm that was thousands of miles away. They were huge. From the breaking point to the sand the sea was foaming white, roiled with splintered waves, twisted by undertow, streaked with clouds of sand.

Hank took one board from the rack on top of his car and walked to the edge of the cliff above the cove. The place was deserted; the beach was empty. As he walked down the path he noticed that the ice plant was dried out and brown, waiting for the winter rains. The path was drifted over where the wind had gnawed into the soft soil of the cliff and made miniature landslides. He walked slowly, feeling his way carefully over the drifts, balancing the board on his shoulder. Halfway down he stopped and rested. Then he went the rest of the way.

The storm waves had narrowed the beach. It was only fifteen or twenty feet wide. Hank put the board down. For a moment he squatted in the sand and looked out to sea. Here, with his eye almost at water level, the long sweep of ocean to the horizon was invisible. He could see to the shallows but no farther. There his vision was blocked by the slow, regular, inevitable heaving of the ocean as the newest wave was formed. The waves reached into the sky, blotted out the sky and the Channel Islands.

The waves exhausted themselves just at Hank's feet. He reached down and touched the last thin edge of the waves. They hissed softly against the sand, turned it gray, and then slid backward.

Hank stood up. He started back up the cliff.

Ten minutes later he had the second board on the beach. He brushed them both off, set them carefully on their sides. He took his pants and shirt off and stretched out on the sand in his shorts.

The early winter sun was very thin. The surface of the sand was warm, but not like the summer sand. Just below the surface the sand was chilled; slightly wet. And there were no sand fleas.

Once Hank opened his eyes and looked at the sun. It was yellow and pale. A thin corona, like a black line, traced its shape.

He thought of the summer sand; the deep swelling warmth that seemed to come from the interior of the earth. He rolled over on his stomach, laid his cheek against the sand. The grains were instantly cool. He turned again on his back.

A gull came in from the sea, kaaing as it slid down a smooth layer of wind. Hank was looking straight up into the sky and saw it for a moment. Its white shape and the pink feet scarred the blueness of the sky and the yellow light between the sky and earth. It looked very small.

He forgot how long he lay there, pulling the heat from the sky, feeling the coldness of the beach against his back. But finally he heard the sound of a car at the top of the cliff. He sat up. He saw Mike's head, and then Georgia's peer over the side of the cliff. Then they started down the path.

Hank picked up one of the boards and stepped to the edge of the water. He waded in until the water reached his ankles. In a well-remembered motion he swung the board into the water and forward and, at the same time, landed on the board while it still had motion. He squatted on the board and began to paddle.

The board chunked into the first shattered wave. It was a wall of foam only a few feet high. The board cut up through the foam, sliced through empty air and then whipped flat. Hank eased his weight onto his arms, lifted his knees slightly from the board and when the board slapped against the water began paddling again.

The next three waves were easy because they were almost spent. But between the waves the water hissed and boiled in a way Hank had never seen. The water moved in quick senseless eddies, was checked by other pressures and tossed aimlessly. The board cut across the eddies, making a slicing neat sound that came minutely to his ear, cutting through the larger sounds.

The fourth wave was difficult. It came combing down on him, four feet of foam, laced through with green strands of water. He paddled hard, with his cheek flat on the board. As the nose of the board hit the wave, he slid his weight back to raise the board, and then, instantly, pushed forward. The board whiplashed into the foam; crashed into the wave with a motion that was arclike, but moving forward. The wave sucked at him, he lost way and then, almost as he stopped, it released him. His eyes were full of water but he was already paddling. He blinked his eyes clear and looked ahead.

This is the moment, he thought. The moment when you see the ocean's worst face; when you are most evenly matched.

Twenty yards in front of him a big wave was forming. It rose silently, steeply, without effort. The mound of water started to peak, to raise itself into the air.

Hank paddled in deep powerful strokes. His whole body was bowed into the effort. He stared at the wave, watched the line of spume suddenly thread along the top. The wave turned concave; became a huge forward-bending wall. He felt a pressure in his ears and knew the wave was about to break. He paddled savagely and just as the tons of water curled down he shot into the concave green substance. He cut through the middle of the wave; he locked his arms around the board. He felt the wave crash down on his ankles; the board shivered for a moment, was almost dragged backward and he heard a great rumbling savage noise as the wave hit the surface of the ocean. Then he was released. He slid out past the surf line.

Hank swung into a squatting position and paddled slowly out for a few more yards. Here the skin of the ocean was flat and smooth and the waves looked harmless. Hank swung the board around and looked toward the shore.

Mike and Georgia were almost at the end of the path. Mike was wearing swimming shorts and was barefooted. They were standing still, watching him. Hank waved his hand and they came the rest of the way to the beach. They stood for a moment talking. They looked out to sea and then at the surfboard. Georgia spoke once, looked again at the waves and then, it seemed to Hank, she became silent. She put her hands in the pockets of her coat and leaned against a rock.

Mike walked to the edge of the water and put a foot in the next wave. He hopped back, pounding his hands across his chest and shouting something to Georgia. She did not reply. Mike picked up the surfboard and walked into the water. With the same skillful, swinging motion that Hank had used he swung the board down and forward and while it was still moving he slid onto it. Then he disappeared as he entered the surf. Hank saw the tip of the board occasionally as it went up over a wave. Once he saw Mike clinging to the board as it whiplashed over a wave. Then as another hump of water gathered itself, heaved into the sky and narrowed out, its powerful green impeccable back was shattered as if a boulder had been thrown through it. It was Mike and his board. They shot through the body of the wave. They came like a sailfish; sharp and flashing, spray flying, cleanly slicing the wave. They slid past the surf line and out into the smooth water beyond.

Hank watched quietly, not moving from his squatting position except to straighten his board occasionally by putting his hand in the water. He felt withered, dried out. His mind was empty and blank. He was aware of the thin warmth of the sun, the swelling of the waves, the sound of the surf and unconsciously he counted the waves and waited for a ninth wave.

Mike's board slid across the water.

"You sure picked a day for surfing," Mike said. "You don't go surfing for ten years and then you pick a day like this."

"You didn't have to come. I just told them at your office that I was going and if you wanted to come I'd have a board for you," Hank said.

"Don't get touchy. I wanted to come. Haven't been surfing for ten years. But this is some surf. I never remember it like this. There must be some hell of a storm somewhere."

"They're humping all right. And they're getting bigger. There'll be a really big one along pretty soon."

"Old Hankus, the medicine man of the sea," Mike said. He brought his board close to Hank's. "Just like old days, eh?"

Hank looked down between his knees. The middle of the board was drying out, leaving a thin film of salt. It was cold. The breeze off the ocean was stronger than the sun. Hank looked up at Mike.

"Just like the old days, only a little bit different," Hank said.

"What's different?" Mike asked. He was grinning; the old, tough, confident, independent, knowing grin. "You're the same. I'm the same. Ocean's just the same; maybe the waves are bigger, but everything else is the same."

"You're not the same. You're different."

Hank did not know where his words came from. He did not think them with his mind or phrase them before he spoke. They seemed to be manufactured by his lungs and lips quite independently. In the withered, brown, desiccated interior of his head Hank felt nothing; he was blank, waiting for some signal.

"You're wrong," Mike said. "I'm just the same. Hank, I haven't changed a bit since the last day we were out here on the boards. Maybe you have, but I haven't. Not the least little bit."

The boards rose on the swell of a wave, dropped into the trough. Hank saw that Georgia had climbed up onto a rock and was sitting with her hands clasped around her knees.

"I guess you haven't changed, Mike," Hank said. "You're just the same. But I didn't really know you before. And then maybe the world changed around you."

Some old long-forgotten sensitivities came alive in Hank. Because of the depth of the trough and the shape of the waves and impulses that came through the board he knew a big hump was coming. He turned and looked over his shoulder.

They both saw it at the same time. It was a long dark blue line that blotted out the horizon. It rose so high above the other waves that it caught the wind and was laced with veins of white foam. Because of its bulk it seemed to move slowly, deliberately, reducing the waves in front of it and absorbing the waves that followed.

"My God," Mike whispered. "It's huge. It's the biggest I ever saw."

Hank backed his board toward the wave, sensing that it would break farther out than the other waves. The big hump was only four waves away when Hank stopped and waited. Mike was beside him.

They watched the color of the wave change. The deep blue faded and it became green and translucent. A delicate filigree of kelp was visible in the wave; the nodules black and solid, the strands as distinct as rope. To one side was a sting ray, caught in the wave. It was like a scarab; motionless, its wings spread, its ugly short tail straight out behind it. In the taut amber of the wave the ray was entombed, harmless.

Then all the other waves were gone and the big hump was all that was left. They lay flat on their boards, looking over their shoulders. Deep in the wave they could see the sea grass trembling, the sharp tips reaching up from the bottom of the ocean and fluttering in the base of the wave. Then they heard the rumbling noise.

They started to paddle. Hank looked over at Mike.

"Don't take it, Mike," Hank called. "Let it go. It's too big for you. You can't ride it."

And Mike grinned. His arms kept pumping. They felt the sea rise beneath them, push against the boards, lift them high. Flecks of foam shot past their boards. Then, just at the tip of the wave, the mass of water gripped them and they started to shoot forward. For a split second they slid forward and upward as the wave continued to gather itself. The roar, the grinding, tearing, rumbling, fundamental sound, grew louder. They could see the tattered surf in front of them, the smaller, minor waves that had gone before and been ruined. They rose still higher and the drop seemed incredible, unbelievable, staggering.

Hank looked down at the beach and he could see Georgia's white face turned toward them. He felt the wave start to break and he looked at Mike.

Mike was getting to his feet. He grinned over at Hank. He was going to ride down the crash.

Numbly, with relief, Hank felt that he had received the signal; been given permission. He started to stand too.

And then the wave broke. The board was hurled forward and in the same instant it slid down the front of the wave. The foam rose around Hank's knees. The board chittered under his feet and his toes worked for a better grip. He looked over his shoulder and saw the mountain of foam and green tossing water behind them.

Hank pressed with his foot and his board angled across the foam, slid toward Mike. Mike saw him coming. Mike did not angle away, he did not look down. He watched Hank's slanting. Hank sensed that Mike knew what it was about; what had to happen; what was coming. And again the relief deepened and Hank felt reassured, decisive.

When his board was a few feet from Mike's he straightened it. Hank stared at Mike for a moment and then he dove at Mike's knees. He felt his ankles slap hard on Mike's board and then they were both in the water.

The broken wave snatched at them eagerly. It was the grip of the entire ocean: ancient, massive, stern. They were swept forward, but were held so tightly they could not move even their fingers. The wave threw them to the bottom and swept them through a patch of sea grass. The tough strands whipped at their bodies. They rolled over and smashed into a great slime-covered rock. The slime was rubbed off instantly and Hank felt the sharp edge of sea rock slice the flesh from his ribs. He was held against the rock and then drawn slowly across the cutting edges.

Then the pressure was gone and they swirled through the green water. Mike reached down and twisted Hank's middle finger loose. He bent it back, almost to the breaking point. Then, quite deliberately, he let go of the finger. Hank tightened his grip.

Hank opened his eyes. Under the wave the world was filled with raging clouds of sand, the black shape of rocks, the twisting blades of sea grass. Closer, just before his eyes, was the solid muscle of Mike's leg. Digging into the flesh were his own fingers.

In the green uneven light he saw Mike's hand come down, grasp his finger and bend it. He threw his head back and there, inches away, was Mike's face. The face was softly distorted by the few inches of water. But Mike's eyes were open and the grin was clean and distinct. Hank closed his eyes.

The finger bent straight back from his hand, a sharp pain came from a great distance, sped down his arm and exploded in his brain. He screamed and bubbles slid from his mouth and floated away. Then, just before the finger broke, Mike let go.

He could have broken my grip, Hank thought. He could have gotten loose.

He made his mind blank, for this was temptation. He dug his fingers into Mike's legs and held more tightly.

They were swirled upward, almost to the surface and then whipped downward. They smashed into rocks again, swept across a layer of sand that quickly, in a few short licks, rubbed the skin from Hank's legs.

Suddenly Mike jerked his legs up and almost tore loose. Hank tightened his grip and with a peculiar distinctness felt the sharp wiry hairs of Mike's leg brush against his cheek.

The wave held them motionless for a moment and then brushed them flat against a shoal of barnacles. Hank felt the sharp, painless slice of the shells as they cut into his back. His lungs were hot and he knew that soon he would open his mouth and the salt water would pour into his throat. He opened his eyes and far away he saw the lively bouncing sunlit surface. Just above him a layer of green water was rushing swiftly past, pierced with beads of foam, flecked white. But, by some oceanic trick, they were held motionless, paralyzed by the great pressures into immobility. The shells sliced his flesh soundlessly.

It's not for you, Hank shouted in his mind. Not for all you stupid cloddish ignorant bastards, walking the face of the earth with plenty of air and sun and clouds. I'm doing it for myself. For selfish reasons. For my own reasons. Not for you.

And then the wave released them. They were lifted up and Mike jerked again, pulling them almost to the green foamy surface. It grew brighter, but at the edge of his vision a black circle was growing, narrowing the light to a contracting circle. Hank knew he was close to unconsciousness. He sobbed and took a mouthful of water down his throat. He clamped his mouth shut. The area of blackness grew.

The wave moved them forward and slammed them against a single rock. There was the sound of a crack, a dull unnatural muted crack. Mike went soft in Hank's arms, collapsed downward upon him. Mike's fingers slid down Hank's back, his head bounced limply from his shoulder. In the center of the tiny circle of vision still remaining to him Hank saw Mike's face. The eyes were open and staring.

Hank let go. He ran his hands over Mike's limp body. Hank pushed upward, very weakly.

His head broke through the surface, but only slightly. The surface was covered with leaping fleck and gobbets of foam. Hank gasped and got a mouthful of foam and some air and was pulled under again. He was pushed to his knees and swept forward. He pushed upward again and this time got more air.

He did not believe he could reach the shore and he did not want to, but he could not control his body. It fought toward the shallow water; weakly, grotesquely, without his help. He came to the surface, snatched a breath of air and swallowed it along with bitter foam. Then he was pulled under. He crawled over rough rocks, patches of sand, the dead sharp bodies of crabs and old shells. Above him the water still rushed and tossed. He sobbed as he crawled and wondered, dully, with a black lassitude, how much his tears would salten the water. The sea rumbled at him; talked of death and oceanic peace and somehow it made him sob more. He got to his feet and found that he was in the shallows. But another wave smashed at him and he went under again. He slid along the bottom, helpless.

Then something caught him by the wrist, held firm. He staggered to his knees. The water was very shallow. He looked up. Georgia was standing in the water and holding him by the wrist. She pulled him to the edge of the water and rolled him on his back.

"Poor Hank," she whispered and her fingers ran over the cuts on his arms and chest, gently touched a long neat slice that was just starting to ooze bright red. "Poor, poor Hank."

Hank tried to speak, but salt water foamed between his lips. He spat. Then he could talk.

"He could have gotten loose," Hank said. "By breaking my fingers he could have gotten loose. But he didn't." He coughed and warm vomit and salt water spilled in a gush on his chest. He whispered, "Why didn't he, Georgia? Why didn't he break my fingers and free himself?"

"Poor, desperate Hank," she said.

His eyes blinked away the salt water. The sun now seemed bright and huge. He could see Georgia. Her face was tight with pity and despair, but also with understanding.

She put her arm around him and pulled him upright. He coughed again. She held him in a sitting position.

They sat there for a long time, waiting for Mike to drift in.

CHAPTER 32

Along the Shore

HANK AND GEORGIA drove to La Jolla in Hank's Ford. They left in the early afternoon, just after Hank came from surgery. He smelled of alcohol and surgical soap. The odor hung about him like something not easily dispelled; tough, penetrating and clean. The odor was dissipated by the gas and oil smells of the Ford, however, by the time they reached Laguna Beach.

They did not talk during the drive. Most of the time Georgia slept. Hank drove very fast and carefully, picking his way in and out of the traffic.

The traffic thickened as they went through the Spanish buildings of Laguna Beach. They drove past the abandoned subdivisions on Dana Point. At San Onofre there was a circle of cars with surfboard racks on their roofs and neither of them looked toward the ocean. They went past the great sweeping emptiness of Camp Pendleton with the long barbed fences broken only by an occasional Marine sentry. On the dunes a few Alligators clawed their way, spewing sand behind in rhythmical spasms. Out to sea a dozen LCVP's circled slowly and helmeted heads showed sharply over the bulwarks. A jet plane slanted down from the sky and a few hundred feet from the ocean it fired a signal rocket with a fierce sound and then banked sharply away. The LCVP's speeded up, formed a line and moved toward the shore and the highway turned inland and the sea suddenly vanished.

It was a racing day at Del Mar and as they swept past the track they could hear the diminutive mechanical cheering of the crowd. They saw the faraway tiny shapes of the horses for just a moment.

They turned off the highway at Torrey Pines and drove toward La Jolla. They went past the neat brushed houses of the retired admirals and colonels and generals and the elaborate Spanish homes of the San Diego rich. The buildings thinned out and then disappeared and they went past the abandoned subdivisions. The hotel they were looking for was right on the ocean. Behind the hotel was one of the most recently abandoned subdivisions. The elaborate bronze street lamps hung over asphalt strips which had been laid down neatly across the sand. Ice plant, heavy with purple buds, crawled over the asphalt, reached almost to the middle of the road and there it was crushed to death by the passage of an occasional car. Lots were still marked by faded flags and stakes and in the middle of the unfinished streets was a colorful little office which, on its windward side, had stopped a large heap of browned and dried out papers that reached almost to the roof.

The hotel was much older. Most of it reached out over the water and was supported by pier pilings. Thirty years before, in the warm millennial glow, the minarets had been bold. Now the stucco had peeled away and the laths and chicken wire showed in big ugly splotches. The sea air and salt water had gnawed patiently at the building and the damages had been repaired singly and over long intervals so that the building had a spotted, irregular look. Also the pilings had settled at different rates so that the hotel had a jerky roofline. Clothes-lines hung between the minarets and held up bathing suits, yellowish towels, bras and shorts to a gray, flat sky. The clothes looked as if they had hung there for a very long time without drying.

In the lobby of the hotel was a large blackboard with the names of the guests and their room numbers. They found Cromwell's name and saw that his room was 213. They went up the stairs and down a corridor. The carpets in the hotel had once been a bright and vivid green, but they were now faded in the center to a rich yellow. The smell in the corridor was not unpleasant, but it seemed very ancient; as if each passing foot and towel and body had left a tiny fragment of itself behind to blend with other fragments and to form the odor of the corridor.

When they came to 213 they knocked. A voice sounded inside, muffled and indistinct. They opened the door and went in.

Cromwell was sitting by the window. He had a light blue blanket over his shoulders. He was smoking a cigar. Clara was sitting on the window seat with a robe over her knees.

"Hello," Cromwell said.

The four of them looked quietly at one another for a long moment. Cromwell blinked. Then he smiled and gestured.

"Sit down," he said.

The room was crowded. Along one wall was a line of old filing cabinets. The opposite wall was lined with stacks of books which were piled up carelessly on one another. Objects spilled into the center of the room: a drying starfish, an abalone iron, a bag of pencils, scratch paper, an old Dictaphone set with two containers of wax cylinders, a box of paper clips that glittered brightly on the carpet.

In the back of the room was a crude kitchen arrangement. There was a small icebox and a hot plate on a table. Waxed milk cartons, cans of pork and beans, ends of bread, a knife with a rusty edge and a cup of spoons were also on the table.

The smell of cigar smoke impregnated the room, as if it had been blended into the paint, soaked up by the books and debris. The ash-trays overflowed with cigar butts; the older ones dried and hard, the top ones still wet and soft.

Cromwell puffed quietly as he watched them.

"Sit down on the window seat," Cromwell said. "We're watching the tide come in. We watch it wash over the rocks."

They sat down and looked out the window. The beach was covered with smooth rounded rocks. Green water surged in among the rocks, reached up toward the hotel. Far down the beach two children ran across the rocks, back and forth, with the fall and rise of the waves. At that hour they were featureless, angular, somehow antic; like crabs shaken loose of their shells.

"Pretty soon the waves hit the pilings under the hotel," Clara said. "The whole place shakes and shivers. But you get used to it. We hardly notice it anymore. Sort of like it."

She turned and smiled at Georgia. For a moment Georgia was con-fused. Then she realized it was the first time Clara had ever looked at her directly, without attempting to shield the birthmark. Clara held her hands in her lap and the birthmark was turned toward the room. Georgia smiled back at Clara.

They watched the tide rise. The waves broke higher on the rocks. When the first wave reached the pilings the hotel shivered. The planks in the floor creaked and the doors rasped. A book slid sideways and collapsed in a small cloud of cigar ash.

"The hotel is really well built," Cromwell said. "The shaking doesn't mean that it's weak. It really rolls with the waves. It's been through dozens of storms. Stood up through all of them."

In a few moments Hank and Georgia were used to the shivering impact of the waves. Hank glanced at Cromwell and saw that he had a notebook in his lap.

"I'm revising my book on Hobbes," he said, holding up the notebook. "The publishers say it finally sold out the first printing and they think maybe a new edition would go. So I'm working on that."

"How about a drink?" Clara said. "I'll make martinis. We don't drink a lot anymore, but we always have something around."

She went to one of the tables and began to pour gin and vermouth into a teapot. She opened the old wooden icebox and chipped off slivers of ice.

"I hear they buried Mike in the Veterans' Cemetery," Cromwell said. "The one out by Santa Monica."

"That's right," Hank said. "He asked for that in his will."

"How many people were there?"

"Two. Georgia and me."

"Just two?" Cromwell said and his voice was calm and steady. "That's funny. He almost had the state in his hand and when he died two people went to his funeral. He was just a little way, just the tiniest slice, from being the most powerful man in the state. Was his wife there?"

"No," Hank said. "She'd taken the kids and gone back to St. Helena. I drove her to the air terminal. She was wearing black and had a veil, but you could see she was relieved. She smiled under her veil when she thought I wasn't looking."

"I should have gone to the funeral," Cromwell said broodingly.

"It didn't matter," Hank said. Hank paused. "John, tell me why you made the speech about Moon just three days after Mike died? I still can't figure it out."

They were all silent. The only sound was the sharp tinkle of the ice splinters being destroyed in the teapot. Clara poured the martinis into water tumblers and passed them around. Cromwell took his glass, sniffed the martinis.

"It was funny having Mike die," Cromwell said softly. His voice was exploring, tentative, as if this were the first time he had formulated the thought in words. "The minute I heard about it something started to go out of me. It was like a knife slit in one of those big

circus balloons. Those big red and white and blue balloons with pictures and advertisements on the side. They float by a cable above the
circus. The gas just started to hiss out. I could feel myself shrink. I
couldn't believe it was happening. I believed all the wonderful words
and pictures on the sides of the balloon. And then they all started to
crumple; get wrinkled and crumple. At first I was scared. More than
I'd ever been before in my life. For three days I sat in a hotel room
and felt the pressure going out of me. I was emptied, crumpled,
baggy. Then it was all over. All that was left was a hulk. The bright
words and the wonderful pictures were all tiny and twisted. The hulk
was drab and ugly. But I knew it was me."

Cromwell paused. He watched a wave foam in around the rocks.
He lifted the glass and drank. Carelessly he pulled the blanket over his
head so that it formed a cowl. He peered out at them.

"Go on, John," Clara said. "Tell us the rest."

"The three days were terrible," Cromwell said softly. "I kept trying to patch up the leak, to hold in the pressure. Actually I held my
hand over my groin as if I had been ruptured; trying to hold everything together. And then at the end of three days it was all over. The
pressure was gone. I was back to normal. I was a carcass that Mike
had taken and blown up. Oh, he didn't do it against my will. I went
along. I asked to have all the wrinkles taken out; to be blown up so
tight. I wanted to sail up above the state and see all the faces looking
up at me and their mouths gaping as they read the words and saw the
pictures. I loved it. I didn't know what all the words were or just
exactly what the people saw, but it was me. Do you understand that?
It was me: John Cromwell. They could paint anything they wanted
on the side. I didn't care. I was just grateful that I could free-float;
that everybody could see me. Except it wasn't really me. It was Mike's
balloon they were seeing."

"Part of it was you, John," Clara said. "Really it was."

"Maybe so, maybe so," Cromwell said. "Maybe a few of the words
and a few of the pictures. But nobody would have seen them if it
hadn't been for Mike Freesmith. He put the pressure in; he took the
wrinkles out; he made me free floating. When the whole thing was
collapsed I could see that. What was left after the pressure leaked out
was old and familiar. Old, familiar, half-drunk John Cromwell. A
kind of bum. A bum who had a trick: he could orate. A bum who
had an itch to see people change when they listened to him. And
when they changed the itch became a great glorious sensation. The

itch was just a minor affliction; without Mike the itch wouldn't have bothered more than a few hundred people in the state. But Mike made the itch something big."

"But why did you make the speech about Moon?" Hank asked again.

"Because when the three days was over I was me again," Cromwell said. "I shrugged back into the old rubbery carcass and the wrinkles all fell in place. And I knew that one of the first things I had to do was to take Professor Moon off the hook. So I had the State Central Committee buy television time and I made the speech. I didn't consult anybody. I just made the speech and admitted that at Fresno I had been wrong about Moon and I apologized. You should have seen the State Committee. They were sitting in the broadcasting studio and they thought I'd gone crazy. They waved their hands, turned red, gave me body English, scribbled notes; anything to get me to stop."

"They think it lost the election for you," Hank said. "They think you might have won if you hadn't made that speech."

"That isn't why he lost," Clara said. "He lost because he didn't follow Mike's plan. John went down and fired all of Mike's research staff the day after he made the Moon speech. They thought he was crazy. They told him they could still win the election for him. But he fired them anyway. God, was I proud."

"She's right," Cromwell said. "The Moon speech didn't make any difference. I still got forty-five per cent of the vote. Just like Mike said I would . . . just by being a Democrat. But I didn't pick up any of the undecided vote. For that you have to do something special. And I wouldn't do what Mike had planned."

"And Mike was right again," Georgia whispered. "He said if you were the Democrat you'd get forty-five per cent of the votes. Without doing a thing. And you didn't do a thing and you got just forty-five per cent."

No one spoke.

The tide passed high water. Its grip on the pilings was weaker. Over the ocean the clouds parted for a moment and a long narrow band of light fell on the water. The light caught a huge shifting clot of kelp. The kelp was blood red and delicate. It writhed as it was washed by the undertow and great swirls of the kelp boiled to the surface and then were pulled down again. The rest of the ocean was smooth and gray, like poured lead.

"Mike was right about a lot of things," Hank said. He watched

Cromwell. "He was right about the people being stupid and irrational. He was right about their being afraid."

Cromwell drank his glass empty. He held the glass up to the window, and watched the bluish film of gin gather into tendrils and slowly form a large drop in the bottom of the glass. He drank off the drop.

"Mike was right about that and lots more," Cromwell said. "They're stupid, frightened, panic-stricken. But they're also wise, courageous, steady. Sometimes they're vicious, sometimes they're generous. They're everything . . . and so they have to be what Mike said they were too. Play a tune well enough, Hank, and someone always comes forward to dance."

"But why did they always act one way for Mike?" Hank asked. "Always the same. Always scared. Always fearful."

"Because he was certain," Cromwell said. "It's the one thing you can't fake. You have it or you don't. The people look up, sniff around . . ." His hands moved, formed and impressed the idea. "They smell out the man with certainty. And if you have it they'll believe you. They'll behave as you tell them."

"Because their own uncertainty is so great," Hank said bitterly. "They're so unsure."

"That's right. They'll believe because they don't have anything else. Or they believe in themselves too little."

"How did they ever protect themselves from the Mikes?" Hank asked.

His voice, thin with strain, asked for something.

"Because there are always some who disbelieve. At some point the disbelievers come together and fight the believer," Cromwell paused. He pulled the blanket tighter around his shoulders and instantly he looked very old. His voice came softly. "Sometimes the disbelievers fight alone. A lonely disbeliever who disbelieves so much . . . so much that you drowned him."

It was loose in the room. Georgia looked up sharply. Hank curled his fingers together into a large double fist and crushed it between his knees. He looked up slowly.

"You knew?" Hank asked.

"Yes. I knew," and from the shadow of the cloth Cromwell's lips hardly moved. "I knew when I read the story in the papers. When I read about you and Georgia waiting on the beach and about the surfboards coming in all broken up. And I knew when I read that you carried Mike up the cliff path. I knew then."

Outside the sea and sky reshaped. The band of light retreated across the ocean, flashed over the great sweep of water, caught an island for a moment and then was gone. The sea was gray and flat.

"Was I right, John?" Hank asked.

"I don't know, Hank," Cromwell said. "I'm not the one to judge."

"I had to do it," Hank said. "No one else was doing anything. So I had to."

"I can't judge it," Cromwell said again.

There was a moment of simple quiet. No one breathed. And then they were all aware of the same thing. It was among them; strange and foreign, although they had made it. It was a curiously solid fragment; almost palpable: Hank would never be judged.

Cromwell and Georgia and Clara were aware of an unwelcome smugness, a relief from judgment. Hank looked at them and saw it. His eyes burned and sunk deeper into his skull. He looked, finally, at Georgia.

"We have to go, Hank," Georgia said. "It's late."

They shook hands with Cromwell and Clara. They walked back down the salt-smelling, moist, ancient hall. They climbed the steps to the roads. They looked at the abandoned tract; at the richness of the street lamps. They looked down the street as if the Ford were an impossible distance. In the sites across the street old tattered flags began to flutter as the wind rose.

Georgia took his hand. She looked at him. His eyes were narrowed, in the middle were thin blue crystals of sparkling agony.

"I'll help, Hank," Georgia whispered. "I'll help you."